FINDING ALEX

Also by Helen Starbuck

THE ANNIE COLLINS MYSTERY SERIES

The Mad Hatter's Son

No Pity In Death

The Burden of Hate

STANDALONE ROMANTIC SUSPENSE

Legacy of Secrets

FINDING ALEX

HELEN STARBUCK

Routt Street Press

2021

Routt Street Press

Who is it that can tell me who I am?

—William Shakespeare

PROLOGUE

"WAKE UP! PLEASE wake up!"

The voice sounded frightened and far away. "Can't," *she mumbled, her mind clouded, drifting, wanting nothing more than to drop back into nothingness and get away from the pain.*

"No!" *the voice sounded…worried…familiar.* "Wake up! You have to wake up and get away…please…he'll come back! He'll hurt you." The voice faded into the nothingness.

Cold. So cold and dark, she thought. *Have to get away, have to get help. Someone told me that…someone…someone.*

The pain in her head felt as if her skull would explode with each beat of her heart. She rolled onto her side and managed to get to her hands and knees before becoming violently ill. The pain in her head surged with each retch.

She waited for the nausea to pass, swaying on her hands and knees, her head hanging down. Slowly she lifted it and saw she was at the bottom of a deep culvert. Overhead, the moon was partly hidden by clouds. She crawled away from the vomit and made her way slowly up the incline, feeling the dry grass and dirt under her hands and knees, feeling the rocks that punctured and scratched them. It would take an eternity to reach the top. Was it worth the effort?

"*Move, keep moving,*" the voice said. So, she moved.

CHAPTER ONE

H E'D BEEN LOST in thought when he damn near hit the woman. If he hadn't had his headlights on high he would have. It was midnight and almost nothing was visible outside the twin beams of his car's headlights.

The fields on either side of Highway 93 and the foothills to the west were invisible in the darkness. In the distance to the east were glimpses of the multicolored lights of Denver. Clouds periodically obscured the moon. His was the only car on the road.

Detective Blake Halloran had been thinking about the case he'd been working on for the last week as he drove on autopilot toward Boulder and the woman he'd been seeing for a couple of months.

Movement from the side of the road at the edges of his headlights brought him out of his thoughts. A woman staggered out onto the highway, into the path of his car. He stood hard on the brake pedal, his tires screamed, and the car fishtailed. His heart was slamming against his chest as the car came juddering to a stop only feet from her.

As he got out of the car on shaky legs, the scent of burnt rubber from his tires surrounded him. The woman's head, face, and neck were bloody, and she swayed as she stood in front of the car. She raised a scraped and bloody arm to shield her eyes from the headlights. Before he could round the front of the car, her legs gave way and she collapsed.

He fished his phone out of his jacket pocket and dialed 911.

"This is Detective Blake Halloran with the Denver Police Department," he said, giving the operator his badge number. "I have an injured pedestrian and need an ambulance south of the entrance to the Leyden dump on Highway 93 going north toward Boulder."

"Is this a pedestrian motor vehicle accident?"

There was no other car in sight. "I don't know," he said his breath uneven, a tremor in his hand made holding the phone difficult. "It could be a hit-and-run, but she's on the highway so it's urgent that emergency services and the police or the sheriff's office are notified." Blake couldn't remember who had jurisdiction on this stretch of highway.

"Is the victim breathing?"

"Yes, but unconscious. Tell them to hurry," he said, disconnecting and dropping his phone into his jacket pocket.

He knelt beside her in the glare of the headlights and felt under her jaw for a pulse to reassure himself that she was, in fact, just unconscious. She was deathly pale. Blood matted her dark red hair and had run down her neck and onto her chest. Purplish-blue bruises wrapped around her neck. Not a hit-and-run then, some sort of assault. He took a deep breath and exhaled, trying to slow his breathing and his heartbeat. He hoped she was strong enough to hold on until help got there.

She wore a very short, tight skirt and a tight stretchy top that didn't leave much to the imagination. Working girl was his first assumption, but he'd seen some high school and college-age girls who wore similar outfits. There was a gash on the side of her head. The palms of her hands and her elbows and knees were scraped and covered in blood and ground-in dirt. Several of her fingernails were broken, and there was a deep cut near the last joint of her left index finger.

Her elbows and knees were still bleeding. He stood up and retrieved his phone activating its flashlight and shining it off the side of the road. The ground dropped off into a deep culvert. Maybe the injuries to her hands, arms, and knees were from crawling up the side of the culvert. The bleeding from the head wound had stopped, so whatever had caused it had evidently happened a while ago.

He ran back to the car, hit his hazard lights, and opened the trunk to extract his triangular hazard warning signs and a blanket. He set up the warning triangles, hoping to prevent any approaching cars from hitting them.

Covering her with the blanket would screw up any trace evidence on her, but she was ice-cold. Figuring it was damned if you did and damned if you didn't, he went with the blanket. Once she was covered, he knelt beside her again to wait for emergency responders.

She moaned and, unable to restrain himself, he stroked the uninjured side of her face. "Help is on the way, hang in there," he said.

He had no idea whether she'd been conscious enough to hear him. She was unresponsive now, and he wasn't sure whether he'd said it to reassure the woman or himself. He took his phone and briefly peeled back the blanket to photograph her injuries and check that there were no other wounds. Replacing it, he tucked the blanket in around her and waited feeling a familiar numbness creep over him.

Five minutes later he saw flashing lights in the distance and heard sirens. A fire truck arrived with lights flashing. Fire fighters emerged and began blocking the highway to divert traffic. Mercifully, there wasn't any at the moment. EMTs unloaded a stretcher from the ambulance that had arrived with the fire truck, and a black SUV with a local police emblem on it pulled up. EMTs rolled the stretcher over to where the woman lay and Halloran was still kneeling.

"What happened?" the EMT asked as he pulled the blanket off and replaced it with a reflective blanket that would help keep her body heat in. He began examining the woman as the other one took the transport board off the stretcher and placed it beside her. They transferred her onto it and the first EMT began taking her vital signs as the other hooked her up to oxygen.

Blake stood up and stared down at the EMT blankly for a moment. It was as if his brain had momentarily short circuited.

The EMT shot him a concerned look. "Are you okay? Any injuries that need looking at?"

Blake shook his head to clear it. "I'm fine, no injuries."

"Can you tell me what happened?"

"She…she stumbled out into the road as I was driving. I damn near hit her." He picked up the blanket and held it against his belly as if for comfort.

A cop appeared at Blake's side and asked, "Where'd she come from?"

"I don't know where she came from. There's a fairly steep culvert leading down from the highway, she could have been down there. She's got bruises around her neck. It looks like an assault to me. Maybe whoever did it left her there, thinking she was dead."

"Dispatch said you're a cop."

"Yeah, DPD. Homicide." Blake pulled his jacket back to show his badge.

"What were you doing up here?"

"I was on my way to Boulder to a friend's house."

"That's quite a drive, and it's late," the cop said, giving him an impassive stare.

"You know the job. It isn't bankers' hours." Blake eyed the guy for a minute. "You asking me for an alibi?"

"You got one?"

"Talk to my partner. I was with him until half an hour ago, when I left to head up to Boulder." He provided his partner Clark Stevens' name and phone number. "If I was the one who did this, why the hell would I call 911 or stick around?"

The cop shrugged. "Stranger things have happened."

On the way back to his SUV he inspected the front of Blake's car, shinning a flashlight on the grill and the front fenders.

Asshole, Blake thought as the cop slid into the SUV's driver's side and pulled out a phone. *Jesus, no trust in a fellow officer at all,* Blake thought. Still, he grudgingly admitted he'd have probably done the same thing. He watched as the EMTs wheeled the stretcher toward the ambulance and loaded her in. Christ, he'd nearly killed her. He followed them to the door of the ambulance.

"Where are you taking her?"

"Saint A's. They're Level 1 trauma."

"Is she going to be okay?"

"We'll do everything we can, sir," the EMT said, climbing into the back of the ambulance and shutting the doors in Blake's face.

The lack of expression on the EMT's face and their rush to leave worried Blake. Would she be okay? The ambulance made a U-turn and took off, lights flashing and siren wailing. Blake watched as the ambulance's lights faded. He knew the lights and the siren meant 'critical patient, no time to lose.'

The sense of responsibility for her and the urge to follow the ambulance washed over him. Maybe he'd call the ER when he got to Fleur's place and see how she was doing. He rubbed his forehead. He must be tired or more shook up than he realized. No one at the ER was going to give him any information over the phone. The question was, did he let this go or stop at the hospital and see what her prognosis was?

"Gonna need you to give me a statement, tell me what happened. I'll let you know when it's ready for you to sign. Gonna need contact info as well," the cop said interrupting Blake's thoughts. He eyed Blake carefully. "You okay?"

"Yeah, just a little rattled," Blake said. He related what had happened and gave the officer his info.

A fireman walked up and stopped. "Need you to get your car off the highway," he said to Blake. "And the sooner you can finish this up, we can get the scene secured and take off, unless you need us to stick around?" he asked the cop.

"No, thanks for the backup. We're almost done here."

The guy nodded and returned to confer with the firemen stationed around the accident scene while they waited. Blake got back into his car and pulled forward into the breakdown lane. He opened the driver's door and waited for the cop to walk over. When finished questioning Blake, the cop handed him a card and said he'd be in touch.

"What happened to your hand?" Blake asked noticing the scratch marks on the back of it.

The cop gave him an appraising stare. "I had a little confrontation with someone earlier who objected to being arrested."

"You might want to have them looked at. They look serious."

The cop raised his eyebrows at Blake. "Thanks, I will," he said. He got back into his car, made a U-turn, and drove away, shortly followed by the fire truck.

Blake realized he was still clutching the blanket. He supposed he should have given it to the cop but was too tired to turn the car around and follow. He'd give it to the guy when he went in to sign the statement. A few minutes passed before he realized he'd forgotten about his emergency triangles. Resignedly he got out of the car, retrieved them, and threw them into the trunk.

On top of the tiredness, the adrenaline was still humming. He sat in his car and looked at his hands on the steering wheel and watched them shake. It'd be a while yet before he could sleep. *You'd think I'd be used to this kinda shit by now,* he thought. Being called to a crime scene never bothered him like this, primarily because he knew what he was getting into. But this had been so unexpected and jarring. Maybe you were never used to emergencies that actually involved you.

As a cop he'd handled other people's emergencies, but only one of his own, and that had been one too many. Lindsey had been the last time he'd allowed anyone to mean anything to him. It was the last time he'd been close to anyone or felt responsible for anyone. That had ended disastrously, so he'd made sure no one got close enough for it to happen again. He closed his eyes tightly, frowning, his breathing speeding up as he fought the images of holding Lindsey in his arms, unable to do anything, as she bled to death.

He forced his eyes open and focused on the interior of the car, remembering what the therapist had said—focus on your surroundings, where you're at, why you're not with Lindsey. *I'm in the car. I'm on the road to Boulder. I'm…here, not there,* he said to himself to counteract the panic that he felt building. He sat and breathed slowly, repeating the phrases, and waiting for his heart rate to drop.

Almost forty minutes later, surprised by the insistent ringing of his cell phone, he didn't know where he was for a moment until he remembered what had happened. Had he fallen asleep? He pulled his phone out of his jacket pocket. Glancing at the screen he saw it was Fleur. He'd planned to pick her up and have dinner, but those plans had been derailed early in the evening. She'd been pissed but told him to come up when he could. She was going to be even more pissed now.

"Where are you?" she demanded, "It's almost two a.m. This is the second time I've called. Are you all right?"

The second time she'd called? He hadn't heard the phone if she'd called before. He wiped a hand over his face. It had been almost six months since he'd had a flashback or lost time after one. Christ, he hoped that wasn't going to start up again.

"I'm sorry, babe, I can't make it," he said rubbing the heel of his hand on his forehead. "Something…came up on the way to your place." There was dead silence.

Finally, she said, "This is getting old, Blake, but whatever. Let me know when you can make some time for me," and disconnected.

He sighed, closing his eyes. Maybe it was time to call it quits and end this. She wasn't happy, and he wasn't entertained enough to continue enduring the sulks and tantrums when he couldn't make whatever they had arranged. Even the sex wasn't enough anymore. Initially it'd been fun, but it wasn't worth all the other nonsense, he thought irritably as he put the car in gear, made a U-turn, and drove toward home.

He'd been seeing her for not quite two months. She was a twenty-four-year-old grad student at the University of Colorado, and he was ten years older. He'd been uncomfortable with the age difference from the beginning. He hadn't thought it would be a huge problem, but it was becoming one rather quickly. Her outlook on life in general was that of someone who hadn't had reality bash her in the head yet. Unfortunately, he had.

He'd met her at a friend's house in Denver. They'd chatted, seemed to hit it off, and exchanged numbers. He'd always been a sucker for blond hair, long legs, and blue eyes, so they had reconnected a week later. The 'relationship'—and he always saw air quotes around it when he thought about it—had sort of evolved from dinner and movies to sleeping together over the course of a couple weekends.

He didn't have a goal in mind in regard to Fleur, and he'd been honest about that, but apparently she had one. He worried that he'd become the fish she was determined to catch and not release. She'd been more and more frustrated and angry as she realized what his job entailed and that he wasn't going to commit or take their relationship any further than it was. He always kept women at a distance, something many of them complained bitterly about before they left or he did. For some reason, women never seemed to believe that he had no interest in a long-term relationship. No matter what he told them.

Blake Halloran wasn't a classically handsome man. He was tall and well-built but he could blend in enough to go unnoticed. Unnoticed until he displayed his quirky smile that, when truly amused, lit up his deep blue eyes and made a dimple appear on his left cheek.

Women seemed to like his startlingly blue eyes and dark blond hair that looked as if he combed it with his fingers, which, about half the time, was true. He liked women, too, but between his aversion to getting too close and his job, relationships never lasted long and there were often hard feelings on the woman's part when things ended.

CHAPTER TWO

ALMOST TWO HOURS after the near accident, he was driving east on Sixth Avenue debating with himself about going to the hospital to check on the woman. He passed the Simms exit that would have taken him to Saint Anthony's Hospital. All the way he kept telling himself he should go home and then rehashing all the reasons why checking on her would be a good idea.

Don't waffle, Halloran, make up your mind, he thought. At last he said out loud, "What would it hurt to check in with the ER?" and took the Federal exit, turned around, and headed back to the hospital.

When he arrived in the ER, he flashed his badge and told the woman sitting at the desk he was the cop involved with the assault victim and wanted an update on her. Eventually she located the doc assigned to the woman.

"She's dehydrated and her temp's still a little low, but she's stable," the doc said when he finally came out to talk to Blake. "At the moment she's in radiology for a CT to determine the extent of the head injury. She regained consciousness, which is good, but she's had a serious blow to the head that'll need to be watched closely.

"Depending on the CT, it's possible she could need surgery if there's active bleeding going on. The hand surgeon on call says it doesn't look like any tendons were cut when her finger was injured, just nicked, so he plans to stitch it up when she gets back from radiology. We plan to admit her for observation for at least twenty-four hours."

The doc paused and yawned. "Sorry, it's been a long night. I'm no detective, but it looks like someone tried to strangle her. Did a pretty decent job, but for some reason stopped before he killed her—maybe he thought he had."

He continued to talk while he yawned. "It's concerning that she's got amnesia. It's not uncommon with head injuries, but she doesn't know who she is or anything else, so we have yet to ID her. People with head injuries usually remember everything but the accident. Any idea who she is?"

"No, not yet. The uniform on scene hasn't shown up to get fingerprints or follow up with her?" Blake had hoped the cop who'd interviewed him would follow her to the ER and get some fingerprints to see if she could be ID'd that way and get her statement.

"No, not that I'm aware of. The only cop I've seen tonight is you." The doc ran a hand over his face tiredly. "You taking over for the uniform?"

Blake shrugged casually and lied. "It's an assault and possible attempted murder, so I got drug in. I figured the guy at the scene would show up too, but looks like he doesn't plan to." He had no intention of telling the doc he was a witness not the cop assigned. "I assume there wasn't anything in her clothing that would help with an ID?"

The doc snorted. "Wasn't enough clothing to put anything in. Is she a prostitute?"

"No idea. Do you have the capability of getting fingerprints?"

"No, I figured you guys either had them or would get them."

"She needed medical attention and the cop on scene didn't get them. Take some samples from under her fingernails, that way if there's anything there and we catch whoever did this we'll have DNA to go on. And run a tox screen just in case."

"Got all that in the works, Detective. We know how to care for assault victims." Tired as he looked, the doc now looked annoyed.

"Sorry, no offense intended. I can get her prints and collect the fingernail evidence and talk to her tomorrow. If for some reason the cop on scene shows up to do that, can someone give me a call?" Blake handed him a card with his cell on it.

"Sure, I'll let everyone know to get in touch."

It wasn't his case, he had no authority to do any of that, and part of him wanted to walk away. Something about this had started to feel wrong—he couldn't put his finger on why—but the idea that it was wrong wouldn't go away, nor would the feel of her face as he'd knelt beside her on the roadside and run his hand down it. It was good to know the woman was stable. That was one worry out of the way at least for the night.

Nearly three-thirty, he thought heading for the parking lot opposite the ER entrance. Whether he'd be able to sleep and whether it was worth trying was questionable.

———◆———

SHE WAS cold and frightened. Her head pounded relentlessly, periodically her vision blurred or she saw two of things, and whatever had happened to her throat made talking painful. She knew she had been hurt and was in a hospital but didn't know why.

"Can you tell me what happened?" the doctor asked.

"I don't know. I…I can't remember."

"What's your name, then?"

"I don't know! *Why don't I know my name?*"

"Probably temporary amnesia from the head injury. It'll all come back to you, don't stress about it."

All she could remember was a voice urging her to move, to get away, being cold, and then stumbling onto the highway and seeing bright headlights. She thought she'd heard a different voice tell her help was on the way. How she got hurt or who she was, was a blank. It was as if someone had taken an eraser to her memory.

The staff in the ER had done their jobs efficiently but they treated her oddly, as if there was something about her that put them off. That made her uneasy. What was it about her that made them act like that? They never touched her without wearing gloves. Did they do that with every patient or only with her?

Thinking about it made her heart race and her mouth go dry. Aside from her pounding head, the cut on it ached and burned.

She knew from what the doctor had told her that she had been hit in the head or fallen and hit her head. He was evasive when she had asked in a hoarse voice what had happened to her neck. When it was clear she knew nothing about herself or what had happened, he patted her on the hand and told her not to worry.

"Don't stress about it or try to force yourself to remember. Amnesia isn't uncommon after a serious head injury, but your memory'll come back."

"When?" She didn't like his patronizing tone.

"There's no way to tell, so you'll need to be patient."

"But I don't know my name or where I live. Where will I go when you release me?" Her heart revved up again and her breath hitched. Underneath it all there was something more serious to fear, but she had no idea what it was.

"You're not going anywhere for a while, maybe not for a day or two, so take a deep breath and try not to worry. When you're ready for discharge, I'll call the cop who's in charge of finding out what happened to you and he'll figure something out."

For some reason a woman, who introduced herself as a sexual assault nurse examiner, had performed a pelvic exam, taken scrapings from under her nails, and then continued to collect evidence swabs from her body. That scared her. They must think she'd been raped.

She took a mental inventory of her body and realized that, despite all her other aches and pains, that was one area of her body that didn't hurt. She had no idea how old she was or what her history was, or what had happened to her. She had no idea whether she'd ever had sex but, apparently, she knew what rape was. When she asked, the nurse said that it was a precaution, in the event that she remembered what had happened and had been raped.

Under all her confusion, it felt as if she knew how to survive and knew not to let her fear take over. She would get through this. She'd figure out something. She had to.

CHAPTER THREE

B LAKE SCREWED HIS eyes closed and pinched the bridge of his nose, trying to force the tiredness away. Three hours of sleep, unsettled sleep at that, hadn't been helpful. He'd probably have been better off staying awake. When the alarm on his phone went off, he was groggy. It felt as if he'd been on a ten-day drunk. He gulped a cup of coffee before he showered and dressed, which helped, but not nearly enough.

It wasn't fully light as he headed west on Sixth Avenue until it curved around and became Highway 93. He drove north until he reached the place where he thought she'd stumbled out into the road and parked on the verge.

He used his big Maglite flashlight to find his car's skid marks. It was odd, there was no crime scene tape, no indication anyone had identified the site. The wind on 93 was notoriously bad though. It was whipping his jacket and hair around at the moment. Crime scene tape, if there'd been any, had probably blown away.

It was early. Maybe they hadn't gotten here yet. There wouldn't have been much to see last night unless crime scene lights had been set up, and based on the cop's attitude, Blake doubted he'd done that. If she'd been assaulted by a john, though, it was unlikely she'd know his name or have a license plate number, and the possibility of finding him and arresting him was low. So it was probably a waste of time unless the guy's fingerprints were found.

He debated about climbing down into the culvert and checking out the scene. The cop who'd interviewed him last night hadn't been all that friendly. If he showed up while Blake was in the culvert, that probably wouldn't go over well. Still, he was here and no one else was. If anyone showed up, he'd have some explaining to do. *Better to ask for forgiveness than ask permission*, he thought. Cautiously he walked to the side of the road and shined the flashlight's beam down the embankment.

He slid and nearly fell twice on his way down. The embankment was steep and littered with rocks big and small. If she'd been left at the bottom, it was impressive that she'd managed to get to the highway in her condition. It was good that she had, the steepness of the culvert would have made it difficult for anyone to spot her as they drove by. Injured and disoriented, she'd managed to make her way to the highway and find help. Luck was on her side there.

Hopefully her memory had returned, and he could find out more about what had happened. No one had called him to say the cop on scene had followed her to the hospital and no one had flagged this area as a crime scene. They might have decided to wait until morning to check it out, which was understandable. But the cop from last night didn't know she couldn't give them a statement because of the amnesia, so he wondered why he hadn't come to the ER last night to try to get one.

He was assuming the cop hadn't. The message to call him if he turned up probably hadn't been passed on. No doubt he'd be hearing from the cop if the guy had shown up and discovered Blake's interference. He was going to have to come up with an excuse for nosing into the case.

And what is your excuse? he asked himself.

What he'd experienced last night—the loss of time, the adrenaline shakes, and the memory of holding Lindsey—hadn't happened in a long time. Initially, he'd numbed himself by drinking until he was anesthetized. That hadn't worked well, but the department therapist he'd been required to see after Lindsey's death had given him a means to pull out of the panic or flashbacks. God, he hoped that wasn't going to start up again. Having this woman lurch out in front of his car last night, seeing her injured and bleeding, seemed to have triggered some sort of guilt or feeling that he was responsible for her.

The sky was turning to light gray as he made it to the bottom of the culvert and began looking for something that would indicate this was where she'd come from, something personal that might have been left behind, something that might help identify her. Maybe something with the fingerprints of her attacker. Eventually, he found a pair of dark red high-heeled shoes covered in red and black crystals, which made it unlikely they'd get any prints off them.

He'd stuffed several evidence bags into his jacket pocket. After donning the pair of gloves he'd brought with him, he pulled his phone out and photographed the area where the shoes lay and some geographical reference points and placed them in one of the evidence bags. He found nothing else, no purse, no car keys, nothing other than the shoes.

It was considerably lighter now. He walked relentlessly around the area where he'd found the shoes but found nothing further. The grass obscured any footprints that might have been left. It hadn't rained in at least ten days, so the ground was dry. It was doubtful he'd have found any footprints even if the ground had been bare of grass. Near where he'd found her shoes, there was an area of blood staining the ground. There was a dried puddle of vomit on the ground near the blood.

There was nothing else out of place or that might offer DNA or fingerprints—no cigarette butts, no used condoms, no littered beer cans—although he hadn't really thought there would be. Fate rarely handed you a solve that easy. He'd forgotten to ask about a rape kit. Maybe the doc had at least assessed whether one was needed.

Eventually he returned to the car and added the shoes to the bagged blanket in the trunk. He used his phone to photograph his car's skid marks and took a few more photos of the surrounding area. On the way into the city, he detoured to Saint A's to check in on the woman and pick up the evidence specimens if the other cop hadn't shown up.

The ER nurse said the victim had been admitted to the neuro floor the previous night and handed Blake the collection of evidence and bagged clothes. She said no one else had called about her or inquired about the evidence. He flashed his badge at the nurse's desk on the neuro floor and was given an update and the victim's room number.

"Well, until she remembers, we can't say for sure if she was raped. There's no obvious signs of it. For now, she's stable," the nurse said. "The laceration on her index finger has been sutured, splinted, and bandaged. She's had a serious concussion and a small bleed from the head injury, but there hasn't been any more intracranial bleeding according to the last CT scan."

The nurse scrolled through the computerized chart. "If no further bleeding occurs, the doc will discharge her. She still doesn't remember anything."

"Okay. Call me when she's ready for discharge, and I'll see that she has somewhere to go until her memory returns."

He kept volunteering for things, which baffled and irritated him. But it was a done deal now, and apparently the other cop wasn't all that concerned. Maybe the assumption that she was a prostitute made it less important for him, which pissed Blake off.

An assault was an assault regardless of who the victim was, or at least it was supposed to be. The cop might have been called to something more urgent, though. He was trying to keep an open mind, but he didn't like the cop he'd dealt with. There was also that niggling little thought that what had happened was important enough for his involvement.

The room was quiet when he pushed open the door, the blinds were drawn, and she looked as if she were asleep. Her face was swollen and bleached of color except where it was bruised. Her neck had ugly dark marks on it. When he pushed the door closed it made a small noise, and her eyes flew open.

"Who are you?" she croaked. Her eyes were huge, and she clutched the call button, clearly terrified.

"I'm Detective Halloran. I'm the guy who nearly ran you over last night." He smiled as he walked toward the bed. She shrank into it, away from him, continuing to firmly grip the call button.

"How are you?" he asked and, to try to reassure her, he pulled his shield off his belt and showed it to her.

"They keep telling me I'm fine. I don't know. My head hurts, my neck hurts. I hurt all over."

"How's the memory?"

"Gone. I don't remember anything including my name. I didn't know where I was, what city, until they told me." She laughed weakly. "I can't even remember what I look like. There's a mirror in the bath, but," she said displaying the bright red band on her left wrist that said "fall risk" in big bold black letters. "They won't let me up by myself and they follow me into the bathroom. I haven't gotten a good look in the mirror, yet. Honestly, I'm not sure I want to see my face if it looks as bad as it feels."

"Try not to worry…"

"*Don't say that!*" she shouted hoarsely pounding a fist on the bed.

She clutched at her neck and swallowed several times, her brows scrunched together tightly against the pain. He stepped up to her bedside and handed her a plastic container of water with a straw sticking out of it.

She took it and sipped, then let her head fall back on the pillow as she closed her eyes. He took the container from her hand and replaced it on the bedside table.

"Everyone says that, and I haven't got a clue who I am or where I belong or what happened to me. I didn't get like this by myself."

She opened her eyes and glared at him. "Somebody hurt me, and I don't know who did it or why."

He nodded, embarrassed. She was worried, who wouldn't be? "Look… uh," he began, but it was awkward. He had no name to use.

He cleared his throat. "Look, I'll take care of getting you a place to stay until we figure out who you are and can contact a friend or relative. I've told them to call me when you're ready for discharge and I'll take care of it." He watched in dismay as tears gathered in her eyes and she angrily wiped them away.

"I have no money, no identification I guess, and no idea what to do. What if my memory never comes back?"

He moved closer to her bed. "The doc says it will eventually, but until it does, I'll make sure you're safe."

She took a shuddering breath and looked at him. She had green eyes in a pale face, with a light sprinkling of freckles across her nose. Out from under the bandage wrapped around her head dark red hair cascaded to her shoulders, some of it still stiff with blood. Despite her injuries she was pretty. She nodded at him and closed her eyes.

"I'm sorry, I'm exhausted. They woke me up all night long, checking on me. I didn't get much sleep. I'm scared." She opened her eyes, looked up at him, and gave him a weak smile. That lost puppy look was like a punch to his gut. "Thank you for helping me."

He mentally shook himself. She was, in all probability, a hooker and had been assaulted by a john who'd gotten a little carried away. If that was the case, she wasn't at all as innocent as she appeared at the moment and he needed to remember that. He'd see she was taken care of until she got her memory back and then, hopefully, she'd remember who had done this to her, he could arrest the guy, and send her on her way.

He shook himself again. *Jesus, it isn't even my case or jurisdiction. What the fuck is going on in my head? Guilt*, he thought, *that's what's going on.*

"You're welcome," he said with a slight smile. "I'll make arrangements for a place to for you to stay and get in touch with Victim's Assistance."

He pulled a mobile fingerprint scanner out of his jacket pocket and reached for her hand slowly, as if she were a frightened animal. "I'd like to take your fingerprints. It could help identify you."

She nodded and held out a hand. He gave it a squeeze before beginning to print her.

———— ◆ ————

HE ARRIVED late to work and was given the fisheye by his partner, Clark Stevens.

"Where've you been?"

"You wouldn't believe it if I told you."

"Give it a try."

"Almost hit a woman going to a friend's house in Boulder on 93 last night. She's an assault victim who staggered out onto the highway in front of my car. I stopped to check on her this morning. She's completely amnesic—doesn't remember her name or anything else."

"Huh. The phone call from the cop last night asking for an alibi for you was a surprise. I vouched for you, so I hope you didn't assault and dump her like the cop seemed to think."

Blake rolled his eyes and said irritably, "The guy's a real asshole. And no, I didn't assault and dump her, or hit her with my car, why would you even think that?"

Stevens laughed. "It was a joke Halloran. You must be tired, you're cranky. You always get cranky when you're tired."

"You sound like my mother. And I don't get cranky."

"Yes, you do." Clark grinned.

"For someone your age, you sound like a twelve-year-old."

"I'm young at heart. And you're cranky." That finally got a laugh out of Blake. He'd been irritable and out of sorts since last night and it was a relief to laugh.

"Don't get comfortable, we may have an ID on the Cheesman Park kid." Stevens said, picking up his briefcase. "I want to go interview the parents who think it's their kid and make sure. Let's go get this over with. As far as the case goes, I hope she's their daughter. But I hope, for their sake, she isn't."

A week ago, an employee of the Botanic Gardens, cutting through Cheesman Park on her way to work, had seen a young woman lying on the steps to the park's pavilion and stopped to offer help. The Good Samaritan discovered the teenage girl had been past the point of needing help for a while. She had been strangled and the tips of her fingers had been amputated.

They assumed she was a runaway based on her age, the clothes she wore, and her general health. The medical examiner said the time of death was most likely between three and five a.m., which wasn't a time when most girls were hanging out alone in a Denver park. With runaways, it was a different story.

A lot of runaways, both male and female, prostituted themselves or sold drugs to survive. The M.E. said there was no obvious indication she'd been raped. If she'd had sex in her last 24 hours of life it had been consensual, and the guy had used a condom. There was no semen present anywhere on her body. There was no physical evidence on her body or drugs in her system to suggest she was a drug addict. Without fingerprints, the likelihood they'd be able to ID her quickly had dropped dramatically.

Polling homeless kids in various parts of the city hadn't yielded much. The ones who would stay and talk didn't recognize her photo, or at least didn't admit to knowing her. The rest took off when they spotted a cop.

Halloran and Stevens had passed out a police artist's sketch of her rather than a morgue photo and asked anyone who might know her to call them. After coming up empty handed, they gave the sketch to the media to see if anyone recognized her. If she was new to town, Blake didn't hold out much hope that would happen. It was possible, though, they'd finally gotten a break on her identity.

CHAPTER FOUR

STEVENS HEADED UP I-25, passing the exit for Highway 36 then Westminster, then Thornton, and kept driving.

"Where the hell are we going?" Blake asked as they passed several more exits for the northern suburbs.

"Wellington."

"Shit, that's almost to Wyoming."

"That's where her parents live."

Stevens was a man of few words, and their initial partnership, despite being something both had agreed on, had been rough. It had begun in the chaotic months after Lindsey's death. Blake felt like he needed to prove himself to Stevens and Stevens had clearly been trying to decide if he'd made the right choice in partners. They'd eventually become friends, and Stevens had taught Blake a lot.

"Why not send the photo to the locals and ask them to talk to the parents? If they thought it was their daughter, we could have brought them in."

"Because I want to do it in person. I want to be able to talk to them if they think she's theirs. I don't like foisting stuff off on other cops."

He probably wouldn't like other cops horning in on his cases either, Blake thought. *I wouldn't, but I've already stuck my nose in the case from last night.*

"'Sides," Stevens continued, "I like to watch people when they get the news. Sometimes it points you to the perp or alerts you that the person knows more than they're saying."

"Wake me when we get there. I didn't get much sleep last night. I don't want to be *cranky* when we get there." Stevens laughed. Blake leaned his head against the window and dropped off to sleep.

————◆————

BLAKE FELT a nudge in his side. "We're here. Try to look professional and not half asleep." Stevens opened his door and stood up. He closed the driver's door, opened the back door, and retrieved his jacket and briefcase. He paused to slip on his jacket and frowned at the house as he closed the car door.

This was not going to be fun, but it had to be done. "Think she's their kid?" Blake asked as they walked up the sidewalk to the front door.

"Who knows? But they saw the police artist's sketch that we released to the media and they called, so chances are…" He let the thought die on his lips as he rang the doorbell and they waited.

A middle-aged woman opened the door. She was dressed in slacks and a cotton top, her hair was nicely styled, but her face looked as if she'd been through hell. She was pale with dark circles under eyes that were rimmed in red. She clasped her hands and brought them to her lips.

"Mrs. Kensington?" Stevens asked. She nodded. "I'm Detective Stevens and this is my partner, Detective Halloran." They both showed their shields, but she barely glanced at them. "May we come in?"

She stepped aside and ushered them in, leading them to a formal living room. The house was relatively new, in a subdivision that looked about five years old.

"Derek? The police are here," she called out and, in a moment or two, a man in his late forties walked in. He was less visibly stressed by their visit but, under his apparent calm, looked just as worn.

"Please sit down. Can I get you something to drink?" she asked.

"No ma'am, but thank you," Stevens said.

It always surprised Blake that people would offer this or make small talk when the reason they were there was clearly not social. Mentally he shrugged. Perhaps the social rituals helped prolong the sense of normality before he and his partner knocked it all to hell.

They all sat, the couple next to one another on the couch and Stevens and Blake in separate side chairs. Stevens pulled his briefcase onto his lap, opened it, and pulled out a piece of paper. He handed it to Mrs. Kensington.

"This is the police artist's sketch of the young woman who was found, that we released to the media. You indicated you saw it on the TV, but please look at it carefully and let me know if it resembles your daughter."

Blake could see from the tears welling in the woman's eyes that the answer was yes. God, he hated this part of the job. The part where you destroyed someone's last chance for a normal life and there was nothing you could do about it.

"It looks like Ashley." The woman began to cry and leaned into her husband's arms.

"I'm very sorry to ask, but I need you both to look at some morgue shots. Sometimes drawings can be misleading." Stevens retrieved the two headshots that had been taken once the autopsy was finished and the M.E.'s staff had cleaned the girl up and made her more presentable. He handed them to the man, who took a deep breath and looked at the photos. His wife glanced at them, stood up abruptly and rushed from the room.

"I'm sorry. She's been so upset since Ashley disappeared." He stared at the photos. "Yes," he said finally. "Yes, it's Ashley. God, what happened to her?"

"She was strangled and left in Cheesman Park." The silence was oppressive. Stevens made no mention of the fingertips. They'd find that out soon enough. "I'm very sorry for your loss."

They gave the man a few minutes to compose himself, then Blake inquired, "When did Ashley go missing?"

"About six weeks ago. She skipped school on the last day and took off. We didn't realize she was gone until she didn't come home from school. My wife called the school and learned she hadn't shown up that day. We called all of her friends but, if they knew anything, none of them would say. The boy she'd broken up with a few months ago seemed clueless."

The man sighed in exasperation. "He'd skipped school with some friends and had been partying outside of town. He didn't know she was missing until I contacted him. At least that's what he said.

"We notified the police, filed a missing person's report. They were skeptical that she was missing. They thought she might be out partying since school was out. But I knew she wasn't. She was gone."

"Is there any reason why she'd run away?"

"No, no reason." Most parents were adamant about that. Even if things had been rocky at home, few would admit it initially. The more they talked, though, the more came out.

"You hadn't gotten into it over her boyfriend, or her behavior, or her plans for the summer?" Blake asked.

"She…was a teenager. We got 'into it', as you put it, all the time. Her ex-boyfriend is a juvenile ass, but so are most of the boys in that class. We didn't care for him, but teenage boys are all asses at that age and she eventually broke up with him."

He slumped back against the couch and ran a hand over his face again, as if trying to wipe the memories away.

"We had fights, disagreements, but Christ, she was a teenager. No one I know with teenagers gets along with them. Over the last year the fights had increased, and lately she'd cut her hair and dyed it black and started wearing all black clothes. She wouldn't talk about it."

"Was she experimenting with drugs or alcohol?"

The man looked at Blake with barely concealed hostility. "How dare you," he seethed.

"Mr. Kensington, I'm not accusing her of anything. I'm asking. Your honesty, even if it's painful to admit, will help us catch whoever did this. It's imperative that you be frank with us."

The man breathed deeply for several minutes. "She indulged in alcohol like most high school kids do, but something had changed over the last six months. She had changed. Her attitude, how she dressed, the people she hung out with, all of it had changed. I wondered if she was using, but I can't say for sure she was."

"Any idea why she'd take off?" Stevens stepped in and took over the questioning.

Kensington sighed. "Things had been difficult at home the last year. Ashley and her mother were at odds. She routinely missed curfew, wasn't doing well in school. She gave us both flack about doing her chores, she argued about pretty much everything—the usual teenage crap."

He paused and seemed to drift for a moment. "Earlier in the year, she broke up with her boyfriend and quit babysitting for the couple who'd used her for several years and refused to go back. She dropped out of the cheerleading squad, quit being active in student government—all the things she'd loved up until then. I don't know why, all she said was she was tired of it. I suppose that's normal. I don't know. She's…she's our only child…" At that, he broke down.

Stevens waited until he stopped crying. "Mr. Kensington, I'm going to need a list of all her close friends and any boyfriends she's had, and how to contact them. I need to know where she spent her time, where she went, and I'll need the names and contact info for the couple she quit babysitting for."

He nodded and sat looking at his hands. "My wife and I will get that for you. When can we see her? When will they let us have her?"

"You can come anytime, call ahead so they know you're coming. The medical examiner's personnel can help you make arrangements for her to be picked up." Stevens fished out a card, wrote a number on the back of it and handed it to Kensington.

"This is my card. I've put the M.E.'s office number on the back. When you're ready call it, they'll take it from there."

They stood up and watched as he sat with his head in his hands.

"Mr. Kensington, my partner and I would like to look at your daughter's room. In the meantime, if you and your wife would write down as much of that information as possible, we'd appreciate it."

Kensington nodded and pointed at the stairway. "Top of the stairs, first door on the right."

Stevens turned to go up the stairs then said, "I'd appreciate it if neither of you would discuss this with anyone. It's helpful if we can gauge a person's initial reaction when we interview them. If they've anything to hide, it gives them less time to come up with a believable story."

Kensington nodded. "We'll get the information together for you."

Stevens and Blake headed up the stairs. Kensington remained sitting on the couch, seemingly unsure of what to do next.

After searching through Ashley's room, and not finding anything of any significance, they headed back to the main floor with Ashley's laptop in hand. "We'd like to take this with us and see if there's anything on it that would help find whoever did this. Are you okay with that?"

Kensington nodded and handed Stevens a list of names and numbers.

"Thank you. We'll return the laptop to you as soon as we've gone through it."

Kensington nodded.

"Again, I'm sorry for your loss. We'll do everything we can to catch the person responsible," Stevens said.

Stevens and Blake walked to the front door and left. Kensington remained sitting on the couch, his head in his hands.

CHAPTER FIVE

T HEY ENDED UP with a list that included the couple Ashley had babysat for, who weren't at home, her friends, and two boyfriends she'd had. The parents had also given them the names of her teachers. It was nearly ten in the evening before they left Wellington. They had pretty much heard the same thing from everyone with whom they'd spoken. Ashley had been a friendly girl and, until the last year, had been social, popular and had performed well in school. Then most of her interests had changed.

"I don't know," her best friend Rachel Lafferty had said when asked what she thought had changed. "She seemed different, quieter, you know? She stopped wanting to go to parties or hang out, but she wouldn't say why. And she spent a lot of time elsewhere, you know, not with us. I think she'd met someone."

"Is it possible she was into drugs?" The girl's eyes widened. Blake spoke up, "Rachel, we're not here to smear Ashley's reputation, or come down on you, but if she was into drugs or in some sort of trouble then we need to know."

"I don't know for sure, but I think so. The last month or so before she took off, we weren't speaking. She seemed unhappy being here, or…I don't know."

"Any idea who would know about that? Who you'd go to if you wanted drugs?" Halloran thought it unlikely she'd say if she did, but it was worth asking.

"No, I don't know who you'd go to." She took hold of a piece of hair that lay over her shoulder and twisted it.

"You said you thought she might have met someone new, someone outside your circle of friends. Any idea who it was?"

"No, I don't. I don't even know for sure that she had. She spent a lot of time elsewhere, you know?"

She hesitated, fiddling with the lock of hair, brought it to her lips, then seemed to reconsider chewing on it and dropped it. "Um, maybe you could talk to Donny Swanson. He might be able to tell you about the drugs."

Halloran nodded and wrote the name down in a small notebook. "That's helpful, thanks."

She reached out and grabbed his arm. "Please don't say anything. Don't say I told you, please."

"We won't." He handed her his card. "If you think of anything else, please call me. Anything at all."

———•◆•———

THE RINGING of the phone in his jacket pocket startled him awake. He'd dozed off, his head resting against the window of Stevens' car on the drive back to the city.

"Halloran," he barked into the phone.

"You want to explain to me why you've been nosing around my case?"

Blake assumed this was the cop who'd shown up at the scene last night. "Who is this?"

"Officer Kyle Jeffries. I spoke with you last night at the accident scene. I called the ER. Apparently, you've been over to Saint A's and talked with the victim and collected evidence. You're a real Sherlock Holmes, except nobody asked for your assistance.

Makes me wonder if you aren't involved in her assault, you're so keen to be a part of it. What gives?"

Blake was fuzzy from sleep, but he'd always been good at thinking on his feet. "You never showed up, and the situation is similar to a homicide we're currently investigating, so I've looked into it. I'm going to ask that it be transferred to DPD so we can handle the investigation." He saw Stevens turn and give him a *'what the fuck?'* look, which he ignored.

"It's not getting transferred, so keep your fucking nose out of it! Got it?"

"I think you need to refresh your memory on how to talk to a superior officer." He didn't add that he intended, based on the call, to make every effort to get the case transferred to him.

"You watch your step, bro, or I'm gonna start thinking you're the one who did her."

"Right," Blake said as he disconnected.

"What the fuck was that all about?"

"I stepped on some toes, that's all."

"What was all that hogwash about a situation that was similar to one we're working on and transferring a case? You got something connected to this Kensington homicide?"

"No, let it go. I just said that to piss him off," Blake said irritably. "I'll catch you up when I have something to tell you."

"You keep your nose clean, partner. I don't want my ass in the wringer alongside yours."

Blake frowned and nodded.

———◆———

HE'D COME to work early the following morning and put in a request for the assault victim's case to be transferred. He'd spoken to the lieutenant in charge and had given him a line about the woman's assault relating to a couple of similar assaults, one a homicide. He wasn't sure it was, but he really didn't like Jeffries' attitude or his lack of follow-through. And he had to admit, what he'd said to Stevens was true—he wanted the transfer if for no other reason than to piss Jeffries off.

Jeffries' lieutenant agreed to transfer it, saying they had other stuff on their plates and that an assault on a prostitute with amnesia who couldn't give them any valuable information wasn't worth fighting over.

Blake disconnected, annoyed by the lack of concern, but he was glad that the case would be transferred. Jeffries was gonna be pissed when he got the news, and that made Blake smile.

He put in a call to the hospital and was told the woman would be discharged by early afternoon. He asked that they call him when she was ready, and he'd come pick her up. He put in a call to arrange for a safe house for her and was told they'd get back to him later in the day.

"Halloran, we got another case," Stevens said as he snagged his suit jacket off the back of his desk chair.

"Yeah, what happened?"

"A guy heading for his car around eight this morning found a woman strangled at the back of a bar parking lot in LoDo." Stevens said, referring to the lower downtown area of Denver.

"What was he doing there at eight in the morning? Most bars I know aren't even open then."

"He's the owner of the place. He closes it down at two most nights and tallies the take from the night. It takes him until at least four to get things shut down. According to the cop who interviewed him, he sleeps in his office until morning. One of the cops knows that area pretty well and says the guy sleeps in his office because half the time he's three sheets to the wind by the time the place closes.

"The uniforms are there now and so's the death investigator, so we need to head over. By the time we get there the DI should be finished. I'll let the crime scene techs know."

Denver had so many homicides and suspicious, accident-related, and unattended deaths that the city had instituted the use of death investigators to assess the scene, take photos, and make a preliminary determination of death. The rule was no one, not even the detectives, were allowed to touch the scene or the body until the DI was done and had released it.

When they arrived, the DI met them and tersely related what she'd determined. The body was minus her fingertips, death was by strangulation, and had probably occurred around two-thirty in the morning. The area where she was found was probably not where she'd been killed as there was no obvious sign of a struggle or blood from the fingertip amputations. The woman had no purse, no car keys. Even her jewelry—assuming she'd been wearing any—was gone.

"She's all yours gentlemen. Not sure when the autopsy will be done, things are kinda backed up at the moment, but I'll email you as soon as I know when it's scheduled."

They nodded as she walked off and they walked into the parking lot toward the body. No purse, no car keys, nothing that would ID her, like Ashley Kensington and the woman he'd nearly hit, Blake thought. The only difference was the assault victim's fingertips weren't missing. But one had been lacerated. Had the perp started to cut her and stopped, or been interrupted? Maybe he was right, and the amnesic woman was connected in some way.

He shook his head. Jane Doe had been left where she was unlikely to be found, but this woman had been left in full view like Ashley. His Jane Doe had a serious head injury that could have killed her, even if the strangulation hadn't, but this one didn't. She might be connected to the other homicides or not. However, in spite of the differences, he thought she might be.

No one in the surrounding LoDo restaurants or businesses that were open had recognized the woman based on the physical description given out or had heard anything. He had the uniformed officers ask around, hoping someone might know her. He wasn't going to have them show a photo around, victims of strangulation weren't pretty sights. The owner didn't recognize her and said the place had been busy and he had been "out front," as he called the main bar area, only sporadically.

He gave Stevens a list of employees working the previous night and had reluctantly given them the customers' credit card receipts so they could be contacted. They'd begin locating and calling them when they got back to the precinct and see if any of them had seen her alive in the restaurant or the parking lot. And, more importantly, whether anyone had noticed if she'd been with someone.

No easy way to ID her. The crime scene techs bagged her hands and canvassed the parking lot for possible evidence. No missing fingertips, so the killer had taken them with him or disposed of them elsewhere. The EMTs bagged her and took her to the morgue.

Her clothes were classy in a high-end sort of way, but also bordered on…Blake wasn't sure what to call them, but they made him wonder if she was an escort. He couldn't say why, maybe he had working girls on the brain since the encounter with Jane Doe.

He did some research into escort services when they returned to the precinct. Stevens assigned several uniformed officers to find contact information for the credit card holders, phone the bar employees, and make arrangements for them to come in for interviews.

Most escorts had a photo and a first name on the sites they worked for, but not much else. Descriptions of them tended toward the banal: "likes talking and laughing and having fun with my date." No mention of sex.

After talking with a detective he knew in vice, he learned the men who hired them provided no last names either, unless they were caught in the act and arrested. The vice detective also said the sites were careful not to offer sex, but most people buying time with an escort probably had sex in mind.

The owners of several escort services assured him they weren't selling sex, merely an escort. When pressed, they said that what escorts chose to do on the dates was up to them. Presumably that might include sex, but that was not what the business provided or guaranteed. What they didn't say was that not specifically offering sex was a way to avoid a charge of prostitution. It didn't fool anyone.

As far as the official business, credit cards were used to pay for the date. If the escort provided sex on the date, there was no record of it because that part, according to the vice cop, was strictly a cash business.

If the dead woman had been an escort, identifying her would require sifting through an awful lot of websites, which is what he'd spent the day doing with no luck. They'd probably have to release her photo to the media to get a hit.

———◆———

"WE'VE DONE a final CT on her. There's no bleeding, so we're going to discharge her," the doc on the neuro floor said when he called Blake.

"I was told you'd pick her up and take care of finding a place for her to stay. I've given her a referral for a therapist who can perhaps help her recover her memory or at least deal with any residual psychological effects of the assault."

"When will she be released?"

"We have to finalize some paperwork, but she'll be ready in about an hour. She's got no name so far or address, so this'll be a write-off. If that changes and she has insurance or some way to pay for it, let the business office know."

He paused. "She doesn't have any clothes either. Everything she had on was taken in evidence. Can you bring something for her? The hospital gets pissy when we send people home in scrubs."

"Yeah, I guess."

They ended the call and Blake gazed blankly at his desk. He'd never bought clothes for a woman before, not even his mother. Where the hell could he get something simple? And cheap, since he would be paying for it.

He'd been told there weren't any safe houses available and probably wouldn't be for quite a while until a gang-related trial due to start in a week was over. A witness had been shot and killed sitting at a stoplight the night before. All the other witnesses had been quickly placed in safe houses. *Maybe a hotel*, Blake thought, *at least for the time being.*

"Halloran!" Stevens shouted from his desk.

Blake jerked. "What?"

"Did you get anything from the escort services you called?"

"No. Maybe I'm wrong about her. It was just a hunch."

"Not a bad one, I had the same thought."

"Stevens, I've got something I need to take care of. I'll touch base with you this evening if that's okay."

"This have anything to do with that case you got transferred to us?"

Blake gazed at him in surprise. "How'd you find out?"

"The captain corralled me and asked what was up. I bullshitted him. Told him we thought it might relate to the kid who was strangled in Cheesman. I don't like getting caught with my pants down, partner, so fess up."

Blake explained what had happened. "I've got a weird feeling about this. And I don't like that the cop on scene basically blew it off until he discovered I was interested, yet he never made an appearance. That was what the phone call in the car was about."

Leaning his elbows on his desk, he rubbed his eyes. "She's ready for discharge and she has nowhere to go and no money. I looked into safe houses, but the DA's office has taken over all the ones we have because of that drive-by the other night. I guess I'll pay for a hotel room for a day or two until I can figure out where to put her. I'll have to pop for it, I'm hoping I can get reimbursed for it."

"She can't remember anything?"

"Nothing, not even her name."

"Hmmm. Not sure you'll get reimbursed, but she's an assault victim and she needs a place to stay, so it's worth a try. Not sure what you'll do with her if she doesn't regain her memory."

"Me either. Um, any idea where I can buy some clothes for her?"

Stevens looked nonplussed. "You've never bought clothes for a woman?"

"No."

Clark shook his head. "My wife shops at Target, Kohl's, or Walmart. One of those should work."

"Thanks. I don't know, I've got this feeling about her. Maybe what happened is related to the kid and the body that turned up this morning."

"You're reaching, Halloran. She still has her fingertips." Stevens waved his hand at Blake. "Go pick her up."

CHAPTER SIX

O N THE WAY to the hospital Blake stopped at a Walmart to the south of Sixth Avenue. He'd purchased flowers and expensive dinners for women, taken a few on mini vacations depending on whether it was near a holiday or their birthday or what he was trying to apologize for, but never clothes.

He looked around the women's section and pawed through a couple of the endless circular hanging racks of clothes. He had no idea what to get, and the clothes ran from child size to gargantuan.

"You look kinda lost. Do you need some help?" An employee with a shopping cart piled full of clothes stood holding one of those price-tag guns used to shoot a plastic thing through the clothing to hold the tag on. She'd stopped affixing the tags and was smiling.

Blake smiled back. "Yeah, that'd be nice. I didn't think there'd be this much to choose from."

"Who are you buying clothes for?"

Blake hesitated. He didn't want to divulge the woman's victim status or that he was a cop. "Uh, it's a woman I know who's getting out of the hospital after an accident. Her clothes were ruined."

"Oh, well then, she'll probably want something comfortable. You can't go to her home and pick something up?"

Blake shook his head no but didn't say why.

She nodded, looking puzzled. "Maybe a pair of sweatpants and a top would be good. What size?"

Blake tried to remember how she'd looked, but the images were all jumbled together. "Um, a medium I guess."

The woman gave Blake another puzzled look but walked off down the aisle, and Blake followed. A few minutes later she had found a soft navy velour top and matching pants with an elastic waistband. "How's this?"

"Good, thanks. This'll be great. I appreciate your help."

"Do you need anything else?"

"No, I think I've got what I need."

She frowned at him. "Does she have undies? You said her clothes were ruined. She'd need underwear and some shoes, won't she?"

"Uh, yeah, probably so." God, he felt like an idiot, like some sort of pervert or serial killer with a kidnapped woman hidden in his basement. "I-I'm not sure what size she wears."

"Well, let's go take a look." She took off toward the underwear section. Blake followed, embarrassed.

She picked out a couple pair of underpants and held them up for Blake's inspection. He nodded his head and threw them in his cart with the jogging suit. They weren't very attractive, but she was an assault victim not a girlfriend, so he supposed their attractiveness wasn't all that important.

She picked out a T-shirt-like top with narrow elastic straps, something he remembered a former girlfriend calling a 'cami.' "I'd suggest that you get her this rather than a bra—it's got a shelf bra with some support but buying a regular bra without a size doesn't really work well."

She held out the top, and Blake took it and tossed it into his cart. God only knew what a shelf bra was. "Thanks, I really appreciate your help and so will she."

He held out his hand and she took it. "Thanks again, I'm going to wander over and get her some shoes. You've been a big help."

Blake pushed his cart in the direction of the shoes.

"You're welcome," she called out. "Hope your friend gets well soon."

"Thanks. Me, too."

He moved off with relief. She had been extremely helpful, but it was clear she was becoming more curious about who he was and who he was buying clothes for.

He arrived at the hospital with his Walmart bags in hand and approached her room. A nurse saw him and stopped him. She took the bags and handed them off to another staff member, pointing her in the direction of the woman's room with instructions to help the patient get dressed.

"I need to go over her discharge instructions and have you sign off on them. I did that with her, but with a head injury we like to make sure someone responsible also gets the info."

Blake cringed. Someone responsible—is that what he'd become? Apparently so, he thought as he listened to the nurse rattle off the instructions, had him sign them, and gave him a copy.

"You can get your car and pull it up front, and when she's dressed and ready, I'll bring her down in a wheelchair."

"Wheelchair? That's just hospital policy, right? I mean she can walk, right?"

"Relax, Detective. It's hospital policy. She can walk just fine."

———•◆•———

WHEN THE nurse arrived in the front entry area of the hospital with Jane Doe—he didn't know how else to think of her—the clothes looked a little bit large, but the tennis shoes he'd bought seemed to fit. Someone had rolled the pantlegs up several times to keep them from engulfing her feet. She was so much tinier than he remembered and frail-looking with her bandaged head and pale, bruised face. She was dressed, that was the important thing he guessed. The nurse helped her into the car, wished them well, closed the door, and left.

Blake looked over at her and smiled, trying, he hoped, to reassure her. "I thought I'd put you up at a hotel for tonight at least, until I can make other arrangements. Right now, the safe houses are full." He saw a flare of panic in her eyes. "Don't worry, you don't have to pay for it."

"Thank you."

Her eyes darted nervously around the car, lighting on him briefly and skittering away. Getting into a car with a man she really didn't know who had told her he was taking her to a hotel probably was unnerving, even if she'd been told he was a cop. A driver behind them hit his horn to get Blake to move. He put the car in gear and pulled farther down the hospital's front drive and parked. He wasn't sure how much she remembered from their first contact, so he pulled his shield off his belt and showed it to her.

"I'm a cop, remember? Detective Halloran. You'll be safe. No one will know you're there. I'll register you under my name." Then he thought saying that might be alarming to her as well. "I know you don't know me other than what I've told you. If you want, you can use my phone to call the precinct and verify my identity."

"No, that's not necessary. The nurses told me they'd confirmed who you were. I just…it's uncomfortable not knowing anything."

Blake nodded. "They gave me some prescriptions to fill for you, some pain pills and antibiotics. Why don't we go fill those and then we can get you settled at the hotel?"

He took a deep breath and exhaled, trying to get rid of the uncomfortable feeling that swamped him. Trying to force images of Lindsey away. As partners they'd had each other's backs, responsible in many ways for each other. Now, he never put himself in a position where he had to take care of anyone. He wasn't any good at it. He'd assumed responsibility for this woman, though, so he'd have to give it a shot.

She nodded, staring out the window as he drove out of the hospital campus. Her hands were clasped tightly together in her lap. He drove into town and found a Walgreens near the hotel he had in mind.

"Do you want to come with me to get these filled?" He hoped she didn't. The way she looked would attract too much attention, but he felt he should ask. She silently shook her head no.

"I'll be right back," he said. He got out of the car, hit the lock button on his key fob, and walked into the Walgreens. While waiting for the prescriptions to be filled, he walked the aisles trying to pick out things he thought she'd need. His phone buzzed.

"Halloran."

"You got the case transferred. I told you to leave it alone," Jeffries said angrily. "You had no right to do that. What the fuck's the matter with you? Are you trying to piss me off?"

"I had it transferred because you did nothing to follow up on the assault. Somebody needed to."

"She's a fucking prostitute who got beat up by her john. It's a case going nowhere, and you know it. You got it transferred to jerk me around. Not a good idea, bro."

"This is the second time you've called me and been insubordinate and I'm tired of it. Call me again, and I'll put you on report. If you'd done your job, the case would have been yours, but it sounds like you had no intention of doing that. Don't call me again unless you want a disciplinary action in your file," Blake said and disconnected.

The guy was a real asshole. It was clear at the scene that neither of them liked the other. Maybe that's what his antagonism was all about. Jeffries didn't like him, and Blake had probably embarrassed him. Or he was one of those cops who did as little as possible to get by and didn't want that called to anyone's attention.

Twenty minutes later he returned to the car with a white plastic bag that urged people to get their blood pressure taken and 'Know your numbers!' He'd been a little shocked at the price of the meds but had put them on his credit card along with the other toiletries he'd purchased.

He handed the bag to her and drove to the hotel. It wasn't far from his apartment, and it was a decent place that wasn't exorbitantly expensive. He planned to talk it over with his captain, but he had a sneaking suspicion that he was going to foot the bill for all of this. At the moment, he had no idea what else to do with her.

He had her wait in the car that he'd parked under the hotel portico until he'd checked her in, wanting to avoid as much exposure as possible. Blake explained to the clerk that she was under police protection and no information about her was to be given out. He asked that if anyone asked about her, they notify him.

"No visitors, no information about her, not even her presence here is to be given out. Are we clear on that?"

"Yes, of course, Detective. Quite clear." The clerk produced two key cards in a packet with the room number written on it. "This is the room number. I've instructed all charges to be put on the card you provided."

"Thanks," Blake said brusquely, taking the key cards.

He went outside and escorted the woman into the lobby. She moved carefully as if the wrong movement would set off a cascade of pain. The clerk stared at her face with its bruises and the bandages wrapped around her head as Blake moved her quickly toward the elevators. Christ, what was he going to call her?

Arriving on the fifth floor and walking down to her room, he handed her a key card. "I'm going to keep one of these until we find another place for you. I know you're probably freaked out about all of this, but you'll be safe here. I won't come in unannounced, I promise, but I think I should have a key."

She nodded, her hand shook a little as she took the card key from him, and they entered the room. She had said nothing since their brief conversation at the hospital. She held her body stiffly, periodically a shudder would pass through her.

The frown hadn't left her face since he'd picked her up, but she wasn't decompensating and that was both a relief and somewhat surprising. Most women he knew would have been pretty rattled if not hysterical. Looking around blankly, she abruptly sat on the end of the bed. She pushed a hank of dark red hair unconstrained by the bandage out of her face and sighed.

"Thank you. I appreciate you doing this. Tell me your name again? I can't seem to remember it."

"Blake Halloran."

"Right, that's right. Now I remember."

"I don't know what to call you. Have you remembered anything about what your name might be?" She shook her head. "Okay, then let's use Jane, like Jane Doe?"

She looked up and gave him a tiny smile. Blake shrugged, embarrassed. "Yeah, not very imaginative, is it?"

"That's fine. It's better than nothing."

Her face looked so bleak when she said that it worried him. "It'll come back to you."

"Let's hope."

An embarrassing thought hit him suddenly. "I didn't ask the nurses. I didn't know what all to get you. Do you need, you know, personal stuff?" He'd purchased the basics along with her meds, but there were other things he'd never thought about.

"Like what?" Then he saw the light go on. She flushed. "No, not at the moment."

God, he thought, *I hope you remember who you are and what happened before I have to go and buy tampons.* Maybe he could convince one of the women detectives he knew into talking to her and finding out whatever else she might need. Maybe he could talk one of them into buying the stuff as well.

He had no sisters and he'd never lived with a woman before. Dated lots of them, spent a few weekends with them, but he had no idea what they needed on a daily basis. He'd never bothered to ask, and he didn't let most of his relationships last long enough to get that intimate.

Lindsey'd been his partner. For some cops, partners were closer than a spouse, and it had been true for them. They'd joked about sex and people they dated. He'd joked about PMS or being hard up for sex if she was in a bad mood. She'd teased him about his brain being ruled by his dick. He'd have done anything for her, but there were limits to what they'd talked about.

After a relationship of more than a few months blew up, he'd find remnants of lotion, perfume, lipstick, and other odds and ends scattered throughout his bathroom and the apartment. Occasionally, he'd find a half-empty box of tampons or a tube of spermicide in the back of the cabinet under the bathroom sink, or a pair of panties that had found their way between the couch cushions or under his bed.

He always tossed everything the former girlfriend had left behind. No point in leaving anything for the next woman to find. *Kind of like policing your brass*, he thought. *Leave no evidence*. There were probably many reasons why nothing lasted, he acknowledged.

"Well," he said abruptly, clearing his throat, "I should go. You probably want to get a shower or something." He pulled his wallet out and extracted a business card. Walking over to the small desk in the room he scribbled something on the back of it. "This is my cell number, just call if you need anything," he said handing her the card.

"I'm going to look into more long-term arrangements tomorrow. I told them to put everything on my credit card, so when you want food order it from room service and charge it to the room."

He didn't want to scare her, but he wanted her to be careful. "I doubt seriously if the person who attacked you will risk further contact, and no one knows you're here, but to be on the safe side, if you order room service, when it comes, look out the peephole and make sure it's an employee. Ask them to hold their ID badge up so you can see it and call the front desk to confirm their name. Or tell them to leave the cart outside the door. Don't open the door until you're sure they've left. Don't open the door to anyone else. Okay?"

She nodded, the crease between her brows was back, and she looked anxious and worried. "I know this is frightening for you, I know you're worried, but you're safe here. I don't live far from here, so call if you need to."

"Thank you." She stood up and he took that as his cue to leave. She walked him to the door.

He opened it and paused. "Be sure and keep it locked. Use the extra locking mechanism they have," he said, showing her the security doorstop. Blake hesitated. He was anxious to go and yet reluctant to leave her alone.

"Okay, well, sleep well. Don't forget your antibiotics and pain meds. Call me if anything comes up." *Jesus*, he thought, *how many times did I say call me if you need me? I sound like a broken record.* She flustered him for some reason he couldn't put his finger on.

She nodded and closed the door after him.

CHAPTER SEVEN

S HE TURNED THE lock and used the security doorstop. *Now what?* she thought leaning against the door. The emptiness in her head—an empty blankness that she couldn't fill with anything before she awoke in the dark in the culvert— was frightening. To have no clue what your name was or who you were, was terrifying.

Christ, she didn't even know what she looked like. Being classified as a fall risk by the nurses, they had helped her into the bath to use the toilet without letting her spend much time there. She'd caught a brief glimpse of a stranger walking past the mirror, but had never been given the time to stare at herself.

What if her memory never came back? What if she never remembered who she was or where she belonged, or why she'd been assaulted? Her heart began to race, and it was hard to take a normal breath. She shuddered and sat down on the bed. She didn't know who to trust, what to say, or what effect it would have on her safety, so she'd decided to say as little as possible. *Better safe than sorry*, she thought.

The sense of wariness felt familiar and she wondered if it was the result of what had happened to her or an integral part of her personality. Had something other than the assault happened to her to make her so wary? The nurses said Blake Halloran was who he claimed to be, and he'd gone out of his way to reassure her, but nothing dispelled the low-level anxiety that plagued her, and which periodically spiked to near panic.

She let her head drop into her hands and tried to breathe slowly. There was no point in putting herself through this right now. The doctors had said her memory would come back. They just didn't know when. She had to trust that it would, hope that it would, but trust was as hard to come by as hope.

Not trusting felt familiar, too. Wary and untrusting. What would make her like that? Was there some reason why she shouldn't trust the people who had helped her?

Although she'd done next to nothing, leaving the hospital and the arrival at the hotel had wiped out any reserves she had. She brought the bag of supplies Blake had purchased into the bathroom and set it on the counter. Looking in the mirror, she saw a face she didn't recognize. Dark red hair fell over her shoulders, green eyes stared back at her, and the face she saw was pale and bruised. A sprinkling of freckles dusted the bridge of her nose. Had she liked how she looked? Other than the bruises, it was a pleasant, maybe even pretty face, but it wasn't familiar.

The bag he'd given her contained a toothbrush, toothpaste, a brush and comb, deodorant, and a package of disposable razors. His priorities were interesting, she thought. The razors would have to wait. There were too many scrapes and scabs on her legs to even try to shave them and she didn't care how they looked.

The nurse had told her she could shower and wash her hair as long as she didn't submerge the wound on her head in water. She removed the bandage on her head and the one on her finger and stripped off the unfamiliar clothes as the shower heated up. He'd tried, and she appreciated the effort, but the jogging suit was a size too big and hung on her.

The underpants were similarly large and granny style, but at least comfortable, as was the little camisole with the shelf bra. He must have had some help there. He wasn't all that familiar with buying women's clothes, if the jogging suit and underpants were any indication. *He's probably an expert at getting them off,* she thought and then wondered where that had come from. How would she know?

He was the only person she had to rely on, but she didn't know him. He was tall and imposing. His height, tousled, dark blond hair, and deep blue eyes made him look interesting, but risky, to know. There was an air of control about him, a seriousness and alertness that made him seem just slightly dangerous. She'd watched him scan the lobby with a thoroughness that was probably natural to a cop.

His face was closed and unreadable, distracted and concerned, seemingly on alert. For what, she didn't know. Other than an occasional reassuring smile he'd graced her with, he would be someone you approached carefully. He'd been awkward and at times embarrassed with her and she got a distinct sense of reluctance about him. She wasn't sure what that was about, but he'd gone out of his way to reassure her.

After letting the water heat up, she stepped into the tub carefully holding onto the grab bar like an old woman. Her thigh muscles protested as she lifted them over the side of the tub one at a time. She stood with a wide stance hoping to add to her stability, afraid she might slip. Maybe taking a shower tonight hadn't been a good idea. If she slipped and fell and hit her head again, it probably wouldn't matter whether her memory returned.

She turned the water temperature up as far as she could tolerate, let it massage her shoulders and back, and felt her muscles relax. It was a relief to finally wash the dried blood out of her hair, and the lemony scent of the hotel's sample shampoo and conditioner was a welcome change from the hospital's antibacterial soap. The scalp wound was tender and prickly with staples—that they'd used staples to close the scalp wound was a surprise—but some of the crusted blood around them had washed away and her hair was clean.

Washing her hair had left her arms aching and weak from the exertion. She felt exhaustion wash over her and ended up bent over with one hand braced on her knee and the other holding onto the grab bar, breathing slowly through her mouth, hoping she wouldn't pass out. She hated feeling this way, she preferred being in control, she preferred to assess a situation and have a plan for dealing with it. Did she? It felt familiar and being in control was preferable to feeling like a helpless dishrag.

When she felt less shaky, she rinsed off and turned off the shower. She held onto the towel bar to steady herself as she stepped out. Reaching for a towel set off a cascade of protests from the muscles of her shoulders. She dried off sitting on the closed toilet. When done, she stood in front of the full-length mirror on the bathroom door and took inventory.

She hadn't recognized her face earlier, and she didn't recognize the slender, well-toned body in the mirror. She lifted her elbows to see the scrapes and saw the muscles of her upper arms stand out and wondered if she'd been used to manual labor or just lucky to have such well-defined muscles. Her knees were scraped and scabbed over. Her thighs and calves were toned and athletic looking. What she saw in the mirror was the body of a stranger.

She was bruised nearly everywhere. Several of her fingernails had broken and a nurse in the ER had used a fingernail clipper to trim them, collected the clippings, and bagged them as evidence. The ugly purple marks stood out against the paleness of her neck and were the most unsettling of her injuries. Why had she been assaulted? Had she done something to provoke it?

Look what the cat dragged in. You're quite a sight.

The male voice echoed in her head and a stab of terror flashed through her. Where had that come from? Had someone said it to her in real life? Was it a friend or family member, or was it the person who had assaulted her? She shuddered. It wasn't the voice she remembered hearing lying in the dark the night of the assault. That voice had wanted her safe and was probably her own mind in self-preservation mode. This voice was sarcastic, critical, and vaguely threatening, and she had no idea who it was.

She took out the brush and comb, toothpaste, and a tooth-brush from the Walgreens bag—for a moment his name had disappeared then flashed back—that Blake had given her. He'd left a small staple remover kit in its sterile packaging in the bag as well. She remembered the nurse who discharged her showing her a pair of staple removers she kept in her pocket and instructing her how to use them.

"Ten days at the very least before they should be taken out. A doctor or a nurse at an urgent care facility can do it, but they're not hard to remove. Maybe that detective who seems so taken with you can do it for you. It'd save you a charge for the urgent care."

Taken with her? If he was taken with her she hadn't noticed, but she had a lot on her mind. He'd been very thoughtful in spite of the poorly-sized clothing, and she was grateful. Ten days seemed like an eternity, perhaps by then she'd know who she was and would know who to go to for their removal. If not, Blake would probably know where to take her.

She smiled, remembering the look of panic on his face when he'd alluded to tampons. She'd been tempted to tell him she needed them, if only to see his face. But she really wasn't in any mood to tease.

Exhausted, she brushed her teeth, combed through her hair, loosely braided it—without anything to secure it—and returned to the bedroom. He'd forgotten to buy pajamas, so she slipped back into the camisole and a clean pair of granny panties.

She took her antibiotics and a pain pill and crawled into bed. Lying in the dark she wondered, again, whether she would ever remember who she was and, if she didn't, what would happen to her. As the pain meds began to take effect, her eyes closed, and she drifted off to sleep.

———◆———

BLAKE SPOTTED Fleur's car in the small parking lot attached to his apartment house as he turned into the lot. He sighed. He didn't need this right now, and he wondered momentarily whether he could turn around and leave unnoticed, but she'd spotted his car. The driver's side door to her car opened and Fleur got out, waving at him.

"Fuck!" he muttered as he pulled into the parking spot next to her car. "Hey, what're you doing here?" he asked as he got out of the car.

There was a momentary flash of irritation on her face before she said, "I met a friend in town earlier and, since I was nearby, I decided to see if you were home. I texted you, but you didn't reply. I haven't seen you in days!"

It's only been three, Blake thought irritably. He checked his phone and, sure enough, she'd texted. But he also noticed that his phone was on silent, so he wouldn't have heard the chime anyway. He wished he had. Had he known about the text, he could have avoided her. *Yeah, it's breakup time,* he thought. *But not tonight.*

"I thought I'd surprise you. I brought some dinner and a bottle of wine."

She was trying, and he'd felt sort of bad about bailing on the evening they'd planned the other night. So, he put on a happy face.

"Sounds great, come on in."

Dinner had been far better than the beer, cheese, and crackers he'd planned on, and the wine had disappeared fast. Although he'd have preferred she go home, he and Fleur had ended the evening in bed together.

He'd never quite made up the sleep he'd lost the night of the near accident, and the wine and sex had sent him into a deep, drugged-like sleep. He wasn't sure how long the phone had been ringing before his hand finally connected with it.

"Halloran," he mumbled. He was so groggy he wasn't sure whether he'd actually said that or just thought it. The line was silent. "H'lo?" He was about to disconnect when he heard her voice.

"I heard someone in the hallway bump against my door. I'm sorry to call, but I don't know what to do."

"You've got the extra security on?"

"Yes."

"Then no one can get in." He rubbed his free hand across his face, trying to rub the fog away. "It was probably some drunk trying to find his room. Probably nothing to worry about."

"Blake? Who're you talking to?" He waved Fleur off with his hand and didn't answer her.

"I'm sorry, I should have remembered about the locks. It woke me up. I…it worried me."

"It's okay. I'd rather you call if you're concerned about something. If it happens again let me know, but I think it's probably nothing to worry about." She didn't respond.

"Are you okay?" She said nothing. "Jane? Are you okay?"

He heard her take a deep breath. "Yes, I'm sorry. I was frightened, so I wanted to talk to someone I knew. I'm sorry to bother you." And she disconnected.

He stared at the phone for a minute, thought about calling her back, then put the phone on his bedside table.

"Jane? Who's Jane?" Fleur demanded, sitting up in bed.

"An assault victim."

"An assault victim who's calling you at two in the morning?"

"Yes. Let it go, Fleur."

"Who is she really?"

"An assault victim. It's not personal, it's work."

"Work!" She flounced out of bed and began collecting her clothes that lay scattered on the floor. "It's always work with you. Work that always intrudes on our time together. I don't know any victims who call a detective at two in the morning."

Blake sighed and ran a hand over his mouth. "I guess you know a lot of victims," he said irritably. He sat up, the sheet sliding down his chest to pool around his waist. "You don't need to go home or be all pissed off. It was just a phone call. I'm not going anywhere."

She pulled her jeans on and snatched her bra off the floor. He watched as she put it on—hooked it in the front, slid it around, pulled the straps on, then leaned over to adjust her breasts in the cups. It never failed to fascinate him for some reason. Even now, when a fight was brewing it was distracting.

Maybe he could talk her down enough to get her back in bed, fool around, and then go back to sleep. He looked at her face in the dim light and thought, *No, probably not a chance in hell of that.*

"It's not just the phone call, it's this whole job thing with you. It always takes precedence over everything, including—no especially—me."

"Look babe, I'm sorry," he said trying to diffuse things to avoid a fight at two a.m. "Come back to bed. It's late. You don't want to drive all the way back to Boulder."

She had pulled her T-shirt on and was stuffing her feet into her sandals and glaring at him. "Yes, I do. I'm not coming back to bed, so you can forget that. I'm tired of your job fucking everything up. Call me if you decide our relationship is important enough to continue without this constant interruption."

That pissed him off. "What d'you want me to do, quit?"

"I want you to be *present* in this relationship. I want your job to quit fucking everything up. I don't want to be a momentary diversion for you."

"This *is* my job. It interrupts my life on a regular basis. Fleur let's not do this now. It's the middle of the fucking night, and I'm exhausted."

"What better time to do it? Call me if you think I'm worth the trouble of one evening, *one* evening, without the job interfering," she said, and stormed out of the bedroom.

He heard the apartment door slam shut. He flopped down onto his pillow, crooked a hand behind his head, and closed his eyes. *Be present* was one of her favorite phrases. Christ, he didn't even know what she meant by that. Apparently, it meant something far different than it did for him. He figured he was present when he was with her, but maybe being physically there wasn't what she was talking about. Whatever it meant, she wasn't going to get it. Being physically present was all he had to offer.

It was a fucking phone call, he thought angrily. If she was going to get all bent out of shape about it, that was up to her. He rolled to his side, then sat up and punched the pillow a couple times before lying down again.

As he began to drift off to sleep, he thought of Jane Doe. He wondered whether it had been a random confused drunk, or if someone had intentionally been messing with her door. Maybe a hotel wasn't such a good idea.

CHAPTER EIGHT

H E HELD HIS phone to his ear as he made coffee and listened to the phone in Jane's room ring without being picked up. Blake left a brief message, asking her to call him, and disconnected. He figured he'd try her again in a few minutes. He'd swing by the hotel on his way to work, he thought as he walked to the bathroom and got into the shower.

Standing in front of the bathroom mirror shaving, his hand jerked when the phone went off and he nicked himself under the jaw with his razor.

"Shit!" He fumbled for the phone, dropped it, and finally managed to get hold of it and answer. "What?" he snapped.

There was silence for a minute. "Detective Halloran?"

"Yeah?"

"It's…Jane. You left a message asking me to call."

He pressed a piece of toilet paper to his jaw. "Sorry, didn't mean to take your head off. How are things this morning? Any more bumps on your door?"

"No, it's been quiet. I was in the bathroom when you called."

"Figured you might be. I'm going to come by on my way to work, if that's okay."

"I'm not going anywhere." He heard her laugh softly.

"I'll be there in about twenty. Make sure it's me before you open the door."

"I will."

"Did you get breakfast?"

"No, I hadn't thought about it."

"I'll pick something up on the way, see you shortly," he said, and hung up.

He showed up with Dunkin' Donuts and McDonald's breakfast sandwiches and coffee. He didn't know what would appeal and figured he'd eat whatever she didn't. He hoped to God she wasn't as fussy as Fleur.

Boulder was jokingly known as twenty-five square miles surrounded by reality and that wasn't far from the truth. With Fleur it was easier to ask what she *could* eat than to ask her what she couldn't. The list seemed to grow daily.

Beggars can't be choosers, he thought as he knocked on Jane Doe's hotel room door.

He handed her a large coffee and her eyes widened when she saw the bags. "Donuts *and* McDonald's?" She laughed and it suited her, made her green eyes sparkle and her face look less pale and battered.

"I wasn't sure what you'd eat."

"I'm not sure what I eat either," she replied. "It's like going to a foreign country—I have no idea if I like the food on offer or not. But McDonald's and donuts ring a bell. It smells great."

"Well, I don't know anyone who doesn't like donuts or McDonald's." Except Fleur and most of the women he'd dated the last few years, he thought. He handed her the sacks. She sat on the side of the bed, emptied the wrapped sandwiches onto it, and opened the donut box. He sat in the chair next to the window and watched as she inhaled a chocolate glazed donut and began to unwrap a breakfast sandwich.

He laughed as he reached for one of the sandwiches. "Guess I'd better grab something while there's something left to grab."

She stopped and put the partially unwrapped sandwich on the bed. "I'm sorry. I didn't mean to be so grabby. I didn't eat last night. I was tired, and the idea of someone bringing the food to the room worried me."

"Please, eat. I was kidding. It's nice to see a woman actually enjoy eating."

She blushed and picked the sandwich up again. She finished unwrapping it and bit into it, closing her eyes and smiling. "Yum. It would appear that I like both donuts and McDonald's. I can add that to the list of things I know. Thank you."

Blake retrieved a packet of sugar and cream from the bed and stirred them into his coffee, watching as she held the rapidly disappearing sandwich in her hands. Her index finger had been splinted, which made it stick out awkwardly.

"How's the finger?" he asked.

She frowned at it. "A little sore, but otherwise okay. My head is more uncomfortable. I'm a little less sore all over, and a night's sleep without being woken up every couple of hours has helped."

She certainly wasn't a whiner, Blake thought. "Once I get to the precinct I'll try to figure out what to do with you. I'm not sure a hotel is a great option—too public, too many chances for information about you to get out. Plus, the food issue. I don't know how much of a risk it poses, it's unlikely the guy who assaulted you knows you're here, but I'm not crazy about you having to open the door for room service." He shrugged. "Employees tend to talk. I don't want the press or anyone else hounding you."

He sipped his coffee as he watched her drink hers black. "You're going to have to spend the day in the room, so don't leave it. I hope I'll have something a little less like a jail cell for you by the end of the day. Will you be okay with TV for entertainment?"

"I'll be fine. I'm still pretty tired, between the TV and sleeping I'll be fine."

"I think it'd be best if you don't use room service, I can bring some lunch by later."

"If you leave the rest of the donuts and sandwiches, I can eat those for lunch and there's a tiny coffee machine in the room. You don't need to bring something over."

She wadded up the wrapper for the sandwich, tossing it at the wastepaper basket, like a basketball player taking a free throw, and actually hitting it. Had she played basketball?

He grabbed another sandwich and watched as she retrieved a glazed donut from the box and began pulling it apart with her fingers and eating each piece slowly, licking the glazed sugar off her fingers. Delicate, slender fingers, full lips, and a pink tongue that darted out to lick off the sugar. He mentally shook himself.

She puzzled him. She wasn't like any prostitute he'd ever had contact with. She wasn't overtly sexual, and she had no artifice to her. She was educated, if her speech and demeanor were any indication, and she didn't act like a druggie.

He shook his head. It was almost impossible to think of her as a prostitute the more contact he had with her, but she could be a very high-class one. The clothing she'd been found in, though, would suggest otherwise. One more puzzle to unravel.

She interrupted his train of thought. "I don't know if it's important, but I was taking inventory in front of the mirror after I showered last night and '*Look what the cat dragged in. You're quite a sight*' popped into my head. I don't know if someone has said that to me before, or whether it means anything at all. I just…I figured I should tell you."

"Okay, if that happens again let me know. Keep track of what pops up. It might help us identify you or where you came from."

He stood up, taking his coffee and moving to the door. "I should go. Put the 'Do Not Disturb' sign on the door and keep the security door stop on so housekeeping doesn't barge in. Will the clothes I got you hold you until I can figure out a more permanent solution to your situation?" She nodded. "Do you need anything else? Makeup or something?"

"I don't use makeup," she said, then stopped. "I guess. Maybe that's how memory comes back. I guess I don't use it."

"That's good. Every little bit helps." He walked to the door and turned. "If you need anything, call me. I'll touch base with you later."

She certainly didn't need makeup. Even bruised and beaten up, she was pretty, very pretty, he thought as he walked to the elevator. But she'd had smeared remnants of makeup on when the accident happened, so maybe she did wear it and didn't remember. Or perhaps only wore it when she was trolling for johns.

He liked her. It wasn't sexual, or maybe only peripherally sexual—he was a guy after all and she was pretty—but he liked her, had liked talking to her while they ate. It was easy to be around her. He had to admit he was impressed with how she managed to get out of the culvert and, now, by her self-control. Most women he knew would have a case of sustained hysteria, but Jane, while worried seemed pretty level-headed.

As the doors to the elevator closed, he reminded himself she was most likely a prostitute. He felt the heat rise in his neck and face as he caught himself comparing her to Fleur and finding Fleur lacking.

I can't get along with a normal woman, he thought, *but apparently, I get along fine with a prostitute.*

CHAPTER NINE

"**LOOK, SHE'S AN** assault victim but she's totally amnesic. She doesn't know who she is or who hurt her. I need to find a safe place for her to stay until she remembers what happened."

He tried unsuccessfully to rub away the frown line between his brows. "I've got her in a hotel room at the moment. Surely you have somewhere? A studio apartment, a shelter, or something that she could go to?"

Blake listened and then slammed the handset of his desk phone down and sat back with his arms folded over his chest. What the hell was he going to do with her?

He'd talked to the DA's office and to Victim's Assistance hoping that some sort of housing had opened up. Neither the DA's office nor Victim's Assistance had offered any solutions. For the foreseeable future, safe houses were unavailable. In desperation he'd contacted several women's shelters, and all but one was full. *It must be domestic violence month*, he thought irritably. The woman he spoke with at the one with a vacancy said they couldn't assume responsibility for Jane once she found out Jane was amnesic.

Hell, he'd even hit up a couple of the women detectives and uniforms he knew and asked if they'd consider housing her with them for a while. The women he asked gave him the hairy eyeball and walked off, shaking their heads.

He leaned his elbow on the desk, dropped his forehead into his hand, and massaged it. He couldn't really afford to keep her at the hotel indefinitely. One more night until he could think of something else wouldn't break the bank.

The escort search wasn't going any better—six sites and no hits. The woman left in the bar parking lot might not be an escort. Maybe he was off the mark there. Assumptions were okay, but it didn't pay to get too locked into them.

It was possible she worked privately. But if so, how would she get customers? Probably a website, he decided, but without a name there wasn't much chance he'd find it. If she wasn't an escort, then who was she and how had she ended up dead in a bar parking lot without her fingertips? And why hadn't anyone called about her going missing?

Stevens was busy interviewing patrons of the bar and so far no one recognized the woman. Steven's said that he planned to go back to Wellington and interview the couple Ashley had babysat for and her former boyfriend the following day. By the end of the day Blake was tired of looking at the sites and their advertisements.

Although he had a lot of objections to the whole process, he could see the appeal of hiring an escort. It'd certainly be less demanding than hooking up with a new girlfriend—or dealing with the current one—he thought as he left the precinct and headed to Jane's hotel.

———◆———

HE ARRIVED with dinner at about seven. "I'm going to have to leave you at the hotel for at least another day since I haven't been able to make any other arrangements," he said when he got to her hotel room. "Do you need anything else? Clothes or anything?"

"I'm fine with being here, but would it be possible to get another pair of pants and a top, maybe some pajamas?"

"Sure. There's a Target nearby"

She nodded. "This outfit's very comfortable, and with all the scrapes and bruises it's good that it's loose. It'd be nice to have a change of clothes, though."

"I think it'd be better if I went alone. Your injuries would cause a lot of curiosity."

"Okay, I'll write down a couple of things I could use and my sizes." She indicated the bag he'd brought with him. "Dinner?"

"Yeah, such as it is. Hope you like Chinese."

"I guess we'll find out. It smells wonderful." She took the bag and carried it to the small table by the window, set the containers out, and hesitated. "Oh dear, chopsticks?"

His face reddened. "I forgot to ask for forks. Can you manage?"

"I don't know, maybe not with my finger in a splint. Are you okay sharing the boxes? There aren't any plates available unless I call room service."

"As long as you don't mind. You know these open up flat, if you take the handle off?" he said indicating the small white boxes with their flimsy wire handles.

She laughed, "No, but that's good."

They sat at the small table by the window and opened the containers. It dawned on him that they wouldn't be able to fill the moo shoo pancakes easily. There were no serving spoons and no plates to put them on.

"Hell, moo shoo pork with no pancakes," he said irritably. "I'm sorry. I didn't think this through very well. I don't have to worry about this when I bring it home."

She smiled, and again he thought how different she looked with a smile on her face. Her hair had been in a braid down her back that morning and now it hung in waves around her face. He wanted to run his fingers through that heavy dark red hair.

Victim, probably a prostitute, he thought, shaking his head to get rid of that train of thought.

"It's okay. We'll figure something out. At least the shrimp will be easy for me to stab with a chopstick. We don't have to put the moo shoo into pancakes, do we?"

"No. Maybe I should call room service."

"Oh, don't bother. I'll manage."

He hadn't enjoyed dinner this much in a while. They laughed when she dropped pieces of food. Using the chopsticks like a two-pronged pitchfork, she managed to eat some shrimp. She really didn't know how to use chopsticks the way they were intended, and the splint made it doubly difficult, so the rice was a huge problem.

"Here," he said, taking her chopsticks from her and picking up a wad of rice between them. She opened her mouth and took hold of his wrist to guide the rice into her mouth. *Pretty mouth*, he thought and, flustered, he retrieved a shrimp from the takeout container and offered it to her.

"I should let you feed me—I'd get more food in my mouth."

He laughed. Then looked at his watch. "We should finish up and I'll go over to the store for those clothes."

He wanted to get out of the hotel room and the close contact with her. It was totally inappropriate, but he wanted her to touch him again. Hell, he wanted more than that. Best go to the store, bring the clothes back, and leave.

———— ◆ ————

"LOCK UP and stay in your room," he told her after he returned with the purchases. "I'll touch base with you in the morning. Call me if anything comes up."

She nodded and he left. He seemed like a nice guy, she thought as she put the new clothes and additional toiletries away. She was getting more comfortable with him now and found herself studying him closely. He was an attractive man, one that intrigued her. She'd caught him watching her eat a donut that morning and the look on his face had sent a flutter through her.

More stiff and sore now than right after the attack, she showered again, mostly for the soothing heat, and took two pain pills. She fell asleep watching TV in the dark and woke up some time later with the sensation of someone pressing the mattress down on either side of her.

A dark form loomed above her. She started screaming and felt his hands clamp around her throat. She thrashed and kicked and grabbed at his hands, trying to pull them away, desperate to draw in air. She began punching into the back of a very solid body with her knees and heard a grunt.

Kicking her legs and twisting her body, she managed to loosen the man's grip on her neck as she tried to flip him to the side. Unable to flip him, she sucked in a huge breath when his grip loosened and screamed, sucked in another breath and, as his hands clamped down on her throat, she began flailing her fists in an attempt to punch him.

Her fist connected with the side of his head and she stabbed the finger with the splint into his face, hoping to hit his eye. He momentarily jerked back, loosening his grip again, which allowed her another quick breath before the pressure returned.

She continued to thrash and kick, as she began to lose consciousness. Frantic, she flailed her hand out and connected with the bedside lamp, which she grabbed and swung at his head. It hit him hard and then crashed to the floor. She heard someone shout into the hallway, "I've called the manager!" and heard a door slam.

The guy's head came up and turned toward the door, and his grip eased slightly. She felt his body shift to the side, and she twisted her body hard, making him lose his balance and fall off the bed. She rolled to the other side of the bed and onto the floor landing on her knees and hoping to make it to the bathroom and shut and lock the door. Instead, he scrambled up, headed for the door to the hallway, and exited the room, slamming the door behind him.

She sucked in huge gulps of air, her heart thumping like a jackhammer in her chest. She staggered up from the floor, her legs barely able to hold her up, and stumbled to the door in the light of the flickering TV screen to relock it.

Shaking all over, and now unable to stand with the adrenaline pulsing through her, she sank to the floor and crawled across the room to the chairs. Using one of the chairs as a crutch to keep her legs from giving out, she pushed it across the room and wedged it up under the door handle.

She sagged back onto the floor. Leaning against the closet door, she pulled her knees up and dropped her head on them. The warm wetness of tears dropped on her thighs as she wrapped her arms around her head and sobbed.

———— ◆ ————

THREE IN the morning, Blake thought as he picked up his phone and answered its insistent ringing. *Must be the witching hour.*

"Halloran," he mumbled.

"He got in somehow. He tried to kill me." Her voice was hoarse and shaky. He could barely make out the words, as if she was whispering, afraid to be overheard.

"Jane? Jesus! What happened?" He sat up abruptly, on alert, swung his legs over onto the floor, and stood up, gathering his clothes and shoving into them.

"He got into my room. I woke up with him trying to strangle me…I can't stay here, he'll come back…I can't stay here."

"No, no, you don't need to. I'll be there in about ten minutes. Lock yourself in the bathroom until I get there. Take the safety latch off so I can get in."

Ten frantic minutes later he walked down the silent hall to her room, wondering how the hell the guy had gotten in with the security measures on. He looked at the door carefully and could see no marks on it. Surely if it had been jimmied in some way the noise would have awoken her, yet the guy had managed to get in unnoticed until he was trying to kill her. Didn't make sense.

He used his card key, saying as he opened the door, "It's me, Jane. You can come out now." There was a chair near the door, and he could see the bed was trashed, sheets and blankets twisted and hanging off the bed, a pillow lying on the floor next to the bedside lamp. He glanced down and saw the 'Do Not Disturb' door hanger lying on the floor inside the doorway.

She cautiously opened the bathroom door. Standing in the pajamas he'd picked out her face was drained of color, her neck was reddened where the assailant had grabbed her, and her eyelashes were wet with tears. She reached out with trembling hands and moved toward him, but he stopped her, holding her at arm's length.

"I need to collect your pajamas before I touch you. Evidence."

She nodded, retrieved the camisole top and a pair of jeans from the dresser drawer, and disappeared into the bathroom.

"Put them on the bed," he said when she came out and held the pajamas out to him.

He followed her, turned her toward him after she'd laid the pajamas on the bed, and held her, stroking her back.

"It's okay, I'll take you to my apartment. You can stay there for now." She sagged into him.

He soothed her for a moment and then untangled from her, grasped her shoulders, and held her away from him.

"I need to call this in and get the crime scene guys over here to dust for prints and whatever else they can find. I brought a bag for you to put your stuff in, so get dressed and pack up while I call."

"One of the guests shouted that he had called the manager. Maybe the manager called the police."

"They'd be here by now if he did. It's not likely. Hotels don't like the publicity of getting the cops involved. The guest may have shouted that to see if it'd stop the noise. If he did call the manager, and the manager came up and found that the noise had stopped, he most likely didn't call it in."

Blake glanced around the room as he called the assault in. Nothing other than the bed and the lamp seemed disturbed. "Did you put the security latch on?" She nodded. "You're sure?"

She turned to him, surprised at the question. "Yes! I put it on. Don't you believe me?"

"I can't figure out how he could have gotten in if that was the case. It doesn't make sense."

"Believe what you want, it was on," she said hoarsely, shoving her clothes into the small carry-on bag he'd grabbed on his way out of the apartment.

He finished the call. "We need to wait until they get here so I can explain what I want them to do. I'll need a statement from you as well, but that can wait. When you're packed, have a seat. I'll take care of this as quickly as I can and then we'll leave."

She nodded without replying as he used the bedside landline to call the front desk and tell them the police were on their way. She slipped into the tennis shoes he'd purchased for her and walked into the bathroom to add the toiletries to the bag. When she returned to the room, she sat on the chair by the table.

Two uniformed cops and a couple of crime scene techs arrived a few minutes later, and Blake explained what he needed to the techs.

"Were you able to scratch him?"

"I'm not sure, it happened so fast." She held up her splinted finger. "I stabbed this into his face. I'm not sure I did any damage."

"Kev, take some scrapings from under her nails and take the outer bandage off and bag it before you get started on the room."

Then he turned to the uniforms. "I'm taking her to another location. You," he said, indicating the officer nearest him. "Stay by the door until the techs are done, then seal it as a crime scene for now."

Turning to the other cop, he said, "Go down and find the manager on duty and tell him what happened. Make sure he understands no one is to go into the room until I've cleared it. Get the security tapes. Don't let him give you the run-around. If he does, let me know and I'll get a warrant. Get his contact information and that of the owner. I'll interview both of them in the morning. When you're done, do a door-to-door on this floor to see if anyone saw or heard anything."

"Guests are going to be pissed at being woken up at four in the morning," the dark-haired cop said.

"It'll be closer to six by the time you get the info from the manager. If people get pissy, tell them an assault happened. That should help smooth things over. See if you can identify the guy who said he was calling the manager and find out if he saw the guy leave. Let me know what you find out."

The cops nodded and Blake guided Jane down the hall to the elevator. They were silent, and he could tell she hadn't liked him questioning her about the security lock. She'd probably be even more unhappy with him after he took her statement.

The whole incident puzzled him. Why would her assailant risk a second contact? If he was a john, a first name at best was all she'd have, and a major investigation into her assault was unlikely with such a slim chance he'd be found. A second attempt, though, that told Blake that there was something seriously at risk for the perp if Jane could identify him.

He wiped a hand over his face. God, he was tired. He'd sort through the details tomorrow.

"You can stay at my place until I can figure out what to do with you."

She nodded.

"Are you okay? Do you need to be seen at an urgent care?"

"No, I'm not okay. As to injuries, I'll probably have a few more sore muscles in the morning and my throat hurts like hell. Otherwise, he didn't have time to do anything other than try to kill me. That's a plus, I guess."

Okay then, he thought, *she's pissed. Well, so be it. At least she's alive.* "I think I've got some tape we can use to keep the splint on your finger. I'll get some gauze in the morning."

She nodded but said nothing.

He scrubbed the back of his neck and yawned. He was tired—no, he was exhausted. The last few days, sleep had been intermittent. He had a headache that felt as if someone was playing a kettle drum in his head.

He realized when they got to his place that it was a mess. He'd gotten used to it being that way and never took much notice of it. Now, it was embarrassing. There were empty beer bottles and an empty pizza box on the floor by the couch. The sheets on his bed hadn't been changed since Fleur had been there. He hoped his other set of sheets was in the closet and not in the laundry hamper.

He didn't want her sleeping on the couch. He wanted to be near the entry door. It was unlikely the mysterious assailant had followed them, but if he had and somehow managed to get in, Blake wanted to be the first person the guy encountered.

"You can sleep here tonight. Have a seat, I need to change the sheets. I'll sleep on the couch. That way I'll be between you and the door, just in case."

She looked like a frightened animal. Her pupils were dilated and the whites showed. "Did he follow us? How would he know I'm here?"

Blake held up his hands. "I doubt he does, but better safe than sorry. Somehow, he figured out where you were. I don't want him showing up here and being able to get to you if he followed us."

He walked down the short hall and disappeared into the bedroom. She heard a door open and heard him moving around in the bedroom. He reappeared a few minutes later and motioned her to follow him. She walked into the bedroom and left her bag on the floor, sitting down on the edge of the bed.

Walking over to his bureau, Blake pulled out a T-shirt and handed it to her. "You can use this until I can replace the pajamas. Bathroom's across the hall."

She nodded and took the T-shirt, balling it up on her lap and staring down at it. He pulled a pillow off the bed and an extra blanket off the top shelf of his walk-in closet and left the room, closing the door behind him with a mumbled, "Goodnight."

⸻ ◆ ⸻

JANE UNDRESSED slowly and slipped his T-shirt over her head. It engulfed her, the arm seams hanging off her shoulders and the hem grazing her mid-thigh. It was soft and well-worn. Pulling the covers back, she crawled into his bed and tugged them up around her shoulders. Unable to get the sensation of the man's hands squeezing her throat out of her mind, the attack replayed in an endless loop.

The sheets smelled of laundry soap, but his scent still clung to the blankets. It surrounded and comforted her, finally allowing her to sleep. But it was sleep plagued by dreams that made no sense. Like a blurred video, she found herself on street corners she didn't recognize, searching, without knowing what was missing or why she was searching. Vague flashes of being in a rural setting made her uneasy. It was like being lost in someone else's dream.

CHAPTER TEN

THE SMELL OF coffee woke her. She was groggy from her restless sleep. Slipping on her clothes and shoes, she walked down the short hall to the kitchen. Her legs were stiff and her muscles ached, bringing the memory of the previous night into sharp focus.

He wasn't the greatest housekeeper, she thought as she made her way into the kitchen. There were dirty dishes in the sink, and the floor could use a broom and mop, but the coffee smelled heavenly.

He turned and held out a mug, raising his eyebrows in invitation.

"Yes, thanks." She took the mug and sat at the table. There were crumbs on its top that she brushed off onto the floor to join the rest of the unidentified muck that was already there. She saw a frown appear on his face.

"Sorry, I wasn't expecting a guest." He sat down at the table and took a drink.

"Do you clean up if you expect one?"

He squirmed a bit and frowned. "Guests don't spend a lot of time in the kitchen."

No, they probably didn't, she thought, remembering the female voice she had heard in the background the night she'd called about the noises at the hotel room door. *His guests, the majority of whom were likely female, probably got moved into the bedroom pretty quickly and were probably moved out just as quickly.*

There didn't seem to be any indication that a woman lived here or had stayed here for any length of time. He was definitely a bachelor if the state of the apartment was any indication.

He got up and returned to the table with a laptop. "I should have done this last night when it was fresh in your mind, but you were pretty shaken up, and I was exhausted, so I figured it could wait." He opened the laptop and tapped a few keys. "Okay, tell me what you remember."

"I took two pain pills because my head was hurting. Well, everything was hurting, that's why I took two. I got ready for bed and checked the locks," she said, giving him a look.

"Then I turned out the lights and turned the TV on for some company. I fell asleep watching it. The next thing I knew I felt someone on the bed. He was kneeling over me and had his hands around my throat."

"You didn't hear anything or sense anything before that?"

"No, nothing. I think he was big, or maybe just heavy. The mattress sank with his weight. He had me trapped between his knees and he closed his hands around my neck." She took a sip, grateful when the coffee relieved the dryness in her mouth.

"I began thrashing around and kicking out. I managed to thump him in the back with my knee several times and I heard him grunt. He didn't say anything. Then I hit him with my fist on the side of his head and stabbed the splint into his face, and he let up on the pressure enough for me to get a breath and scream."

Her hand went involuntarily to her throat, covering the once-again purplish marks where someone had tried to strangle her for the second time.

"I tried to twist my body, hoping I could lever him to the side and off me. It didn't work. He was pretty big, but he lost his grip enough that I got another deep breath."

She cleared her throat and grimaced in pain. "I felt for the bedside lamp with my hand and grabbed it. Then I smashed it against his head, and it fell to the floor. He eased up and I got another breath."

She shuddered and took sip of her coffee. She wanted the warmth of it to soothe her throat but the caffeine wasn't doing much to ease the shaking of her hands. Blake was typing furiously as he listened.

"I heard someone in the hall yell that he'd called the manager, then I heard a door slam. I think it was the door of the guy who'd yelled. My attacker lifted his head and angled toward the door."

She frowned and rubbed her neck as if remembering his hands on it. "I felt his weight shift when he looked toward the door, so I jerked myself to the side and managed to topple him off onto the floor. I rolled off the other side of the bed and was going to make a run for either the bathroom and lock the door or the hallway, but he jumped up and ran for the door and left. I managed to relock the door and barricade it with a chair. Then I called you."

He stopped typing. "Think about it for a minute. Were you able to see him? Was there anything else you felt or sensed? What did he smell like? Could you see what he had on or see any identifying marks or tatts?"

"I couldn't see him clearly. It was dark and the light from the TV was behind him. He was big, at least he looked big to me, but I can't really tell you what he looked like."

"Anything else you remember?"

"He smelled badly of sweat." She sat with her eyes closed for a moment. They flew open suddenly. "He had gloves on and long sleeves. I could feel them when I grabbed at his hands. I'd forgotten that."

She shuddered. "I couldn't pry his hands away. He was very strong, so instead I pounded on him with my fists and knees, hoping I could hurt him enough to get him to let up so I could get a breath."

The coffee cup shook as she raised it to her lips and drank. "When I jabbed my splinted finger into his face and hit him with the lamp, he eased up enough for me to get a breath. The guy yelling about the manager was the only reason I was finally able to throw him off me. I doubt though, if the guy across the hall hadn't said he'd called the manger, that the man would have given up or that my efforts would have had much effect."

"It probably saved your life. All the noise, enough to rile someone up, that was key. What else? Any other smells or impressions, anything that comes to mind?"

"I'm sorry, that's all I remember."

"Okay, Jane…"

"Alex," she said suddenly.

"Is that his name?" he asked, going on alert.

"No," she said with a baffled look on her face. "I…I think it's mine."

"*Your* name? It's a guy's name."

"Not necessarily. It could be a nickname—like a shortened version of Alexandra or Alexis." She frowned at him. "It popped into my head when you called me Jane. I think it's my name. It feels familiar."

"Okay, we'll assume it is. I can check missing person's reports for those names and see if anything turns up. Your fingerprints didn't ring any bells. You're not in the fingerprint databases, I'm not sure why. It's hard to avoid these days. Anything else? Take your time, don't force it."

She drank her coffee and closed her eyes. "Oily."

Blake frowned. "Meaning what?"

"I don't know, a whiff of something oily." The smell was somehow familiar, but what it was and why it seemed familiar was elusive. It felt like it was something she was used to, but something that made her uncomfortable, something that felt…dangerous?

"What kind of oil? Hair oil, furniture oil, car oil?"

"I don't know!" she snapped. "I don't remember, just oily. The smell seemed to come from his hands." She was afraid to say it was familiar because of the discomfort it caused her.

She heard him sigh, and it annoyed her. "What do you want me to do, make something up?"

"No, of course not. It's frustrating. None of this will help us find the suspect." He let out an exasperated breath. "Well, maybe the techs will have found something that'll help. I still want to figure out how he got in, if the security was on."

"*If? If it was on?* You don't believe me, do you?" The anger swelled and made her head hurt.

He raised his hands in frustration. "I don't know how it could have been on. If it looks like a duck, it's probably a duck."

"What the hell does that mean?"

"It means that, *logically*, the latch probably wasn't on. *Logically*, it makes sense that you forgot to use it. In that case all it would take to access the room is a master key, and every damn maid in the place has one. One of them is probably missing. But master keys don't open a security latch."

"I *know* the security was on—I don't care if you believe me or not!" she snapped standing up, grabbing her coffee, and returning to the bedroom. The sound of the slammed door reverberated down the hall.

CHAPTER ELEVEN

"**D**O YOU KNOW anyway someone could get past a security latch on a hotel room door?" Blake asked his partner.

Stevens looked up from his desk, puzzled. "What?"

"A security latch, you know those angled pieces of metal you flip over to make sure no one, like a maid, can enter if you're in the room. Do you know if they can be opened from the outside?"

Stevens leaned back in his chair and cast his eyes up as he thought. "Nope, try Googling it," he said, returning to upright.

"You're a big help," Blake said, sitting down at his desk. He was going to have to touch base with the uniforms who were there last night and get the contact info for the owner and the manager and arrange to interview them. He wondered whether it was worth the time to Google it. In all probability, she'd forgotten to use it.

"You trying to break in somewhere?"

"No. Why do you always assume I'm doing something questionable?"

"I like to jerk your chain," Stevens said with a laugh.

"Well knock it off. I'm trying to figure out whether it could be done if the latch was thrown."

Stevens frowned at him. "Why?"

"According to my amnesic victim, who I had to stash in a hotel room because I couldn't arrange anywhere else for her, someone did just that and tried to kill her last night."

"She didn't throw the latch, then."

"She swears she did."

He raised his eyebrows. "When I was single, I couldn't remember some days whether I'd turned the coffee pot off. I'd figure I did, then I'd come home to a place smelling of burnt coffee and the pot would be wrecked. She could be mistaken."

"I think she probably is. Doesn't matter, I guess—he found her and got in anyway. I have no idea how he knew where she was or why he'd bother to come after her. If he was a john, it makes no sense."

"Did you see this?" Stevens asked as he hit some keys on his computer and brought up 9*News* on the screen. "It ran on the six o'clock news the day you installed her at the hotel. One of the uniforms told me about it this morning. I thought you'd seen it."

Blake looked over his shoulder and watched the video clip from the previous day's news. "Well shit, who talked to that reporter? It gives my name and details about her, including the hotel she was at. Fuck me. If I find out it was someone here that leaked the information, I'll make them wish they hadn't."

"That one's good-looking," Stevens said, indicating the reporter. "If she's like any other reporter I've ever met, she's a bulldog when she goes after a story. Hell, with that face? She could have gotten a hospital employee to talk to her or cajoled someone here into talking to her. Might have even been someone working at the hotel. Maybe all three. Most guys will tell a pretty woman anything."

Stevens closed down the news site and pulled out some files. "She okay?"

"Yeah, mostly shaken up. She defended herself well until another guest yelled that he'd called the manager because of the noise. The guy cut his losses at that point and took off."

"Where is she now?"

"My place."

Stevens looked up at him and raised an eyebrow. He was the only person Blake knew who could raise one eyebrow independently of the other. "Your place? I'm not sure that's a great idea."

"Well, it's all I can fucking come up with right now," Blake snapped. "There are no safe houses and the hotel didn't turn out to be very safe. It's only until I can arrange something else."

Stevens gave Blake a skeptical look then opened the file on the woman found strangled in the bar parking lot. "Got the autopsy back," he said as he held the file out, and Blake took it.

———•◆•———

FOR LACK of anything better to do, and to keep her mind off the previous night, Alex picked up the beer bottles and pizza box in the living room and disposed of them, then stacked the magazines on the coffee table. She folded the blanket Blake had used last night and placed it on the pillow, leaving them on the couch, then gathered the discarded socks and running shoes on the floor by the door and returned them to his room.

She cleaned the bathroom. Standing in the kitchen she unloaded the dishwasher, put the dishes away, and added the dirty dishes from the sink. Then she went in search of a broom and mop. She was jumpy and restless. Cleaning was mindless, channeled some of her restlessness, and took her mind off the anxiety.

But seriously, she thought, *who knew one man could make such a mess?* For some reason, the disorganization and careless housekeeping bothered her more than she thought it warranted. Putting things back in order soothed her. Maybe she'd been a clean freak or had OCD before the amnesia.

A place for everything and everything in its place, you never know when you'll need something in a hurry. She stopped and held still. That voice again, the man's voice, the voice that sounded as if he would brook no argument. She ground the heel of her hand against her forehead. *Who was he?* She took a deep breath. God, when would her memory return? And, if it did, who would she turn out to be?

A few deep breaths more and she walked to the tiny utility closet in the hallway near the kitchen that held a broom and a small, most likely useless vacuum. No mop. There was a metal box on the top shelf. Out of curiosity, she took it down and opened it.

It was his gun cleaning kit and the oily solvent smell hit her, sending her back to the night before and swamping her with terror. She slammed the lid on the box closed and hastily stuffed it back on the shelf of the closet, closed the door, and leaned against it.

The memory of breaking down a gun suddenly overwhelmed her. She could feel her hands disassembling the pieces of the gun, feel them coming apart, and watched her hands moving automatically over the familiar weight of each piece. She could smell the solvent and oil—and then the memory was gone.

She let her head fall back against the closet door and closed her eyes. What the hell? Why would she know anything about guns or disassembling them? What did it mean? Was the guy who assaulted her someone she knew? Was he the voice she kept hearing, someone associated with guns? Someone who had a good reason for wanting her dead? Was she involved in something illegal?

Her head began to throb, keeping pace with her heartbeat. She walked down the short hall and into the bedroom, digging out the bottle of pain pills from the bag Blake had loaned her. She dry-swallowed two.

Her headache wasn't bad, and her body aches and pains were tolerable, but there was a scared part of her that wanted the oblivion the pills would provide. She forgot about the kitchen and crawled into Blake's bed, pulling the sheets up around her. Surrounded by the scent of him, she closed her eyes and waited for the pills to send her to sleep.

CHAPTER TWELVE

"I'M TERRIBLY SORRY, Detective. I can't imagine how it could have happened." The manager frowned and looked embarrassed.

"Regardless of how sorry you are, it did. I want to know if there are master keys missing and when they went missing. And I want to know who was working the day I checked her in here. Her location was leaked to the press. If I find out it was you, I'll have your balls for it."

The man looked affronted. "We guard the privacy of our guests religiously. No one here released that information."

"You know that for a fact, do you?" The man looked uncomfortable. "That's what I thought. Names. Of everyone working here when I checked her in and the day after. Now."

The manager nodded and disappeared.

"Now get the head of housekeeping here," Blake said when the man returned and handed him a list of names and contact information. "If any of these people are working here today, find them and send them to me. I want an office to work out of until these interviews are done."

"Yes, of course."

Four hours later, he'd discovered that a master key went missing the day he'd checked Alex in. The head of housekeeping had discovered it was missing the morning of the attack. She hadn't told the manager because she was sure it would turn up, that it had been misplaced. It had happened before. The keys had always been found, and nothing untoward had happened as a result.

An employee who was on duty when he'd checked Jane in was probably the one who'd talked to the reporter. He looked guilty as sin, but Blake had no way to prove that he'd done it.

"Your big mouth almost got a woman killed. I'm gonna dig on you, buddy, and if I find any proof it was you, you're dead meat." He got up and opened the door of the small office the manager had allowed him to use and opened it.

"Any more information about this incident gets leaked to the press, I'm coming for you first thing. Now get out."

The kid scuttled out of the office and disappeared.

———◆———

"WHAT'D YOU find out from the couple Ashley babysat for?" Blake asked Stevens when he returned to the office.

"Wife said Ashley babysat for their two kids throughout high school. This last year she'd changed a lot, but the couple continued to use her. She was good with the kids, but they began to worry about her behavioral changes. About six months ago she said she wouldn't be available to sit for them anymore. Didn't say why. The wife said she was relieved in a way, as Ashley's change in behavior had begun to worry her."

"Sounds like something happened. Could you get them to speculate or talk about it?"

"The wife was the chattier of the two. She said Ashley had changed, started dressing differently, was moodier, not herself. She tried to talk to her several times, but the kid wouldn't talk to her. She says she wondered if she'd met someone who was influencing her."

"And the husband?"

Stevens scratched behind his ear and frowned. "Less chatty, not altogether happy to talk to me. Although he pointed out several times they'd agreed to talk willingly and wanted to help. He was twitchy, nervous. A little sweaty. Made me wonder if he knew something he was reluctant to share."

"Maybe he's the reason for the change. The girl was attractive and young—maybe he hit her up one night and things got a little out of hand."

"That's a possibility, although I didn't get that vibe off him. I'm going to keep dogging him. See if I can find out whether anything happened between them, whether he knows anything important."

Stevens looked tired. "I'm gonna have a couple chats with the boyfriend she broke up with and her other friends, see what pops. I don't think any of them, including the couple she babysat for, are likely suspects. But they may have information that could lead us to one."

"Yeah, there's that. Any luck getting an ID on the woman behind the bar?"

"Nope, nothing yet."

"Okay, I'll keep trolling the escort sites and see what I can find. If you need help with the interviews, let me know. I'll ride herd on the uniforms and the calls they've made about the credit card charges from the bar."

"I'll take care of the interviews, you deal with the escort stuff and the uniforms. See if you can get an ID on her."

⸺◆⸺

IT WAS nearly eight when he returned to the apartment. He let himself in, unlocking the two keyed deadbolts in the door, one of which he'd added after he moved in. He set a pizza box on the table inside the door.

"It's me," he called, not wanting to alarm her. There was no reply. "Ja…Alex?" He hadn't adjusted to using the name she thought was hers. She was still Jane to him. No answer.

He closed and relocked the door, dropping his briefcase onto the floor. He walked quickly down the hall to the bedroom and saw a lump under the covers he assumed was her. At the bedside, he reached out and put a hand on her shoulder. She came up abruptly, crying out and fending his hand off with a defensive swipe of her arm, her eyes wide and fearful.

"Hey, it's okay. It's me. Sorry to scare you."

She scooted up against the headboard, blinking at him with owl eyes a few times. Clearly, she'd been deeply asleep. He supposed the original assault and then the one last night had exhausted her, but if she routinely slept that deeply it was no wonder the guy had gotten in without waking her.

"Are you okay?"

"I…I'm fine. I took a pill 'cause my head hurt. I guess it really snowed me."

He nodded and walked to the doorway. "I picked up pizza on the way here. When you're ready come on out."

He set the open pizza box on the surprisingly clean kitchen table and laid out a couple plates, tearing off two segments of paper toweling for napkins. He opened the fridge and offered her a beer as she entered the kitchen.

"Maybe not, not with the meds onboard."

"How about a Coke?" She nodded and sat down at the table.

They ate in silence. The pizza was nearly finished when she spoke up. "May I see your gun?"

He rocked back and stared at her. She couldn't have taken him more by surprise had she pulled a gun on him. "My gun? Why do you want my gun?"

"Please. I want to see if what I remembered earlier today is real or just a fluke."

He frowned and made no move to retrieve his gun from its holster. "What'd you remember?"

"The oily smell…It was the smell he had on him. I remembered handling a gun."

He watched her a moment and then unsnapped the safety strap on the gun in his shoulder holster, removed the clip, and checked that the chamber was empty. He handed it to her butt-first. "Be careful."

After she had taken it, he wondered what it meant if she knew how to handle a gun. He trusted her, or he thought he did, and maybe that was a mistake.

She nodded and pushed the pizza box and plates out of the way. He watched dumbfounded as she confidently and effortlessly disassembled his gun and had it lying in pieces on the table in a matter of minutes.

"Where the fuck did you learn to do that?"

"I don't know."

"What d'you mean *you don't know?*" he asked incredulously, nearly shouting. "Why would a memory of doing that suddenly pop into your head? What the hell is going on?"

"*I don't know!*" She got up and started to leave the kitchen. He stood and grabbed her arm.

"Don't you walk off! What the hell's going on? Are you jerking everybody around with this 'I don't remember who I am' bullshit?" She didn't answer, and he shook her arm.

"Who *are* you? What happened to you the other night? And don't you *fucking* lie to me."

Alex jerked her arm away from him and rubbed the spot where he'd grabbed her. "*I don't know!*" she hissed at him. "I. Don't. Know."

"Then what triggered your memory, if that's what it is. People don't know how to do what you just did unless they're intimately familiar with guns."

"I was cleaning up. I needed something to do to get my mind off what had happened at the hotel. I opened your utility closet, looking for a broom, and saw that metal box on the shelf."

He watched as she moved away from him, as if to put a safe distance between them, a worried frown on her face.

"I took it down and opened it. I saw it was your gun cleaning box and the smell hit me and…and it was like a video playing in my head. I wasn't sure if it was real, that's why I asked for your gun."

He pushed past her into the living room and dropped down onto the couch. "You better not be lying to me."

"I'm not lying to you, for God's sake!" she cried, following him into the living room. "I'm trying desperately to figure out who I am and what happened. The smell, that oily solvent smell, was what I smelled on him. That's why it hit me so hard when I opened the box."

"Why didn't it register last night? Why didn't you mention it this morning when you told me about the attack?"

"I don't know. I don't know how this memory thing works. Right now, it's one body slam after another. I never know when I'll remember something or what it'll be."

She sat on the edge of the only chair in the living room and gripped its arms. Her knuckles were white. "I'm *not* lying to you."

He rubbed both hands over his face, tiredly. "Fine. It'd be nice if you could remember where you learned that."

"It apparently doesn't work like that."

He rolled his eyes and shook his head. "More's the pity."

They sat and stared at each other wordlessly. He wondered what the hell her familiarity with guns meant. Had she been involved in something illegal that resulted in the assault? A sudden knocking on the door startled both of them. Blake got up and motioned her to the couch as he walked to the door. He wished his gun wasn't lying disassembled on the kitchen table.

Oh, fuck me, he thought when he opened it cautiously and saw Fleur standing there. "This isn't a good time, Fleur."

Her eyes went wide with surprise then narrowed, brow furrowing as she stared at him. "Why not? It's Friday night."

"It just isn't. I wish you'd called. I could have saved you the drive. I'm tied up right now. I'll call you tomorrow."

He could see he'd angered her but was surprised when she pushed past him. "Don't brush me off, Blake, I…" She stopped when she saw Alex and turned on him. "Who is she, and what is she doing here?" she demanded.

"Jane Doe, the assault victim," he said, holding the door and sweeping his hand toward Jane—Alex, whatever—as if in introduction. "Fleur Williams," he said to Alex.

"It's bad enough she calls you in the middle of the night, but since when do you bring victims to your apartment?"

He sighed. "Fleur, it's an open case and I can't discuss it with you. Please, let it go. I'm beat and I don't want to do this tonight. Go home and we'll talk later."

"Talk later? I don't think so. You blow me off every chance you get, supposedly because of your job, and now this!" she said pointing at Alex. "We're done, Blake. Don't call me, ever again." She turned and left, slamming the door after her.

He blew out a breath and turned toward whatever the fuck her name was. "I'm sorry about that."

"No, I am. I've caused problems for you."

"Actually, you've solved one for me. I don't have to figure out how to break up with her now. So, thanks."

Alex raised her eyebrows and said nothing. It pissed him off. "Yeah, I'm a shithead. I know it and now you do, too. But until I figure out what to do with you, you're stuck with me, so deal with it."

He turned abruptly, walked into the kitchen, and grabbed the clip to his gun. Taking it with him as he disappeared down the hall and slammed the bedroom door shut. *Women,* he thought as he stripped and pulled a T-shirt and cargo shorts out of his dresser. *They complicate everything.*

He left his slacks, briefs, and shirt lying in a puddle on the floor, hanging his jacket over the closet doorknob. He jerked the door open and walked across the hall to the bathroom without bothering to cover up.

The shower went a long way toward relaxing his shoulder muscles, and his mood had settled by the time he'd dealt with the clothes he'd left on the bedroom floor and walked into the kitchen wearing the T-shirt and cargo shorts. She held his reassembled gun out to him, and he took it. He'd check later to make sure she'd put it together correctly.

The clip and gun rested in his shorts' pocket, heavy against his thigh. He wasn't letting the gun out of his sight. After her little demonstration, he was wary of her. Who the hell was she? Did she really not know who she was?

He'd let his guard down because she was pretty, easy to be with, and at times seemed so helpless. But she wasn't, not entirely. She'd managed to avoid being killed twice and was uncomfortably familiar with guns. From now on, he thought, he'd keep a careful eye on her.

"Tomorrow's supposed to be my day off. I'll get some food in here and whatever else you need. Make a list of what you want and leave it on the table."

He finger combed his still-wet hair. "I may have to go in for at least part of the day. I'll check in with my partner in the morning and see what's happening. I'm sorry about yelling at you."

She nodded. They stared awkwardly at one another. "I think you've got a lot on your plate," she said at last. "And I've added significantly to it. I hope you can find a safe place for me to stay so you can at least have your apartment to yourself."

She got up, walked to the bedroom, and closed the door.

Jesus, he thought as he sat down at the table. *She even makes it hard to be pissed at her.*

He disassembled and reassembled his gun and shoved the clip back into it. She'd put it together perfectly.

Who the hell was she?

CHAPTER THIRTEEN

"DID IT LIKE a fucking cop, like someone who handles guns all the time."

Stevens nodded. "Huh. Still no idea who she is?"

"No." Blake sat at his desk. "Her fingerprints aren't in the databases. That's hard to avoid these days, so I don't know what that means. I don't think she's from Colorado, Georgia, California, or Texas 'cause they all require at least thumb or index prints to get a driver's license. That assumes she's got a license to drive. And that's about all I know for certain."

He pressed the heels of his hands against his eyes for a few moments. The headache was back. "I'm gonna search missing persons for women with names that begin with Alex and see what pops. If that bombs, then I'm going to have CBI search the military databases. If she was a cop, she'd be printed and in the database."

He tipped back in his chair. "If she's undercover, then who knows? Christ, it's hard to avoid having your prints on record. I can't figure out why hers aren't. It's…worrisome."

Stevens nodded noncommittally.

Blake scratched at the edge of his collar and yawned. "I'm gonna be tied up with this most of the day. Catch me up on where we stand with the other two homicides."

"As far as finding a reason or a suspect, nothing so far. I searched for similar crimes and, interestingly enough, there've been similar homicides in Aurora and Golden, and one here in Denver about six weeks ago. At least that's where the bodies were found."

Stevens held up his fist, raising a finger as he ticked off things. "One, they're connected—no fingertips for prints. Two, both of the bodies in Aurora have been ID'd as prostitutes through photos the assigned detectives showed around."

He raised another finger. "And three, I'm thinking you're right about the woman from the parking lot being an escort. There's no ID on her yet, and none on the body from Golden or the recent Denver homicide. All three were missing their fingertips, and visual IDs haven't turned up anything so far on the one in Golden or the one here. I'm gonna contact the detectives assigned and see if I can get a copy of the files on all of them. Maybe there'll be something in them we can use."

"I'll pick up where I left off on the escort sites."

"Good, but don't spend too much time on it right now. I'd like to get your girl ID'd. You said she looked like a prostitute, or at least was dressed like a low-end one."

"She's not my girl," Blake muttered as he scrolled through Colorado missing persons reports.

"Right. If you can ID her, maybe we can tie her to the others and get a description of the guy. I'm not convinced she's connected but, if she is, she could be the only living witness to whoever's killing these women. Maybe it's a good thing she knows how to handle a gun."

Blake snorted. "Maybe, but I tell ya, after that demonstration I'm not letting her near a gun until I know who the fuck she is."

Stevens nodded and both went back to their computer searches.

An hour later Blake pushed back from his desk. "Christ, who knew there were so many variations of names beginning with 'Alex,' or that there were so many missing women?"

"Find any that look like your girl?"

"Will you stop calling her my girl?" Blake rubbed his neck. He didn't want her to be 'his girl,' but he guessed she was. "I haven't found anything. Makes me wonder if her name is really Alex. No one's reported her missing. Maybe no one cares enough to file a report."

"If she's a working girl, that may be the case. You gotta have a family or friends who care enough to file a report. That profession doesn't lend itself to either."

"The photos I've seen of missing women with similar names so far don't look like her, but they don't always look much like the missing people. Remember Ashley's graduation photo? Didn't look like the kid we found at all."

The high school yearbook photo of Ashley Kensington bore no immediate resemblance to the body they'd found in Cheesman Park. You could see the resemblance if you looked closely, but she'd dyed her hair black and chopped it off. Her face had looked gaunt.

She didn't look like the full-faced, smiling girl with the long, glossy, brown hair pictured in the high school photo taken at the start of the year. It had required an artist's rendering shown on TV for her parents to get in touch and seeing a morgue head shot to ID her. Parents always knew their kids, even when others didn't.

"It's only been seventy-two hours for the woman in the bar parking lot, and not much longer for your girl. Something may pop up."

Blake was beginning to think otherwise. None of the photos he'd seen matched Alex's face or physical description or that of the woman from the bar.

"I'll be back. I want to check on something."

———◆———

KAYE JAGERSKI grabbed her wallet. "Let's walk across the street and get a coffee."

"It won't take long, we can talk here."

Kaye was a vice cop he knew. She was a petite brunette, but anyone who knew her knew she was formidable. Despite her last name, she had always looked Italian to Blake with her dark, curly, chin-length hair, dark brown eyes, and olive complexion. He'd worked with her on several drug-related homicides, and she could put you in touch with just about anyone. Her network of contacts was legendary. Maybe she could help him find out about Jane. Alex. Whatever. Jesus, if this kept up, he'd end up calling her Whatever.

"No, I'd like a cup of coffee and a break from desk work. My eyes are starting to bleed looking at all these files."

They sat outside the coffee shop at one of the small tables on the patio, among people working on laptops and chatting with friends. They took a table as far away from the others as possible.

"Let me see her photo."

Blake found it and held his phone out to her. "Pretty, in spite of the injuries. If she works the streets, she hasn't been doing it long."

"Why do you say that?"

"The bloom fades pretty quickly. It's a shitty life. You don't stay this good-looking—fresh, if you will—for long. At least not on the street. As you might imagine, men who want or have to buy sex off women standing on street corners aren't the cream of the crop. Their behavior isn't always predictable, and women can get into trouble pretty easily. Beatings, rough handling, drugs, things like that."

He nodded and thought of the beating that Jane had been subjected to. "I can't find any missing persons' report on file. It's been more than seventy-two hours, but if she was a prostitute then she might not have been reported missing. I hoped you could check with some of those contacts of yours to see if anyone recognizes her."

"Sure, I can ask around. Send me her picture and I'll see what I can find out." Kaye watched him for a minute while she sipped her coffee. "What's bugging you, Halloran?"

Blake put his coffee down. "She amnesic from a bad blow to the head. Doesn't even remember her name. A few things have come to her over the last day or so, including the fact that she *thinks* her name may be Alex, but nothing helpful."

He sighed, rubbing his eyes. The light was too bright, and his head was pounding. He should have brought his sunglasses, and he needed to find some ibuprofen. Sleeping on the couch on alert for an intruder and trying to solve the puzzle that was currently occupying his bedroom wasn't all that restful.

"She asked to see my gun last night, and when I gave it to her, she disassembled it in a matter of minutes. Like a professional. She couldn't, or wouldn't, say how she knew to do that. She's no prostitute, in my opinion. I think she was posing as one. There's a reason why, and it's not to experience selling sex to perverts. I'm not sure what it might be."

Kaye laughed. "They're not all perverts." She watched Blake irritably wave the comment off. "Interesting she knows how to do that. Sure she's really amnesic?"

"I think she is, but I gotta say the demonstration weirded me out."

"What d'you think's going on?"

He thought for several minutes. "Okay, you're going to think I'm nuts, but after the demonstration I wondered if she might be a cop or something similar. Maybe she's undercover—maybe that's why there's no missing persons' report. I don't know."

"Possible, I suppose, but there should have been prints on file if she's a cop."

"And she's not in any of the databases. Hell if I know why. Stevens ran a search for crimes like we picked up recently and came up with a couple in Aurora, one in Golden, and one here in Denver—that's in addition to the Cheesman Park kid and the woman we found in LoDo.

"My Jane Doe was dumped off Highway 93, not far from Golden. Of the two recent homicides that Stevens and I picked up, one was a runaway who probably was soliciting to survive, and the other one may be a high-class escort."

He rubbed at his face and took a final sip of the coffee. "There's a tie-in between those two and the others because of the missing fingertips. I think my Jane Doe is connected, too, but I can't figure out how. She was strangled but the perp didn't kill her, maybe he thought he had, and she has all her fingertips."

The thought of her index finger swathed in a bandage flashed through his mind. Maybe whoever assaulted her had meant to amputate her fingertips…but why stop?

"Why deviate from the pattern?" Kaye asked, seeming to pick up on his thought process.

Blake shrugged. "All I can come up with is he'd strangled her and given her a major head injury probably he thought he'd killed her, and dumped her there. I don't know why he didn't do her fingertips. Her index finger had a pretty good slice on it, so maybe he planned to cut them off and didn't for some reason."

God, the whole puzzle was so frustrating. "The reason he's killed the other women seems to be connected with prostitution. It's the only commonality. It's possible he discovered she wasn't one, and it didn't matter to him if she was identified. There's part of me that wonders if he didn't get interrupted for some reason and couldn't finish the job."

"You don't know that she isn't a prostitute."

Blake sighed. "No, I don't. It's just a gut feeling. She was dumped in a spot that wouldn't be seen easily, and it's possible by the time her body was found she wouldn't be in any condition to ID. Who the fuck knows? He might have been in a hurry or couldn't be bothered. That's assuming it's the same guy and not just a john who got carried away."

"Send me the photo and I'll ask around. Something may turn up. A cop going undercover to find a perp who's killing prostitutes doesn't make a lot of sense. With the murders in three different cities, being investigated by three different divisions, I can't see any reason to do that. Each jurisdiction would handle the investigation separately."

"I know. I can't figure out what's going on." As they walked back across the street, he asked, "D'you know any way to break into a hotel room if the security latch is on?"

She looked at him speculatively. "Don't tell me, she broke into a room with a security latch in place."

"No, but somebody who wants her dead did—broke into her hotel room and tried to kill her. She swears she had the door locked and the latch on. I wondered if that was even possible."

"I've got someone I can put you in touch with who might be able to answer that." They entered the police station and rode the elevator up.

When it stopped on her floor, she said, "Keep an eye on your gun when you're around her. You never know. Sounds like she's got a serious enemy, and the reason she knows about guns may not be a good one."

That's just great, he thought as he got off on his floor and walked to homicide. *I potentially have a gun-happy prostitute living with me.*

CHAPTER FOURTEEN

H E WAS TROLLING escort sites and wolfing down the burger and fries that Stevens had dropped on his desk before he left to follow up on some information, when he saw a woman hesitantly walk into Homicide. She seemed lost, so he stood up and walked over to her.

"Can I help you?"

"I was told to come speak to Detectives Halloran or Stevens about a friend."

"I'm Detective Halloran. Who directed you here?"

"Um, another detective. I'm sorry I can't remember his name—he was in Missing Persons. He took my report, then said to come talk to you. I don't know why."

Blake's interest picked up. He'd let it be known that they had two unidentified victims and asked that anyone coming to report a missing woman matching her description or Alex's be sent to him or Stevens.

"Okay, why don't you come with me and we can talk privately."

He led her to an interview room and closed the door. The room was bare, with only a metal table bolted to the floor and four chairs. The paint was drab and unappealing. Being in a room with an unaccompanied woman made him glad the cameras in the room were motion-activated.

"I should warn you, what goes on in here is automatically recorded. So if that's a problem, let me know."

"No, it's fine, I guess," she said, looking uneasy.

"What can I help you with, Ms. . . .?" He indicated a chair and they both sat down.

"Carolyn Treacher. My roommate, Katia Beneš, never returned from a date the other night. I think something's happened to her."

"When was the other night?" He listened with a sinking heart as she told him it was the night before they had been called to the parking lot in LoDo. "Do you have a photo of her?"

The woman held out her phone and he realized he'd been right. Her friend was in the morgue. It was a relief to get this woman ID'd. Now if someone would just come in and report Alex missing.

"Tell me about the date," he said, postponing the inevitable. "Do you know his name? I'm assuming it was a guy."

She nodded, then corrected herself. "Well, not his full name. He booked the date as Calvin."

"Booked the date?"

She blushed and nodded. "We...we work for an escort service—Elite Escorts. They book the dates and send us a first name and a general description—you know, age, dark hair, blue eyes, glasses, wearing a red tie—and where to meet the guy. They don't give the guys our real names to prevent them from trying to contact us outside the service."

She spoke as if she was discussing a business meeting, and he guessed it was in a way. "The service makes a reservation at a restaurant or a bar under the guy's first name, so we know what to tell the hostess. It's somewhere public so we can check him out from a distance, see if we want to continue the date."

"And if you don't?"

"We call the service, let them know, and leave. The service calls the guy and arranges another girl or refunds his money."

"And does the date include sex?" She stared at him for a moment. "Look, I'm not interested in arresting anyone. I'm trying to get a handle on what happens."

She watched him for another minute, then said, "No, that's not what the service charges for. There's no guarantee, implied or otherwise, that the guy will get laid. And he's told that up front."

She shifted on her chair and looked uncomfortable. "Are you going to arrest me after I've given you details?"

"No, I'm not. Unless you confess to committing a felony, you get to skate on this one."

"If we decide the guy's someone we want to have sex with, that's between us and the guy. We charge them two grand in cash, paid before leaving the restaurant or whatever. They get four hours. It's four grand more if a guy wants an overnight. We get to keep half the cash and the service keeps the money for the date."

"That's a chunk of change. I guess these aren't johns off the street."

He saw her eyes flame with anger. "We are not prostitutes—we're escorts. And we decide whether to have sex, like you would on a regular date. It's not required. These men are usually classy and well-heeled."

Well, you're charging money, a good-sized chunk of it, in return for sex, he thought. *Doesn't matter what you call it, that's prostitution.* He chose not to say that.

"Do you know whether she contacted the service and changed her mind about the guy or whether she went with him?"

"No, according to the service, she didn't call them. They assumed she went on the date." She twisted her hands in her lap. "It's not like Katia. If she was going to spend the night or longer with him, she'd have texted me. We do that. To be safe."

Safe. Providing sex to strangers for money. He didn't think safe was possible under those circumstances. It was time to tell her. He sighed. He hated this.

"I'm sorry to tell you, but your friend was killed."

She looked as if he'd slapped her and blinked her eyes rapidly. "What? No, that can't be right."

"Ms. Treacher, a woman's body in the morgue looks like the photo of Katia that you showed me."

"No, that can't be right. You're wrong, it's not her."

"I suppose there's a small chance it's not her, but I don't think so."

"You're wrong, it's not her."

"Well maybe not, but," he said as he reached over and slid the box of tissues toward her. "If you're up to it, I'd like you to view some photos of the woman in the morgue to rule Katia out. Would you be willing to do that?"

Tears were running down her cheeks, but she nodded as she pulled a tissue out of the box and wiped the tears off her face.

"I'm going to need contact information for the service and who I should talk to." He called the morgue to arrange for photos of the woman he knew was Katia Beneš to be emailed to him.

She reached back into her purse, pulling out a card and searching for a pen. After scribbling a name and phone number on the back of the card, she thrust it at him. He nodded as he heard someone at the morgue pick up the phone.

———— ◆ ————

AFTERWARD, SITTING in the conference room, she sobbed. He said nothing—what could you say? There was nothing nice about looking at a morgue shot. Thankfully, identifying Katia didn't require a trip to the morgue.

Saying 'I'm sorry for your loss' never felt like enough, certainly didn't comfort or soothe a victim's friends or family. Nothing anyone had said to him after Lindsey's death had made any difference other than to piss him off. Blake never could figure out what else to say, and he dreaded the phone call to her parents.

When she had stopped crying he asked, "Did you drive here?" She nodded. "Show me to your car and I'll drive you home. I can Uber back to the station. I don't think you should drive right now. You've had quite a shock."

He followed her directions to a high-rise apartment building that ran for a block along Speer Boulevard. Apparently, she and Katia were making decent money—the smallest apartments started at thirty-five-hundred dollars a month. He'd inquired once thinking, quite mistakenly, that he might be able to swing the rent. She directed him to her parking space in the underground garage.

At her apartment door on the fifth floor, she turned and gave him a watery smile. "Thank you. You've been very kind. I don't quite know what to do. I guess I'll contact her parents in Florida and see what they want to do about her."

"You don't need to do that. I'll contact them at the number you provided and break the news."

Her smile wavered, and it looked like the tears were going to resume, so he preempted them by saying, "Take a day or two off, Carolyn. You need some time to recover. I'm going to give your name to Victim's Assistance, if that's okay with you. They can help you through this."

She shrugged her shoulders and opened the door. "That's fine, if you think it'd help."

He caught a glimpse of the view out the living room windows. A block away, the tall treetops that ran along both sides of the Platte River separating north and southbound Speer Boulevard didn't interfere with a picture-perfect view of the foothills in the distance. A view like that didn't come cheap, especially in downtown Denver.

She hesitated, her hand on the doorknob. "Would you like to come in?"

He might have under different circumstances, but he wasn't going to. "I'm sorry, I have to get back to the precinct. Will you be okay? Maybe you should call a friend."

"Katia was the only person I'd had a chance to make friends with. I moved here a couple months ago, and she needed a roommate to swing the rent on this place."

Her eyes teared up again and he knew it was time to leave. His life was complicated enough right now. He didn't need this. Couldn't afford her anyway, he thought.

"I'm sorry." He handed her his card. "If you have questions or concerns, give me a call. I'm going to give her parents my name and number. I'll help them make arrangements to get…to take care of her."

He hoped Katia and her parents weren't estranged. He didn't want to have to contact Carolyn again if Katia's parents refused to take care of her body.

He turned to leave, then paused. "Find something else to do, Carolyn—what you're doing now is dangerous."

She stared at him blankly, nodded, and closed the door. He doubted she would find a different job. Money was its own addiction, and it was clear from the apartment that she and Katia had pulled in a fair bit.

He wondered, as he rode the elevator to the lobby and arranged for an Uber, whether she'd be able to maintain her current lifestyle any other way. Probably not, he decided. He hoped he wouldn't be staring at her body one of these days.

CHAPTER FIFTEEN

"SERIOUSLY? YOU DON'T know how?" Mick, the guy Kaye had put him in contact with, sat across the table at a local bar and laughed.

He was skinny, with coal-black hair combed straight back from his forehead. A wispy moustache crawled across his upper lip, which didn't do much to help his looks. There was little that *would* help with his looks, Blake thought. The guy was ugly, in a way that was hard to describe. It was as if his face had all the normal parts, they just didn't fit with each other. As if his face was at war with itself.

Blake glared at him. "No, I don't. If I did, I wouldn't be wasting my time talking to you."

The guy laughed again. Nothing seemed to annoy him. He opened a slim case that had been resting on the table in front of him and pulled out an iPad.

"You should try watching YouTube some time. It's amazing what's on there." He brought up the Internet, searched for a second, then handed the iPad to Blake. "Watch," he said, tapping the 'play' arrow on the screen.

Blake had to concentrate on not letting his jaw drop as he watched a several-minute video, accompanied by music that made him think of old silent movie comedies. A heavy, nerdy-looking guy showed how to unlock a u-bar latch, a regular square bar lock like the one on Alex's hotel door, and a security chain.

He used headphone cords for the u-bar, a Do Not Disturb sign for the square bar, and some sort of gum and string thing to slide the security chain off. All you needed was a card key or master key to open the door enough to get to the security features, and the rest was simple.

Blake remembered the Do Not Disturb sign lying on the floor inside hotel room. So she *had* flipped the security bar, hadn't forgotten to do that, and in the end it hadn't mattered. The guy got in anyway.

"Christ. Anybody could watch this and break into a hotel room. How is this legal?"

"Freedom of speech, man, plus he says it's for demonstration only and not to use it for nefarious purposes. I had to look that up, never heard of nefarious purposes before." He laughed. "It means wicked or criminal. Got myself a new word now."

"Aren't you lucky." Blake handed the iPad back and stood up, tossing twenty bucks onto the table for the guy's time. *I should have Googled it and saved myself twenty bucks*, he thought. "Appreciate the help. Don't get up to anything nefarious. Wouldn't want to have to arrest you."

Mick laughed and slapped his palm on his thigh, then pointed a finger at Blake. "See, dude? Now *you've* got a new word."

"Yeah, great." Blake had a weird urge to tell the idiot that he'd known what nefarious meant since he was about ten but chose to resist it. At least Mick had wanted to know what it meant enough to look it up.

———— ◆ ————

"**CAN YOU** believe that?" Blake asked Stevens, pointing to the video he'd pulled up on "hacking a hotel security latch" as the guy had called it.

"Jesus, you know some days, as much help as it is, I think the Internet is part of the problem." Stevens sat back in his chair. "Well, I guess your girl did use the latch."

"For the last time, she is *not* my girl. Knock it off."

"Well, what do you want me to call her? We haven't got a name."

"Hell, I don't even know what to call her. I started calling her Jane because she was a Jane Doe, then she came up with this news flash that she thinks her name is Alex. Who knows? Go with Jane."

"What did the parents say about this Katia?"

"Parents moved the family here from eastern Europe when she was a kid. She grew up in Florida, moved to Denver a year ago, and she told them she was working for a dating service as a counselor. Said she interviewed and set up dates for members, like an online dating site but more personal. They didn't seem to have a clue she was an escort or that she was selling sex. I felt like a total shit, telling them the truth, but I didn't see how I could avoid it."

"Once the press gets hold of her identity, they'd find out anyway. Better you break it to them than have some reporter shove a mic in their face and ask how it feels to have your daughter working as a high-class prostitute."

"I suppose."

"Good that you got her ID'd. You going over to talk to her bosses?"

"Yeah, I thought I'd hit them up on the way home."

"How's the roommate situation working out?"

Blake made a face and ran his hand through his hair, as was his habit when frustrated. "Fine, I guess. The gun thing rattled me, so I've been keeping it close. The sooner I can find a safe place for her, the better. I'm not used to sharing space. I don't like..."

"I know, getting close to people," Stevens said. When Blake scowled at him, he said, "Well, get used to having her around. I heard the safe houses are going to be booked for a while. The DA's trial won't be over for at least six more weeks. You could try the women's shelters again, but I hear a lot of them are pretty full, too."

"I'll survive. She's not hard to live with. It's just not something I'm used to."

"Plus," Stevens said with a chuckle, "my guess is you're not getting any benefits."

"She's a witness, for Christ's sake."

"I'm glad to hear you're behaving yourself."

———— ♦ ————

CALVIN N. Hobbes, Blake thought on the drive home. Very funny. That was the name given and the name on the pre-paid credit card the guy used when he arranged the date. No one had caught the reference to the popular comic strip. Surely Blake wasn't the only one who remembered the kid with a stuffed tiger for a friend.

The owner of the service had reluctantly given him the name, the physical description the guy had provided—dark hair, black glasses, wearing a navy sports jacket—and the credit card slip. To get those Blake had resorted to threatening to get a warrant to search the entire premises and the business's books and interview all the escorts. He wasn't sure he'd have been able to get a warrant, if push came to shove, but the guy caved and gave him the information.

The guy's name could be Calvin N. Hobbes—parents often had bizarre senses of humor—but he doubted it and he'd bet the name had been a deliberate choice. If this guy was the killer it would be a dead end. What was frustrating was the owner of the service said they never met face-to-face with the men contacting them for escorts.

The men would choose the escort they were interested in off the website after being allowed to access the page with all the women's photos. If they wanted to go ahead, they paid the fee via the website and provided a description of themselves and what they'd be wearing at the arranged meeting. The service then passed that info along to the escort. The men had the advantage of knowing what the escorts looked like, and the escorts only knew a general description. A perfect set up for trouble.

Katia had no purse or money on her when found. And the medical examiner had determined, as with Ashley Kensington, that Katia had no vaginal trauma and there was no semen to be found anywhere else on her. End result was no one knew if she'd had sex, consensual or otherwise, just that if she had, the guy had worn protection.

Blake couldn't charge or arrest the service owner for prostitution, which was a damn shame, as he deserved it. With no proof that Katia had accepted money for sex, or had sex for that matter, Blake had to walk away. It didn't mean he wouldn't be keeping an eye on the place, though.

CHAPTER SIXTEEN

"**I**'**LL NEED SOME** time to evaluate her. Amnesia's tricky, and what you're describing is rare. It could be the result of the head trauma but, coupled with the assault, it could also be dissociative."

"What does that mean?" Blake asked, watching Dr. Gwen Caswell. They stood near his desk where she'd approached him after hearing about Alex through the department grapevine. He was surprised, but somewhat relieved, when she offered to see Alex and perhaps help her recover her memories.

The department shrink wasn't someone who was particularly popular. Among other things, any officer who used lethal force, or had been involved in an incident where a police officer had been killed, was required to be cleared by her before returning to work. As a rule, cops—well, guys in general as far as he knew—weren't big on talking about upsetting things in therapy, or much of anything personal. They handled it or they didn't.

Blake certainly wasn't into talking about problems with anyone. His only contact had been the required meetings with Caswell following the shooting that resulted in Lindsey's death and that had been bad enough, despite her giving him some ways to short circuit the panic attacks and flashbacks.

He didn't know much about her personally. He had no idea if she was married or single. She didn't share personal information. Caswell was in her late fifties, if he had to guess, and not what Blake would call gorgeous. She was more pleasant-looking and comforting in appearance. Her face was placid and she had a calm, unflappable demeanor, and was able to listen to all sorts of unpleasant things without flinching.

She also had a steel core that refused to allow the cops she dealt with avoid issues that needed addressing. Caswell was, if not liked, respected. She seemed eager to connect with Alex and try to help. Maybe the lure of working with an amnesia victim was hard to resist.

"What it means is the person experiencing it often has no memory of their name or anything else about themselves," she continued. "In other words, they've dissociated from the trauma and their life prior to it. The trauma has made it too unpleasant to remember. That's simplified, but essentially it."

"Is there anything you can do to help her recover her memory? The guy who attacked her is probably the same one who made the second attempt on her life at the hotel, so it's vital that she provide some information about the assault so we can try to find this guy."

"I understand the urgency, but you can't pressure her. It doesn't help. Her memory could come back all at once on its own, or it could be triggered by something in her environment."

Blake told her about the gun incident, leaving out the fact that Alex was at his apartment or that it'd been his gun cleaning kit that had triggered the memory.

"That's interesting. So, what she smelled triggered her memory of disassembling a gun, but nothing else?"

"No, the guy who got into her hotel room and tried to strangle her smelled like gun oil. I…I guess when she remembered the smell, it triggered her memory. But she has no idea how she knew about guns or anything else."

He shrugged in frustration. "She's remembered that her name may be Alex or some variation of that, and nothing else."

"Well, her situation is fascinating. I'd like to see her. Can you bring her here tomorrow morning, say nine?"

Blake nodded. "Do you think you can help?"

"I don't know, but I can tell more once I see her."

"We need her to remember what happened. If you can help her remember, that'd be great."

"She'll have to give me consent to discuss whatever we talk about with you, so you may want to sort that out ahead of time."

"Why wouldn't you talk to me about it? I'm the detective on the case!"

"Detective Halloran, you may be the detective on the case, but she will be my patient. She's not a police officer. I'm not seeing her because of a departmental issue that requires reporting to higher-ups. Therefore, she has to give me permission to discuss it with you."

She folded her arms across her chest and raised her eyebrows at him. "That's how it works, so discuss it with her and we'll go from there. Nine a.m. works for me. If you can't make it, let me know."

"Fine, I'll have her here." He watched her start to walk away and, as an afterthought, said, "Thanks. This is going to have to go to the department for reimbursement."

She waved him off and left.

———— ◆ ————

THE SCENT of food hit him when he opened the apartment door and walked in, making his stomach growl. "It's me," he called out. *Next thing you know, I'll be calling out, 'hi honey I'm home,'* he thought and sighed. *I'm in this disaster because of you, Lindsey.* Lindsey didn't reply, but he imagined her rolling her eyes at him. Sometimes he wondered if he was losing his mind. Thoughts of her seemed to always be there. Four years and he still struggled with the memories.

Jane, hell he couldn't get used to calling her Alex, poked her head around the kitchen entry. "Hungry?"

He nodded and she ducked back into the kitchen. He shrugged out of his jacket and draped it over the living room chair, undid his tie, and opened the top button of his shirt. *The apartment has to be at least eighty degrees*, he thought as he rolled up his sleeves. The A/C apparently wasn't working, again, and the building was old enough that the insulation, if there was any, was useless at keeping the heat out.

The A/C units installed in each apartment routinely conked out at some point during the summer, and the residents would go a week or two living in sweltering apartments until the landlord could get the units fixed. The heating system seemed to do the same in the winter. One of these days he was going to move. Somehow, he never got around to it.

He walked into the kitchen to find her standing next to a pot of boiling water on the stove, a box of pasta on the counter, and another pot containing some sort of red sauce. Her face was flushed, and her hair was tied up in a messy bun on top her head. Escaped tendrils of hair curled in the humidity. She'd found a pair of his shorts and was wearing the camisole top. He was surprised at how scabbed up her legs and arms were. It was easy to forget those injuries when clothes hid them.

"You cooked dinner." It smelled delicious, but he wondered briefly if this was another recovered memory or whether it lent more weight to the idea she was bluffing about the amnesia.

"Did you know you could cook?"

She smiled. "I don't think this qualifies as cooking. I'm boiling the pasta according to the directions on the box and used a jar of sauce I found in your cupboard. It's not a recovered memory, if that's what you're asking."

He remembered a former girlfriend who'd left the pasta and jarred sauce in his pantry right before he'd decided she was getting too comfortable in his space and had broken up with her. Leaving clothes in his closet or cooking for him had always been red flags indicating break-up time. Offering to do his laundry, he'd discovered, was deadly.

"Smells great, wherever it came from." He wanted a shower desperately and to change into some shorts and a T-shirt. She must have read his face.

"Go get comfortable. This won't be ready for a little bit."

He stood under the shower, soaping up and trying his best not to picture her in his shorts and the camisole while he was naked in the shower. Despite the scrapes and bruises, she was beautiful and he'd been unable to look away from her breasts.

He shook his head to dispel the thoughts and his physical reaction, which persisted in spite of him. Embarrassed by his response, he grasped the shower control and abruptly lowered the temperature, and that got rid of the erection and thoughts about what she'd look like naked. He rinsed off and got out.

What am I going to do with her? he wondered as he toweled off. He wasn't sure how to even ID her. Running her prints had drawn a blank, and he'd searched the missing persons reports till his eyes were ready to shrivel up and die with no success.

He had no name and no idea where she lived, so trying to get any other records was impossible at the moment. He couldn't put her picture on the news, not with the guy who assaulted her waiting for a chance to kill her. Maybe Kaye Jagerski would come up with something. He shook his head. He had to let this go for tonight at least or his brain would explode.

Looking around he noticed with some surprise that the bathroom looked clean, really clean. He couldn't remember the last time he'd cleaned the bath. It had been a while.

He didn't spend much time in the apartment. It wasn't a refuge.

It was more of a stopping-over place. A place he returned to for sleep, to zone out in front of the TV, or a place to clean up and, occasionally, a place to bring women. He guessed that one perk to having her here was that it was at least clean. He dressed and returned to the kitchen.

"I appreciate it, but you don't need to clean the place, or cook for that matter. You're not a maid, and I don't expect payback for you being here."

She had dished up the spaghetti and searched the fridge until she found a rather ancient plastic container of grated Parmesan cheese that he used to shake on top of pizzas. He cringed. He wasn't sure how long that'd been in the fridge. But that brand seemed to be like Twinkies—it never went bad as far as he could tell.

"I'm here all day with nothing to do but think. I didn't clean the place or fix dinner because I thought you expected it. If I thought that, you'd be an old man before I complied."

He grinned. She had some bite to her, and he liked it.

"I did it to keep from worrying about everything and trying to force my brain to remember. Plus, you really are a pig. I had to do something."

"Well, I wasn't expecting a roommate," he said indignantly.

"No, you weren't. I wasn't expecting to be here, either. In any event, I like things clean and we both need dinner, so sit and eat. It's not fancy, since you don't have a lot of food here." She offered him a plate heaped with pasta.

"I don't eat here often," he muttered, sitting down and taking the plate from her and shaking the grated Parmesan on the pasta.

"No shit, Sherlock."

He laughed. "I don't think anyone's ever said that to me before."

"I used to say that to my—" her face went blank for a moment. "Sister."

"You have a sister?" he said sharply. "What do you remember about her?"

She rested her elbows on the table and her chin in both hands. Her fingers fanned over her face, and she pressed them against her closed eyes.

"I must have," she said, sounding puzzled.

"What's her name? Does she live here?" he demanded.

She turned her chin into her left hand and held up her right. "Stop. Please, just stop. That's all I know. I used to say that to my sister, I guess, or she said it to me. I don't know anything else, so stop going at me like that."

Blake sat back in his chair, thumping his hands on the table on either side of his plate. "God! It's like pulling teeth. There has got to be a quicker way to get your memory back than waiting for these bit and pieces to make sense."

She sat quietly and picked at her spaghetti. He shook his head and returned to his plate, shoveling the spaghetti in, and trying to think of a way to dig out more information without harassing her.

"Look, it's not your fault," he said at last, putting his fork down. "I'm tired. Ignore me."

"I have no idea whether this is real or not, but there's something sad about the thought that I have a sister. It feels like…like grief or worry? If I remember anything, I'll let you know. It's so unpredictable, and I don't seem to have any control over it. I'm sorry."

"No, don't be sorry. You're not to blame."

He turned his attention back to his plate. It was good to come home and eat some decent food rather than the crap he got at drive-thru places, or having a beer and chips for dinner some nights. He hadn't shared an apartment since college when he was getting his criminal justice degree, and he hadn't cared much for it then. Having her around, though, wasn't bad. The fact that there was another person in his space took some adjusting to. But she was at least easy to be with.

"The department shrink talked to me today. She heard about your amnesia and wants to work with you. She wants me to bring you in for an eval tomorrow."

She looked up from her plate, confused. "A shrink? Why?"

"She thinks she might be able to help you regain your memory. I think it's worth a shot. In fact, the ER doc suggested it and gave me a name. I'd prefer you be seen by the department's shrink rather than taking you somewhere else. At least at the police department no one's going to try to kill you."

He finished his pasta and lay his fork down. "And I can't pay for an outside shrink, so..."

"Are you having to pay for this? For the hotel? For my clothes? You're not being reimbursed?"

He was surprised by her reaction. "Not at the moment. I'll probably get reimbursed eventually. I hope."

"Why are you doing it?"

"What the hell else am I going to do with you?" he asked in exasperation. It felt as if she was angry about what it was costing him, and it pissed him off. It wasn't as if he had much choice in the matter, not after insinuating himself in the case and taking it from Jeffries.

She pushed back from the table. "Nothing, I guess. Set up the shrink and I'll talk to her if that's what you want." She started to walk out of the kitchen, then paused. "I cooked, you clean. That's the deal, roomie," she said, and left him sitting at the table.

⬤

SHE HEARD him banging around in the kitchen as she walked from his bedroom to the bath and closed the door. The idea of seeing a shrink was intimidating, and she wasn't sure why. It made her uneasy. She wanted to know who she was and what had happened, but there was some reticence she couldn't figure out. Was there something she *didn't* want to know?

The less you tell anybody, missy, the better. Who you are ain't nobody's business.

That voice again, who *was* he? The use of *missy* made her wonder whether he was her father or brother. If so, why was he so paranoid?

She was beginning to get stir crazy. The trauma had started to fade slightly, and she felt safe here. The amnesia still sent her heart racing if she gave in and thought too much about it and that voice that kept surfacing worried her. Being confined to a one-bedroom apartment with nothing to do was wearing on her.

What the hell would he do with her if her memory never returned? What the hell would she do? She had no idea what she'd done before the assault, no idea what skills she had other than taking a gun apart and putting it back together.

That discovery worried her, and it had clearly unsettled him. He'd kept his gun close since that demonstration. How had she learned to do that? What had she done that required that knowledge? Did the man attached to the voice she kept hearing have something to do with it?

The man who'd attacked her in the hotel smelled like gun oil. Was he the voice she kept hearing? Had she worked with him? Had they been involved in crimes? Had she done something that goaded him into trying to kill her? Until she could figure that out, she had no intention of sharing anything more the voice said with Blake.

The snippets she knew about herself didn't help. She had no way to verify her name or that she even had a sister. The emptiness inside her head and the inability to find what was lost kept her scurrying away from thoughts about it to avoid the despair it caused. What if she never remembered?

Maybe talking with the shrink would help. It would at least get me out of the apartment, she thought, stepping into the shower.

CHAPTER SEVENTEEN

"**I** MIGHT HAVE SOMETHING for you," Kaye said over the phone. Alex was in the bedroom and had kept the door shut since dinner. He wasn't sure what that meant but was glad he could talk to Kaye without Alex overhearing.

"I have a woman who recognized your victim's face. She's not the most reliable witness—she's high a lot of the time—but she seemed sure about this."

"Great, what's her name and how do I get in touch with her?"

"I'm texting you her photo. Name's Sally Howard. As far as getting in touch, you'll need to check out the area around Colfax and Logan, near the Cathedral. Sometimes she wanders all the way down to Clarkson. She lives in an apartment near there and that's where she hangs out."

"Okay, what'd she have to say?"

"Recognized the face, said she'd seen her around, intimated that she knew more but wanted to be paid for the info. I told her you'd take care of that."

"How much will that take?"

"Slip her $20 unless the information is really good, then it's up to you depending on how generous you feel. And don't go in all cop. Hit her up like a john, then you can let her know I sent you once you're off her corner. I don't want to cause problems for her—she's been helpful in the past."

"Thanks, Kaye. I owe you."

"Buy me dinner sometime, otherwise we're square. Hope she can help. You never know with Sal. She can be helpful, or she can be a stoned pain in the ass. Depends on the day."

———— • ♦ • ————

BLAKE SAW her standing on the sidewalk in front of the McDonald's on Colfax near the Cathedral of the Immaculate Conception. It was an odd neighborhood. Weird little restaurants and a used bookstore surrounded the cathedral. To the west, the state capitol with its gold dome could be seen, and there were a number of low-rent properties and fast food places in the area. It hosted a fair number of homeless people, who mixed with people from surrounding businesses and restaurants.

It was seven, not dark yet. Daylight savings time kept the night at bay until often eight or nine in the evening. She slumped against an RTD bus sign, looking bored until a car slowed down, then she'd perk up and smile invitingly. Most drivers who slowed sped up again after a closer look or, not being on the make for sex, didn't notice her at all.

He saw a parking spot on the street about twenty feet from where she roosted sucking on a straw protruding from a McDonalds super-sized soft drink. He pulled into it and got out. He'd left the apartment in knee-length cargo shorts, a T-shirt and flip-flops, adhering to Kaye's advice not to look like a cop. He'd let Alex know he was leaving, telling her he'd be back in an hour or two but declining to say where he was going or why.

He saw Sally perk up when she saw him walking toward her. "Hey, handsome, you wanna have some fun?" she asked.

"What kind of fun?

She looked at him appraisingly, saw his shorts—well-worn and baggy—his flip-flops, and the figure hugging navy T-shirt. He might not go all-out moneywise, but as far as his looks, she'd hit the jackpot.

"Well that depends on you, doesn't it? Why don't we go somewhere more private and we can discuss it?"

"Okay, my car is over there. Let's go."

She dropped the drink in a garbage can they walked past. They returned to his car and got in.

"How much?"

"Fifty for a blow job, a hundred for the works."

He nodded and drove to a nearby parking lot, pulled in, and parked.

"This isn't very private, dude. We could get arrested. I know someplace we can go that's more secluded." She leaned over, laid her hand on his chest, and smiled suggestively.

Blake turned to her and took out his shield. "I don't think getting arrested is going to be a problem, Sally. Kaye Jagerski gave me your name and photo. I need to ask you some questions about a woman you may know."

"A cop, wouldn't you fucking know it," she said, rolling her eyes and flopping back in the passenger seat. "Well, there goes my money."

"Tell me what you know about her," he said, pulling up Alex's photo on his phone, "and you'll get your money if what you know helps. Do you know her?"

She squinted at the photo, then reached for his phone and spread her thumb and index finger on the screen to enlarge the image.

"I know her, some. I told Jagerski that. She showed up about a month ago. I seen her chatting up some of the other girls down in the park by the City and County building."

Sally handed his phone back. "She started hanging out near my block here. We had words about that, but she said she had no intention of taking work away from me. Said she was new to town and just wanted to hang out. She didn't seem to be keen on finding customers, just talking."

She pulled a cigarette out of her tiny purse that hung from a cross-body strap. "You mind?"

"I do, actually. What else do you know about her?"

Sally frowned and replaced the cigarette in her purse. "Said her name was Alexandra, but to call her Alex."

"She give you a last name?"

"No, and I didn't ask. After we talked for a while, she showed me a photo of a woman. Said she was looking for her, asked me if I'd seen her. I hadn't."

Sally fidgeted with her purse and Blake wondered how badly she needed a cigarette. "I couldn't figure out what her game was. She dressed the part, had these gorgeous sparkly red heels that she always wore, but I didn't get the feeling she was street material."

"Why?"

"She was different, friendly. Talked like she was educated. Most women like me aren't college grads." She laughed and started to cough.

"You ought to give up the cigarettes."

"And everything else that's bad for me, I know." She waved him off. "This Alex said the same thing to me, but it's an old habit so that's not likely. A few days after I met her, she offered to get me a coffee at Mickey D's or lunch if I wanted. She was more interested in information than tricks."

"What kind of information?"

"Turns out the woman she was looking for is her sister. Showed me a couple more photos on her phone, old ones. They looked sort of alike, hair was the same color, but she said her sister might have changed it. They both had green eyes, but the sister looked older. I hadn't seen anyone who looked like her photos."

"Did she say where she was from? Did she tell you her sister's name?"

Sally thought for a few moments. "No, she never volunteered where she was from, said her sister's name was… hang on, give me a minute. I'd think better if I had a cigarette."

"Fine," Blake said, opening his car door. "Let's go for a walk. I don't want you smoking in my car."

"A stroll with a good-looking man is nice, but let's go sit on that RTD bus bench and talk. It'll look like we're waiting for a bus. I start walking around the block, chatting with you, and someone I know sees me, they'll want to know who you are."

"You could tell them I paid to walk with you."

That made her laugh and cough, as they walked toward the bus stop. "Honey, I've had some weird customers in my time, but no one's ever paid me to walk—unless it was on his chest."

She lit up, sat down on the bench, took a deep drag from her cigarette and blew it away from him. The cloud of smoke caught the breeze and it drifted back toward him, God he hated cigarettes, but he said nothing.

"Said her sister's name was Suzanne, or maybe Susan. I forget. Something like that, but no last name."

"Did she say why she was looking for her?"

"I think her sister had ended up on the street and then went missing, or she hadn't heard from her in a while. She said they texted a lot. Her sister had sent her photos of the area, you know the tourist shit—the Cathedral, the capitol building. She figured her sister hung out around here so she was asking around to see if any of the girls here knew her sister. Alex said she wanted to fit in so we wouldn't be wary of talking to her. Think she was also hoping some guy who knew her sister would pick her up."

"And did any of the women know her sister?" Christ, she didn't volunteer anything. He hoped he could remember to ask the right question.

"Well, I didn't. Not sure about anyone else. She may have hung out in Civic Center Park, and I don't hang out there. The girls around here and me, we're not best buds, you know? They're competition." She took another drag.

"Then Alex was gone as well, about a week or so ago. I figured she'd found her sister and gone home. Didn't see her anymore."

"Did you see her with anyone when she was around? Did she manage to attract a guy?"

"If a guy approached her, she'd talk to him for a while then the guy would leave. I saw her talking to a guy one night. He'd seen her and pulled to the curb. She stood at his car window, leaning on it and talking to him for a while."

Sally took another deep drag from the cigarette and blew it out. "Looked like she showed him her phone, maybe she was showing him the photos of her sister. Then she got in the car with him and he drove off."

She dropped the cigarette butt and ground it out with the toe of her sandal. "I got offered a job at that point, so I don't know if she came back or not. But it was a longer conversation than I'd ever seen before. Then I didn't see her around anymore. It must've been about a week ago I saw that."

"Get a look at the guy, or what the car looked like?"

"Never saw him really, he was just a presence behind the wheel leaning toward the window. The windows were tinted dark. Big guy. Other than that, I can't say. The car was black—an SUV."

"Make or model? Or a license plate?"

"Dude I was working, for Christ's sake. Who notices that? Might have been a Ford, maybe."

Blake sighed, and rubbed his eyes. He wanted nothing more than to go home and lie down on the couch and zone out in front of the TV. He watched Sally then said, "Any idea where she was from?"

She screwed up her face in an effort to remember. "I don't think she ever said, but I got the impression she was from out of state."

"Why?"

"She wasn't all that familiar with Denver. I guess that was why."

"But she had a phone, right?" Sally nodded. "What'd it look like?"

Sally thought for a moment. "An iPhone. Not sure what version. It looked pretty new. Had one of those high-impact cases on it. Black case."

Blake fished around in the pocket of his shorts and pulled out his wallet. "I really appreciate the help. If you think of anything more, get in touch. If any of the other women you know have information, get in touch. If it's helpful, you'll get a kickback."

He handed her a hundred dollars and saw her eyes light up. "Keep your eyes open for that guy and his car. If you see him, get a description of the car and license plate number and call me immediately. Don't go with him no matter what he offers you, understand?" He handed her his card with his cell number on the back.

"What'd he do to her?" she asked apprehensively.

"Tried to kill her. So be smart, don't go with him. Get the license plate and call me if you see him."

She nodded, stuffing the bills into her purse. "Thanks, man. I appreciate the money. I'll call if I see or hear anything."

"Come on, I'll drop you off on your corner," he said as they walked back to his car.

CHAPTER EIGHTEEN

BLAKE HAD LEFT a message for Dr. Caswell, relating what he'd learned about Alex's movements before the assault and her sister's name. He figured he'd better get used to calling her Alex, now that he was sure that was her name. He'd gotten fond of Jane, though and was reluctant to give it up.

It was good to know about the phone. If Alex remembered the number they might be able to track it, assuming the guy hadn't taken the SIM card out. If they could find the person who'd assaulted her and he'd kept the phone it would be solid evidence. It was a lot of ifs, the most insurmountable was Alex's memory returning. Blake wasn't hopeful.

When he got back to the apartment, she was watching some period piece playing on PBS. He thought about telling her what he'd learned, then decided to let the shrink handle that. No telling what her reaction would be—there were too many questions still, and he wasn't sure he could handle it if the information really set her off. Tomorrow, he'd call the morgue and ask about the uniden-tified bodies they had.

He got a beer from the fridge and sat in the chair next to the couch. He was antsy, unsettled, not totally sure what to do with the information he'd gotten from Sally. Not professionally, he knew what he had to do in that regard, but he had no idea what to say or do when it came to Alex.

She cocked her head at him. "What's up? You seem twitchy."

"The shrink can see you at nine tomorrow. I couldn't remember if I'd told you that." He took another swig of beer and tried to stop the one nervous tic he had of letting his leg bounce when he sat in a chair.

"She says she needs your permission to talk to me about what happens. Without that she can't discuss it with me. I can't solve this unless I know what you remember."

"Okay, I haven't got a problem with that." She muted the TV. "That doesn't seem like the problem, though. You've been unsettled since you returned. Can you talk about it?"

"I'd rather not." It unsettled him even more that she'd picked up on his unease.

She turned back to the TV for a few moments, watching the actors' mouths move silently. "Does it relate to me?"

He sighed.

"And you don't want to tell me."

"I'd rather you talk about it with the shrink." He didn't want to share what he'd learned.

"If it's about me, I have a right to know."

"Do you remember what you were wearing when I found you?" he asked suddenly, thinking he should tell her.

"No. All I remember is bright lights and someone telling me to hold on, that help was coming. Was that you?"

"Yeah."

"The next thing I remember is waking up in the ER. What does my clothing have to do with anything?"

He looked at her delicate features, shadowed still by the healing bruises, her serious green eyes, and had no idea what would happen. He took a long swallow of his beer and a deep breath.

"The clothes you had on were…I'm sorry, I don't know how else to put this…they were slutty."

He rubbed the cold beer bottle across his forehead. "My first impression was that you were a prostitute who'd been assaulted by a john who got carried away, freaked out, and dumped what he thought was your body."

He watched her face drain of color and then suddenly flame with red. "I see. That explains the weird attitude toward me that I kept picking up on from the hospital staff, like I was distasteful or something."

She turned the TV off and swiveled around on the couch to face him.

"So, I'm a prostitute. I wasn't expecting that at all." She looked as if she was on the verge of tears, but they didn't fall.

"No, wait! I didn't say you *were*. I said you were dressed as if you were. I don't think you are."

Now that he'd opened that can of worms, did he tell her the rest? Christ, he wasn't equipped to handle this at all. He wished he'd kept his fucking mouth shut or made something up.

"Well, what you think and what the truth is may not jibe. I… if you'll excuse me," she said, rising from the couch abruptly and walking quickly toward the bedroom.

"Ja—Alex! Wait, you didn't let me finish!" he said, following her. He reached out and grabbed her shoulder. He was unprepared for and shocked as hell when she grabbed his hand, twisted it, spun him around, and had him face first against the wall with his hand pinned up against his shoulder blade before he could prevent it.

"Don't grab me!" she said sharply. Abruptly, she let go and backed away. Turning he saw a mask of confusion on her face. "Oh God," she whispered, holding a trembling hand to her mouth and backing away from him into the bedroom.

"Oh God, who am I?" she said again as she slammed the door in his face.

———◆———

SHE WAS curled into the fetal position on the bed, heard him knock on the door, and ignored him. She heard him walk away. Who *was* she? It terrified her. The gun disassembling and now what she'd done to him, how did she know that? What had she been before the assault?

Was she a prostitute? Had she learned those skills to protect herself? That didn't seem possible. The idea was so foreign to her. She wasn't sure whether she wanted to know. The idea flitted through her mind that she should take the clothes and other stuff he'd bought for her and disappear. Somewhere. Hide until her memory came back to her, and if it didn't? She had no money, which made that idea ridiculous. She shuddered and curled more tightly into a ball.

"Alex?" He knocked on the door again and opened it.

"Go away."

"Listen to me please," he said, walking over to the bed and sitting on its edge next to her. He started to reach out and touch her, then withdrew his hand.

She moved away from him. "Please, leave me alone. I don't know how I knew to do that. I can't answer your questions, so please go away."

"Look, I'm sorry. I shouldn't have dumped that on you." He rubbed a hand over his face. "I don't think you're a prostitute. I think it was a front, I think you were searching for someone. Does the name Susan or Suzanne mean anything to you?"

She rolled away from him, couldn't bear to look at him, "No. Oh God, what's going to happen to me?"

She felt him lean over and stroke her back. She stiffened. "Go away," she said. "If I am a prostitute I'm choosing not to be right now. I'm not paying you back for your hospitality with sex."

He pulled his hand back abruptly as if he'd been burned and pushed off the bed. She heard him walk to the door.

"I'm not asking to be paid back, and I wasn't hitting you up for sex!" he said angrily. "I wanted to…oh, the hell with it. Forget it." And he left, slamming the door behind him.

———— ◆ ————

THAT'S WHAT happens *when you try to be nice, when you get involved,* he thought as he blasted through the living room, snatched his keys off the hook by the door, and slammed out of the apartment. He paused long enough to lock the deadbolts and then headed for his car.

He hadn't wanted to fuck her, for Christ's sake. Well, not at that particular moment anyway. He'd had some pretty explicit dreams since he'd picked her up at the hospital, but his subconscious was out of his control. He was a guy with a gorgeous woman living in his apartment, so no surprise there. But in that moment, he'd been overcome with pity for her and wanted to comfort her somehow. *What woman would want a guy to stroke her back after he'd told her she might be a prostitute?* he thought.

"You're an idiot," he muttered as he got in his car and left.

When it came to handling and interviewing suspects, casual social interactions, or seduction, he knew what he was doing, but this was deep water that he'd always tried to avoid. All he'd wanted to do was comfort her and try to reassure her that his initial impressions about her were wrong.

He should have told her about Sally and everything Sally had told him right away and let her sort it out with the shrink in the morning. By the time he'd tried to tell her, she wouldn't listen to him. *Shoulda, coulda, woulda,* he thought. That opportunity was gone, and he'd fucked things up royally.

When he returned to the apartment near midnight, the bedroom door was closed, and he couldn't see a light on under the door. He'd wanted to apologize, to explain himself, but that opportunity had passed as well. He lay down on the couch and dropped off to sleep, unsure what tomorrow would bring.

CHAPTER NINETEEN

H E'D AWAKENED AT seven and made coffee, then, because the bedroom door was still firmly closed, he'd taken a shower and shaved. His clothes, however, were in the bedroom and he couldn't go to work in cargo shorts and a T-shirt. Towel wrapped around his waist, he knocked on the door.

"Alex? It's seven-thirty. I need to get dressed and we need to be at the shrink's by nine."

No answer.

"Alex?"

She jerked the door open. He took a hasty step backward, stumbled, and lost his grip on the towel around his waist. He grabbed frantically at it as she pushed past him and walked into the bathroom, closing and locking the door.

Well fine, be pissed, he thought as he snatched the towel off the floor and re-wrapped it. She didn't look like she'd slept well. Her face was pale and her eyes were shadowed. He hadn't slept well either. Tired, stressed, at odds with each other, today was off to a bad start.

Grabbing the clothes he needed, he headed to the living room where he quickly pulled on boxer briefs and his slacks, in case she popped out of the bath at an inopportune moment. It hardly mattered now, he thought. She'd gotten an eyeful when he'd lost hold of the towel. Standing in bare feet and slacks at the kitchen counter, he fixed a cup of coffee and blew on it before taking a couple of cautious sips.

Looking out the small kitchen window at a lovely view of the brick wall of the apartment building next door, he shook his head. He really needed to move. He was so absorbed in the coffee and his thoughts that he didn't hear her walk into the kitchen.

"I'm sorry. I overslept," she said.

He jumped, managing to spill hot coffee on his bare chest. "Shit!" he swore, quickly moving the cup away to prevent it from dripping on his slacks, which made it slop over onto his hand. Setting the cup on the counter, he grabbed for a paper towel to wipe his chest and hand off. Both burned like hell.

"What the fuck are you doing sneaking up on me like that?" he snarled as he wiped at the coffee dribbling down his chest, perilously close to the waistband of his slacks.

"Sneaking up on you? I wasn't sneaking up on you." She shook her head and moved by him to get a cup of coffee. "When it's time to go let me know." She picked up her cup and walked back to the bedroom and closed the door.

In the car on the way to the precinct, neither spoke. Alex spent most of the drive looking out the window, and Blake spent the time trying to figure out a way to apologize for the night before.

At a stoplight near the precinct he finally said, "Look, I didn't mean anything last night. I wasn't trying to…I wasn't making a move on you. You looked like you could have used some comforting, but I was out of line. It won't happen again."

She said nothing in return, and it pissed him off. The least she could do was nod her head, but she didn't. They rode in silence the rest of the way. He escorted her to Caswell's office and waited with her, neither speaking, until the doctor opened her door and invited them in.

"Alex, it's nice to meet you. I'm Dr. Caswell. Detective Halloran made this appointment so we could talk and see if we can make any headway toward restoring your memory."

Alex nodded at her and Caswell indicated she should sit in one of the chairs. "Detective Halloran, I'll call and let you know when we're finished." She held the door, indicating he should leave. He scowled and left, heading up to Homicide.

"What's biting your ass, Halloran?" Stevens asked when Blake sat down at his desk and said nothing as he rifled impatiently through the papers on the desktop.

"Nothing."

"Trouble in paradise?"

"Shut the fuck up, okay? Leave me alone."

Stevens held his hands up in surrender and listened to Blake pick up the desk phone and make a call.

"Have you got any unclaimed or unidentified females staying at your place at the moment?" Blake asked. "Okay, I'll be over in about half an hour; I need to see them. I may have an ID for one of them."

Stevens let the silence hold for a few minutes then said, "So why are you calling the morgue and who're you trying to find?"

"Jane Doe's sister."

Stevens' eyebrows went up. "Her sister? How'd you find out she has a sister?"

"She suddenly claimed to have a sister the other night, but of course has no further information on that—no name, no idea what she looks like. Kaye Jagerski asked around and put me in touch with a prostitute who recognized Doe's photo."

"Thought her name was Alex."

Blake scowled at him. "I have no proof of that." He did, based on Sally's information, but calling her Jane Doe was a nasty little dig at her. It was petty of him, but he wasn't feeling very charitable toward her at the moment. The burning sensation on his chest from the coffee kept him pissed.

"The contact of Jagerski's said Doe was looking for her sister and showed her a couple of photos. Her description of the sister was that she looks 'sort of' like Doe, so I'm going on the assumption she may be in the morgue and unidentified. If she is, I hope she's in good enough condition to identify."

"By you or Jane Doe?"

"By me at the moment. She can't tell me what her sister looks like, and she doesn't recognize the name Suzanne, which the woman I spoke to said she called her sister."

"You're coming down on her pretty hard, Halloran. What's happened?"

"I'm fucking up right and left is what's happening, and she gets more puzzling as time goes by. I told her about my suspicions when I first found her, which was idiotic. What woman in her right mind wants to be told she's suspected of being a prostitute?"

Blake sighed and leaned back in his chair. "It upset her, and she headed for the bedroom for some privacy. I followed her to try to explain why I don't believe that's true."

He shook his head, still finding what had happened hard to believe. "I grabbed her shoulder to stop her and she had me pinned against the wall with my arm wrenched behind my back faster than I could say 'fuck me.' The only thing she didn't do was cuff me. I've never been so surprised in my life."

Stevens raised his eyebrow. "That would lend some credence to your idea that she may be in law enforcement of some kind, or maybe the military or personal security."

"But she's not. She can't be; her prints aren't in AFIS or the military or government databases."

"Unofficial paramilitary maybe, although that's not helpful. They're not likely to want their fingerprints on record. Is that it?"

"What d'you mean is that it? Is what it?"

"Well, if it was me, that'd surprise the hell out of me. And it's odd that her prints aren't on record, but it wouldn't put my nose as far out of joint as yours is at the moment."

"I don't want to talk about it. With you or anyone else."

"Little misunderstanding between roommates?"

"Fuck you." Blake stood up and walked off, pushing past a couple of detectives standing near the door, and left.

He had to find other accommodations for her. Having her at his place was a disaster waiting to happen, but he was out of ideas at the moment.

He almost wished he smoked so he could go sit outside and do something that would make him feel better. Instead of bumming a cigarette off one of the people standing around the entrance and taking up smoking, he drove to a nearby coffee place and stuffed his face with a huge muffin and a large coffee.

Caffeine, sugar, and fat should do the trick, he thought.

———◆———

DR. CASWELL had taken her time, asking Alex about any residual effects from the head injury. All that remained were headaches if she was very tired or tried to watch TV for too long, Alex explained. The anxiety about the amnesia was always there, along with worry about the man who'd tried to kill her. And now, the guns and self-defense puzzle.

Caswell quizzed Alex thoroughly about what she had remembered since the assault and talked about amnesia in general. Alex found her reassuring, which was good, but was still anxious about where the therapy would lead her. She kept remembering the caution about revealing too much from that unidentifiable voice. She was both desperate to get her memory back and terrified of what she would learn.

"I believe you have a combination of traumatic amnesia caused by the head injury and what is called dissociative amnesia.

The first is pretty easy for most people to understand and recover from. Amnesia often centers around the time of whatever caused the injury but doesn't affect memories formed before the accident or the ability to recall or form them afterward."

Caswell leaned back in her chair and folded her hands over her stomach. "Dissociative amnesia is more complicated. It occurs when something happens that is frightening enough or disturbing enough that a person forgets or dissociates from the event. That dissociation is sometimes seen in sexual abuse survivors or others who have experienced something extremely traumatic and they have no memory of the incident.

"For others, like yourself, it often means that, in addition to not remembering the trauma, they have no memory of who they are, don't know or recognize family members, don't know where they are, or where they came from. It's a self-protection mechanism."

"Is there any chance my memory will return?" Alex asked, fearing the answer but needing to know.

Caswell smiled. "The brain is a miraculous organ. It can heal from all sorts of insults if given time."

"I don't *have* time. I need to know now. I need to know something! *I can't live like this*," Alex shouted, and then pinched the bridge of her nose in the hopes that she could stop the threat of tears. *Crying gets you nowhere, missy.* Alex blew out a breath and rubbed her hands over her face. That fucking voice again, who was he?

"I'm sorry, that was rude. I'm just at the end of my rope."

"What has Detective Halloran told you?"

"About me?" Alex snorted a laugh. "That he thought I was a prostitute when he found me after the assault. He says he doesn't think I am, but when I freaked out at hearing that he tried to get into bed with me."

Caswell pulled her head back in surprise. "He *what?*"

"He sat down on the bed beside me and rubbed my back. I took it as him wanting sex, which didn't sit well particularly at that moment."

"Are you staying with him?"

"There's nowhere else for me to go. The guy who assaulted me tried to do it again at the hotel where Blake—Detective Halloran—put me up, so he took me to his apartment."

The look on Caswell's face worried her. She didn't want to get Blake into trouble, and it didn't look as if Caswell liked the idea of her being at his apartment.

"He looked into safe houses but, apparently, they're taken because of some major trial where a witness was killed," she added quickly. "The women's shelters he talked to were either full or were unwilling to take an amnesic assault victim who someone had attempted to kill twice."

"That's really not an acceptable solution. I'll talk to him. Tell me what happened between you."

After Alex related what had happened, and what Blake had told her on the way to the precinct, Caswell said, "Is it possible that you misinterpreted his actions? By that I mean is it possible he's telling the truth, that it was a very awkward, and certainly inappropriate, attempt to comfort you?"

"I guess. He's been very…he's done nothing inappropriate." She flashed on him trying to grab the towel as it dropped to the floor. The sight of him naked—broad shoulders, dark hair drifting from his chest, down his firm belly, and flaring around his sex—had sent a jolt of arousal through her, but that hadn't been intentional or inappropriate on his part. Her thoughts about him on the other hand…were best left unexplored at the moment.

"I feel safe with him. Last night, I don't know what happened. He left immediately when I told him to; he didn't press or force himself on me. Then, this morning, he seemed sincere."

"Did he tell you he'd talked to a prostitute one of the detectives in Vice had sent him to?"

"No. Maybe that's what he was upset about, he found out that's what I am."

"Quite the opposite, apparently. The woman told him you didn't seem at all interested in customers. All you wanted to do was talk to her and others. She said you were trying to find your sister, who'd gone missing."

"Why didn't he tell me? Why let me think the opposite?"

Caswell smiled. "It sounds like he tried to. Based on what I know about him, interpersonal relations with women have been difficult."

She watched Alex then said, "He left a message for me last night, telling me what he'd found out, and said he didn't want to tell you for fear of upsetting you." Caswell laughed out loud. "Then he basically tells you enough to upset any woman."

"I pressured him to talk to me, even though I knew he didn't want to. I wasn't prepared for what he said."

Caswell smiled at her. "He did tell you he didn't think you were a prostitute. And, as I said, it sounds like he tried to tell you the rest. But by then you were obviously upset, and without the other information it would have been hard for you to believe."

They sat in silence for several minutes. "I'd like to try some hypnosis and see if it will help. I suspect that what happened was traumatic enough to result in this amnesia, but I doubt seriously that the blow to the head is the cause. Would you be willing to undergo hypnosis?"

Alex was scared to, but even more afraid not to. She nodded. "All right. Now?"

"No, I have another appointment in fifteen minutes." Caswell picked up an iPad and tapped on it for a moment. "How about tomorrow afternoon, say three o'clock?"

"Okay." Alex shrugged. "I haven't anything else to do."

"And you're okay with me discussing our sessions with Detective Halloran?"

"Yes."

"I'll speak to him about the living arrangements and see what we can come up with."

"No! Please, don't. I feel safe with him. I'm afraid to be alone. I think that I misread his intentions."

"Alex."

"No, I don't want you to talk to him. I'll talk to him. Please."

Caswell gave her a long stare and finally said, "I will speak with him. I have a duty to. If, after I've spoken with him, I feel it's safe for you to remain there, I won't press to find another place for you to stay."

Alex nodded. "Thank you."

Caswell stood and opened the door to the office, indicating a chair in the waiting area. "Sit here and I'll let him know we're done for the day."

CHAPTER TWENTY

H E SHOWED THE medical examiner the photo of Alex and watched the man carefully. "Any of the unclaimed or unidentified women look even vaguely like her?"

"There may be one. Come on and I'll let you take a look."

She was pale, with a bluish cast to her waxy skin. The vapor that escaped from the drawer was unsettling. Her hair was a brassy blond, but a half-inch of roots was red like Alex's hair, and it made him shudder.

"We weren't able to ID her."

"What color eyes?"

The M.E. looked at the autopsy record. "Green. Is she yours?"

Blake stared at the corpse's face. She was obviously older than Alex, but there was a resemblance. It was a resemblance, but not enough for him to make a positive ID.

"I think so, but I can't say one hundred percent. Hang on to her for a while longer. I have a woman who may be her sister, but she's amnesic and, so far, can't remember anything helpful."

Blake rubbed his forehead. "She was posing as a prostitute to look for her sister, so apparently that's how her sister made her living. I don't suppose you can determine that on autopsy."

"All I can tell you is this woman wasn't a virgin, probably hadn't been for some time, and had never had a child."

"If the woman I'm working with remembers anything that makes me think this body is her sister, I'll get some photos from you and ask her to look at them. If she thinks it's her sister, but isn't sure, I'll bring her here for an official ID."

The M.E. nodded. "Photos are best for relatives to look at—corpses not so much. I'll email you some photos. She had nothing on her that would ID her—no purse, no license, nothing. And," he said, pulling the sheet down, "she had no fingers to print."

"Christ, another one." Blake sighed. "Yeah, she's mine."

The M.E. pulled the sheet back up. "We'll hold on to her for at least another month. After that she'll be cremated and her ashes disposed of, unless there's some official reason not to. We could take DNA swabs from your witness and compare them to the DNA from this woman to see if they're related."

"All DNA would tell me is she's related, but I'll see if there's a way I can collect that and get it to you without alerting her. I don't want her to know about this woman yet. We're trying to get her memory back, and I don't want to do anything that might traumatize her unless I have to."

"Okay. But we can't keep this one forever. She's almost used up her allowable time before we cremate and dispose."

"I realize that, but she's now part of an ongoing homicide investigation. Don't do anything with the body until I clear it. And send me the autopsy report and photos." Blake sighed in frustration. "If it looks like it'll be a long-term thing, I may bring her here anyway. Maybe seeing the body will shake something loose. But if I do, for God's sake don't mention the fingers."

"I'll wait to hear from you." He closed the drawer and walked Blake out to the reception area. "Good luck. It'd be nice to get her ID'd and out of here."

Blake's phone rang as he walked to the parking lot. "Detective Halloran, this is Dr. Caswell. Alex is done and ready for you to pick her up. Before you come, however, I want to discuss last night."

Fuck me, Blake thought. "Okay," he replied warily.

"I was not aware that Alex was staying in your apartment. While that's really not acceptable, I understand the dilemma you're in. I want to hear your side of the story before I make any decisions about whether to allow the living arrangements to continue."

"Well if you don't think the arrangements should continue, then she's your problem. I have no other solution to the current housing situation."

"Don't get into a pissing contest with me, Detective. You won't win."

No, he probably wouldn't. He huffed out an exasperated breath. "I made the mistake of telling her some, but not all, of the information I'd heard about her. Then I tried to tell her the rest, but she freaked out and wouldn't listen."

He reached his car, opened the door, and got in. "I should have kept my mouth shut and let you handle it but, dipshit that I am, I didn't. She…"

He paused, she what? "She looked so alone and so torn up about it, I wanted to comfort her, tell her the rest that I'd learned. Like an idiot, I reached out and stroked her back."

He leaned back and let his head drop onto the headrest. "I wanted to comfort her, that's all, but she thought I wanted to have sex in return for letting her stay with me. I had no intention of doing anything else, none. She told me to go away, and I did. It was a mistake. It won't happen again."

"I'm glad to hear that. I'm also glad to hear you respected her rebuff."

"There wasn't anything to rebuff, since I wasn't planning on fucking her!"

"No need to be that graphic, but as long as you remain professional, I see no reason to alter the arrangement. I have checked about safe houses and shelters, and it appears that this is the perfect storm—none are available."

He heard her shuffling some papers. "I will check in with Alex periodically about the arrangements. She wants to stay with you, but if I get any sense that something has changed for you or that she is at risk staying with you I will see that she's moved. Understood?"

"Understood. Just so we're clear," Blake said through gritted teeth, "I've never forced myself on any woman, *ever.*"

"I'm glad to hear that," she said, and disconnected.

I've never wanted to. I know what no means, he thought, shoving his phone in his jacket pocket and driving off.

———•◆•———

ALEX WATCHED him carefully when he entered the waiting area. His face was shut down, but irritation radiated off him in waves. Whether it was because he was angry with her or had his mind on other things, she couldn't tell.

"Let's go," he said shortly, and walked out of the waiting area without checking to see if she was following him.

Angry with me then, she thought as she followed him to the garage and got into his car. "I want to apologize for misinterpreting your actions last night," she said stiffly.

He snorted a laugh and said nothing.

"I wish you'd told me the entirety of what you'd found out."

"Yeah, well, I'm a fucking idiot, so not surprising that I didn't handle it right. I did try, but you wouldn't listen."

Okay, really angry, she thought. *I wonder what Caswell said to him.*

His driving was as irritated as he was. It looked to her like he was driving in the direction of the apartment. She hoped that Caswell hadn't interfered with her living there. It was true, she did feel safe with Blake. If she had been less upset the night before, the stroke of his hand on her back would have been welcome, would have been a comfort. And the thought struck her that comfort was not something she was used to.

"Would you mind if we stopped at a grocery store?" she asked hesitantly. "Um, there isn't a lot of food on hand."

He nodded. A few minutes later he pulled into the parking lot at a King Soopers grocery store. He found a parking place, pulled into it, hit the brakes, and jerked the emergency brake on.

Yep, she thought, *really angry.*

"Come on, then," he said brusquely, opening his door and getting out.

They walked the aisles and she picked out bread and sandwich fixings, some milk, some Coke, bottled water, and the same coffee she'd seen in his cupboard, then drew a blank.

"I don't really know what else to pick out. I don't know what you like. I...I don't know what to suggest, and I can't pay for any of it."

He looked so angry and had been so silent, that she finally said. "I'm sorry. God, I'm sorry. I wish there were somewhere else for me to go."

He stopped and turned to her and could see tears shimmering as she blinked them away. "It's okay. It's not your fault." He looked uncomfortable. "I'm sorry, too. I'm an idiot. I should have known better last night."

He shrugged as if not knowing what else to say about it then said, "Let's get some eggs and bacon, some cereal, and maybe some more pasta and sauce—the spaghetti was easy, and pretty good."

That got a small laugh out of her. "Then let's look around and see if anything appeals," he said. "I'm not much of a cook, so we should keep it simple. We'll figure something out."

She nodded. They finished shopping and afterward he drove to a nearby store that carried electronics and prepaid phones and said he'd be right back. Returning to the car twenty minutes later, he took out a phone and played with it for a few minutes, then handed it to her.

"This is yours. I should have thought of this sooner. It's charged. Keep it handy. I've programmed my cell into it. If you need me hit '1' and it'll autodial."

She nodded and took the phone, sliding it into her pocket. She turned around and added the bag with the phone charger and instruction manual to the collection of grocery bags in the back seat as they returned to the apartment.

Unloading the groceries, they carried the bags up the stairs. In the hallway in front of the apartment door, he put his bags on the floor, but before he could put the key in the top lock an older woman from the apartment opposite his, opened her door. She was attractive, her silver hair cut in a short bob. Her face was friendly and open looking, but Alex saw Blake frown.

"There you are, Blake, I've been keeping my eye out for you." She turned to Alex. "I don't think we've met. I'm Connie Holtz, most people in the building just call me Mrs. H." She held her hand out. Alex offered hers. The woman patted it, and let it go. "Are you one of Blake's lady friends?"

Alex blushed, but before Blake could reply, she said, "No. I'm Blake's sister, Jane."

"I didn't realize Blake had a sister. It's nice to meet you. It looks like you've had a bump on the head—is everything okay?" The woman gave her an appraising stare.

She was looking less beat up, but the evidence of the attacks was still pretty obvious. "Yes, I'm fine. I was in a car accident and my car is out of commission. I'm staying with Blake until I get it back."

"Oh, well, I'm sorry to hear that, but I'm glad you're better."

She turned to Blake. "I didn't know you were having problems with your locks."

"What?" he asked.

"I wondered what the problem was since that locksmith was here earlier this morning."

"Locksmith?"

She took a step back at the look on his face. "Why, yes…the man who was here working on your locks. He was in a uniform…"

She clutched at a small heart locket at her throat and fiddled with it nervously. "I heard noises out in the hallway, so I checked though my peephole and saw this locksmith working on your door."

"When was this?"

"Well, I guess a little before ten this morning."

"Did you speak to him?"

"No, I don't meddle in other people's business."

Alex saw the look of incredulity on Blake's face. "What'd he look like?"

"I didn't get a good look because his back was turned to me. He was a big man— looked muscular. Tall. He had one of those ball caps on, but I think his hair was dark based on what I could see around his neck."

"When did he leave?"

"My program was set to start at ten, and he looked official, so I turned on the TV and forgot about him. Should I have called the police?"

"No, but thanks, Mrs. H. I guess I forgot he was coming today; I thought it was tomorrow. I appreciate you keeping an eye on things," he said, hoping to get her to go back in her apartment.

"Anytime Blake, anytime. Nice to meet you, Jane."

Alex nodded, and by some miracle the woman actually did go into her apartment and shut the door. Turning his back to her door, Blake unlocked the apartment and drew his gun out of its shoulder holster. Alex's eyes went wide and her pulse rate kicked up.

"Stay here," he said softly, barely above a whisper. "Here are my car keys. If the shit hits the fan get the hell out of here, go to my car, and drive to the precinct. Don't hang around, understood?"

She nodded and he slowly pushed the door open and moved into the apartment. She heard him moving around carefully, quietly. When he finally returned, she felt her pulse rate start to drop.

"No one's here," he said softly. "Come inside and close the door, but no talking unless I ask you something, okay?"

She nodded, puzzled. She put the groceries away to give herself something to do while he continued to prowl the apartment one room at a time.

CHAPTER TWENTY-ONE

MRS. H SEEING the locksmith tampering with the door was fortunate, but worrisome. Why would the guy risk coming here and tampering with the locks? It made no sense. Even if Alex could ID him, if he was a john that she'd gone with thinking she could get information on her sister, all they'd have was a description, no name, nothing to help find or arrest him. To Blake, that meant that something significant was at risk if Alex remained alive.

Mrs. H was a busybody, regardless of what she told people. Alex's comment about being his sister had surprised him. Alex seemed to lie easily and spontaneously. One more worrisome puzzle about her.

Blake had seen nothing missing or disturbed when he'd checked out the apartment. *If nothing's missing,* he thought, *maybe something's been added.* He walked into the living room and switched on the TV.

"Let's put the groceries away," he said over the TV noise as he walked to the kitchen. He held a finger up to his mouth as he entered the kitchen and moved close to her, his mouth next to her ear. He felt her unexpectedly shiver when he spoke close to her ear.

"I need to check for listening devices so keep conversation to a minimum, and don't say anything about the locks. If he planted bugs, I don't want him to know Mrs. H saw him and told me about him being here. I sure as hell don't want him coming back and killing her to keep her from identifying him." Alex nodded anxiously.

Back in the living room Blake said aloud, "I'm going to flake out and watch the game. I'll think of something to eat in a while."

He flipped through the channels until he found a game and then began quietly searching the apartment. He found a bug in the living room under the coffee table, and one in the bedroom affixed to the back of the bedside table. He left them there for the time being. Maybe he could use them to his advantage. If so, he'd tolerate them for a few days. If not, he'd get rid of them.

The guy's lock picking had been professional, and once he'd done what he came for he'd left. Without nosy Mrs. H, Blake would have been none the wiser that they were being monitored. He'd have to get her some flowers or something; or not. A gift might encourage her.

Blake was worried. The guy who'd attacked Alex obviously knew she was here. He must have followed Blake from the precinct and scoped the place out for a few days to know that most residents were gone during the day, and he'd come prepared with a uniform. If he'd gotten in and Alex had been here, he'd have killed her. But he'd prepared for all eventualities by bringing the bugs.

"Here, I fixed sandwiches." Alex handed him a plate with a sandwich and some chips, and then a beer.

He took it gratefully and watched as she retrieved her own food and sat in the chair next to the couch. He downed half the beer and most of the sandwich before he spoke.

"Thanks for making this, it's good."

"You're welcome," she replied cautiously.

He made a few comments on the game as if watching it. She said nothing, eating slowly and wondering why he'd left the bugs in place. When they'd finished, he motioned her to the kitchen.

Standing next to the fridge, close to her, he said quietly, "This break-in's brazen as hell and risky, which tells me the stakes are high for whoever this guy is. Something important is in jeopardy if you remember what happened. Something more than simply being able to ID him. I'm going to stick around the rest of the day, just in case."

"In case what? I don't understand. If he came back when I was here alone, I would hear him messing with the locks and would call you."

"And it wouldn't make much difference. He's skilled at picking and opening locks, so chances are he's quick. If he was trying to get in with you here, he'd be quiet. You weren't here, so he planted the bugs. If you'd been here, he'd have killed you before anyone could have gotten here, including me."

She gasped and raised her hand to her mouth. She pushed past him suddenly and ran toward the bath. He heard her lose the food she'd eaten a few minutes before, while he tried to think of what to do.

He heard the toilet flush and the water in the sink run for a few minutes before she returned, opening and taking a long drink of a Coke. She looked so pale her skin was nearly transparent. Blake's stomach flipped uneasily as he remembered the woman in the morgue. Seen in this light, there was a resemblance.

"You clearly know how to break down a gun and put it back together, so I need to find out if you know how to shoot one."

"Why?"

"Because I can't leave you here with nothing but a phone and no way to defend yourself. I can't be here 24/7."

"You want me to have a gun?"

He paused and walked to the entrance to the living room. "Man, these guys are putzes. I can't believe they missed that shot." Returning to the kitchen, he said, "Yes, any objections?"

She shook her head.

"Good, 'cause other than taking you to work with me and making you sit at my desk all day I don't know what else to do."

"Then let's hope I know how to shoot."

They passed the evening uneasily. At ten she announced she was going to bed, so he motioned her into the kitchen again.

"There's a bug in the bedroom, but as long as we don't have any serious conversations there it should be fine. I'll think of something. Maybe the bugs are a way we can force his hand. Try not to worry and get some sleep."

———— ◆ ————

HE'D RETRIEVED his other handgun from the small locked box he kept in his closet and took her to the nearest shooting range. She knew how to shoot and was pretty deadly at hitting the target. He'd once heard an instructor say that women were disconcertingly accurate at hitting the kill zone on targets, even women who had never shot a gun before. Clearly, she had.

"When I'm not here," he said as they sat in his car after returning to the apartment, "keep this on you at all times. Keep it by your bedside, too. There may be nights I can't be here because something has come up that my partner and I have to handle."

"Do you honestly think he'll come back?"

"I don't know, but he's made two attempts on your life. I don't want to find out that third time's the charm. When he didn't find you in the apartment, he put the bugs in place so he could keep track of us. Probably so he'd know when you were here alone."

He saw the terrified look in her eyes and watched her face blanch. "Alex, I have no place to move you right now, and I doubt a safe house or a shelter would be any better than here. I don't know what else to do. You obviously know how to use a gun, so I think it's the best option right now. Just don't shoot me, please."

"Then don't sneak up on me."

"Trust me, I won't," he said with a grin.

The smile did wonders. Instead of the harried, always some-what-pissed-off-looking detective, it rendered him boyish and charming. He saw her cheeks flush as she watched him and she tugged on her lower lip with her teeth. The smile faded, however, as he dropped his head into his hands and rubbed his face.

"I can't figure out who you are. You're not military or a cop. Your prints aren't in any of the databases that they should be in if you were. I can't explain your familiarity with guns or self-defense. Does anything come to mind that might?"

"I keep asking myself that, but I have no answers. It's muscle memory and I'm on autopilot, I guess." She frowned. "Is it possible that there's a less than legal reason I can shoot? I worry about that."

"All I can say is, if there is you've never been arrested or finger-printed, because I can't find your prints anywhere. So, either you're very good at what you do or very lucky."

"What if I'm some sort of off-the-grid hit woman?" She blushed. "I mean, I know that sounds dramatic, even silly, but it's a possibility, right? If I were, I'd have to be pretty good and probably would never have been arrested."

Blake had wondered about that, or at least whether there was some criminal reason she knew what she knew. He realized he was letting his attraction to her to get in the way, but he seriously doubted she was the kind of sociopath that normally took on con-tract killing. As for being off the grid, for all intents and purposes she was and he'd found no way to ID her.

"I don't know for sure. I suppose it's a possibility, but I don't see it. You don't fit the profile, personality-wise." He smiled at her and watched as that slight flush returned to her cheeks. "You're too nice."

"But maybe that's only because I can't remember who I am. Maybe if I did, I'd be different. I can't stand this uncertainty and the fear of finding out who I really am." She hesitated. "I keep hearing this man's voice, saying things he may have said to me once. It's rough and there's a mean edge to it. I don't know who it is, maybe it's the person who attacked me."

"What does he say?"

"Things like don't tell people anything about myself, that the less people know the better. What if I-I'm a criminal or some sort of horrible person? What if the reason I was attacked is because I killed someone he knew, or I double-crossed him somehow?"

He could see her anxiety rising and was worried she'd work herself into a panic attack. He leaned over and took hold of her shoulders.

"Stop. I think the likelihood that you're any of those things is pretty low. I don't know what the voice means. Ask Caswell, but my guess is amnesia wouldn't change your basic personality—not that much anyway."

"What if I never know who I am or who this voice belongs to? What if the person who attacked me is never found? What'll I do?"

Without thinking he pulled her into his arms. "*Shh*, we'll figure this out. Caswell is good. I don't like her, but she's good. She'll help you figure it out. You'll remember, and who knows? Maybe I'll figure out who you are if you don't."

He held her close, taking in the scent of her. Her hair was soft against his face, she was warm and yielding in his arms, and desire flared as he held her. Abruptly he came to his senses.

He let go and pulled back. "I'm sorry, I shouldn't have done that. For God's sake, don't tell Caswell."

"It's okay, it helped."

"Well, Caswell won't see it that way, so..."

"Blake," she said touching his arm with her hand. "I'm not going to say anything. I don't want to move. I feel safe with you. At least I'm with someone I know, sort of."

CHAPTER TWENTY-TWO

BLAKE LAY AWAKE on the couch, his gun next to him. It didn't make a good bed partner, nor did his concerns. What the hell was he going to do with her? He didn't know where to take her and having her stay here was getting complicated—for him.

It was becoming too easy to forget and take her in his arms and harder to let go. And the random thoughts about her, about how she felt in his arms, were getting far too frequent. He tried, when he was awake, not to think of the dreams he was having about her to avoid embarrassing himself in public. The only downside of having a dick, in his mind, was it often decided to make its presence known at the most inopportune times.

It was difficult not to think of the dreams, though. They were so erotic—imagining how she'd feel, how she'd taste, what they'd do, how she'd look and sound when she came—that he woke from them painfully aroused. His cock wasn't happy that there was only one self-inflicted outlet for all that desire. He wanted her, badly, but acting on the urges would only cause a shitload of trouble.

Emotions got in the way of doing his job, got in the way of everything, which was why he avoided them. Here was as safe as anywhere for her, and here she had him to keep an eye on things, but he worried. If he wasn't around and the guy who was listening surprised her, would she be able to protect herself? And what the hell did the voice she'd told him about mean? Was it her memory or some sort of psychosis?

He figured it was only sheer luck that the guy hadn't killed her the night Blake had nearly run her over. And if it was the same guy as the one who was killing the prostitutes, why hadn't he made sure she was dead and cut off her fingertips? Did the fact that she had a laceration on the joint of her index finger mean he'd intended to and been interrupted?

And why hadn't he killed her in her hotel room? Blake still didn't understand why he hadn't finished the job. Instead, he'd taken off at the first sign of trouble.

Why? he thought. *Why'd he bail?*

In both instances, the guy could have strangled her and slipped away after she was dead, before anyone was the wiser. Blake shuddered at the thought of how close she'd come to being murdered.

The noise Alex had made and the fight she'd put up in the hotel room had resulted in the warning from the other guest. Dead, there was no chance she could ID him, which made his leaving the hotel room with her alive even more puzzling. Apparently, he couldn't chance being seen leaving the hotel room or being caught near the room by a manager who'd been alerted to the noise and would find a dead body and remember him. Maybe that was why he bailed.

Other than being arrested, what else would make it important that he not be ID'd? Was *who* he was not worth the risk of being seen? Was he connected to the deaths of the women who'd had their fingertips cut off? Too many damn questions.

Blake's mind drifted, as it often did when struggling with a puzzle, and he'd learned over time that it was his way of searching for answers. If he let his mind drift, answers sometimes arose. Doing that, he fell into a restless sleep.

The woman in the morgue opened her eyes and he lurched back.

She reached out with her hand that had no end digits and grabbed his arm. "Promise me you'll find him."

He nodded wordlessly as she let go and closed her eyes.

"Why can't you find who did this to me?" Ashley Kensington cried, materializing on the other side of the dead woman lying in the morgue drawer.

"We're trying."

"No, you're too busy trying to protect that woman."

"She's part of this," he said.

"No, you want her to be. You want her, period, and you don't care about finding my killer."

"What about me?" Katia said, appearing at the head of the morgue drawer.

"We're trying, for God's sake. We're trying."

"No, you're not," they said in a chorus as they reached out with their bloody hands and tried to grab his arms.

He woke with a hoarse shout, gasping, his heart racing, frantically brushing at his arms to dislodge the hands that he could still feel grabbing him. He forced himself to look around and reorient himself. *I'm here, in the apartment, not the morgue,* he thought as he took several deep breaths. *It was just a dream. It wasn't real.*

He heard Alex's quick footsteps before she materialized in the dark and sat on the coffee table next to the couch. "What's wrong? Are you all right?"

He sat up and scrubbed his hands over his face. "Yeah, fine. Bad dream I guess." He leaned his head back against the couch and exhaled slowly, trying to force the images of the dead women and the feel of their cold hands out of his head.

"Sorry I woke you."

"It's okay. Can I get you something?"

"No," he said, pushing up from the couch. "Go back to bed. I'm fine."

"Okay," she said, apparently for the benefit of the bug since she didn't return to bed and instead followed him into the kitchen.

She pushed him into the corner by the fridge and said in a whisper, "You're not fine. What was that all about?"

"A bad dream, I told you. I'm gonna get a drink then go back to bed. I'm fine."

He poured himself a scotch and drank it down like medicine. His hand shook slightly and he could feel his heart pounding against his chest wall. *I'm here, not there, I'm here, not there,* he thought, repeating in his head the mantra that helped to bring him back from flashbacks.

"You can talk to me. You don't have to carry all this on your shoulders…"

He heard the sympathy in her voice and it sent a little jolt of panic through him.

"*I'm fine!*" he hissed, leaning into her face. "I don't need to talk about it. I don't *want* to talk about it! I need you to go to bed and leave me alone!"

He saw the shocked look on her face and regretted what he'd said. "I'm…I'm sorry."

He reached out without thinking and stroked her hair, letting his hand slide around and cup the back of her head, pulling her toward him until their lips met. *Soft,* he thought vaguely as he touched his lips to hers and began exploring. *I want you,* he thought more urgently.

He pulled back abruptly. Taking hold of her shoulders, he spun her around. "Go. To. Bed," he hissed in her ear as he propelled her out of the kitchen, down the hall into the bedroom, and pulled the door closed before he walked back to the living room.

He lay down on the couch, knowing it would be a long time before he slept.

CHAPTER TWENTY-THREE

LEX HAD SEEN his hand shake, had seen the panicked look when she'd offered him the chance to talk, and been taken by surprise when he cupped her head in his hand and began kissing her. She'd felt the jolt that had run through him, both the sexual one and the one that made him pull back as if he'd been hit with a cattle prod. She'd felt her own jolt and responded to his kiss. He'd tasted of scotch. His tentative then hungry kiss had aroused a deep longing in her, and she hadn't wanted the kiss to stop. She'd wanted to comfort him and take that panicked look away. And she wanted him.

Alex supposed it was a good thing he'd cut off the kiss. She wasn't entirely sure she'd have had the control to do that. Despite knowing that getting intimately involved with him was risky, she realized that was exactly what she wanted. Her situation; his decision to move her to his apartment, their odd, uncertain friendship, and her reliance on him had put them in quarters that were far too close.

In the dark, in his bed, in a room that still smelled faintly like him, she knew she had to hold back. She had no idea who she was or what her real life was like. She didn't know whether she had a husband or a significant other or children. More worrisome was whether she was someone he'd have to arrest when it became clear who she was.

In spite of all the reasons to avoid getting involved with him, reasons she needed to remember, she wanted to ignore them. He could be frustrating and irritable and hard to read or deal with at times, but she felt safe with him and she didn't want to keep her distance.

The comfort she felt in his arms was addictive and his kiss had set off deep, seemingly long-neglected needs. Once she knew who she was and why she'd been assaulted, though, she had no idea what would happen between them. If she had a husband and a family, would she take one night with him before she went back to her real life?

Yes, she thought. Yes, I would.

She wondered what had jarred him awake with that hoarse cry. Caswell had said he had issues with relationships. How would she know? Had Blake been a client? Why? What had happened to him? What had caused that haunted, panicked look she'd seen on his face?

What put that look of pity in his eyes lately when she caught him staring at her? What did he know about her that he was holding back? She heard the TV go on, turned low. The dream was still bothering him apparently.

------- ◆ -------

"THE KID knew something was wrong but wasn't sure what it was. He said she cut it off with him early in the school year and wouldn't say why," Stevens told Blake as they sat in the department break room.

"That's not very helpful. Even her parents knew something was wrong."

"Well, I'm going up tomorrow to talk to the two girls who were her best friends, according to her parents. Not sure I'll get much more out of them. They're teenagers, pretty self-involved. Plus college is about to start, so they're focused on that."

"Maybe she ran away just for the hell of it."

Stevens snorted. "They run away 'cause something's not right or something appeals enough to lure them away. I don't know any kid who just up and decides to run away. Something in the home, something that happened outside it, who knows? But they don't make a turn-around like she did and then run off for the hell of it."

"Honestly, I'm not sure how important that is. It'll give us a reason she ran away, but it won't help identify the guy who killed her and the other women. He seems to prefer killing prostitutes. He could have mistaken her for one, or she may have been selling herself to survive and made the mistake of going with him."

Stevens shrugged. "I gotta follow through. One of her friends might have stayed in contact or knows something."

Blake nodded and yawned. He hadn't slept much last night. Hell, he hadn't slept well or for a full night since he'd almost hit Alex with his car. The dream and the kiss had kept him awake long after he should have been asleep. He could have sworn the alarm on his phone had sounded only ten minutes after he'd dropped off.

"You look like hell, Halloran. What's going on?"

"Had a rude surprise when I got home day before yesterday. My next-door neighbor, who's quite the busybody, came out to tell me some guy had been working on my door locks."

Stevens raised his eyebrows. "The guy who attacked your girl?"

"Jesus, she's not my girl!" Blake said irritably.

He rubbed his forehead to ease the headache that seemed to have taken up residence since he'd woken up. "Yeah, it's gotta be him. He managed to get in and plant two bugs and leave. I left them in place at least for now, and I'm trying to figure out how to use them to get to him. It's not very conducive to sleeping."

"Interesting."

"It pisses me off. The guy has serious B&E skills. He knew how to breach the hotel security, and he managed to pick the locks on my apartment. Now he'll know where both of us are."

"It wouldn't be hard to keep an eye on you or her. The press leaked your name and the hotel. All the guy would have to do is watch for you to leave here and follow you to your apartment once, then he could come and go as needed."

"I realize that, but I didn't think he'd be that ballsy. And why? Why put this much effort into killing her? If he was a john and she went with him to get information on her sister, at best, all she could tell us was what he looked like. There's more going on here than that." Blake took a slug of the bottle of water he'd purchased from the soda machine in the break room.

"I'm going to talk to Caswell and see what she thinks about having Alex look at photos of the body in the morgue. If it's her sister, then her assault is connected to the other women's murders. Seeing the photos might bring her memory back. I think, if we find this guy, we've got our killer."

"I don't know. It's possible I suppose," Stevens said. "If the guy who attacked her is the same guy, why didn't he make sure she was dead and cut off her fingertips? Why didn't he strangle her and be done with it when he got into her hotel room?"

Blake had dropped his head into his hands. "I don't know. The first time he may have thought she was dead and got interrupted before he could cut her. Maybe he reserves the finger-cutting for prostitutes and knew she wasn't one. I don't fucking know, and I can't explain it."

"Well when you can, let me know. Until then, we operate on the assumption it's two different guys."

———— ◆ ————

"NO. IT'S a very bad idea. It could shock her even further and delay any movement toward her remembering anything."

Blake had debated whether to tell Caswell about the break-in and decided not to. If she thought Alex wasn't safe she'd find a way to move her, and he didn't want her moved. For a lot of reasons, and not all of them were professional.

"I'm pretty sure it's Alex's sister, but I can't prove it without someone who knew her ID'ing her. I gave the M.E. hairs from Alex's brush for a DNA sample, but results take forever. It could be weeks before we know if they're related. If it is her sister, then that'd tie Alex's assault to the other women who've been killed. She could help us find the guy if she could remember what happened."

"For now, Detective, that's your problem. I can't support you putting her through that, because I cannot guarantee it would help her or you."

She sat behind her desk and stared holes through him. "And while I realize you're frustrated my concern is for her welfare, so tread carefully here. If I find out you've followed through with that, you'll be in deep shit."

"I know you don't have a very high opinion of me, but I do care about her welfare. This guy needs to be found. He's tried to kill her twice, and we have no way to ID him."

Caswell looked surprised. "Whatever gave you the idea I think poorly of you?"

"I may not be a shrink but I can read people, too."

"And you've deduced what?"

"That you can be a pompous bitch sometimes, and that you think I'm an idiot who can't see beyond what I want. That I'm a bumbling fool."

"I can be pompous at times, but I wonder if what you think you see in me isn't how you feel about yourself."

Blake shot up out of the chair and moved to the door of her office. "I think we're done here. If she remembers anything important, I want to know immediately."

"You'll be the first, Detective."

CHAPTER TWENTY-FOUR

WELL, I WALKED into that one, Blake thought as he headed back to Homicide. He scowled at nothing in particular, but the look sent several people scurrying out of his way. He was sure if Alex saw the photos of the woman in the morgue, she would remember at least something. Maybe her last name, maybe more, but Caswell had him hamstrung.

He didn't care for her shrink tactics, and he knew what he knew. He had an instinct for people and an ability to read them, and he knew, regardless of what she said, that she didn't like or respect him. He didn't know why. Did he care, was the question.

How much trouble could she cause him if he showed Alex the photos? Probably a lot if it went wrong, he decided. The effect of that trouble wasn't clear, yet.

He had the photos as his ace in the hole. If nothing else broke soon, he'd use them and take whatever blowback it caused. His only concern was what effect showing Alex the photos would have. He didn't want to make things worse for her.

Blake leaned back in his desk chair. He'd finally gotten hairs from Alex's brush and given them to the M.E. to test for DNA, but as he'd told Caswell, it'd be weeks before any results came back.

The easiest tactic would be to show her the photos, but he'd hold off on that a while. Maybe Caswell would be successful in helping Alex remember the assault, or at least her last name.

He wasn't sure about Caswell or her techniques. She'd seen Alex every day so far. Alex never had much progress to report after the sessions, and often seemed distant and uncommunicative after them. Each time she met with the shrink, she seemed more despondent to him. She would put on a happy face, or at least try to conceal her feelings, but he'd gotten used to her and knew that something was bothering her. She seemed puzzled after the sessions, distracted, forgetful. It made him wonder if the hypnosis was a good idea.

He wished he could be a fly on the wall and observe one of their sessions. Not much he could do about any of that at the moment, so he picked up the files that had been sent to them from the Aurora cases and began to read through them.

━━━◆━━━

"HOW HAVE things been for you?" Caswell asked.

Alex sat in her usual spot in the chair across from Caswell's desk. She had come to dread these appointments. Each time she left one, a weight would descend on her leaving her with a vague sense of anxiety. To avoid Blake's curious stares and questions, she'd retreat to the bedroom trying to figure out what triggered the uneasiness.

What sessions she could remember were vague, and there were others she had no memory of at all. Was she losing her short-term memory now as well? Had the head injury caused far more serious damage than the neurologist had believed?

"I haven't remembered anything. I can't even remember most of the hypnosis sessions."

Caswell nodded. "I understand, but you must be patient. You don't look as if you've been sleeping well."

"I'm not."

"That's not uncommon after a traumatic experience, and you almost always fall asleep during the hypnosis sessions. That makes remembering them harder. I thought we'd work on some relaxation techniques that may help you sleep at night." Alex nodded, although she was not at all sure they would help.

"And living at Detective Halloran's, how is that going?"

"It's become home, I guess. It's the only one I have at the moment. I feel safe there."

"And Detective Halloran, is he behaving responsibly?"

Alex frowned at her. "If you mean has he tried to have sex with me, no. He would never do that unless I invited him to." She thought about the kiss and put it out of her mind. She wasn't going to mention it to Caswell.

"Alex, living in close quarters with a man, any man, often breeds expectations and unwise intimacy especially when you're vulnerable. It would be far better to move you to a more neutral place."

Caswell leaned back in her chair and linked her fingers together across her abdomen. "You're stressed and at a disadvantage because of your reliance on him. If he pressures you for sex, how will you turn him down if that means jeopardizing staying somewhere you feel safe?"

Alex could feel her anxiety spike. She didn't want to move. She didn't want to be alone and vulnerable. "Blake would never pressure me for anything. He's been nothing but professional. I feel safe there, and I'm not moving. I have the final say in this."

Caswell stared at her. "You do, but if I feel things have gotten out of hand I will insist and take the issue up with his lieutenant, who I'm sure is unaware of the situation."

Both were silent for several minutes when Caswell said, "Well, let's get started on your hypnosis session."

And Alex's anxiety rose another notch.

BLAKE ASKED a uniformed officer to take Alex to the apartment after her session with Caswell. It was late in the day, and he had several things he needed to do before he could leave. The officer walked Alex into the apartment and said, "Halloran asked me to hang out until he gets here."

Alex nodded, and watched the cop search the apartment carefully and without speaking. It was quiet and less stifling. The air conditioning unit had, for some unknown reason, started working again.

When the cop was through checking things she said, "Feel free to turn the TV on. Can I get you something to drink?" He shook his head no.

The suffocating weight of the hopelessness of her situation followed her like her shadow. She wasn't sure the hypnosis sessions were helping, and the depression seemed to grow daily. Not wanting to be social, Alex walked into the bathroom and closed the door. Standing in front of the medicine cabinet mirror, she looked at her reflection. There were dark shadows under her eyes and her face was pale. She looked lost. She pulled the cabinet door open and looked at Blake's razor. He used what looked to her like an old fashioned razor that he had to screw open to insert razor blades into. She'd never asked why.

Between the anxiety about the amnesia, the second attempt on her life, and now the listening devices her sleep was totally disrupted. So far, Caswell's response had been to tell her that was normal. It might be normal, but it was hard to live with.

At night she would go to bed exhausted and was able to fall asleep rapidly, but she would startle awake a few hours later with her heart pounding. She would lie awake sometimes for several hours, trying unsuccessfully to figure out what had woken her and worrying about what her future held.

Doing the relaxation techniques Caswell had taught her would finally allow her to drop off to sleep, but a few hours later she would startle awake to begin the cycle all over again. As a result, she fell asleep during the hypnosis and had no memory of what had taken place.

Caswell kept assuring her this was common, and not to worry about it. But she did, and it bothered her that she didn't know what suggestions Caswell had given her. It added to the increasing sense that there was no way out of this situation.

Alex knew Blake was impatient for her to remember something he could use to identify her or to arrest her attacker. And she knew he was keeping something from her. Something that made him look at her with pity, something he was afraid to tell her.

Despite the trust she had in Dr. Caswell, she debated before each session about refusing to undergo more hypnosis but, when there, couldn't manage to bring it up. The fear of actually remembering who she was and what had happened was certainly enough to make her uneasy, but the pervasive depression seemed to grow each day.

She kept coming back to the worry that if her memories returned, she would be sorry they had or that she might never know who she was, might never find her way out of this predicament. She exited the bath and walked to the kitchen wondering, as she stood by the sink, if it wouldn't have been better if her attacker had succeeded.

The cop poked his head around the kitchen entrance and said quietly, "Halloran texted me, says he'll be home shortly, and I could go. He told me not to announce it because of the bugs. Are you okay with that?"

"I'll be fine, thank you."

She walked him to the door without comment. He left and Alex returned to the bathroom.

"**ARE YOU** sure the woman was from Golden?" Blake asked the detective assigned to the case.

"No, we're not. We hit a wall. No one near the dump site knew her or would admit to knowing her. No one in town recognized her. We had no way to ID her because of the missing fingertips, nothing on her that might help, and no response to the media blast, so the whole case went cold. I think she was dumped out here for those exact reasons."

"You know about the two prostitutes from Aurora, right?"

"No, not until you contacted me. Aurora PD never contacted us. No real reason for them to do that. They were unaware of our body. Now you supposedly have an unidentified body, too, which we didn't know."

"We didn't know we had a serial on our hands until the second body turned up. We didn't know about the unidentified body here in Denver until recently. I'd like to coordinate these cases, see if something pops. Can you send me your files? I'm happy to share mine. Sometimes a fresh eye sees something."

"Yeah sure, I'll scan and send them to you. Looks like they're connected. It'd sure be nice to get her ID'd."

"It would, thanks for sending the files."

Blake hung up and prepared his files on Ashley, Katia, and the unidentified woman he knew, but couldn't confirm, was Alex's sister. When they were scanned, he decided he'd wait until he got the files from Golden first before he sent his.

That's what's wrong with all of us, he thought. *We're too territorial.*

That reminded him of Kyle Jeffries, suspicious, almost belligerent at the scene, then pissed off, territorial, and in his face about his interference with a victim Jeffries failed to follow up on. The second run in with Jeffries a few days after his lieutenant passed the case off to Blake had puzzled him. By Jeffries' own admission, the assault was unimportant to him.

Blake didn't like Jeffries or his lieutenant on general principle based on their attitude toward Alex's assault, and it was pretty clear Jeffries didn't like being one-upped. Perhaps there'd been fall-out from whatever confrontation he'd had with the person who'd objected to being arrested and Blake taking the case away had added to his belligerence.

I should have put him on report after the first call, Blake thought, but it hadn't seemed worth the trouble. Looking at his phone and realizing he'd stayed far longer than he'd planned, he emailed the files to the Golden detective, and left.

As he was walking into the apartment building, he texted Alex to let her know he was on his way up. They'd agreed to this to prevent her from freaking out and shooting him when he came through the door. He walked up the stairs to avoid using the elevator. He'd always been slightly claustrophobic, and the elevator was a little too small for his comfort.

As Blake put his key in the lock, he realized Alex hadn't texted him back, which sent a cold spike of fear through him.

He eased the door open. "Alex? It's me." No response. *Ah Christ, he'd told the cop to go home too soon and she'd been here by herself. Let her be okay*, he thought. *Please let her be okay.* "Alex?"

He drew his gun and nudged the door open wider, scanning the room and seeing nothing out of place. He moved into the living room and peered cautiously around the dividing wall into the kitchen. Nothing. Moving down the hall, he checked the bedroom first and saw her phone and the gun he'd given her lying on the bedside table. Seeing no one and nothing out of place, he turned toward the bathroom door and opened it.

Alex sat on the floor, back against the tub, holding her wrist, one of his razor blades lying on the floor beside her. He reholstered his gun and dropped to the floor next to her, grabbing her wrist and examining it.

"Jesus," he said, his heart hammering in his chest. "Jesus Christ, Alex, what happened?"

She shook her head and said through tears, "I didn't know what else to do, but it didn't work very well. It hurt too much."

Thankfully, she'd done what a lot of people did when attempting suicide, she'd cut across her wrist, which never sliced anything important enough to bleed to death. The wound was bleeding and looked as if it'd need stitches. Christ, he'd have to take her to the ER and have it stitched, but if he did, he knew they'd slap her with a 72-hour hold at the hospital or a psych hospital. The last thing he wanted.

CHAPTER TWENTY-FIVE

"**S**HE'S AN ASSAULT victim the perp has tried to kill twice. She can't stay here."

Blake stood with the ER doc outside the treatment room where Alex lay on a gurney, her wrist sutured and bandaged. "Well Detective that's not up to you. She's on a 72-hour hold at the very least, until psych can evaluate whether she's safe to go home."

"I'll see that she's supervised. Her life is in danger if left in the hospital or a psych facility." Blake hesitated. "Is there…something I can do to persuade you to let her go?"

The doc snorted a laugh. "No, there isn't. It's not in her best interests and I could lose my license if I let you bribe me into releasing her." The doc sighed seeing the look on Blake's face.

"Get an officer to sit outside her room. She isn't physically in any danger, she didn't lose enough blood to be a concern, but I'm keeping her here until psych can arrange an eval. It could be a while. She may not have been serious enough to follow through, but you know as well as I do, it's a cry for help. She needs assessment." He strode off, clearly frustrated and disappeared into another treatment room.

Blake swore and tried to decide what to do.

He returned to the treatment room and stood next to the gurney, watching her. Her eyes were closed, and she cradled her bandaged wrist on her abdomen. The doc had said she'd cut a couple of small superficial veins but nothing major. The wound required stitches, but otherwise hadn't done serious damage. The blood she'd lost was minimal. All in all it could have been much worse.

Jesus, he thought. *What the fuck had gone wrong?*

He reached out and stroked her hair and her eyes fluttered open. "Hey, how're you feeling?" he asked, then felt the heat rise in his face. *How was she feeling? Suicidal? Ya think?* he chastised himself.

"Stupid," she said, looking anywhere but at him.

"Alex, I…"

At that moment, a nurse bustled in. "We're admitting you to the floor, we've got a couple of emergencies coming, and we need the bed. You're under a 72-hour hold so one of our psych docs can evaluate you. We'll take you up to your room, once the floor nurse lets me know they're ready."

"I don't need to be…"

The nurse shot her a sympathetic look. "Alex, it's not up to you, it's not a choice."

Alex frowned and turned to Blake. "Can't you do something? I don't want to stay here, I want to go home." She looked on the verge of tears.

It struck Blake she'd called his apartment home and despite all the other complications, it pleased him. "I can't Alex. But I'll stay with you to make sure you're safe. I have to call Stevens and talk to him, let him know what's going on."

Turning to Blake and lowering her voice so Alex couldn't hear, the nurse said, "If they discharge her after the assessment, I'd advise you to keep the pain meds in your possession. Frankly, I wouldn't leave her unsupervised. A person doesn't need a razor blade to successfully commit suicide."

Blake nodded, annoyed, it wasn't as if he didn't know that. The thought that she could have used the gun far more effectively made him sick to his stomach. He wasn't sure what to make of that.

Half an hour later, she was ensconced in a private patient room, while Blake stood outside talking on his phone to Stevens. He wanted the entire incident kept quiet, especially from Caswell. He was sure she'd insist on moving Alex and causing trouble for Blake.

"Fuck, she musta been serious. Hurts like hell to intentionally cut yourself."

"It's weird, but I'm not sure she was serious." Stevens grunted his disbelief. "Hear me out. She was fine, has been so far. She's tolerated the anxiety and the not knowing pretty well. Then, all of a sudden, she tries to off herself?"

"Any hesitation marks?"

Blake sighed. "I didn't really look. She sliced across her wrist, so no serious damage, but she needed stitches and they're insisting on keeping her for the next 72-hours."

"Regardless, slicing your wrist is serious, Halloran."

"They don't need to keep her, but I couldn't talk them out of it."

"You're a doc now? They don't have a choice. You know that."

"What I want from you is your word you won't say anything about this to anyone, especially Caswell."

"Why? Seems to me she should be the first to know."

"She'd insist on hospitalizing Alex more long-term, or at the very least moving her out of my place. And I can't guarantee her safety if that happens."

"Well, you're not doing a bang-up job of that at the moment. She tried to kill herself. How does that make sense?"

Blake shifted from one foot to the other uncomfortably. "I'm going to stay here. You know the bugs were in place. Whoever put them there knows what she did, knows she's vulnerable. I can't just leave her here."

"You're too close to this—too involved. What am I going to tell people about where you are? You can't just disappear for three days. Let me arrange for a uniform to sit outside her door."

"No, I'm staying." Blake insisted.

He heard Clark sigh. "You couldn't save Lindsey, Blake. That wasn't your fault," he said at last. "Are you sure that's not what you're trying to do now? Make amends for not saving her by taking responsibility for this woman? She'd be perfectly safe with a uniform outside the door."

"That is not up for discussion, not with you or anyone else," he said angrily. "What's going on with Alex has nothing to do with that."

"You sure about that?" Then, knowing a brick wall when he ran into it, he let the subject drop. "What're you going to tell Caswell about her absence?"

"I'm going to tell her Alex came down with the flu, and the doc said it was because of all the stress, and that she probably hadn't had a flu shot. That'll put her out of commission for at least ten days."

"Jesus, what a stupid idea. I'm not lying for you."

"Then don't. Say you don't know. Or that as far as you know she's okay but hasn't regained her memory."

"Fine," Stevens said.

"And as for me…"

"Don't worry about it. I'll come up with something."

Blake paused. "Do you know any other shrinks attached to one of the other precincts that I could say would see Alex when they release her?"

"U-Hills has got one who's pretty good. Dave Kendall. Want me to call him and give him a heads up?"

Blake felt his gut relax. "Please. Clark, thanks for the help."

"I must've lost my mind. I'll text you his number after I talk to him."

"I know I haven't convinced you, but I'm sure she's connected to our dead prostitutes. I can't prove it yet, but I'm sure."

Stevens sighed. "Maybe she is, who knows? I haven't turned up anything to lead us to the perp. Neither of Ashley's girlfriends had a clue what was going on. All they said was she got into drugs and alcohol, and she stopped hanging out with them. They thought maybe she'd met someone who was into that but had nothing reliable to confirm it. And I've got nothing further on Katia.

"We may never find this guy unless he does something stupid and gets caught or leaves something behind that'd ID him. I see you got the files from Golden, so maybe that'll help. I'm gonna go out to Aurora and have the guy on the case find the women who ID'd the bodies. Maybe they saw something."

"I'm sorry I can't help you with this right now. I know she's connected, and I know if I don't stay with her, the guy will make another try for her."

Blake heard another resigned sigh from Clark. "You know this is going to backfire on you, right? If it does, it'll leave your ass hanging in the wind. And I don't want to see you go off the deep end again."

Blake murmured something noncommittal and disconnected. The thought that Alex could have been more successful using the gun he'd given her, made the coffee he'd had earlier rise up and burn the back of his throat.

———•◆•———

"I'M SORRY, Blake."

He scrubbed his face with his hand. "What the hell happened? Jesus, Alex, it was the last thing I expected to find." He took the container of water she held out to him and put it back on the bedside table.

She shrugged, looked puzzled, and began to cry. He'd never seen her cry, tear up a little, but never actually cry, and it worried him. He sat next to her on the side of the bed. "I didn't know what else to do. I don't know who I am, and I'm not sure I really want to know. I'm afraid to know. I can't sleep. I've been getting more depressed by the day. I feel like I'm losing even my short-term memory some days. I'm so strung out I…I couldn't see any other solution."

"This is not the answer to anything. I need you to promise me you won't do that again. Please."

She watched him, and he could see how tired she was and how frightened of all the unknowns. But there was something else there he couldn't put his finger on.

"Did you remember something? Is that what triggered this?"

"No, nothing."

"Alex, something set this off. You've been relatively okay through most of this, so why now? Why today?"

He saw the panic in her face. "I don't know!" she exclaimed. "I…all of a sudden I couldn't take it. I've been feeling weird the last few days. Hopeless. Scared."

She paused and looked at him pleadingly. "I thought about all the things I don't know, all the things I might not want to know, and I cut myself. But I couldn't do it right. I tried, but it hurt too much."

Blake nodded and sighed. "Before anyone shows up to assess you, we need to get some things straight. It's fine to tell them you've been depressed, but don't mention Caswell or the hypnosis. I don't want her to know about this. She'll insist on moving you out of my place at the very least or press for longer hospitalization.

"The guy who planted the bugs probably got an earful and he'll know you're vulnerable. I can't keep you safe if Caswell knows. Stevens is going to get me the name of a shrink outside my precinct. Maybe they'll let you go early if they think you're not in immediate danger and have a shrink to go to."

"I'm so sorry," she said and began to sob.

He reached for her, gathering her into his arms. "It'll be okay, it will. Let it go, Alex. Let it go. You need to sleep. I'll be right here."

She nodded and he let her lie back against the bed. He took her hand in his. "Sleep, you're safe." A little while later he felt her relax.

In the dark, listening to her deep, even breathing, he leaned over, kissed her forehead, and whispered into her hair, "I don't care who you are or, God help me, what you've done, I'll see you safe."

CHAPTER TWENTY-SIX

I T HAD TAKEN nearly the full seventy-two hours for a person from the psych team to arrive and evaluate Alex. After talking to Dave Kendall, whom Blake had called and filled in on the situation, they agreed to release her.

Blake took her home in the late afternoon and destroyed the two bugs. He spent the evening working on his laptop while she watched TV, and they pretended that everything was fine. When she announced she was going to bed, he nodded and told her to sleep well. An hour later she reappeared and stood uncertainly in the entrance to the living room.

"Need something?" Blake asked looking up from his laptop.

"I wondered…wondered if you were finished working."

"Pretty much, why?"

"I can't sleep. I got kind of used to you being in the room at the hospital. Would you sit with me till I fall asleep?" Blake looked surprised and she quickly said, "It's okay, I just thought I'd ask."

"Sure, I can do that if you want me to."

Blake got up and followed her back to the bedroom. She crawled into bed and pulled the covers up and turned away from him. There was no chair and it felt awkward as he sat down on the side of the bed.

"Thank you," she said quietly in the dark.

A few minutes later he noticed her surreptitiously wipe at her face. "Alex? You okay?"

"Not really," her voice sounded tear clogged. "Blake, I'm so sorry. I've caused you so much trouble. I wish there was somewhere for me to go so you could have your life back."

Without giving it too much thought, he stretched out next to her on the bed, on top of the covers, and slid his arm under her neck. He pulled her close and held her against him. "Stop," he said. "You don't need to apologize, it's been hard for you, and I'm happy for you to be here. I don't have a very exciting life anyway, so there isn't much for you to mess up," She laughed a little. They lay quietly for a few moments.

"Just sleep Alex, things will look better in the morning, they usually do."

———•◆•———

ALEX SAT on the closed lid of the toilet as Blake removed the bandage. He winced at the sight of the sutured wound that ran across her wrist, but he cleaned it and added a new gauze pad, holding it in place as he reached for the rolled gauze to wrap around her wrist. He tried to ignore the worry. He couldn't take her with him, and he couldn't leave her alone or with access to the gun or the narcotics.

"You're going to Mrs. H's for the day. I talked to her last night while you were in the shower," Blake said quietly. Alex began to protest, and he frowned at her.

"I don't have a choice, Alex. I can't leave you here, and I sure as hell can't leave the gun or the narcotics."

Alex sighed. "Blake, I promised. I won't do this again. I'm okay by myself."

"The guy who's been listening got an earful the other night, and without the gun you have no way to protect yourself, so you can't stay here. I can't take the chance. I'm—No. I started to apologize, but I'm not sorry. I can't leave you alone. Not right now."

Alex watched as he wrapped her hand in addition to her wrist with the gauze. He reminded her that Mrs. H knew her as Jane, not Alex.

"When she asks, and she will, tell her you were cutting up vegetables or something and the knife slipped and cut your palm badly. Or maybe tell her that a glass broke in your hand and cut your palm. I told her I wanted you to stay with her today to make sure you were taken care of."

"Okay. What about tomorrow? Is Mrs. H's my new home away from home?"

He glared at her. "I don't know. Maybe."

He continued to wrap her hand and wrist, and applied tape to hold the gauze in place. "I'm taking the pain meds with me. I want you to take two before I leave. I'll leave some ibuprofen with Mrs. H, I…I don't want to leave the narcotics here."

"That's fine," she said resignedly.

"Whoever the guy is who's been listening, he'll know you're vulnerable. He won't know you're at Mrs. H's if he shows up."

Alex nodded.

He took hold of her uninjured hand. "I thought you were handling all this until I found you the other night. I don't know what to do, Alex."

He frowned and squeezed her hand. "I can't take you with me. I don't want Caswell to know what's happened. She'll insist you go to a psych hospital and she'll for sure insist that you can't live here."

It scared him to think about what she'd do if left alone. Even if he took the gun, she was too vulnerable here. He remembered holding her through the night, and how she'd relaxed into his arms. How she seemed to trust him. The chance that she might try again and succeed was unacceptable, and it wasn't going to happen if he had anything to say about it.

"Blake, I swear to you, *swear to you*, I won't hurt myself again."

Her hand rested in his and he squeezed it. "I'm so sorry for what happened. I…I don't really know why I did it. They say sleep deprivation makes people crazy. I couldn't finish it. I think there's a stronger part of me that doesn't want to die."

He sighed heavily. "I hope to God you're right. Alex, if you need me call. I'll stop whatever I'm doing and come home."

"I will. What about my appointment with Caswell tomorrow?"

"I'll take care of that. I'm calling a halt to the sessions for the time being. I plan to tell her you have the flu. I don't think she's helping. I think maybe her attempts to dig out your memories could have contributed to this. You may not be ready to do that."

And maybe, Blake thought, *maybe, Caswell had been right about not showing Alex the morgue photos.* At any rate, he certainly wasn't going to do that now.

He stood up and reached for the bathroom's doorknob. She reached out, took his hand, and turned him toward her. "Thanks for staying with me at the hospital and last night. The last few days, it's the first real sleep I've had since the assault."

He nodded. Emotionally and physically exhausted, they had slept through the night— Alex in pajamas under the covers and Blake fully dressed on top of them. Desperate for sleep, they had both dropped off quickly. Despite the physical closeness, he'd slept surprisingly well, too.

As the sun came up and the bedroom began to lighten, Blake had turned to her half asleep and wrapped his arms around her. He'd sighed and pushed his erection against her back, letting his hands begin to drift over her, grasping her hips to pull her toward him, sure he heard a sigh from her and felt her push her bottom up against him. God he wanted her, wanted to be inside her, wanted…

He'd jerked awake when his phone alarm sounded and sat up abruptly, hoping, regardless what he thought she'd been doing with her bottom, she hadn't been awake enough to be aware of what he'd been doing while half asleep.

The memory of waking up, fully aroused, intent, as he'd often been when a woman stayed over, on making love one last time before the demands of the day took over embarrassed him. He was grateful, and somewhat resentful, that his phone alarm had gone off before he'd been able to continue with his intentions.

Returning to the moment, he mumbled, "Um, sure." To lighten things up he said, "We could make the sleeping arrangements permanent, all in the interests of a good night's sleep." He grinned at her.

She smiled back at him, and it soothed him to see it. "I'm not sure we'd get much sleep if we made it permanent," she said.

The comment sent a jolt of arousal through him. "Probably not," he said turning quickly and leaving the bathroom to conceal what the thought of making love to her had brought on. *So, it's making love now instead of fucking her? Jesus*, he thought. *I'm in way over my head.*

"Right, well, I'm ready to hit the road. I'll walk you over to Mrs. H's," he said briskly trying to hide his discomfort as he walked down the hall to the living room and began gathering up his things. "Call me if you need anything," he said as she entered the living room and walked toward the door.

"I will," she replied as he escorted her across the hall to Mrs. H's.

CHAPTER TWENTY-SEVEN

"**S**HE'S SICK AS a dog. I had to take her to urgent care night before last. She was burning up with fever," Blake told Caswell over the phone.

"The flu," Caswell said with an edge to her voice.

"Yeah, the doc said it was most likely from all the stress she's been under and that she probably hadn't had a flu shot. My neighbor is checking in on her over lunch." That was a lie, but he didn't want her to know Alex was essentially on a suicide watch at Mrs. H's.

"I see." There were several moments of silence before she said, "Did you show her the photos? Is that what this 'flu' is all about?"

"No, I didn't. Thanks for the vote of confidence."

"Don't get pissy with me, Detective. I know you wanted very much to push this along by showing her. Now, she's too sick to come in for our appointment. It's odd, to say the least."

Blake decided to call her bluff and hoped she wouldn't take him up on the offer. "If you don't mind getting exposed to a pretty nasty case of the flu, then come over after work and check it out. Seeing as you don't trust me."

"I don't trust you, Detective. Perhaps Alex and I could conduct our sessions at your apartment."

That made his heart rate triple. "Not for the next few days, you won't. She's miserable. Chills, fever, coughing, and she aches all over. She doesn't want to talk to anybody. The doc said to let her rest."

Blake was winging it here, spewing symptoms that he vaguely remembered from a bout of flu he'd had several years previously.

"All she said to me when I got her back to the apartment last night was she wanted to go to bed and die." He closed his eyes as he said that, willing away the thought of Alex cutting her wrist.

There was momentary silence again before Caswell said, "You'll keep me informed of her condition?"

"Of course," he said as the phone went dead.

———◆———

THE NARCOTIC pills had begun to dull, but not erase, the throb in her wrist that pulsed with each beat of her heart. A pulse of pain that reminded her of the nasty, but totally ineffective, slice she'd made over her left wrist.

The memory of that sharp, searing pain as she'd forced the razor into the skin of her wrist made her shudder as she sat at Mrs. H's kitchen table, where her self-appointed nurse had offered her breakfast.

Once she had eaten, Mrs. H bustled around, chatting as she settled Alex on the couch with a pillow to rest her hand on, an ice bag, and a glass of orange juice on the coffee table in easy reach. And, of course, she inquired about Alex's hand.

"What in the world happened?"

"It was a stupid accident. Mom always said never use a knife unless it was pointed away from you. Turns out doing that can make just as big a mess. I really sliced my palm."

"You've had quite the time lately. The car accident and now this. My husband always said a bad accident can shake you up pretty good, make it more likely for other accidents to happen. Do you need a dressing change or anything?"

The woman was relentless. Blake was going to hear about this when he got home. She wanted to rest, to be left alone to think.

"No, the doctor said not to mess with the bandage for a few days, and I took some ibuprofen so I'm fine. But thank you."

"You're not taking pain medication? Didn't the doctor prescribed any?"

Crap, she thought. "Yes, he did," she said, playing for time. "But I…I can't take narcotics they really mess me up."

"Well, I hope the ibuprofen helps."

"It usually does. I'm really tired since I didn't get a lot of sleep last night. I'm going to close my eyes and rest."

"That's a good idea. I'll be quiet as a mouse. My show comes on at one, but you have plenty of time to sleep. When one o'clock rolls around, you can watch it with me."

Alex smiled convincingly, she hoped, and closed her eyes.

———•◆•———

LIKE THE detective from the GPD, Blake didn't think the woman whose body had been dumped outside Golden had lived there either. The town was tiny, and while it catered to students at the School of Mines, tourists, and people who liked the new restaurants and wine bars, there wasn't an active or obvious solicitation area in or near the town.

Going through the file that the detective had sent him, it was clear no one knew her. They couldn't place her as an employee or a student at Mines. The guy had even checked at the Coors Brewery complex and was assured that she didn't work there either. Although she looked as far from a teacher as possible, he'd also asked at the local public schools to see if anyone knew her but had drawn a blank.

The assumption the detective had made was that she was a transient who'd solicited the wrong guy. Maybe even picked him up in Central City or Blackhawk, the gambling towns up the canyon from Golden. He'd made enquiries at the casinos in both towns, to no avail.

Blake certainly couldn't fault the guy—he'd done all that could be done. The story had run on the local news stations but had produced no calls from anyone who recognized her. Maybe she'd been passing through Colorado on her way somewhere else. It was anyone's guess.

The Aurora cops had better luck. Showing the photos of the two dead women around, they'd managed to ID both of them within a week of finding the bodies. The few friends and family members who existed had been contacted and alibis checked, and none were suspects.

Reading through the interview with one of the prostitutes who'd recognized one of the women, Blake noticed she'd mentioned a dark car whose occupant she'd seen the woman talking to. She'd ID'd the car as a black Ford SUV. When pressed she thought it might be an Explorer but wasn't sure. She mentioned the windows had been darkly tinted, which prevented her from getting a good look at the guy. All she would say was he was a 'big guy.' None of which was much help.

Blake sat back in his desk chair and rubbed a hand over his mouth several times. That sounded like the description Sally had given him for the car and the guy she'd seen Alex talking to and leaving with.

He shook his head. Why any woman who didn't have to earn her living soliciting would do that baffled him. Alex had to know it was risky and dangerous, yet she'd gone with him. What had he said to her? What had she talked to him about? Had she known him?

His best guess was Alex had asked about her sister, and the mystery guy had indicated he knew her and knew where she was. Thinking about the self-defense tactics she'd used on him, and her attacker at the hotel, Alex most likely thought she could handle the guy if he made any moves. And that had been a mistake.

If the guy Sally had seen was the same guy, he was the one who'd killed the other women and probably the one who'd tried to kill Alex. Blake huffed out an exasperated breath. And so what? He had no idea who the guy was, and he was no further along in identifying Alex or the woman in the morgue. And the woman in Golden might never be identified unless they caught the killer and he had kept fingertip trophies or a purse with an ID.

He heard his cell ring from inside his pocket and fished it out. "Halloran."

"Hey, it's um, Sally, you know? We talked a few days ago? About Alex?"

"I remember. What's up?"

"I, um, asked around about Alex. She didn't recognize Alex, but I think one of the girls I talked to maybe saw the guy you were asking about."

Blake sat up, scrambling for a piece of paper and a pen. "Great, Sally. Will she talk to me?"

"Uh, maybe. Long as you don't try to haul her in."

"Not my job. She gets a free ride if she'll talk to me. I'll pay her for her time, and I'll pay you as well."

"Okay, well, she should be around tonight. I'll talk to her and get back to you."

"When did she last see him?"

"She says she saw him night before last."

"Did she tell you anything about him?"

"Said he looked like he'd been in a fight."

"Why?"

"Didn't say, just said he looked like that."

"Okay, thanks. Call me when you get something set up." He paused then asked, "Did she say whether anyone left with him?"

The line was quiet for a moment. "She said one of the girls left with him. She doesn't know the girl real well, but she hasn't seen her since."

"Shit, okay, set something up as soon as possible and get back to me. Tell her I'm going to want a description of the girl who left with him, a picture would be better, and as much information on the guy as possible."

He closed his eyes and rested his forehead in his hands. If she set something up for tonight, what the hell was he going to do with Alex?

CHAPTER TWENTY-EIGHT

ALEX WOKE TO the smell of soup. She opened her eyes and saw Mrs. H setting a tray with two bowls and small plates with a sandwich on each on the coffee table.

"Oh good, you're awake. I made some soup yesterday, it's vegetable beef. I think soup's always good when you're recovering from an injury."

"Thank you," Alex said, pushing up into a sitting position on the couch. "It smells wonderful."

"I thought I'd eat in here with you, keep you company. Here's some iced tea. I wasn't sure if you took sugar with it."

"No, this is fine."

They ate companionably for several minutes until the older woman said, "I worked as a nurse in the ER for years. Did you know that?"

"No," Alex said cautiously, unsure what had brought the topic up.

Mrs. H smiled and fluttered her hand in front of her face dismissively. "Well of course you didn't, silly me. Blake probably doesn't either. He's gone a lot, so we don't have a chance to talk much."

"That must have been interesting."

"Oh, it was. You know, most nurses who work in critical care areas will tell you it's either boring as hell or it's chaos and terror. There never seems to be any middle point."

Still not sure why the topic had arisen, Alex asked, "Did you enjoy it?"

"Yes, I did. I learned so much." She paused and took another bite of her sandwich and a sip of tea. "One of the things I learned was that there's always a better solution to life's problems than suicide."

The word hung in the air, and the bite of sandwich Alex had taken seemed stuck in her throat. She coughed to dislodge it and took a drink of tea to wash it down.

Mrs. H turned, smiling at her. "I also got very good at reading injuries. Your injuries when I first met you didn't look like they were from a car accident. It looked like someone had beaten you and—despite your attempt to cover it up—if I had to guess, tried to choke you. Now you have a bandaged wrist, and Blake wouldn't leave the narcotic pain pills here for you to take or leave you alone."

"I told you—"

"Yes, I know, you said that you couldn't take narcotics," she said, interrupting Alex. She smiled wryly. "Neither you nor Blake is stupid. If you're his sister, he'd know about that. If not, surely you would have mentioned it to the nurses or the doctor. Will you tell me what really happened last night?"

Alex didn't respond except to put her plate on the coffee table, her appetite having faded quickly.

"Is your name really Jane?"

"No, it's Alex."

"Short for?"

"I don't know. Not for sure anyway."

"You don't know?"

Alex got up from the couch and walked over to the window. "Mrs. H, please. Please let this go. I can't really answer your questions, because I don't know. And the not knowing is responsible for this," she said, holding up her bandaged hand.

"Tell me what you do know, then. I may not be able to do much, but I can listen."

Alex blinked her eyes rapidly to try to prevent the tears that threatened to fall. "You're very kind. I didn't realize that before."

Mrs. H laughed. "I imagine Blake told you what a busybody I am. I am, I guess. I'm retired, my husband died seven years ago, and I haven't a lot to do. I volunteer several places, but I miss the camaraderie that you have with coworkers in a hospital, so I chat with people."

She stood up and brought Alex's tea over to the dining room table and indicated a chair. Alex sat at the table and took a sip.

"I like Blake. He's a nice man, for all the bluff and gruff he shows people. Cops have a hard life and I know I irritate him. I wish I didn't. But aside from all that, you can talk to me and, regardless what Blake may say, it will remain a confidence between us."

Alex aimlessly moved her glass in a circle for a few minutes. "It's true, what I said. I don't remember what happened to me or even who I am. Bits, tiny irrelevant bits, come back to me here and there. But not my full name, not what happened, not who I am. I guess it finally overwhelmed me. I'm not really sure."

"The amnesia is from the head injury?"

"Possibly. Or it may be that what happened, or who I am, is so traumatic I don't want to remember. I could be anyone. I could have done all sorts of horrible things. Maybe my attack was payback for something I did."

Mrs. H drank her tea and let her eyes drift around the room. "I don't really know you," she said at last. "But Blake has had ample opportunity to get to know you. I think he'd sense if that were the case. He's very perceptive."

She chuckled. "Except for the women he dates, his perspective goes out the window then. But I don't think he'd have you in his apartment or be as protective of you as he is if you were somehow…wrong."

"Maybe, but he needs me to remember so he can find and arrest the guy who attacked me. Whether I'm a criminal or not, he needs me to cooperate."

Alex stood up and paced the tiny dining area. "There's another agenda in there somewhere, something he's holding back. I know it. I see the way he looks at me when he doesn't think I'm paying attention. Like he knows something, something that makes him pity me. It's frightening."

"Have you asked him?"

"No, I'm afraid to."

"Alex, it's been my experience that nothing is as bad as not knowing. There's a lot you don't know, that you won't know until your memory returns, but you can find out whether Blake is holding something back. Ask him. It'll be one less thing for you to worry about."

BLAKE ARRIVED to pick Alex up at about seven and something had obviously changed between her and Mrs. H. Instead of being glad to leave, Alex had hugged the older woman and thanked her for allowing her to stay. It was quite a turnaround from not wanting to go to almost not wanting to leave. At least if he had to go out later perhaps neither of them would mind another visit.

He was preoccupied with worry about the woman who'd been seen leaving with the suspect, the woman who had yet to reappear. He worried that instead of returning unharmed they'd find her mutilated body somewhere. Sally hadn't gotten back in touch and Blake knew the longer it took to get information on the missing woman, the higher the chance she was already dead.

"What?" he said, realizing that Alex had been talking to him and had asked him a question.

She cocked her head at him. "What's wrong?"

"Nothing, it was a long frustrating day," he said, walking into the kitchen and retrieving a beer from the fridge.

Alex followed him into the kitchen and sat at the table. "Can you talk about it?" she asked quietly.

He guzzled the beer for a moment then shook his head. He turned and opened the fridge again, searching for something to eat. Then shut it.

"How about we go get some Mexican food? We've been living on pizza and spaghetti for too long. You could probably use some time out of jail. Maybe it'd help." he said as he quickly finished the beer and fished his keys out of his slacks' pocket.

Alex nodded. They left the apartment and drove off quickly in Blake's car.

The tiny restaurant was a hole in the wall—or a hole in a strip mall. Bedraggled *piñatas* hung from the ceiling here and there and dusty neon signs for *Dos Equiis* and *Corona* beer and *Patron* and *Herradura* tequila were mounted on the walls. Of the two that were actually on, one was flickering. The restaurant was packed with people, though, and smelled wonderful.

Blake guided her to a booth at the back of the restaurant that allowed him to see the whole room easily. He didn't want any surprises. He ordered a beer for each of them, and when the beers arrived, they put in their food order.

Blake shifted his beer bottle around in a circle after a few sips. "So how was your day?" he asked, not sure he wanted to know but not knowing what else to say.

"Good."

He watched her and frowned. "Seems like you and Mrs. H got pretty chummy. That surprised me."

"She's actually a very nice woman. You should cut her some slack."

"Hmmm."

"She was an ER nurse."

"Didn't know that, never asked."

"Have you bothered to get to know anyone who lives in the building?"

He'd had a bad day and was worried about a potential dead prostitute and what the hell he was going to do with Alex in the short term and long term. The criticism pissed him off.

"Not unless they're fuckable and, generally, I pass even on those. Too close for comfort when things go down the tube."

He saw her face flame with color. "I see. Sorry I asked."

"My policy is don't ask unless you want to hear the answer."

"I'll try to remember that. How about you try to remember not to be a jerk?"

CHAPTER TWENTY-NINE

THE DINNER THAT followed was quiet, and Alex figured it wasn't a good idea to ask him what he was withholding from her. Blake had another beer and the frown had returned and stayed. He was distracted, glowering at his food, not looking at her, and saying little. She ate and didn't try to carry on a conversation.

When they returned he hustled her into the building and into the apartment without comment, then went to the fridge to get another beer. The night was not shaping up well, and he seemed intent on getting drunk.

"Will you tell me what's wrong?" she asked, following him to the kitchen.

"No. Now leave me the fuck alone," he replied irritably, opening the beer and taking a long drink.

"Why are you being so hateful?"

He set the beer on the counter and stepped close. She took a step back, bumping up against the edge of the sink. He put his hands on the sink, trapping her between them, and leaned in until his face was nearly touching hers.

"Because the last few nights and today have been shitty, and tonight may be shitty as well if I get the call I'm expecting."

She could feel his breath on her face. It smelled cool and hoppy with the beers he'd drunk. "If I get it, I've got to figure out what to do with you so I don't come home to a corpse. That tends to add to a man's crappy mood. If that happens, things are going to be shitty for quite a while. So, unless you want to fuck my brains out and let me blow off some steam, leave me alone."

Alex slapped her hands against his chest and shoved him away from her. "You really are an asshole. I'm sorry if you've had a crappy day, but don't take it out on me, understand?" Her heart was pounding from the intensity of the confrontation. She pushed away from the sink, shoved past him, and headed for the bedroom.

She had no idea what the call he was expecting was about, but clearly it worried him. And there was no way she could make up for what she'd done or convince him she didn't intend to make further attempts on her life. She couldn't explain that it didn't feel as if cutting herself had been her idea in the first place. She knew he was afraid she'd make another attempt, a successful one, and she had no way to reassure him, but that didn't excuse his behavior. Talking to him, asking for answers, was going to have to wait.

⸎

WHAT THE *fuck's the matter with me?* he thought as he lay on the couch in a beer haze, the noise of the game on TV registering vaguely in his consciousness. He was so…what? Insane? Chasing his tail? Caught between wanting to fuck her and wanting to keep his distance or wishing at times he'd never taken responsibility for her had only added to his frustration and anger. Yeah, insane for sure.

He was worried about her, about the outcome of all of this. And it had taken her suicide attempt to get him to realize how afraid he was that her attacker would find her and succeed in killing her or, now, that she would do something rash and succeed in ending her life.

One thing for sure, he was calling a permanent halt to the hypnosis sessions. Caswell concerned him. She seemed determined to thwart his attempts to push things along with Alex. He wasn't sure it was a good idea to push things, but he hadn't thought she'd be so against it. After all, wasn't she trying to do the same thing?

He'd researched hypnosis online. He was never sure how accurate the information you got there was, but it offered some help. According to one article, you couldn't be made to do something you didn't want to do. But other articles suggested that you could be indirectly pushed toward doing something under the right circumstances, with the right suggestions.

Maybe that's why Alex had said she didn't know why she'd done it. Maybe with the precarious situation she was in and all that had happened to her so far, maybe Caswell pushing her to remember what had happened made her decide to end it rather than face reality.

"God!" he exclaimed under his breath. If he could only get a last name or some hit on Alex's fingerprints. Who she was and what had happened couldn't possibly be so bad it was worth her life. And he realized he had gone so far over the line when it came to her, he honestly didn't care who she was. If it was that bad, he'd figure out a way to extricate her from whatever she'd gotten into and take her away. Somewhere.

Maybe Clark was right. Maybe he was trying to atone for not being able to save Lindsey. He knew it wasn't his fault, at least he did in his head, but that had never assuaged the guilt for the situation that had resulted in her death.

"You're the dumbest fuck in all creation," he said to the empty room and the TV.

THE CALL from Sally didn't come till midday the following day. At least he hadn't had to go out unexpectedly last night and leave Alex alone or at Mrs. H's, but she would be with Mrs. H while he was working. She seemed happy to have Alex, and Alex hadn't objected.

He had a sneaking suspicion that Mrs. H knew that it had been a suicide attempt, not an accident. He wasn't sure how he felt about that. Maybe being a nurse, she would help Alex. He didn't know how. Last night's confrontation had left him and Alex uncomfortable and uncommunicative.

"Kelly says she'll meet you at that diner on Colfax and Speer and you can buy her lunch. She didn't want to meet at night, didn't want anyone knowing she was meeting with a cop. Didn't want to risk losing business."

"What time?"

"One—she doesn't get up that early. She asked me to come so I could introduce you. Guess she feels safer if I'm there. I told her you'd promised not to arrest her."

"Good. I'll see you there."

Blake checked his wallet and decided he'd have to hit an ATM on his way. He hoped he had enough to cover the expense. If not, he'd pay Kelly and arrange to pay Sally when his paycheck arrived. Stevens walked into the squad room and sat at his desk.

"You look like the cat that swallowed the canary. What's up?" he asked.

"I may have a lead on the suspect who's killing the prostitutes. I'm meeting the person at one."

"Who is it?"

"A friend of a connection that Kaye Jagerski gave me, but it's possible another body may turn up."

Stevens' eyebrows shot up. "Yeah? Why?"

"This person told my source that she'd seen another girl leave in a car with a guy who might be the guy we're looking for. She hasn't seen her since."

Blake stood up and prepared to leave. "I'm hoping to get a description, maybe a photo of the woman so we can start looking for her. I'll let you know. It's the best potential lead we've got, so keep your fingers crossed."

Stevens sketched a salute as Blake moved past him. "Keep me posted. How's your girl?"

"She's not my fucking girl, and it's…complicated," Blake replied irritably.

Stevens shook his head and opened his laptop. "No doubt it is," he muttered as Blake left.

———— ✦ ————

"WELL, HE looked big from what I could see," Kelly said. "That's about all I can tell you. The tinted windows made it hard to see him."

"Tell me about the car—can you describe it?"

"A black SUV. I don't know the make, and I never thought to look at the license plate. I never really paid the car or the guy much attention, or thought about it, till Sally talked to me."

"Tell me what the girl who left with him looks like. What's her name?"

"Carla Russo. She's tiny. Italian, I think. Shoulder-length, dark hair and brown eyes. About five foot, and maybe a hundred and ten pounds dripping wet."

"You don't happen to have a photo of her, do you?"

The woman frowned and pulled out her phone. "Maybe, give me a sec to look."

Blake took a sip of his water and looked askance at the congealed mess on his plate. He'd made the mistake of ordering enchiladas and couldn't for the life of him figure out why since he and Alex had eaten Mexican food last night. They seemed like the most innocuous item on the menu, but they were inedible.

"Here," she said suddenly, thrusting her phone at him. "She's the one on the left."

The face that looked back at him was heart-shaped and lively. Dark brown eyes looked out from a smiling face surrounded by a halo of black curls. Jesus, he hoped she was still alive.

"Send me that photo," he said, rattling off his phone number. "If you see her, call me immediately so I know she's safe."

"Why wouldn't she be?"

Blake eyed Sally. "I didn't get a chance to tell her. I figured you would," Sally explained.

"The guy she left with may be someone who's killing women. If you see him, *do not* go with him. Call me right away. I need a license plate if you can get one and a more detailed description of the guy, but don't put yourself at risk to get either. Pass the warning around so others know not to go with him."

She nodded, her face pale.

"I've got to get back to the precinct. You've got my cell. Call me if you see anything. And if Carla shows up, call me. I'll want to talk to her."

He paid them for their time, despite the strain on his bank account, and left. When he got back, he sent the photo out for all units to be on the lookout for her and alerted the morgue to call him if a body that looked like her showed up. He said a silent prayer that wouldn't happen.

"What'd you find out?" Stevens asked as he returned to the department and took a seat at his desk.

Blake sighed in frustration. "Black SUV, no license plate number, no ID of the driver except 'he was big,' which seems to be the general consensus from everyone who's seen the guy. I did get a photo of the girl who went with him and sent out a BOLO for her. I hope to God we find her alive."

"If she's alive that'd mean that whoever she went with isn't our guy."

"At least there wouldn't be another dead body."

"True. What's eatin' at you, Halloran?"

"This whole fucking thing's eating at me!" Blake exclaimed, massaging his temples.

"I'm hog-tied by Caswell. She doesn't want me to ask Alex to look at the morgue photos of the unidentified woman for fear it'll cause further problems for her. I can't ID the guy who attacked her without her memory coming back, and it's not—except in tiny bits and pieces. None of which are significant."

Blake sighed loudly. "And then the whole thing that happened the other night. I feel responsible, like I missed something that could have ended in her suicide. I've felt responsible for her since I nearly hit her and that's not like me.

"End result is all I've got on this guy is he's big and he drives a black SUV. For fuck's sake, that could be anybody, and it might not even be the guy responsible for the murders."

"So how much trouble would it cause to show Alex the photos?"

"I don't know. I don't want to make matters worse for her, and I don't know that showing them to her would help at all."

Blake tipped back in his chair. "When I asked her if she knew anyone named Susan or Suzanne, which is the name of the woman my contact said Alex was supposedly asking people about, she denied knowing anything. The name meant nothing to her and didn't result in any recall."

"Well maybe showing her the photos wouldn't solve anything, but it might not cause problems for her, either."

"Maybe." Blake scratched his chin and neck. "I worry that right now might not be the best time to spring something like that on her."

"Because of the suicide attempt?

"No shit. Jesus, there seems to be no solving any of this."

"Well, I got a little more info on Ashley."

"Yeah, what?"

"Mom contacted me and finally admitted that they'd been having problems with her for some time. She said her husband had wanted to shield the family from public opinion and hadn't been totally honest with us."

"What kind of problems?"

"Oh, the usual teenage bullshit. You know, constant rebellion, impossible to get along with, acting out. But then it sort of took a serious turn. She got involved with a guy who apparently got her into drugs, and she took off with him once she graduated. They didn't know where she'd gone, but the mom gave me his name."

"Do you think he's the one who killed her?"

"I don't know. I'm looking for him, and I'm going to pull him in and grill him to see what went on. I guess he's a possibility."

"Why wouldn't they tell us that initially?"

"You don't have kids, so I don't expect you to get it. She's dead. It doesn't matter to them who killed her so much as their need to make her into what they'd hoped she'd be—the good kid, their little girl."

Stevens leaned back in his chair. "Finding the guy who did it won't bring her back. But they have to live in that community, and they'd prefer her reputation not be tarnished."

"You'd think they'd want him caught and punished."

"I'm sure they do, but they have to live with the memories. You've probably never been caught between doing what everyone thinks is right and caring about someone so much you want to protect them even if that means lying."

That pushed a button. "Thanks a lot."

Stevens held his hands up. "Not a criticism, Halloran. Merely an observation."

The problem was, he'd never felt that way about anyone since Lindsey. He'd never had to, but he'd have lied, done anything for Lindsey. That part of him had been firmly shut down until Alex had shown up in his life. She'd blown his sense of right and wrong all to hell and forced him out of hiding.

CHAPTER THIRTY

"NO, MAN, I never hurt her. She was messed up. I finally had enough and took off. She was fine when I left her."

Stevens had tracked down Carl Jones and had him in an interview room. He'd taken up residence with another young woman and was living in a ratty apartment in Aurora and working nights at a local convenience store.

"Left her on the street to make her way alone. That doesn't seem fine to me."

"Well, what was I supposed to do with her? I offered to take her back home but she refused to go. She was messed up. Her mood swings were nuts. She hated her parents and I don't know why. Maybe they got tired of dealing with her, I know I did. She wouldn't talk about them other than to say she was glad to get away."

"When was the last time you saw her?"

He gave them a date two weeks before her death, which couldn't be verified, but his whereabouts when the M.E. had determined she was killed was solidly alibied. He had been on a bender with three friends, and all three vouched for him.

The bartender where they'd been partying remembered all of them because he'd had to throw them out after they started a fight.

After he left her, Jones said he had no idea what she'd been doing or where she'd been living. They let him go.

"Jesus, I'm glad I've got boys, and I hope we taught them better than that," Clark said. "What is it with girls and dirtballs?"

"You got me. I have no clue."

Blake's phone rang. "Halloran." He listened and a frown settled on his face. "Okay, thanks for letting me know."

"Not good news, I take it?"

"They found her dead, no fingertips, no witness." He slumped into his desk chair, closed his eyes, and shook his head.

"The M.E.'s got some hair that doesn't belong to her. But Christ, the hair could be from anyone of her johns. It'll help convict the guy if we find him and it's his. Big 'if' so far, and it isn't going to ID him."

"Where'd he dump her?"

"The canyon heading to Blackhawk. He seems to like that area around Golden and Highway 93. A bike rider stopped to fix a flat and he happened to see the body at the bottom of the ravine and called 911. It was pure luck. She wasn't easily visible. Her body could have lain there for years."

"You're gonna have to show Alex the morgue photos. We have to know what she remembers. I'm beginning to think maybe you're right and the guy who attacked her is our perp."

"Finally convinced you, eh?"

"I'm not totally convinced. I want to know what happened to her and rule her out if it was a different guy. If it's not our guy, we still need to find both of them."

Blake was sure they were one and the same. He just couldn't confirm it.

———◆———

BLAKE SURPRISED Alex when he picked her up at Mrs. H's. After escorting her into the apartment he dropped onto the couch and stared at his hands. "Look, I'm sorry about last night. It's no excuse, but I'd had a miserable day and I drank too much and… acted like an asshole."

Alex stared at him for a few moments before replying, "You scared me, you were so angry."

He scrubbed his face with his hands before dropping them back into his lap. "Before you were staying here, when I was in a foul mood I could come home and have a few beers, flake out on the couch, and wind down. I didn't have to talk to anyone. I didn't stay in relationships long enough for anyone to get close. Nobody felt sorry for me, there wasn't anybody who wanted to help, and nobody asked questions. I don't know how to deal with that, I guess."

He sighed and glanced at her. "This isn't your fault, and I don't want you anywhere else, but I'm not used to a roommate."

"Do you want to talk about it, or not? If not, I'll go to the bedroom and read."

"Read? Read what?" he asked, not addressing her question.

"Mrs. H gave me some books," Alex laughed. "They're romances. The one I started is surprisingly good. I asked her why she read them, and she said it was the only sex she was likely to get at her age."

"Umm, I guess that's good." He blushed hard, then looked at her quizzically. "Is it?"

"Not sure. She's an attractive woman in her sixties. I don't know why romance novels would be her only outlet for sex, but who knows?"

Alex walked over and sat in the chair next to the couch. They sat quietly for a few minutes until she said, "I don't know why, but I feel like there's something you're not telling me—something that pertains to me. If you can't tell me then I'll manage, but if you can I wish you would. My imagination fills in the blanks with all sorts of things. Frightening things."

He nodded but said nothing.

"I'm not going back to Dr. Caswell," she said softly.

"That's okay with me, but I thought you liked her."

"I do, but the last few times I've felt so…I don't know. Hopeless, I guess, like there's no solution to this, and that when I remember it'll make things worse, much worse for me. I feel like I'm forgetting something important, and I can't figure out what it is. Every time I'm in her office that sense that I've forgotten something important just overwhelms me, and the depression was getting worse with each session. I'd rather try to remember on my own."

She got up and paced in front of him. "Plus, she really doesn't like you. She's always pumping me for information about you. I don't like it. I don't want her causing problems for you or insisting that I move."

He was surprised. Caswell's interest was something he'd been unaware of. "She's got plenty of reasons not to like me. We got into it over you, and I got in her face. Now she thinks I'm working against her." He didn't plan to tell Alex that the reason he didn't particularly like Caswell were the sessions he'd been forced to undergo to get cleared to return to duty after Lindsey's death.

Alex smiled at him. "You're looking out for me, she should be grateful for that."

"Yeah," he said, pointing at her bandaged wrist. "Doing a bang-up job of that. It's a good thing she doesn't know about it or she'd go to my lieutenant and force me to move you."

Alex blushed and stared at her wrist. "I'm sorry to put you though that. Connie, Mrs. H, has been helpful. She told me to call her or come over if I felt like hurting myself again."

She paced a few more times then turned to him. "I don't want to go back to Caswell. I don't want to be hypnotized again."

"Why, what has she been doing?"

"I'm not sure."

"You don't remember her suggestions or what you talk about?"

"For the most part, no. I often fall deeply asleep when I'm with her and I stop hearing her voice. I know this sounds crazy, but I'm wondering if whatever she talks about or suggests is at the heart of this," she said, holding out her wrist.

"From what I've read, a hypnotist can't make you do something you don't want to do—can't make you hurt yourself."

"But what if all it took to magnify the fears I have about who I am and push me in that direction was continual suggestions that it was a hopeless situation, that I'd be better off not knowing? Or dead?"

"And you think that's what she's doing?" he asked incredulously.

Alex shrugged. "I don't *know* what she's doing, that's the point. She may be doing nothing other than trying to help me remember, but maybe that's what triggered my suicide attempt. I…I don't want to go back."

"If you feel that way, even if she's not doing anything weird, I don't see the point of going. But you're going to have to call her and tell her. She'll never believe me. She already thinks I've manufactured this flu because I…"

Fuck. Opened my big mouth. Fuck, fuck, fuck.

"Because you what?"

Blake squirmed. "Because I don't want her to know about your suicide attempt."

Alex frowned then sighed. "But she doesn't know about that. Why would she think you'd done anything that made me want to stop seeing her?"

God, I must be off my game, he thought. *Can't even lie well anymore.*

"Okay, obviously you can't or won't talk about whatever it is you're withholding. Get me her phone number and I'll call her in the morning."

"Alex, I can't tell you. Not yet. Please trust me. When I can, I will."

He saw the worry on her face and relented. "I can tell you a little. I was upset last night because there's a guy who's killing prostitutes, and a woman was seen getting into the car of a possible suspect a couple nights ago."

He ran his hand distractedly through his hair. "I had patrols looking for her. I hoped she was okay. But she turned up dead this morning, and now the only person who might be able to identify him is dead."

Except you, he thought. *And I'm not going there tonight.*

She sat down next to him on the couch and touched his hand. "Oh Blake, I'm so sorry. I shouldn't have—"

"It's not your fault, Alex. I had no right to treat you like I did. It's…so frustrating. I don't know that we'll ever find the guy."

"You'll find him, I know you will. Thank you for telling me. I didn't know what was going on last night…I thought you were angry with me." She squeezed his hand.

"No," he said. "Never you."

She smiled, let go of his hand, and stood up. "Are you hungry? I'll see what…"

He reached out and grasped her hand. "Alex, I don't care about dinner. Stay with me a while."

She sat down beside him. "Okay."

"I'd appreciate it if you'd sit here for a while."

"Of course. Blake? You've seemed so upset the last few days. Aside from what I did, what's going on?"

"Just…the usual chaos at work. I'm tired. I need to turn my brain off for a while."

She offered a tiny smile. They sat quietly for several moments. He played with her hand which he'd refused to release. Suddenly, he leaned into her and brushed his lips against hers and said, "I've wanted you for a long time. Wanted this."

She slid her hand into his hair and touched her lips to his, teasing them with her tongue, and he felt all the tiredness and frustration dissipate. "I wondered if you did."

"The morning after I brought you here from the hospital," he said picking up her wrist, "it was a good thing my phone alarm went off. And last night? I was angry about a lot of things, but I wanted you so badly I could barely control myself."

His teeth nipped at her lips, his tongue slipped into her mouth, his desire spiked, and he pulled back. "I want you, Alex."

She smiled. "But not just to relieve your frustration?"

The use of his own words made him grin. "Christ, no." He pulled her in and claimed her mouth, tasting, teasing, making love to it. Then pulled back.

"Is that what you want?" he asked hoping to God she said yes.

"Yes," she said.

He smiled, slipped his hand around the back of her neck and pulled her in for another kiss reveling in the softness of her mouth, the taste of her.

"Touch me. I want you to touch me," she sighed.

His hand dropped to her breast and then reached to pull the camisole up. He slipped his hand underneath it and cupped her breast, thumbing her nipple that was as hard and erect as he was.

She let her head fall back and held his head against her breast when he found it with his mouth. He could hear her ragged breathing, feel her heart pounding.

He pulled away at last and stood up, bringing her with him. "Not here. I'm not going to make love to you on the couch."

He walked with her toward the bedroom, shedding his shirt and shoes along the way, easing her out of her top. He stopped in the hallway, working frantically to undo her jeans and push them down onto the floor. As she stepped out of them, he slid his hand into her panties, cupping her, sliding between her legs and slipping his fingers into her. She moaned softly.

He stroked her and used his mouth to make love to her breast. "God, I want to be inside you," he gasped.

She moved against his fingers as she undid his jeans and freed him, pushing his jeans and briefs off his ass and downward, where he kicked them off. She stroked him, feeling the small bead of moisture on the tip of his penis, running her thumb across it and teasing him with her thumb. He let go of her breast, closed his eyes and moaned as she continued to stroke him, as he pushed into her hand bracing himself on the wall behind her.

"I want you, now. Here if we have to, but now," she said.

She released him as he knelt to pull her panties off, nuzzling his face against the soft curls of her pubic hair, then stood and kissed her quickly. "No, not here. Maybe another time, 'cause there will be other times."

She smiled as he grasped her hand, pulling her into the bedroom, and dropping onto the bed with her. She stroked him and nipped his ear, whispering what she wanted him to do to her.

"Oh Christ, wait—wait a second." He rolled over and blindly rooted in the bedside table drawer until he pulled out a condom packet and tore at it frantically. He wanted inside her so badly he wasn't sure he could wait long enough to get it on. He heard her giggle.

"Let me help," she said.

"God, no. If you touch me like that again, I'll forget the condom."

He got it on and nudged her knees apart, lying between them. He teased her breast with his tongue, sliding his fingers inside her, pulling them back and sliding in again, stroking her with his thumb.

"I want you inside me. Please." He moved up against her, watching her as she lifted her hips in invitation. "Now."

He thrust into her as deep as he could go and she shuddered, wrapping her legs around him, pulling him hard against her, and vising around him as her orgasm pulsed, milking him. He heard her moan as he thrust faster and harder until he came and collapsed onto her, his breath ragged, his heart racing.

A few minutes later he whispered, "We are so fucked," his breath hot against her ear.

"Wasn't that the idea?"

"Oh, that was definitely the idea, and it was the best idea I've ever had." He withdrew and turned onto his back, sliding the condom off and dropping it into the small wastebasket by the bed.

He turned back to her and smoothed a strand of hair off her face. "I meant, if anyone finds out about this we're screwed. Or I am for sure."

"Then no one will know. I certainly won't tell anyone." She stroked his back letting her hand drift down to the cleft between his buttocks and back up making him shiver. "Blake?"

"Hmmm?" he asked, burrowing into her neck.

"Let's have one worry-free night."

"I like that idea." He wrapped her in his arms and pulled her tight against him.

"It won't be so rushed next time. I intend to take my time with you the rest of the night," he said kissing the top of her head as she nestled against his shoulder.

She ran her hand across his chest, her fingers drifting in the dark hair that grew there.

"Why don't you let me take my time with you," she replied, planting a soft kiss on his cheek as she let her hand drift downward through the hair on his belly until she found him ready and waiting for her.

CHAPTER THIRTY-ONE

BLAKE ARRIVED AT work and sat at his desk, staring at, but not seeing, the papers and folders that littered it. He found it hard to concentrate. His mind kept drifting back to Alex flushed and sated in his arms or the feel of her beneath him. He vividly relived the kissing and exploring, the tastes and sensations that he'd discovered making love to her.

He shook his head. All he needed was to be called away from his desk with a major hard-on. He had to find something else to think about, but it was hard. He laughed to himself. Yeah it was hard, and so was he at the moment.

Stevens arrived, looking at Blake with a quizzical expression, which got rid of the erection. He nodded hello and shuffled through some paperwork on his desk. A few minutes later he took a call. After a brief conversation, he got up and left without saying anything, and Blake wondered what was up.

Stevens' look had made him squirm. He felt as if there was a blinking sign on his forehead that said, "We fucked." He had to quit with the paranoia. No one knew he and Alex had made love most of the previous night, and no one would unless he slipped and said something.

A half-hour later Stevens called him and asked him to come to an interview room in Missing Persons. He walked into the room to find Stevens, Jacobs from Missing Persons, and a woman he didn't recognize sitting around the table waiting for him.

She was late-middle-aged and looked as if she was used to the outdoors. Her face and arms were tanned and strewn with age spots. Wrinkles creased the outer edges of her blue eyes. Her mousy brown hair was short, cut in a very masculine style, and shot through with silver.

"This is Sharon Lowry from Freed, Montana. Ms. Lowry, Detective Halloran."

"Freed? That's one I've never heard of," Blake said, wondering why she was here and why he'd been asked to join the group.

She smiled. "Almost nobody has. It's a very small town. Fewer than five hundred people."

"Nice to meet you," Blake said, sitting down across from her.

"She knows Alex," Stevens said. "Came to Denver to try to find her and contacted Missing Persons."

Blake raised his eyebrows in surprise. "You know Alex? How?"

"She grew up in Freed. I knew her and her family."

"Last name?" Blake demanded.

"Kincaid."

"What makes you think she's missing?" That got a raised eyebrow from Stevens, but he remained quiet.

"She came to Denver to look for her sister. They kept in touch via text messages and phone calls. Suzanne had stopped responding to calls or sending texts, and Alex was worried something had happened to her. Not unwarranted since, from what I heard, she was working the streets."

The woman frowned. "I tried to talk Alex out of it, told her to call you guys, but she's pretty bullheaded. Now I can't reach Alex on the phone either. Her phone goes directly to voice mail and at the moment it's full. Probably from all my messages that she hasn't answered."

"Hang on a sec," Blake replied, leaving the room and heading for his desk to retrieve the photos of the woman in the morgue. When he returned, he hesitated. "I'm sorry to have to show you this, but is this her sister?"

"Yes, that's Suzanne." Her eyes filled with tears, and he grabbed at the box of tissues that sat on a small table near the door and handed it to her. "She's dead, isn't she?" Blake nodded.

"Well, I'm terribly sorry, but can't say I'm surprised."

"Ms. Lowry, what can you tell me about Alex and her sister?"

"Is Alex dead, too?"

"No, ma'am. She's fine."

"Thank God."

Jacobs left and returned with a bottle of water and handed it to her. She dabbed at her eyes, took a sip of the water, and, looking down at the table, began to talk.

"Her family lived on a farm outside of town. Her daddy raised cattle and grew hay to feed his herd and sell if it was a good crop. Ed was a strange man, one of those survivalist types. He was ex-military, I never knew which branch. He was so paranoid. He had some sort of safe room under the house, where he stockpiled food and supplies to survive a disaster."

She blew her nose. "He could be really normal, and then the right comment would trigger all his weird beliefs, and he'd go on about it until people walked off. Most people in town gave him a wide berth."

"What kind of beliefs?"

"He believed that there would come a time when the government would be in crisis and would try to subdue everyone by taking away their guns and their rights. He had guns, lots of guns, and he trained with them all the time. Made the girls do it, too—made them learn self-defense techniques."

That explained the familiarity with guns and her ability to subdue someone, Blake thought. *At least she didn't get it from criminal activity.* Hearing that, the knot in his gut started to relax.

"Suzanne refused to participate once she hit her late teens. Alex went along with it to keep the peace, and she was good at it. I think she enjoyed it on some level. Her dad had wanted a boy, which is why he always called her Alex instead of Alexandra. Suzanne always called her Lexie."

She sighed and swiped at her eyes again. "I took the girls under my wing. Their father made it really hard for them to fit in socially. It wasn't the guns, everybody has them where I live, but his rants when he got agitated had earned him a reputation. Kids figured their father was crazy and so the girls must be, too. I felt sorry for them."

She fiddled with the tissue in her hand, folding it over and over until it was about the size of a postage stamp.

"Their mother was cowed by Ed. She wouldn't stand up to him or defend the girls. Can't say I blame her. He was verbally and physically abusive to all of them."

With a shrug she explained, "It's a small, isolated town in Montana. A lot of men, including the sheriff, believe 'discipline,' which is what they call it, is needed to keep kids and wives in line. And if it gets a little out of control, they turn a blind eye to it because they won't interfere between a man and his wife. It's why I never married."

She took a deep breath and continued. "Suzanne was the oldest. She ran off before she graduated from high school. I don't think anyone, including Alex, knew where she was initially. She'd get letters from Suzanne periodically. Alex told me they were from all over, so Suzanne must have been moving around a lot. Then about a year ago, Alex told me Suzanne had started contacting her periodically by text."

"When did Alex leave her family, or did she?"

"She waited until her mother died, that was four years ago.

Honestly, I was surprised she stayed that long, but she said she wouldn't leave her mother alone with her father. She'd just turned twenty-eight. After seeing her mother buried, she moved to Bozeman and worked in a restaurant. She kept a very low profile but stayed in touch with me. I missed her, but I was glad to see her go and stop wasting her life."

She smiled faintly. "Ed passed this year. He left the property to Alex. Ed disowned Suzanne, but Alex said she didn't want it. She hasn't done anything with it yet. Not sure she will."

Blake hesitated. "Alex says she hears a male voice periodically that says things like not to tell anyone about herself, not to trust anyone. It rattles her because she can't identify whose voice it is. Do you think that could be her father's voice?"

"It sounds like something Ed would say." A frown settled on her face as she continued. "I think on some level her father's paranoia affected her. She never went to college or applied for anything that required a background check. She was smart. She read all the time, anything and everything."

Blake hid a slight smile, remembering the romance novels Mrs. H had given Alex. "She could have gone to college and ended up with a better job, but she seemed content.

"Then Suzanne stopped contacting her, and she told me she was coming here to try to find her. She never altogether trusted the police, so she didn't contact you. That was partly her dad's fault and partly because she knew Suzanne was soliciting. She figured you would arrest her if you found her."

The woman sat back and took another drink of water. "I tried my best to talk her out of it, and when I couldn't, I insisted she contact me regularly so I knew she was safe. That stopped about ten days ago. I called and got kinda shunted around here, so I decided to come in person. I don't tolerate being ignored."

"Ms. Lowry, I very sorry that happened. We didn't have an ID on either Alex or her sister, so that may have been the problem."

"What do you mean you didn't have an ID? Couldn't Alex identify herself or her sister?"

"Alex was assaulted about the time she stopped contacting you. She had nothing on her that would ID her—no phone, no purse. Nothing," Blake said. "She has amnesia, total amnesia, and for a while didn't remember her name. Then all she could remember was Alex."

Blake stuffed the morgue shots back into the folder. "I discovered that she was looking for her sister, and the woman I spoke with said the sister's name was Suzanne or Susan. Alex didn't recognize either name when I asked her about it."

He tapped the folder with the photos. "The therapist who's been working with her told me not to show her these photos. We didn't have any way to ID the woman in the morgue or determine whether she was Alex's sister." Blake didn't intend to mention her missing fingertips unless pressed.

"Lord," she sighed. "At least she's safe. Can I see her?"

"I'd like to talk to her first, prepare her. The therapist has been adamant that we not surprise her with anything."

"Of course. I'm staying at a nearby hotel. Will you let me know as soon as I can see her?"

"Yes, let me get your contact information."

Blake stepped out to get pen and paper. As Lowry was writing the information down, he said, "I hope seeing you will bring back her memory, but from what I've read it might not. At least we have someone who can fill in some of the blanks for her and give her some reassurance."

She handed him the paper and stood, holding out her hand to all three detectives and shaking their hands one at a time.

"Thank you. And thank you for keeping her safe."

CHAPTER THIRTY-TWO

"WELL KUDOS TO you. You were right about her attack being connected. Why the guy didn't follow through like the others doesn't make sense. You gonna tell her?" Stevens asked him as they made their way back to Homicide.

"Yeah, I've gotta figure out how, though. I've got to get her to remember somehow. She's our only lead to the guy."

A few steps down the hallway Blake said, "She refuses to go back to Caswell. She thinks working with her to recover her memory set off the suicide attempt, so I'm scared to dump this on her."

"Seems like it'd be a relief for her to find someone who knows her and who can reassure her that she's not a criminal. You said she worried that her knowledge of guns and self-defense meant she'd done something to cause the attack."

They entered the homicide department and made their way to their desks.

"Yeah, it probably would help but, oh hell, who knows?" Blake dropped down onto his desk chair and looked up at Stevens. "I need to talk to someone other than Caswell about this."

"What have you got against Caswell?"

"She doesn't like me at all, and I really can't figure out why. I mean, she knows me from before…after Lindsey…but I don't recall any issues with her. I resented being there and didn't really like her much, but there was no real animosity."

Blake stared off into space. "We had a confrontation when I said I wanted to show Alex the photos, and after I told her about Alex's 'flu,' but we haven't had that much contact since then. And Alex said she pumps her for information about me."

"She knows Alex is staying at your place. Makes sense she'd want to know about you and whether that's a good idea."

Blake fiddled with a pencil on his desk. "I suppose. You know that buzz you get off some people, people you take a dislike to almost immediately? I kinda have that buzz about her. I didn't like being forced to talk to her about what happened. All I wanted was to get it over with and go back to work. I didn't like how she kept picking at me. Now…it's like she sees me as a threat. At any rate, I don't want Caswell to know about Lowry. I don't want her in the middle of this."

"Why don't you talk to Kendall?" Stevens asked. "Let him know what's going on. See what he says"

"I suppose I should. He's scheduled to see Alex day after tomorrow. I'll be back. Call if you need me."

———•◆•———

BLAKE WALKED into the modern, nearly new University Hills cop shop near the University of Denver campus. He was escorted to the office of Dave Kendall, who welcomed him and offered him a chair. Blake noticed he sat across from him, not behind a desk, and he liked that.

"I'm scheduled to meet with Alex, have there been other developments I should know about?"

Blake explained about Sharon Lowry showing up. "Caswell has been pretty adamant that Alex not be shown the morgue photos, which I guess I can understand. But it's like…"

"Like what?"

"Like she's obstructing things instead of helping Alex. Alex told me last night she didn't want to see her again."

He took Kendall through what had been happening. "She keeps saying that it felt like she didn't have a choice, like things were so bad that suicide was the only option."

Blake pulled at his ear in frustration and frowned. "That's not the case, at least in my opinion. She's safe, and, even before Lowry showed up, I'd have sworn there was nothing criminal or weird for her to remember. What I want to know is whether Caswell could have somehow given her the suggestion to cut herself."

"That's highly unlikely. Caswell's a good therapist and I can't think of any reason she would do that. Alex doesn't remember what happens during the hypnosis sessions?"

"No, she says she falls deeply asleep and can't hear Caswell's voice, can't remember anything. That worries me."

He stared out the window of the psychologist's office at grass, trees, and the I-25 overpass. "The only thing she has to be afraid of is the guy who tried to kill her twice."

Blake rubbed his forehead then let his hand drop into his lap. "I can't *find* him until she remembers what happened. And I know, now that her sister's been ID'd, that it's the same guy whose been killing the prostitutes. So, I *need* her to remember."

"I realize that, Detective, but this kind of confrontation with reality can backfire. Especially when what she remembers is that traumatic. I definitely wouldn't show her the morgue photos—not now at least. I would suggest that you introduce her to Ms. Lowry in an indirect way."

"Meaning what?"

"Put Lowry somewhere neutral and bring Alex in and ask her to wait in the same room. See whether seeing this woman helps Alex remember something."

"And if it doesn't? Then what?"

"Then perhaps join them and introduce Alex to her. Let the woman talk to her and see if that triggers anything. If not, then her need to forget is far more important than the need to remember right now and forcing it could be disastrous."

"And in the meantime, women are being killed, and I have no leads on this guy at all. And he's a threat to Alex as well."

"According to you, Alex trusts you. Your presence would reduce her anxiety over meeting this woman and hearing her out. At the very least, she can reassure Alex that her skills and knowledge, and most likely the reason for her assault, aren't criminal in origin. That should ease her mind and perhaps let her remember."

Blake nodded. "Okay. I appreciate you being willing to step in regarding the hospitalization. I don't want Caswell to know about it, and Alex doesn't want to see her anymore."

"I'm happy to see Alex, but you realize I'd have to ask Caswell for her notes. That's going to cause problems for you."

"Could you see her without having those?"

Kendall frowned. "I could, but it would be best if I had them."

"I'd appreciate it if you hold off asking for them. Caswell could make serious trouble for me and Alex."

"In what way?"

Did it again, Blake thought. *Opened my big mouth.*

"Alex is staying at my apartment." He saw Kendal frown, but forged on. "I made the decision on the spur of the moment. Housing her at a hotel turned out to be too risky, and at the time there were no safe houses available. That hasn't changed. And the women's shelters were either full or they didn't want to take responsibility for her."

Blake paused, and knew he was risking Kendall reacting like Caswell. "Caswell wants her moved. I don't. Alex doesn't want to move. She says she feels safe at my place. This guy has been pretty successful at finding her, and I can't guarantee her safety if she's elsewhere."

Kendall raised his eyebrows and gave Blake an appraising stare. "That's an unusual way to solve the problem. Is it working out?"

Blake nodded, afraid to say much more.

"I can't say I'm in favor of it either, but that's your decision and Alex's."

CHAPTER THIRTY-THREE

THE PHONE CALL did not go well. Caswell was convinced that Blake was to blame for her decision to stop the hypnosis.

"Blake had nothing to do with this." Remembering the flu story, Alex continued, "I don't feel well and, to be honest, I don't think the hypnosis is helping. I haven't remembered anything, and my anxiety has skyrocketed. In any event, this is my choice and I don't want to continue. If I change my mind, I will let you know."

"I don't like this at all, Alex. I told you a while back that staying with Blake made you vulnerable to pressure from him to do things the way he wants. You shouldn't be staying there, and you shouldn't stop the hypnosis."

"That's your opinion. Where I stay and what I choose to do is mine. Blake has put no pressure on me to do anything. I don't want you harassing him or me about this."

There was silence on the line before Caswell replied tersely, "If you change your mind let me know."

To warn Blake, because she was sure Caswell would confront him, she called his cell.

"Are you okay?" The first words out of his mouth when he picked up sounded a little panicky.

"I'm fine. I'm at Connie's, Mrs. H's," she clarified. "She went to the grocery store, so I called Caswell. She's very unhappy and is sure you're the reason I don't want to continue. I wanted you to know so she doesn't blindside you."

She heard him exhale sharply. "Okay. I'll keep my eye out for her. Kendall will hold off asking Caswell for her files, at least for now."

"I'd rather not see him, please. Can I think about it some?"

"I suppose. You've been released from the 72-hour hold, so there's not much they can do if you don't see him, but it might help."

"I'll think about it."

Blake paused. "I'd like to take you out for dinner. I know it gets boring staying at the apartment and…anyway, I'll come pick you up in about an hour. I have to come back by the precinct briefly, then we can head out."

"Dinner?"

"Are you up for it?"

"Yeah, but I thought you didn't want Caswell to see me. To see my wrist."

"I don't, but I have to stop by and check on something briefly… to…see if it's come through," he improvised. "I'll put you in an interview room. It'll be fine, trust me."

"You're the only one I do trust." She wasn't sure she should go on, but at last said, "Last night would never have happened if I didn't."

She could hear the smile in his voice. "Then I'm exceptionally glad you trust me."

She chuckled. "So am I."

———— ◆ ————

BLAKE HAD barely disconnected when he saw Caswell approaching. She did not look happy.

"I'd like to talk to you privately, Detective Halloran."

"Okay, follow me."

She nodded and walked down the hallway with him and into one of the interview rooms.

"What's up?" he asked as he closed the door. Figuring it was better to play innocent and see where this was going, he stood there and waited.

She glared at him. "Don't act as if you don't know what this is about, Detective. It won't fly. Why did you coerce Alex into stopping the hypnosis sessions?"

"I didn't. In fact, I didn't know she had. When did this happen?"

Caswell looked momentarily surprised. She must really think he was an idiot.

"She called not long ago and told me she wasn't going to continue. You had no idea about this?"

"She'd mentioned it, but she's been ill. Which is what I told you the other day. I figured she meant she wanted to stop until she was feeling better."

"No, she wants to stop entirely, and I don't believe that's in her best interests."

"Maybe not, but that's her decision. Not my place or yours to try to talk her out of it."

Caswell narrowed her eyes at him. "You think you're very clever, don't you? When this backfires on you, don't say you weren't warned."

"Warned?"

"I intend to inform your lieutenant about her staying with you and what I believe is your manipulation of her."

Blake laughed. "Well feel free, but she's not living with me anymore."

"Where is she staying?"

"I'm not divulging that. Someone has tried to kill her twice, so I have no intention of revealing her whereabouts. As to coercion, seems to me like you're the one pressuring her to do something she doesn't want to. If I were you, I'd be careful."

"This isn't over, Detective," she said as she stormed off, the door to the room banging against the wall from the ferocity of her exit.

No, it probably isn't, Blake thought.

If pressed by his lieutenant, he might have to lie and say she was staying with a friend of his. He wasn't going to say who the friend was or where Alex was, not even to his lieutenant. Mrs. H wasn't really a friend any more than Alex was staying with her, but it would suffice. And from now on Alex would be with Mrs. H when he wasn't at the apartment.

———◆———

ALEX DISCONNECTED from the call and stood looking out the window of Mrs. H's apartment. She wasn't seeing the front lawn of the apartment complex, the blue sky, or the clouds scudding across it. She was remembering Blake's face this morning lying across from her, relaxed in sleep.

His face had been peaceful, something it rarely was when he was awake. The frown line between his brows had relaxed and his lips, often drawn into a tight line, were full and vulnerable looking and the corners quirked up in a faint smile.

Without thinking she'd reached out and stroked his cheek, smiling at the feel of the dark stubble that graced it. Stubble that had taken its toll on her face and breasts.

His eyes fluttered open and he smiled. "What a beautiful face to wake up to," he said sleepily.

"I was thinking the same thing."

He chuckled. "I'm hardly beautiful."

"You are to me," she said and was rewarded with an embarrassed smile.

"Couldn't sleep?"

"I slept fine. I'm sorry to wake you, I…wanted to touch you."

He turned to glance at his phone. "Well, the alarm would have gone off in about half an hour anyway. And waking up this way is a lot more pleasant than the alarm."

He slid his arm under her neck and pulled her close. "Wish I had the day off."

"That might be dangerous. We might not get out of bed."

He was already half-aroused, but her comment sent his cock to full alert and he pressed it against her.

"We may not get up for a while whether I have to work or not," he said, sliding his hands down her flank in a caress.

Alex had slept well despite the interruptions for making love. She'd relaxed with him next to her and slept, but during the night, she was startled awake when she felt him jerk suddenly and moan as he whispered the name Lindsey followed by another moan. She'd held him and stroked his back until he'd slipped more deeply into sleep. Who was Lindsey and why did the name cause him such distress?

Staring out Mrs. H's window, an uneasy feeling writhed in her gut. He wanted to take her out to dinner and wanted her to wait at the precinct, the last place she thought he wanted her to be. What was going on? Had he figured out who she was or what had happened to her? Did he want her at the precinct so that what he'd discovered could be handled officially?

Blake had told her to trust him, and she did, but it took all her effort to tamp down the fear that rose up in her every time she thought about going to the precinct.

Alex heard the door being unlocked and turned to see Connie coming through it loaded with grocery bags. "Here, let me help with those."

"Oh, thanks. Put them on the kitchen counter and I'll go get the others."

She returned several minutes later with a few more bags. "You look tired, Alex. Why don't you go lie down on the couch and take a nap? You look like you had a restless night," she said, and shooed her over to the couch.

CHAPTER THIRTY-FOUR

BLAKE SEEMED NERVOUS when he arrived to pick her up. He'd walked her over to his apartment and she'd found him pacing and rubbing his neck when she returned to the living room after she'd changed. There had been no kisses, no caresses, no banter, and she was on the edge of panic. What had he discovered? Was he going to arrest her? She couldn't find the courage to ask, so she tamped the fear down and waited.

The Homicide department was busy when he escorted her in and walked toward an interview room. He situated her at the table, asked if she wanted anything to drink, said he'd be right back, and started to leave.

"Tell me why I'm here, for God's sake! Don't…" she faltered to a stop.

"Alex, it's okay," he said squeezing her hand. "Trust me, it's okay."

Before she could reply the door opened, and a man escorted an older woman into the room. "Sorry, Halloran. Didn't know you were in here. I need to leave Ms. Lowry here briefly, okay?"

"Sure," Blake said as the woman came in and sat down. He turned to Alex and whispered to her, "Sit down, I'll be right back." He squeezed her hand again and left.

Alex sat down and smiled hesitantly at the woman, who watched her closely and seemed curious about her.

After several minutes of silence, the woman said, "You don't recognize me do you, Alex?"

Alex jolted back in her chair. Who was this woman? Is this what Blake had brought her here for? Her breath came in short gasps and she felt faint.

"Should I?" she asked fearfully.

"It's true, then. You don't remember anything?"

Alex looked at her apprehensively. "Oh God, what did I do to you? How do you know me?"

"Sweetie, you didn't do anything. I came looking for you when I didn't hear from you. I'm a friend."

"Why don't I know you?"

"I don't know. You've had a hard time, I guess." The woman picked at the edge of an old purse she had set on the table. "My name is Sharon Lowry. I knew your family. I was close to you and your sister. You came…"

She stopped when the door opened, and Blake stepped in. Alex rose and turned on him. "You bastard! You fucking bastard! You knew who I was all along, and you let me *torture* myself? Was it your idea to spring this on me?"

"I…no, Alex, I thought it'd help. Help reassure you."

"*Help me?* Why couldn't you tell me? Instead you let me worry myself into slitting my wrist because I couldn't remember. Because I was afraid to remember. What were you waiting for?"

She stepped up to him and got in his face. "How long have you known?"

"Since yesterday. Only since yesterday when Ms. Lowry showed up."

"I assume there's no warrant out for my arrest?"

"Why would there be a…?"

"Good, then I'm leaving." She pushed past him and out the door.

"Alex, stop! Please wait!" He reached for her but thought better of grabbing at her. He danced in front of her, holding his hands up for her to stop.

"I don't want to be around you right now."

"Okay, okay. I get that, but please let me take you back to Mrs. H's. You can't leave."

"Oh, yes I can. Get out of my way."

He grabbed her shoulders then and held on to her. "You can, but you have no place to go. He'll find you. He'll finish the job. Please, let me take you back. I'll leave you alone once we get there. I'll stay somewhere else if need be."

"I hope he does finish the job! I'm sick of this!" she hissed in his face. "I don't know her. I don't remember ever seeing her before. How do you even know she's who she says she is?"

Behind her he saw Stevens usher Lowry out of the room and shoot him a worried look. "Alex, come back into the interview room so I can explain. I don't want Caswell to see you, and she might if she gets wind of this."

Alex stared at him with contempt. It hurt that this man she'd made love to the night before, this man she had trusted, had betrayed her. *You can't trust 'em, missy, no matter what they tell you.* She tapped her forehead with the heel of her hand and willed the voice to go away.

"You have five minutes," she said angrily.

"Fine," he said, guiding her back into the interview room and closing the door.

They stared at each other, neither speaking until, at last, Blake said, "I'm sorry. I should have told you, but I was told this way would be better for you. Jesus, Alex, I'm lost here. I was trying to do what was right by you."

"Answer my question. How do you even know she's who she says she is?"

He shook his head, let out a long breath, and said, "She has family photos of you and your sister, and she said you'd come here to find Suzanne. Which is what another person I spoke with a few days ago also said."

"And?"

She watched him debate with himself and then give in. "And, God, I'm so sorry, but she identified a body we have in the morgue as your sister."

Alex flew at him and beat against his chest and screamed, "And you *didn't tell me?* You *knew* and you didn't tell me? You bastard!"

She collapsed against him and began to sob. "You bastard."

He cautiously wrapped his arms around her, held her, and hoped desperately he hadn't totally fucked everything up.

"I'm sorry. I'm so sorry."

"SHE WON'T talk to me," Blake said to Stevens. He'd left Alex in the interview room when she'd pushed away from him and told him to leave her alone. As a precaution, he'd stationed a uniformed cop outside the door to prevent her from taking off.

"So much for the shrink's advice, I guess." Stevens scratched his head and pursed his lips. "So, what're you going to do with her?"

Blake snorted. "Arrest her if I have to. I can't risk her taking off." He shook his head. "Who knew I could fuck things up so badly?"

"Well, women," Stevens said with a shake of his head. "They're unpredictable. Maybe she'll calm down if given some time."

"She's been in there for more than an hour and still won't talk to me."

"Want me to be the bad guy?"

"Meaning what?"

"I'll tell her I've remanded her into your custody because she's a material witness in the killings, whether she can remember anything or not. I'll tell her unless she wants to be put in protective custody in jail until we find this guy, she has to go home with you until we can find her another place to stay."

"She may opt for jail." Blake shrugged. "Give it a try."

"Want me to have Lowry try to talk to her again?"

"Not right now. Give her some time to get over this before we try that again."

"Okay, sit tight."

A few minutes later Blake got a text from Stevens:

<Come get her but wear a steel jock strap.>

That made Blake laugh, but he figured it was probably good advice. Alex glared at him when he entered the interview room. She stood up and crossed her arms over her chest.

"Since my choice is your place or jail, I'll go home with you. But I'm not happy about it."

Blake nodded and held the door for her, choosing the better part of valor and saying nothing. The frost in the car on the ride home was palpable and cold enough to freeze his balls off. A steel jock strap would have made it even colder. They entered the apartment and Alex started toward the bedroom, then turned.

"FYI: after that little stunt, don't expect an invitation for sex."

"You're unbelievable!" Blake said in exasperation. "You act like I did this to hurt you, like I haven't spent the last few days trying to decide what to do, worrying about how it would affect you."

He paced the living room. "*I* wanted to tell you what I'd found out. *I* wanted to show you your sister's morgue photos. *I* wanted to tell you about Lowry. But *everyone*," he said, raising his voice and sweeping his arm around as if a chorus of people stood in the living room with him. "Everyone said no, it'd be too traumatic. It's a bad idea. Don't show her the morgue photos, it could make things worse for her. Don't tell her what Lowry said. Put her in a room with Lowry and see if it triggers anything. And because I took their advice, *you're pissed at me?*"

He turned to the door and jerked it open, looking back and glaring at her. "I wouldn't fuck you now if you paid me."

And he slammed out of the apartment

ALEX SANK onto the side of the bed and dropped her head into her hands. Apparently, she had a sister. She'd been right about that. She'd been right about the sense of grief, as well, but neither the name Suzanne nor the photo of the woman in the morgue, that she'd insisted on seeing, meant anything to her. If the woman was her sister, she couldn't say. Why didn't she recognize her?

And Sharon Lowry? She could be anyone for all Alex knew. She'd had no chance to listen to what the woman had to say or ask questions. The one huge relief was knowing that she wasn't a criminal, or a prostitute. But why she'd been assaulted and who had done it was a mystery. Still.

What if she *never* remembered anything? What then? Try to go back to a normal life and hope that whoever had assaulted her would leave her alone because she couldn't implicate him? And what kind of normal life could she go back to?

She lay down on the bed and curled into a ball. The bed smelled like Blake again, like their lovemaking, but it was no longer comforting. It embarrassed her. She'd trusted him. What choice did she have? But he'd withheld information that could have reassured her. He'd made love to her under false pretenses. He'd let her be scared.

She was furious with him, and yet she yearned for him, cared for him far too much—and that embarrassed her as well. Caswell was right: she was too dependent on him. Maybe Connie would let her stay with her. But for now, she'd try to sleep, try to forget him and everything else.

HE SAT on the bar stool and gazed into the amber liquid in the glass. It wasn't making him feel better or even getting him drunk, which would have been preferable to sitting here beating himself up. It surely wasn't defusing his anger at her, at everyone who'd told him not to tell her, and at himself for listening to them.

And now she thought he'd lied to her, kept things from her, taken advantage of her. He hadn't really lied. He hadn't told her things, had kept things from her, but he hadn't lied.

And that, he could imagine Lindsey saying, *is bullshit*.

"Go away," he mumbled, taking another sip of his Scotch.

He hadn't been honest with Alex, but it was because he was afraid to dump everything he knew on her, and he hadn't listened to his own intuition. What he'd said to her was true—he was lost. He'd never dealt with anything like this or anyone like her.

He regretted what he'd said as he left the apartment. She'd infuriated him with her snotty remark about sex and he'd retaliated. That anger was dissipating now, and he realized he'd probably permanently burned that bridge. It was a bridge he wished he hadn't burned, but he had no idea how to repair it. He was lost there, too.

He pulled his phone out of his jacket pocket and looked at the time. Almost midnight. She'd most likely be asleep and he could come back without another confrontation. He'd make sure he was up and gone before she woke in the morning. He fished a credit card out of his wallet and signaled the bartender for the tab, paid it, and left.

CHAPTER THIRTY-FIVE

HE HATED THAT couch, he thought driving to work. He'd never spent more than an hour or two napping on it. Sleeping on it night after night was misery, especially now when he'd much rather be in bed with Alex. As soon as possible it was going to Goodwill. Where Alex was going to go was another subject entirely.

The apartment had been dark and silent when he got home. He quietly opened the door to the bedroom to make sure she was there. Standing in the doorway he watched her, taking in her face and how she was curled into herself, the palm of one hand resting on the pillow next to her face. More than anything he wanted to slide in next to her and take her in his arms and apologize as many times as it took to get her to tell him it was okay between them.

At last, he closed the door softly and returned to the living room. He took off his clothes and carefully hung his jacket off the back of the living room chair. He sniffed cautiously at the underarms of the shirt he'd worn and decided it could get him through another day and the pants looked clean, so he carefully folded them and left them on the seat of the chair. He'd go commando tomorrow. Wearing the same briefs two days in a row seemed like a bad choice.

He sure as hell wasn't going into the bedroom in the morning to retrieve fresh clothes or spend time cleaning up at the apartment. He didn't want to bump into her every time he turned around. The fewer face-to-face events he had with Alex right now the better. He'd strip and shower when he got to work. Hopefully that'd keep him presentable enough until things settled down between them.

"So, how's your inmate?" Stevens asked when Blake finally appeared, clean but unshaven, at his desk.

"No idea. She was asleep when I left, and we aren't talking."

"Any ideas about what to do from here?"

"None."

"I think we ought to let Lowry talk to her, see if what she tells her rings any bells."

Blake threw his hands wide. "Feel free to set it up—I'm not touching that with a ten-foot pole. I'm going to start looking for somewhere else she can stay."

"Just FYI, the department can't foot the bill for her security—no cops guard-dogging her."

"You know what? I am sick and tired of people saying, 'just FYI' to me." He glared at Stevens then ran a hand through his still-wet hair, leaving it in total disarray. "Never mind. You arrange it with Alex—about talking to Lowry. I'm staying out of it."

"She'll get over it, Halloran. Me? I wouldn't disrupt everything yet. Let things settle down, give her some space."

"Thanks, Dr. Phil. I'll keep that in mind." Blake saw Stevens' eyes widen.

"Mayday. Trouble on the way," he muttered, and stood up abruptly and walked away.

Blake turned and inwardly groaned. Could this day get any worse?

Caswell strode up to him. "I hear you dumped a visitor on Alex in an attempt to get her memory to return. What happened?"

"That's really none of your business."

"I'm making it my business. She's a patient of mine."

"Not anymore, she isn't."

Caswell frowned then took a deep breath. "I'm sorry. We've been at odds for a while but Alex takes precedence. I'm only concerned about how she is. I would appreciate an update on what happened."

Blake raised his eyebrows. Her apology and contriteness seemed out of character, but he relented. "A family friend came looking for her when Alex stopped responding to her phone messages. She verified that Alex was looking for her sister and confirmed what I had suspected all along, that the woman in the morgue is Alex's sister."

Caswell nodded. "How did the meeting go?"

"Not as planned."

"Meaning what?" He could see Caswell beginning to get annoyed with him again for not disclosing freely, making her pump him, and secretly it pleased him. He really disliked her.

"Meaning she didn't remember anything, and the woman and Alex didn't have much time to talk. So, not as planned."

"And where is Alex now? I'd like to touch base with her."

"As I told *you* before, I'm not revealing her whereabouts. She's fine. You'll have to take my word for it."

He could see that pissed her off, but she held her temper. "Fine, tell her I'm here if she wants to talk." She turned and walked away.

He fished his phone out of his pocket and texted Alex.

<Caswell says hi. I told her I'd moved you and didn't tell her where. She may have saved your phone number when you called to cancel the sessions. If she contacts you please don't talk to her, don't even pick up the call. I would really appreciate it if you would stay at Mrs. H's today until we sort out a safe place for you to stay.>

There was no response, so with a muttered curse he returned his phone to his pocket and sat down to go over Suzanne Kincaid's file and autopsy report. Lowry had told Stevens that she would wait for Alex to decide what to do with her sister's body.

It was cowardly to refuse to approach Alex about talking with Lowry, but he was baffled about what to do. He had no idea how things had so totally backfired or how to fix that. He was pissed at himself for how it had all unfolded.

Against his wishes, he kept thinking of Alex, replaying memories that caused a weird ache in his chest every time he thought about her. He remembered the look she had given him in the hospital, that lost puppy look that had hit him like a brick. He remembered how tiny she looked sitting in the wheelchair at the hospital entrance in the track suit he'd bought her. He remembered her laughing and reaching for his hand while they ate Chinese in the hotel room.

He wasn't sure he'd ever forget the softness of her lips, her scent, the feel of that curtain of dark red hair brushing his chest as she moved over him in the semidarkness of his bedroom. Or the freckles on her nose, or the giggle that had somehow escaped while he had searched frantically for a condom.

It surprised him that his memories weren't so much erotic as they were tender. That was an adjective he'd never used before when thinking about a sexual conquest. He closed his eyes and rested his chin on his hand. She wasn't a conquest, he realized. She was what he wanted, more than he'd ever wanted anything.

He could easily remember the eroticism of their lovemaking, but it was the small things that kept haunting him. What surprised him was that making love to her wasn't all he'd miss if she was no longer around. He rubbed his temples, trying to erase the tiredness and attempt to focus on the work at hand, when his phone rang. He didn't recognize the number.

"Halloran."

"Blake, this is Connie Holtz."

"Is everything okay?" he asked anxiously.

"Yes, sort of. Alex wanted me to call and let you know she's spending the day with me. She's resting in my room. She says she didn't sleep well last night. Blake, what's wrong?"

"What do you mean?"

"Why wouldn't Alex call you herself?"

"Did you ask her?" he asked irritably.

There was silence on the line, and then she spoke up. "I'm assuming something has happened between the two of you. You're not being very talkative, and neither is she. She looks exhausted and upset, and you sound like that. I wish one of you would tell me what happened."

Blake heaved a sigh. "A woman came in to report Alex missing. My partner and I arranged for Alex to meet her without really introducing her, to see if Alex recognized her or might remember something. It didn't go well. At all."

He ran his hands through his hair. By now he looked like an irate porcupine. "She's mad at me, thinks I lied to her or at the very least kept things from her, and she's upset because she didn't recognize the woman."

He was silent for a few seconds. "And she now knows her sister, who she came to Denver to try to find, is dead. So, all in all it was a cluster fuck."

"I see. Well, I'm sorry for both of you. Is there anything I can do to help?"

"Keep her at your place when I can't be there until I find another place for her to stay. She's not safe at my apartment alone. If you'd do that it'd be a big help."

"Of course." She paused, then said, "She'd be more than welcome to stay with me all the time if you felt that would be safer for her."

"Thanks, that would probably be a good solution." Blake hesitated, then plowed on. "If you think she's open to it, ask her if she'd be willing to talk to Sharon Lowry again. She's the family friend. If I ask, Alex will probably refuse."

"You two!" Mrs. H said in frustration. "I'm not getting in the middle of this. You're both grownups—at least I think you are.

You need to talk to each other and work this out. The sooner the better. If Alex brings up the subject I'll ask if she'd be willing to talk to the woman, but I'm not carrying messages for either of you from this point on."

She waited, and when Blake said nothing she said, "It's plain as day, to me anyhow, that you two care about each other. Whatever's gone on between you, talk about it, get it sorted out. If you think about it, not talking to her is what set this off. Don't be an idiot. I'll tell her the same thing."

And she disconnected.

Meddling old biddy, Blake thought. He shook his head. *Not fair. You brought her into this, she's got a right to an opinion and she's been a big help.* But it rankled that her opinion wasn't far from Alex's. He should have told Alex the truth. All of it. He wondered if he'd get a chance.

CHAPTER THIRTY-SIX

"DETECTIVE HALLORAN?" THE voice sounded familiar, but he couldn't place it.

"Yeah?"

"It's Kelly. We talked the other day about Carla?"

"Yeah. I'm sorry...I'd hoped we'd find her alive." *Christ,* he thought, *All I seem to be doing these days is apologizing. It's just one fuck up after another.*

"I know."

"Thanks for trying to help."

"That's why I'm calling. I've got a friend I think you should talk to. She may have seen this guy."

"When can I talk to her?"

"Now, if you want. We're at the same place I met you the other day."

"Be there in ten. Don't let her leave, tell her she's in no trouble."

Blake pulled out his wallet, which was distressingly empty. He wasn't sure his bank account would stand another withdrawal until his paycheck arrived on Friday. He looked up and saw Stevens heading back toward his desk.

"Caswell's gone?" he asked warily.

"Yeah, you chicken shit, she's gone." He returned his wallet to his pants pocket. "Have you got any cash on you?"

Stevens raised his eyebrows questioningly. "Yeah, why?"

"The prostitute I talked with about Carla Russo says she may have a witness who's seen the guy who's been abducting these women. I need to pay her for her time, and my bank account is nearly empty. Payday is this Friday. I'll pay you back."

"How much?" Stevens asked, fishing his wallet out of his back pants pocket.

"Can you spare a hundred?"

"A hundred?"

"Um, that seems to be the going rate these days."

Stevens counted out five twenties and held them out toward Blake. "You're not paying for a blow job on my dime, are you?"

Blake gave him a withering stare and Stevens laughed. "Had to ask, you know that. How could I resist?"

"Resist next time. I'll be back in an hour or so. We might have gotten our first break in this case. And FYI, blow jobs are only fifty bucks."

Blake walked away to the sound of Stevens' laugh.

———◆———

"HE HAD ample time and opportunity to tell me what he knew, all of it, and he chose not to." Alex got up from the couch and walked to the living room window.

"He knew how worried I was about who I was and what I might have done to incur the assault, and he said next to nothing."

Mrs. H listened quietly to Alex, allowing her to talk without interruption.

Alex turned and held out her bandaged wrist. "He let me worry enough that this happened! If he'd told me anything maybe I wouldn't have done it."

Mrs. H looked at her with a pained expression. "And you care for him, don't you?"

Alex shrugged a shoulder, then nodded wordlessly.

"Why do you think he didn't tell you?"

"He says that everyone told him not to tell me. He says they told him it wouldn't be safe to tell me, even though he wanted to."

"So, he paid attention to the people around him, including the therapist who you'd been working with, right?"

Alex reluctantly nodded again, not wanting to let go of her anger toward Blake. "He says he's lost, that he didn't know what to do. I don't either. He should have told me and taken the chance it would help."

"But he cares for you, doesn't he? And he didn't want to make it worse for you."

"How could it possibly be *worse* for me? I don't know who I am, I don't know who tried to kill me, nor do I recognize my sister or the woman who says she's a family friend. He should have told me. He should have shown me the photos of my sister as soon as he had them."

Alex rubbed her temples. "I don't know what to do! I may never remember anything. I didn't even recognize the photos of my sister!" She sat down on the couch and began to sob. "I didn't even recognize her."

Mrs. H leaned over and wrapped her arms around Alex. "If you remember nothing, then you build a life with what you do know and go on. This woman knows who you are, and perhaps if you spoke with her things would start coming back to you."

She leaned away from Alex and, with a frown on her face, said, "I hesitate to suggest this, but perhaps seeing your sister's body would be more effective than the photos. But first, talk to this woman who knows you."

Alex nodded as she wiped the tears off her face. "I was so mad at Blake, I refused to talk to her. If I do and nothing she says connects, then I'll ask to see my sister."

"And try to see Blake's side of things. He was trying to protect you, and he was doing what others told him to."

She brushed a lock of hair behind Alex's ear. "I will help in any way I can. I told Blake you can stay here if needed. You two need to talk. But for now, let it go. Rest, and when he gets home go talk to him and ask him to arrange a meeting with Sharon Lowry. And now I'm going to butt out. This is up to you and Blake to resolve."

Alex leaned over and hugged Mrs. H "You must have been a great nurse, Connie."

She smiled. "Once a nurse always a nurse, they say."

———◆———

CANDY SLIPPED into the booth, followed by Kelly, and watched him suspiciously.

"You swear you're not going to arrest me?"

"I am not going to arrest you. All I want is information."

"Okay, good."

"What did you see and when?"

"Couple of weeks ago, I talked to a guy in a black SUV. He was trolling, offered me five hundred bucks to go with him to a motel and stay the night. I decided not to."

"Why? That's a lot of money."

"It is. It was a hell of a lot of money and I was tempted." She glanced around the restaurant. "You've got to listen to that little voice if you want to survive in this business, and there was something off about him. I got weird vibes. I thought it was odd that he'd offer that much money right off. Nobody wants those of us on the street to sleep over, and he was pushy about it. But to be honest if I'd been hard up for money that week, I'd have probably gone with him."

She shifted in her seat, sucking on the straw she'd stuck into a virulently red drink the waitress had just delivered.

"We hadn't discussed what he wanted, other than the overnight, or talked price, and he offered the money. Most guys usually want to knock the price down or at least haggle. So, I turned him down. It pissed him off. I walked away and stood with some people at a bus stop, figuring he wouldn't make a stink if there were other people near me."

"And he left?" She nodded. "Tell me what he looked like."

"Big guy, black hair, blue eyes."

"Big as in fat, or muscular, or tall?"

"Tall if I had to guess, and muscular, not fat."

"Curly hair or straight?"

"His hair was cut short, kind of a military cut, nearly shaved sides and a flat top, so I have no idea about curly or straight."

"Okay. Did he have any visible injuries on him?"

"Injuries?"

"Yeah, like scratches or bruises or cuts on his face or neck, or… hands?" Blake's voice trailed off as he thought of Kyle Jeffries and his short black hair and the scratches on his hand.

"I didn't see anything."

So not Jeffries, Blake thought. Not liking someone didn't qualify them as a suspect.

"He wasn't a bad-looking guy, which made me wonder why he was trolling for sex. Seems like he'd be able to get it for free with his looks."

"Did you see him pick up any other women after he left you?"

"No, he was pissed. He pulled out into traffic and shot off like a rocket."

"Did you get a license plate number or part of one?"

"No, I never thought to look."

"Any stuff in the car strike you as odd?"

Candy frowned and closed her eyes for a moment. "He had some tools lying on the passenger seat. I remember because he brushed them off onto the floor when he said to get in the car."

"What kind?

"A big wrench and a pair of those plier-like clippers; you know, with the big sharp blades on them?"

Blake felt the tingle. It was the guy. He was sure of it. The information wasn't much help in finding or identifying him, but he didn't want to tell her that.

"You've been a big help. If I find a suspect, I'll want you to come in and look at photos. Here's my card. Call me if you see him again. Try to get a license number if you can and pass the word around not to go with him no matter how much money he offers."

"I will. Kelly told me what he's been doing. We've both been telling people we know."

Blake held out the money to her, but she pushed his hand away. "No, I don't want to be paid for this. You're a good guy. You're trying to help, trying to protect us, and I appreciate that. Keep your money. Just find this guy."

"We're trying. Believe me, we're trying."

CHAPTER THIRTY-SEVEN

LAKE TEXTED <I'M on my way home. If you'd rather stay with Mrs. H, I'll bring your clothes and stuff over. Let me know.>

Blake waited for a response, but when none came, he started his car and drove toward home. Halfway home he heard the text chime, ignoring it until he pulled into the apartment parking lot.

<I can get my clothes if you want me to stay with Connie. Let me know when you get to the apartment.>

He made a face at the phone and shoved it into his jacket pocket, got out, locked the car, and headed up.

"*I can get my clothes if you want me to stay with Connie,*" he said in a snarky voice. "Fine, come get your fucking clothes. Go stay with *Connie*. Stay pissed. Fine with me." Except it wasn't.

He didn't text back and was surprised ten minutes later by the knock on the door and to see Alex standing in the hall.

"You shouldn't be standing in the hall."

"You didn't text, so I thought I'd check to see if you were home yet."

"I hadn't gotten around to it. You should have called or texted me that you were coming over. Standing in the hall isn't safe."

She nodded. "I'll get my clothes."

She started to push past him, but he took hold of her arm and turned her toward him. "You don't need to. I'd like you to stay with Mrs. H when I'm not here, but you don't need to make it 24/7. Unless you want to."

"It would be best, don't you think?"

He dropped her arm and stood back and allowed her to enter, saying with a shrug, "Up to you. I won't hit on you, if that's what worries you."

She frowned and he saw a flash of hurt on her face before she walked to the bedroom to gather her things.

"May I borrow your carry-on, the bag you gave me at the hotel?" she asked, walking into the hallway.

He sat on the couch, keeping a neutral expression on his face. "Sure."

He wasn't going to try to stop her or convince her to stay, but he wished he could find a way to do it without losing face, without having to beg. This is what came of getting involved, nothing but pain.

When she'd packed her things, she walked back into the living room and stopped a few feet from the couch. "I'd like to talk to Sharon Lowry, but not at the precinct. Maybe here, if that's okay with you."

"Fine with me."

"And…and if what she tells me doesn't bring back any memories, then I'd like to view my sister's body. Perhaps seeing her in person would jar something loose."

"Okay." He sat very still and watched her. "Before you go, do you remember a man with black hair and blue eyes, tall and muscular, with a high and tight haircut?"

She frowned. "High and tight? What does that mean?

"Military-style haircut, shaved sides, crew cut on top."

She shook her head. "Should I?"

"I hoped you would."

"Is he the man who assaulted me?"

"No idea at this point. If he's the one, you're the only one who's seen him up close and survived who might have more information, so until you remember I've got nothing."

"Where did the description come from?"

"A woman who talked to a guy I think is probably the perp, but there's no way to ID him or locate him. Unless you remember a license plate or something I can use to find him."

She dropped her head momentarily then looked at him. "I'm sorry. I wish I could remember."

He shrugged as if it didn't matter and said, "We'll find him eventually, with or without your help. A few more dead prostitutes won't matter."

"You don't think that."

"You don't know what the fuck I think."

"Then tell me."

"Why? You didn't believe me before, so why waste time repeating myself?"

"Because I asked you to."

His anger surged at her demand. His face lost its neutral expression and he saw her flinch.

"Fine. I think you're wrong about my intentions. I did what I did because I wanted to protect you, and everyone told me to keep my mouth shut. That's what I get for listening to so-called *experts* or caring what happens to you."

He stared at her hard. "If you were any other witness, I'd have shown you the photos and told you everything, and if it backfired so be it. And the frustrating thing is I have nothing. Nothing to ID this guy and no way to stop him, unless you remember details this woman didn't have.

"But there's nothing I can do about that, so it is what it is. Sadly, you're right. I do care that more women will probably die, but I have no way to prevent it. It eats at me."

"What else eats at you Blake?"

He frowned. "What d'you mean? Isn't that enough?"

"Who's Lindsey?"

It was as if she'd punched him in the gut. How had she heard about Lindsey? "None of your fucking business."

He stood up and walked to the door and opened it. "*Connie*," he said with an edge to his voice, "is probably waiting for you. I'll let you know when I've arranged something with Lowry."

He didn't want to explain Lindsey, didn't know how she knew the name, and he was angry she'd asked. As angry as he was, he wanted her to turn to him and ask to stay, to tell him she wasn't angry with him anymore. But she wasn't going to do that, and he had no intention of talking to her about Lindsey. He walked her next door and left when Mrs. H opened the door.

———— ◆ ————

THE ROOM smelled like potpourri instead of Blake's bedroom, and the bed smelled like laundry detergent not Blake. She missed the feel of him. She missed the sense of security he gave her. The anger for withholding the information from her was still there, but she could see that he'd been pushed into not telling her.

She felt guilty that she couldn't remember anything to help him. She felt responsible for the dead women and for the sister she couldn't remember. Maybe she should go back to Caswell and try once again to remember something, anything.

The thought of Caswell brought a deep wash of depression over her. She rolled to her side and pulled the other pillow to her and hugged it. No, not Caswell, perhaps the other therapist Blake had mentioned. First, she needed to talk to Sharon Lowry and see what she could tell her. Maybe it would help her remember something, she thought as she finally slipped into sleep.

She stood in Caswell's office and turned around and around. There was something here. Something important. But what was it?

Nothing she saw seemed to be what she was looking for. Being in the office frightened her.

The dream shifted and the woman she'd been told was her sister stood in front of her in a small, dated kitchen. She was younger, a lot younger. They both were.

"Don't go, please. I don't want to be here alone," she heard herself say.

"Then come with me! Don't stay here. You don't have to stay here."

"But we're not done with school. We're underage, he'll find us and bring us back. How will we survive, Suz?"

"Fuck school, it's filled with teachers and kids who think we're crazy. And he's not going to bother trying to find us. He never really wanted either of us. He tolerates you because you do what he asks. He doesn't want me around at all."

"What about Mom? I can't leave her here alone with him."

"Fine, then stay, and good luck with that. I'm leaving. come if you want or stay. I don't care."

The kitchen disappeared and it was cold and dark, and her head and throat hurt. She heard boots crunching on the ground and felt herself being carried down an incline, the person slipping once. Each step jarred her head. Then the steps stopped, and she was dropped carelessly onto the rough ground before everything went black.

Alex jolted up in the dark, clutching her arms around herself protectively, her breath rapid, her heart racing. Caswell's office unsettled her, and the person who'd carried her down the incline terrified her.

The kitchen conversation floated back to her. Her sister had left, and she had stayed, somewhere, but where? Her sister who was dead, and other than what the dream had shown her, someone she didn't remember. Maybe, though, the dream meant her memories were coming back.

"I'm so sorry. I'm so sorry I don't remember you," she whispered as tears ran down her cheeks and splotched onto the blanket.

CHAPTER THIRTY-EIGHT

LEX'S PHONE CHIMED and the text read <I'm bringing Lowry to the apartment at one. I'll text you when we get there.>

She glanced at the clock on Mrs. H's kitchen wall. Half an hour, then. An uneasy sensation roiled her stomach. Despite the previous contact triggering nothing, she hoped this meeting would. The scene from her dream returned. Maybe Sharon Lowry would know more about that, perhaps be able to fill in the gaps.

Blake arrived and walked her across the hall without saying anything. Sharon Lowry sat on the couch and stood up when they entered.

"Alex," she said, holding out her hand. "It's so good to see you."

Alex took her hand, gave her a tentative smile, and nodded. "I'd like to hear what you have to say. I'm sorry, but I don't recognize you. I'm hoping some of what you have to tell me will change that."

"I hope so, too."

Sharon sat back down on the couch and Blake indicated Alex should as well. He took a seat in the chair. He didn't ask if either minded his presence. It was his case, she was his witness, and he was staying.

"Tell me about my sister."

Sharon nodded. She pulled her purse up off the floor and opened it, pulling out an old fashioned wallet with photos in plastic sleeves. She removed several from the wallet and handed them to Alex.

"These are photos of the two of you at various times. I took them. Your dad didn't believe in photos." She held the photos out and Alex took them.

"Why didn't he believe in them?" It was an odd statement. What was there to believe in?

"Ed, that was his name, didn't want any visual record of your family. He didn't know I took these or he'd have been furious." She smiled hesitantly. "He was pretty paranoid about the government. He didn't want the government to be able to identify you by sight."

Alex looked through the photos. She and Suzanne stood on either side of a horse in one. They both looked like teenagers, she perhaps thirteen or fourteen and Suzanne a couple years older. Another of her sitting on a porch in a swing, with Suzanne sprawled on the porch floor laughing about something.

They were all similar in nature, two young girls at various ages in a place where they were relaxed and happy. That wasn't what she remembered from the dream. In the dream they were far from happy.

"Why did she leave? We look happy in these photos, but I don't think we were."

"No, you weren't. At least not at home. All these were taken at my place. Both of you were able to relax and be kids at my place. Your dad allowed you to come over because I told him I'd hired both of you to help me out around the property. I gave you each twenty bucks a week to back that up." She brushed her bangs away from her forehead.

"Suzanne hated your father and hated the town and the people in it. She waited until September of her senior year, when she turned eighteen, to leave. She refused to stay and finish the year."

"I begged her not to leave," Alex said.

"Did you remember that?" Blake asked sharply.

Alex glanced up from the photos. She had forgotten he was sitting there. "I don't know, I dreamt about her last night. I was begging her not to leave me there. She asked me to go with her, but I told her we weren't finished with school, and I was afraid to leave my mother there. At least I was in the dream, it could be a memory."

"I'm sure she did ask you to come with her. She would have. She always protected you from your father when he was in one of his moods. She'd have wanted you to go with her so he wouldn't take his rages out on you."

"And I guess I didn't."

"No."

"I let her leave by herself and now she's dead."

"Alex, she was leaving whether you went with her or not. Her death is not your fault."

Alex lay the photos on the couch cushion and looked at Blake and then Sharon Lowry. "I don't remember that, but I remember the dream. I can't tell you what we were doing in the photos, or where we were, or even what the damn horse's name was."

She rubbed her neck. "I see she looks like me in some ways, but for all I know she could be anyone." She gestured at the photos.

"Why can't I *remember* her? Or you? Or my parents? Am I ever going to remember? Or do I fill in the blanks with other people's memories?"

Blake watched her and could see the panic and the frustration. "Alex, listen. Don't try to force yourself to remember. Let Sharon talk and tell you what she knows and just listen."

She listened for the next hour as Sharon Lowry talked about her parents and her sister, their farm, the town, and its residents. She listened to how Sharon had taken Alex and her sister under her wing. She'd given them a place they could be free to laugh and be girls. And although she couldn't remember it, she was grateful to the woman for giving them that.

When Sharon seemed to have run out of things to tell her, Alex said, "Thank you for what you did for us. For what you're trying to do for me now."

She sighed. "Maybe it'll come back to me now that I've heard you out. I don't know. All I know is that I don't remember it. What you've told me seems like a story about someone else."

"I'm going to stay in town for another couple of days, then go home. I can't be gone for too long. My horses need tending to. My neighbor is taking care of them while I'm gone, but he has a farm to run as well," Sharon explained.

"If you need to, go home. I know most of what I needed to hear. Remembering it may take a while."

"I thought I'd stick around in case you have questions or wanted to come home with me."

Alex took her hand and smiled. "Thank you for that, but I can't leave yet. If you'll give me your phone number, I can call you if I need to know something."

"What do you want to do about Suzanne?" Lowry asked hesitantly.

Alex frowned for a moment then said, "If I have her cremated would you take her ashes home with you and bury them, or spread them on your property? I think she'd like that."

"Of course. I'll stay until that's taken care of and then take her with me."

They both stood and Alex hugged her. "Thank you. I'll let you know as soon as it's done."

Blake rose from the chair and walked to the door with Lowry. He stopped and turned to Alex.

"I'd like to talk to you when I get back. If you'll go back to Mrs. H's, I'll text you when I return, or you could wait here. I won't be long."

"I'll wait here."

He nodded at her and left.

CHAPTER THIRTY-NINE

I T HAPPENED SO fast that Blake could remember it only in flashes. The passenger window shattering, bits of safety glass and blood spraying his face and shoulder. Jerking in surprise and making the car fishtail. His curb-jumping turn into a near-by parking lot, yanking the emergency brake on, and bolting out of the car. Pulling the passenger door open to see Sharon with her hand clamped to her neck, blood pulsing through her fingers. Blood spraying on his chest as her hand dropped, and he covered the wound and pressed hard all the while wondering when the kill shot would come for both of them.

Someone must have heard the shot or seen his car veer into the parking lot and called 911. In moments, he heard sirens. A police car arrived, followed by an ambulance, and Blake moved aside allowing the EMTs to take over. They moved Sharon quickly into the ambulance and took off, siren wailing and lights flashing. Blake sat on the ground near the front of the car and held his head in his hand, trying to get his breathing to slow.

"Are you hit?" the cop asked, then repeated himself several times before Blake could hear him over the pounding of his heart that seemed to block out all other sounds around him.

"No. I…here," he said, pulling his jacket back so the cop could see his badge. "I need to get to the hospital, now."

The cop nodded. A second patrol car arrived.

"I have to get him to Denver Health. Secure the scene till I get back."

The cop offered Blake a hand and pulled him up off the ground, then helped him into the patrol car. "They're taking her to Denver Health. Tell me what happened while I drive. I'll connect with you later to get a full report. Give me your card."

Blake fished clumsily in his jacket pocket and handed him one, leaving a bloody fingerprint on it. In the ER, he found a nurse and asked where Sharon was.

"She's on her way to the OR. You can go up to the second floor and wait in the surgical waiting area. I'll let the OR know you're there. Someone will keep you informed."

"Is she going to make it?" Blake asked, knowing the answer but hoping he was wrong.

"I can't say at this point, I'm sorry."

Blake waved his hand in frustration and found his way to the surgical waiting area. He was grateful that it was empty. His shirt, jacket, and hands were covered in blood, and there was a spray of it on his face and neck. After the shakes had passed, he found a men's room and tried to at least clean his hands and face. Returning to the waiting area, he paced as he frantically called Alex.

———◆———

HALF AN hour after Blake and Sharon had left, there was a knock on the door, and Alex heard Mrs. H call to her through the door.

"Alex, it's Connie. Open up, please, and hurry."

"What is it?" Alex asked opening the door.

"Blake called on your phone—you left it at my place. You're to come with me, now," she said, catching Alex's hand and pulling her out the door as she closed it, half dragging Alex down the hall.

"Wait, stop! What's going on?"

"Alex, please stop asking questions and come with me. I'll tell you in the car. Here," she said, handing Alex a beanie she had been carrying and a large T-shirt with a silly cat on its front. "Slip this on over your shirt. Put the beanie on, tuck your hair up into it, and pull it down as far as possible so it covers your hair and your face isn't as exposed."

She saw Alex hesitate, and said in a voice no doubt many recalcitrant patients had heard over the years, "Alex! Put the damn hat and T-shirt on and hurry up!"

They reached the opposite end of the hall and took the back staircase down to the main floor. Connie cautiously opened the door and peered out.

"My car is parked in the first row—the white sedan there. We're going to walk normally so as to not draw attention but get in quickly and then keep your head down until I tell you to sit up."

She grabbed Alex's hand and pulled her out the door. Once in the car, Connie pushed Alex's head down below the dash.

"Stay there till I tell you it's okay to sit up."

"For God's sake, Connie, what's happened?"

"There's been an accident. Blake wanted me to get you out of the apartment and take you somewhere safe until he can come get you."

"Accident? What accident? Is he hurt?"

"He says he's fine, but..."

"Oh God, not Sharon?"

Connie nodded. "She's on her way to the hospital. He was at a stop light, and the car was shot at. Sharon was seriously injured. I don't know how badly. Blake said he'd explain later."

"Where are we going?"

"To a detective he's friends with, Kaye Jagerski. He talked to her, and she said for us to come there."

Connie drove silently for some distance before she indicated

Alex could sit up. They arrived at a small brick bungalow in a neighborhood filled with similar houses. Connie pulled around to the alley. As they approached the garage, she tapped her horn twice. The door went up, and a uniformed officer stood inside and motioned them in next to what Alex assumed was Kaye Jagerski's car.

The officer closed the garage door and hurried them across a small backyard and into the back of the house. Alex saw a woman speaking on the phone.

"Yeah, they just arrived, intact and unharmed. I have two uniforms here for backup. How's the victim?" she asked.

"No, that's fine. I have a small basement apartment I rent out through Airbnb and it's empty at the moment, so they can stay here as long as needed." She paused. "I'll tell her. Keep me posted," she said as she disconnected.

"Sharon?" Alex asked anxiously.

"She's in surgery. The outcome's uncertain at the moment. Blake's at the hospital and will update me when he can. Come in and sit down."

Kaye ushered them into the living room and sat across from them. "Blake's sure that the shooter is the man who assaulted you, and that he either thought Sharon was you or he wanted to keep Sharon from imparting any more information to you. He wants both of you to stay here until he can figure out what to do. That may be a while."

She leaned forward, elbows on her knees. "I provide basic things for guests—extra toothbrushes and sample toiletries—so you'll be good for those until I can arrange for your things. Blake isn't going to stop by because the guy may be following him, and he doesn't want to lead him here."

Kaye stood up. "Let me show you where you'll be staying. The stairs are a little steep, so watch your step."

AN ANXIOUS several hours passed before Kaye came down. She had locked the exterior door to the apartment, and put the chain on it and told them not to open it for anyone.

She handed Alex her phone. "It's Blake. Bring the phone up when you're done."

"Blake what's going on?"

"I'm glad you're at Kaye's. She'll make sure you're safe. Please listen to her and do what she says."

"I will. You're okay?"

"I'm fine." He didn't sound fine.

"Sharon?"

There was a long pause. "She didn't make it. I'm so sorry." He huffed out a breath. "I tried, Alex. I tried to stop the bleeding, but I couldn't." His voice broke slightly. "I called Kaye on the way to the hospital. I needed you safe."

"Blake, it's not your fault," she said, but he interrupted her.

"I called your phone, and Mrs. H picked it up. I guess you left it in her apartment when you came over to talk to Sharon. I wanted you out of the apartment, out of the building. I wanted you…safe." His voice broke.

Alex waited and said nothing. "God dammit! We can't catch a break on this case. I'd hoped talking to her again might help. Now she's dead."

She heard the anger in his voice and sadness. "She was a nice woman, and she cared about you and your sister. Now she's gone, and you have no one. God, I'm so sorry."

"I have you."

He laughed ruefully. "Yeah, for all the good that's done. I'll be in touch. Do whatever Kaye asks you to do."

And he disconnected.

Alex sat for a moment staring at the phone and then went upstairs to return it.

"Could someone go to Connie's apartment and retrieve my phone and charger?" she asked Kaye, handing her the phone.

"I'll talk to Blake. He can retrieve it, but I don't want him bringing it here. I can have one of my plainclothes guys bring it over."

"Thank you. I can manage without it if necessary, but I'd like to be able to contact Blake without tying up your phone."

CHAPTER FORTY

HE NEEDED TO change; there was blood all over his jacket and shirt. He could smell it, feel it stiff and uncomfortable on his chest, and he needed it gone. Needed to stop the panic it set off. He'd washed his hands in the men's room near the surgical waiting area, but his cuticles were still dark red with dried blood. He saw it as his hands gripped the steering wheel. He shook his head hard. *I'm in the car. It's not Lindsey. Alex is safe,* he kept thinking to himself and breathing slowly as he left the hospital.

His phone rang as he drove home in a car from the motor pool. He answered it through the car's Bluetooth speaker.

"It's me," Kaye said. "You going home or avoiding the apartment for now?"

"Going home. What's up?"

"Alex would like her phone, which is in your neighbor's apartment. Can you get it and take it to the precinct? I'll have a plainclothes officer bring it over here."

"I don't have a key."

"Connie said to go to apartment 2D and talk to Mason. Tell him what you need and give him the code word 'jellybean.' That way he'll know it's okay."

"Jellybean?" In the face of everything that had happened the word seemed incongruous.

Kaye laughed. "Yep. She said Mason would give you her extra key."

"Okay. I'll let you know when I get to the precinct."

"You okay? It's been a rough day."

"I'll survive," Blake said, getting out of the car and walking into the apartment building.

"I'm sure you will, but are you okay?"

Women, they kept pushing at you, wanting inside your head, wanting to help. "I'm as fine as I can be," he said biting back an angry retort. "Frustrated as hell and no leads. No one saw anything, as usual. We think he was across the street behind some commercial garbage receptacles."

"But nothing that could identify him?"

"Nada." Blake let himself into his apartment and walked to the bedroom, putting his phone on speaker and leaving it on the bed as he shrugged out of his jacket and shirt. There was blood on his chest and abdomen as well. Seeing the blood on himself had triggered flashbacks about Lindsey in the surgery waiting area that had threatened to overwhelm him before he'd forced them away, compartmentalized them, and locked the compartment tight. Now he just wanted it gone.

"I don't think this guy is your average weirdo," he said.

"Meaning what?"

"He's too good at not leaving evidence, breaking into places, making it hard to ID the victims. I keep getting the feeling he's somebody associated with law enforcement or forensics or, Christ, who knows?"

"He'll screw up eventually. They always do."

"I just hope I can keep Alex alive till then and that she remembers something helpful."

"These things percolate in people's heads. Her contact with Sharon may have been more helpful than it seems."

Kaye waited for a response and, getting none, continued, "Alex mentioned wanting to see her sister's body. Maybe that'd help."

"Maybe. I have to figure out how to get her to the morgue without her becoming a resident there."

"Get cleaned up—you probably need it—and I'll think about how we could get her there anonymously. Text me when you get the phone to the precinct."

"Will do, and thanks for keeping them at your place. It was all I could think of."

"No problem. I'm glad to help." Kaye hesitated. "If you want… need to talk, let me know."

"Thanks," he replied disconnecting.

———◆———

IF I could stand under the hot water forever and not have to get out, he thought, *I might feel human again.* But he had things to take care of. Things that couldn't wait for him to feel better.

The blood was gone from his chest and abdomen. He'd scrubbed until there no longer was a dark red stain around his cuticles. That was something, some movement toward what needed to be done, he thought as he dressed in jeans and a clean shirt.

He picked the stained shirt and jacket up off the floor. He'd have to dispose of both of them. Maybe the shirt would wash clean, but he wasn't sure he wanted it now. Looking at the dried blood that had saturated the jacket, he doubted his cleaners could remove the stains or would want to have to handle it. It was a biohazard now. It hadn't been that great-looking anyway. Not having the energy to walk to the kitchen and get a garbage bag, he dropped them back onto the floor.

He sat down on the edge of the bed and flopped back onto it, staring at the ceiling. He'd held it together until he was sitting in the surgical waiting area and had gotten the shakes. It could have been Alex. That thought had continued to run through his mind. He couldn't get it to stop. Nor could he stop imagining that it could have been her blood pouring out of the neck wound that the bullet had inflicted on Sharon. Like the blood that poured from Lindsey. Blood that he'd tried frantically and unsuccessfully to stop with both women.

He covered his face with his hands. What good did it do to keep thinking about what-ifs or regretting something that couldn't be changed? It had been Sharon, it had been Lindsey, and that had caused enough guilt and regret. He closed his eyes and inhaled. There it was—Alex's scent. He felt himself starting to drift off to sleep and abruptly sat up. All that kept the thoughts at bay was work. *Back to work*, he thought, getting up and heading for the apartment door.

"Connie said to tell you 'jellybean.' I'm a cop and I need to retrieve something from her apartment. She said you had an extra key." Blake flashed his shield.

"I do, hang on."

Blake had expected a man Mrs. H's age, but Mason looked about twenty, had half-sleeve tatts on his forearms, and gauges in his ears. The not so faint smell of marijuana drifted out of the apartment. It surprised him she'd make friends with the kid. He had a lot of preconceived ideas about her, he realized.

"Here, man. You going to keep it or bring it back?"

"I'll keep it for now. She's not going to be home for a few days, so don't worry about it. If anyone shows up looking for her call me, okay?" He handed the kid his card.

The kid raised his eyebrows in surprise. "She's not in any trouble, is she?"

"No, it's for her safety. Anybody asks, you don't know where she is, you don't know her all that well. You know nothing as far as she's concerned. Get a description of anyone asking about her, got it?"

"Got it. Take care of her, she's cool. Tell her I'll keep an eye on things for her."

Blake nodded and walked back down the hall to Mrs. H's apartment. Letting himself in, he began looking for Alex's phone and found it and the charger in the spare bedroom. It was a comfortable place, and he was grateful for the help she'd given Alex. Guess he'd have to be nicer to her from now on.

Stuffing the phone and the charger into his pocket, he left and locked up.

———— ◆ ————

<PHONE'S ON the way. Jack Michaels is bringing it. How are things?>

<Quiet. No problems. I had an idea about the morgue visit. Call me.>

"What'd you come up with?" Blake asked when Kaye picked up the call.

"I have a friend who's been going through chemo and has lost her hair, so she's been wearing wigs. If my friend comes over wearing one and brings another with her, Alex can wear the one my friend is wearing and wear her clothes. If the guy is watching he'll think it's my friend, not Alex. I could bring her, and my friend could stay here until we get back."

"Let me call the morgue and find out when we could bring her over."

"I'll call my friend and get her over here."

———— ◆ ————

ALEX FELT silly in the wig and apprehensive standing in the lobby of the morgue. Blake walked in and her heart leapt at seeing him. She felt calm wash over her. He looked exhausted. His face was blank and dark circles hung under his eyes.

He walked over to her and asked, "Sure you're up for this?"

"No, but I need to do it. I need to remember."

"It may not work."

"It may not, but I have to try for my sister and for Sharon." Her eyes welled with tears.

Blake drew her into his arms and held her. It felt so good to have his arms around her. She saw the surprise in Kaye's eyes and then a curtain dropped, and Kaye's face took on a very neutral expression. A cop face.

Blake let go and stepped back. "Okay, let's go."

"I'll hang here," Kaye said.

The place was quiet, hushed almost. It smelled like the hospital—industrial strength cleaning products and other unidentified, but unsettling, smells hung in the air and set Alex's heart to racing. She didn't know for sure, but she didn't think she'd ever seen a dead person before. She'd probably seen her mother. Sharon had said she'd waited until her mother died to leave, but she had no memory of it. She would see one now and only hoped it would be bearable.

The attendant ushered them into a viewing room, where Suzanne's body lay on a gurney covered to the neck with a white sheet. He backed out of the door and closed it behind him.

Blake took hold of her elbow and walked with her to the gurney. "We can leave anytime, all you have to do is say so and we'll go."

She nodded and walked closer. The sight of the woman's still, pale face, immobile and bereft of life, shocked her. But more shocking were the images that burst into her brain. Images of her sister alive—angry, funny, laughing, crying, belligerent, and sweet.

Alex shuddered. Blake stepped up, and she felt him rest his hand on her back. "Are you okay?"

"I remember some things about her. I remember I loved her. I missed her, I worried about her. Oh, Suz!" She leaned over and lay her head on her sister's chest. There was no give to it, no warmth, no movement, no reassuring beat of her heart, and as the icy cold seeped through the sheet she lifted her head. Before Blake could prevent her, she reached under the sheet for her sister's hand.

"No, Alex, don't!" he said, reaching to stop her, but it was too late.

Alex jerked her hand away and pushed the sheet back, staring in horror at her sister's hand. "What did he do to her? Did he cut off her fingertips? *Did he torture her?*"

She let go of the sheet, stumbling away from the gurney as she began to sob.

Blake pulled her to him and held her tightly. "No, no he didn't torture her. The M.E. said it happened postmortem, so she didn't feel it. She didn't feel it, Alex. She didn't feel it."

She sobbed into his shoulder, and he surreptitiously left a kiss on the top of her head. A few minutes later she disentangled herself from him and approached her sister's body and stroked her hair.

"I remember you, Suz. I know you. I won't forget you again. I'm so sorry I didn't find you in time." She stayed silent for several minutes then turned to Blake. "Please, I want to go now."

———•◆•———

IT WAS dark, and it was his bed, but he couldn't sleep. He couldn't forget the look on her face when she'd seen her sister's hand, couldn't forget her sobbing on his shoulder. Couldn't forget the feel of her hair as his lips had skimmed a kiss on it. Couldn't forget how good it felt to hold her.

He never cried. He hadn't cried at his mother's funeral, despite feeling her loss deeply. Nor had he cried for his father on whom he'd relied as his moral compass. By the time he'd found himself standing in the church next to Lindsey's casket in his dress blues, he was numb, dazed, and just drunk enough to numb the pain and get through the ceremony without embarrassing himself. But he had no tears to cry. When Alex laid her head on her sister's chest, he'd nearly broken down. It had rendered him barely able to talk with the hard, painful lump of unshed tears in his throat.

She hadn't remembered anything except her sister and memories about her. He hadn't pushed Alex or questioned her. It had been difficult enough for her to see the body and he didn't want to add to it. And she had volunteered nothing other than that she remembered her sister. Seeing her sister's body had been a bust, too, as far as the investigation went.

He turned over for probably the tenth time since lying down. Sleep was going to be elusive. He got up, went into the bathroom, and took two ibuprofens. He felt as if he'd had a headache since he nearly hit Alex with his car.

Probably a brain tumor with my luck, he thought.

Wandering out into the living room, he detoured to the kitchen and poured himself a scotch and sat on the couch in the dark. The couch had been his bed for long enough that he stretched out on it and rested the glass on his chest, sipping from it and staring into the darkened living room.

The scotch had given him a warm glow. As he finished it, he felt his eyes grow heavy. He set the glass on the coffee table, and a few minutes later dropped off to sleep.

She stood next to the morgue gurney and watched him.

"Take care of her," Suzanne said.

"I'll try, if she'll let me."

"Take care of her whether she lets you or not. It's your job," she said. "Find him. Stop him. It's your job."

"I know how to do my god damn job!" he shouted at her.

"Then do it."

It was his job, he thought—jolting awake and lying in the dark. But he couldn't do it unless something broke, something that would lead him to the guy. And being lectured by a dead woman didn't help.

"Fuck me," he said and closed his eyes, hoping to go back to sleep.

CHAPTER FORTY-ONE

"NOTHING, HUH?" STEVENS asked him the next day. "She remembered her sister, so I guess that's a start. That memory might lead to others, but who knows?"

"Forensics got some black carpet fibers off the last victim that match fibers off one the early victims. Unfortunately, it's from a Ford Explorer, which makes it pretty much useless. There are so many Explorers in Colorado it'd be like trying to find a needle in a haystack to ID the one it came from."

Blake leaned back in his chair. "I wonder if this guy is in law enforcement or some type of forensic or legal job. He's too good at not leaving evidence."

"Could be," Stevens said. He covered his mouth as he yawned widely. He looked as tired as Blake felt. "What's your girl gonna do about her sister's body and the friend's body?"

Blake didn't bother to tell his partner—again—that Alex wasn't his girl. He'd given up, and Stevens seemed attached to the moniker. *Alex had been, briefly. But not now after all that's happened*, he thought.

"I haven't asked. She had quite a shock at the morgue. Jesus, I wish I'd anticipated her wanting to hold her sister's hand. I thought she was gonna come unglued when she saw the fingers."

Blake pressed his fingers against the bridge of his nose. "I just…I don't want to harass her or overload her with questions right now. The two bodies aren't going anywhere, so there's no rush on deciding what to do with them."

"Well, that's true. I'm sorry about Ms. Lowry. I liked her, and she clearly cared for both of the girls. I keep hoping this fuck'll make a mistake and we'll catch him, but it doesn't look that way."

"No, it doesn't. I hope I can keep Alex alive until she remembers something, and we can put him away."

"I've been thinking, there's this Vidocq Society…"

"The what?"

"Stop interrupting and you might find out. It's a group of law enforcement people who review cold cases and help solve them. I heard a guy who participates in it talk once, and he said fresh eyes often see things that the people who've been working the case didn't."

"Our case isn't cold."

Stevens snorted. "Might as well be. We've got nothing."

"You want to contact them?" Blake asked incredulously.

"No, I think they only look at actual cold cases, but if we had someone here look at the files, they might see something we haven't."

"Did you have anyone in mind?"

"I don't know, maybe Roberts and his partner Adams."

"I doubt they'd have time. They're tied up in those drive-by gang shootings. What about Frost? He's out on sick leave, but he could review the case files. He won't be back for another three weeks or so."

"Yeah, that might work. Lemme think on it."

"How about I call and see if he's up for it."

———— ✦ ————

BLAKE SAT in Detective Alex Frost's cluttered home office. He looked much like he always had. He had receding brown hair shot with gray and a cynical expression on his face that seemed permanent. The bags under his brown eyes were still there, but he looked less tired and he seemed relaxed. The job took its toll on everyone. Blake knew Frost was in his late fifties, but before his surgery, he'd looked older. Not so much now.

"I was hoping to have someone who hasn't been involved in the case look at the file and see if anything jumps out that we've missed."

"I can look, not sure I'll find anything. You two are a good team with a high solve rate, so I doubt you've overlooked anything," Frost said.

"We'd appreciate it. Are you up for it?"

"You mean am I recovered enough?" Frost asked, raising his eyebrows.

Embarrassed, Blake said, "I guess. I don't know anyone who's had heart surgery, and I didn't want to impose."

"I'm fine, Halloran. I'll be back at work in a couple of weeks." He settled back in his office chair and watched Blake. "Before I look at the file, tell me what's happened and where you're at with it."

Blake described what had happened so far and how little evidence or breaks they'd had. "We're at a standstill, and I can't guarantee he won't get to our witness before she can remember what happened or we get a break and can arrest him."

He rubbed his forehead. "If she can't tell us anything, then the threat to her persists. If it were me, I wouldn't take the chance that she'd never remember me."

"Neither would I, and clearly he doesn't plan to either. He's tried to kill her twice, and he succeeded in killing the one person who might help her remember eventually, or it was a third attempt on her life if he mistook the woman for your witness," Frost stated.

Eyes closed, Frost absently scratched at the middle of his chest. Blake wondered if that was where his surgical scar was. "If I were you, I'd sit down with the witness and go over everything you've found."

He opened his eyes and stared at Blake. "Tell her about everyone who's been killed, about the tools the one woman saw on the guy's car seat, and what you think is going on. See what happens."

He leaned forward. "If that doesn't result in anything then I'd take her out to the spot where she was assaulted, take her down into the culvert and walk her around. Tell her what happened as you know it. Maybe seeing the culvert will bring back memories of the assault."

"I don't know, seeing her sister was pretty traumatic."

"True, but it brought back memories of her sister. Impress on her that you can't get rid of the risk to her if this guy can't be found and arrested. My opinion, for what it's worth, is it'd be worth the risk. If she totally freaks out, have a shrink ready to take over."

Blake nodded, not entirely convinced. "I appreciate the help. Let me know if you spot anything we should follow up on."

"I will. Keep me posted—this is an interesting case." He laughed. "And I'm bored out of my mind."

They shook hands and Blake left.

———◆———

BLAKE DROVE to a nearby fast food place, and then thought better of it and found a restaurant with a drive-thru that offered a little healthier fare. It might not be a bad idea to eat better. He really didn't want to end up having heart surgery. Frost looked good, but heart surgery wasn't something Blake wanted to go through.

He thought about talking to Alex like Frost had suggested as he ate his turkey sandwich. Talking to her was a risk, no question, but it'd been what he'd wanted to do all along. And seeing her sister had brought back some memories.

Taking her to the site of the assault, though, that felt downright dangerous. They'd be exposed if the guy showed up. Blake thought that was unlikely. The guy most likely had to work. He couldn't monitor them 24/7 unless he was working with a partner, which Blake doubted. But Alex might be irreversibly traumatized by being there or what she remembered, and he didn't want that.

He should talk to the shrink at U-Hills. If they went to the site, maybe the guy would go with them and be there if she needed help. Blake pulled out his phone and texted Kaye.

<I want to come by and talk to Alex, but I'm worried I might be tailed. Any thoughts on how to accomplish that?>

A few minutes later, she texted back. <I'll swing by the house later and pick her up. I'll have her wear the wig my friend left so she'll be less recognizable. I'll text you and you can come talk to her in one of Vice's interrogation rooms.>

<Thanks, text me when you're there.>

Blake sat at his desk for several moments then texted Alex.

<I'd like to talk to you about the case. Kaye will come by and pick you up, if you're willing to do it.>

He debated about apologizing again, but decided it was probably pointless and waited, hoping she'd text back and agree.

<When?>

<Today, not sure what time, she'll let you know.>

<Okay.>

Not very chatty, he thought irritably. He wasn't sure what he'd expected. He knew what he'd hoped for, some sort of reconciliation. But that was unlikely.

He dialed the shrink at U-Hills and explained what he wanted to do and asked whether Kendall would come, observe, and intervene, if needed.

"I'd like to meet with Alex first, establish some sort of relationship with her. Otherwise she may not trust me enough to listen if things get out of hand. It would be best if I could talk to her ahead of time in the interview room."

"Sure, that'd be fine." Blake hesitated. "Do you think this is a good idea?"

"Under normal circumstances, no, but with the escalated threat to her life it may be the only solution. According to you, she held up after viewing her sister's body, so at least talking to her would probably be safe."

"And the visit to the site of the assault?"

"Unknown. I'd like to accompany you, in case things go south."

"I'd appreciate that. I have no idea whether she'll remember anything or how it will affect her."

"Neither do I."

"I don't know what else to do, but it worries me."

"We do what we have to do, Detective."

"I guess so. I wonder though whether the collateral damage is worth it."

"Let's hope it's minor."

CHAPTER FORTY-TWO

"WHEN WE GET to the garage, I want you to keep your head down, so the wig's hair falls forward and helps obscure your face."

Alex nodded as she climbed into the passenger seat of Kaye's car. The wig was hot and itchy in places, and she couldn't wait to take it off.

Connie, who had remained at Kaye's house with Alex, had tried to reassure her, but she was on edge. Neither Blake nor Kaye had said what he wanted to talk to her about other than the case. What that meant was anyone's guess. If there'd been a break, if they'd caught the guy, surely one of them would have given her the good news.

When they arrived, Kaye hustled her into the precinct and up to an interview room like the one where she'd first met Sharon. It was still hard to think about her. Alex didn't have any concrete memories of her, a few hazy ones seemed to be trying to surface, but it had been clear that Sharon cared deeply for her and her sister. And now, because of her, Sharon was dead. Guilt and sadness washed over her for Sharon and her sister.

Blake entered the room with a man she didn't know. "Alex, this is Dr Kendall. He's the therapist I mentioned to you after you stopped seeing Caswell. I'd like to talk to you about the case and I asked him to be available if whatever we talk about…causes problems for you."

He wanted to take her hand but resisted. Hell, he wanted to hold her and reassure her that everything would be fine. And, if it wasn't, that he'd be there for her. But he couldn't, not with Kendall standing there.

"If you'd be willing, he'd like to talk to you before we get started and get to know you. Okay?" She looked worried but nodded. "I'll let you two talk, then."

He walked out of the interrogation room and into the observation room where he switched on the audio and video feeds and listened.

Kendall sat down after Blake left. "Alex, it's good to meet you. I'm Dave Kendall. I'm a therapist at one of the other precincts. Blake contacted me because of your suicide attempt and because you and Dr. Caswell apparently weren't a good match. I thought it might be helpful if we talked before he goes over the case with you."

Alex nodded. "I wasn't comfortable with her any longer." She fingered the edge of the now-small bandage on her wrist. "I know this sounds crazy, but I felt like the hypnosis caused this."

"Do you still have suicidal thoughts?"

"I'm not sure I did when I did this to myself." She saw the puzzled look on his face.

"It wasn't so much the thought that I wanted to kill myself as it was the thought that I had to cut my wrists—that doing that would end this limbo I'm in. I guess that's suicidal ideation. I can't explain it. With every session, I felt more hopeless and frightened. Like I had no choice."

"And now?"

"I have Blake's next-door neighbor, a nurse, to talk to, and that urge has lessened. As if the farther I get from the hypnosis sessions, the less pressing that idea is."

Alex ran her hands through her hair, relieved that she'd been able to take the wig off. It lay on the table where she had dropped it, looking like some sleeping animal.

"Remembering a few things about my sister and hearing what Sharon had to say has given me some hope that things will be better. But I'm still scared to know what I've forgotten about the assault."

"That's understandable. Seeing your sister must have been difficult and upsetting for you."

"It was, but it was also like a curtain going up. I remembered her, but nothing else. It was a relief to remember her, to know her, not just hear about her from Sharon Lowry." Alex took a deep breath. "And both of them are dead."

"What you've gone through has been very traumatizing, and your inability to remember may be a protective mechanism."

He leaned forward and rested his forearms on the table. "Normally, I would advise Detective Halloran not to pursue his idea. Forcing someone to try to remember can be risky. But the threat to you is very real, as I'm sure you know.

"I think that talking with Detective Halloran might help you remember and that would help him and his partner find this man and put a stop to him. Are you willing to take the risk?"

Alex nodded silently.

"I will be nearby. If you want or need me, ask. If you need to stop, ask. Detective Halloran has agreed to stop if you ask him to. Okay?"

Alex nodded again as Kendall stood up and moved to the door. "I'll let him know you're ready."

Kendall met Blake in the hallway. "I think she'll be fine, but I'd like to observe so I can intervene if needed," he said.

Blake nodded and took him to the observation room and turned everything back on. He hadn't mentioned observing their conversation. He hadn't asked permission, either, but he needed to know what had been said to be prepared for his conversation with Alex.

Kendall turned to him as Blake opened the door to leave. "If I think this is putting her at risk, I will put a stop to it. Understood?"

Blake nodded and closed the door. He approached the interrogation room door with the files clutched under his arm. He paused, taking a deep breath and blew it out before he opened the door and entered. Alex sat with her back to him and didn't turn. Sitting across from her, he didn't know what to say.

"So, what are we going to do?" she asked finally.

"I'd like to go over everything that we know so far, including how I found you the night of the assault. I'm hoping it may help you remember something we can use to find this guy."

Alex stared at him for several moments before she nodded her head and waited. Blake began by relating what they knew about Ashley Kensington. He showed her the police artist's sketch, hoping to make Ashley more real to Alex.

"I was thinking about her when you stumbled out onto the highway and I nearly hit you. As I told you, the way you were dressed made me think you were a prostitute. Your skirt was very short, and your top was pretty skimpy."

It made Blake uncomfortable telling her all the things he'd assumed about her, all the things that turned out to be untrue. But he had vowed to tell her everything and take the consequences.

"You'd taken a bad beating, and it looked like the person who assaulted you had tried to strangle you. I figured you'd picked up the wrong person and things had gotten out of control."

He watched her blush. "The cut on your index finger stuck in my head, and later I wondered if the same guy who had killed Ashley and cut off her fingertips had assaulted you. But I couldn't figure out why he'd stopped. I still haven't figured that out."

He went on to tell her about arriving at the hospital and finding out the cop who'd taken the report hadn't followed up.

"At the scene, the cop was belligerent with me, but not interested enough to follow up at the hospital. That puzzled me, and his attitude irritated me. It's why I requested your case be turned over to my partner and me. That and I thought you were connected to Ashley's murder. I'm not sure why I thought that, but I felt like it was my responsibility to find out what had happened."

He told her about returning to the culvert and searching it, finding the shoes but nothing else. She didn't flinch or act as if anything had jarred any memories loose. So, he cautiously laid out the morgue photos of Katia and Carla. They weren't pretty, and he was worried about showing them to her. Kendall was watching and listening. If something triggered her, he would be there for help.

Blake told her about finding them, about discovering her sister in the morgue. Alex sat impassively listening, showing no sign that anything was resonating for her.

"Eventually, I was introduced to a prostitute who had almost gone with the guy I think is the perp. He was in a black SUV and offered her a lot of money to go with him. She described him like you described the man who attacked you in your hotel room—large—but she saw him more clearly. Said he had black hair and blue eyes."

Blake paused, wondering whether what he was going to say would produce any sort of reaction. So far Alex had simply sat quietly and listened.

"She said he had tools on the front passenger seat. A wrench and a pair of cutting shears." There was an almost imperceptible flicker in Alex's eyes that made his pulse jump. "Does that mean anything to you?"

"I...no...it just made me think of Suzanne's fingers." She quickly swiped at her eyes with the back of her hand.

Blake wondered if that was all, but he continued. "She turned him down. He kept trying to pressure her into going with him until she walked off, and he left."

Alex glanced down at the healed cut on her index finger and absently ran a thumb over it. "You think he intended to cut off my fingertips but didn't for some reason?"

"I do."

"But you don't know why?"

"No. I have some ideas, but there's no way to tell until we catch him and ask. That's assuming he'll talk."

Blake sat back in the chair and gazed at her. She was pale and anxious, and he had no idea whether he was doing the right thing or not.

"I think he was interrupted somehow, like the night he got into your hotel room, and he cut his losses and left. I'm pretty sure he thought you were dead. Maybe, as long as you were dead, at that point it was irrelevant whether he cut off your fingertips or not. For some reason, he abandoned what he thought was a dead body rather than completing his ritual.

"His first mistake was assuming you were dead. His second mistake was not finishing you off in the hotel room. It wouldn't have taken much more effort to do it and leave before the manager appeared, but I think he didn't want to run the risk of being associated with the hotel if anyone saw him."

Alex flinched and Blake regretted his bluntness. He knew that memory was a fluid thing. It could be distorted over time and it was susceptible to leading questions or suggestions, but he hoped that Alex would recall something valuable that would help identify the guy who'd assaulted her.

"Does any of this mean anything or bring back any memories?"

"No. It breaks my heart about my sister and all the other women he's killed, but the only thing I actually remember is the hotel attack. Some memories about my sister seem to be coming back, but nothing else. I'm sorry, Blake." She looked pained.

He shook his head. "It's okay. I'd hoped that something might shake loose." He sighed. "If you remember anything text me, let me know."

"I will."

He stood up. "I'll let Kaye know we're done."

He wanted to hold her again, feel her relax into his arms, touch her, kiss her—something to help take away the anxiety and distress he saw in her face. But with Kendall watching from the observation room he couldn't.

He cleared his throat. "I'm sorry for what happened. I should have told you all of this before…"

Alex stood up and rested her hand on his arm. "I know you're sorry. You did what you'd been told to do. I understand that now."

He shrugged his shoulders. "Water under the bridge," he said and turned to the door. "I'll let Kaye know we're done."

He left and closed the door after him.

CHAPTER FORTY-THREE

"HOW DID THE meeting with Blake go?" Connie asked when Alex returned.

Alex shrugged. How did it go? It was hard to take in all the information and see the photos. It was hard to be in the same room with him. She could smell the subtle cologne he usually wore, but it was faint. He hadn't shaved that day, and his face had that distracted, closed-down look she knew meant he was struggling with something.

She wanted to wrap her arms around him and hold him, but she suspected that Kendall was observing them and listening. There was no two-way mirror, like you saw on TV, but she was sure that there was some way to record and observe what happened in these rooms. And she couldn't think of a way to bridge the gap between them that she'd created.

"It was unsettling and difficult to see the photos and listen to him talk about what had happened to those women," she said. "I don't know how he does that day after day. I can see why he's so frustrated. He and his partner haven't been able to discover much that would lead to an arrest. And other than the attack at the hotel, nothing came to me; nothing that would help."

She rubbed her neck and slumped down onto the couch that occupied the living room of Kaye's small basement apartment.

"What if I never remember anything? I feel like it's my fault now that these women are getting killed, because I can't remember the guy who assaulted me."

"Alex, try to think of it this way: if you hadn't survived, they'd be in the same predicament, only your name would be on the list of victims."

Connie sat down next to her. "Feeling guilty about something you have no control over is pointless."

"But I do. I have to remember *something*. If nothing else, at least what he looks like."

"The more pressure you put on yourself, the less likely you'll remember anything." She was quiet for a moment.

"It's like when I forget a word or a name or where I met someone. If I keep struggling to remember, I can't, but if I let it go and figure it'll come to me eventually then all of a sudden there it is."

Alex leaned back on the couch and sighed. "I'm exhausted. I feel wrung out after seeing and hearing about all of that."

"Let's eat, I fixed dinner. Then you can go to bed and get some rest."

"I'm not really hungry."

"I'm sure you're not but eat at least some of it. You need it."

———◆———

SINCE LISTENING to Sharon and viewing her sister's body, Alex had the sense that something wanted to surface, some memory or some information. It was like Connie had said, though, the harder she tried to search for it, or get it to materialize the further it receded. Over the last few days thoughts of Caswell's office and working with her kept surfacing, but they made her uneasy, so she'd forced them away.

She had tossed and turned in bed for more than an hour, sleep elusive. Eventually, she used the relaxation techniques Caswell had taught her and finally dropped off to sleep.

She stood in Caswell's office. It was dark and being there frightened her. Something was here, something she needed to find or remember, but she had no idea what it might be.

"You can't help solve the murders, because you don't remember."

Alex whirled around and saw Caswell sitting behind her desk.

"Living the rest of your life without any memories except what you know since the accident—I'm not sure how you stand it."

"What's here that I need to know?"

Caswell smiled, but it was more of a grimace. "I can't tell you. This is a dream, Alex. I'm not real."

Alex turned around again, searching the room and the bookshelves, until her gaze returned to the desk where Caswell no longer sat. She had disappeared. Alex turned around again searching the room for…something. As her gaze fell on the desk, she found her sister sitting where Caswell had been.

"Lexie." A warm memory of her sister using the nickname only Suz had used washed over her.

"I don't know how to remember what I've forgotten. Tell me if you know."

"I can't tell you, Lexie. It's like the shrink said, I'm not real."

Her sister disappeared and left Alex standing alone in Caswell's office. Alone and afraid.

———◆———

"NOTHING. NOT one fucking memory." Blake scrubbed his face. It was late. He and Stevens had been poring over the case files since Alex had left with Kaye, and he wanted nothing more than to lay his head down on his desk and sleep.

"I have no idea where to go from here. Kendall says to let her think about it for a day or two and then maybe take her to the culvert."

"That's what I'd do," Stevens said. "Any word from Frost?"

"No, it was his suggestion to talk to her and take her to the culvert. Frost also said, based on what I told him, he wasn't sure he'd come up with anything. He said he'd call if he found something."

Blake rested his chin on his hand, elbow on his desktop, and closed his eyes. It wasn't until Stevens spoke that he realized he'd fallen asleep.

"Yo, Halloran!" Blake jerked awake. Stevens was standing by his desk, ready to leave. "Go home and get some sleep. That's what I intend to do."

Blake shook his head. "Christ, I'm so tired I'm not sure I could drive home without falling asleep. I think I'll go down to the bunk room and sleep for a while."

"Well, wherever you do it, get some sleep. We can start this again in the morning. See you then," Stevens said with a huge yawn.

In the bunk room, Blake stretched out on one of the lower twin bunk beds that filled the room. The mattress wasn't all that comfortable, but tonight—or he guessed it was morning now—he could probably sleep on the floor and it wouldn't have been a problem.

———◆———

OH GOD, now what? he thought, hearing his phone ring. He fumbled for it in his jacket pocket that he'd hooked over the bed post. It was nearly four in the morning and he'd only been asleep for three hours.

"H'lo?" He couldn't muster the energy to say his name.

"Blake?"

"Mm-hum," he mumbled, then realized it was Alex, which brought him to full alert. "Are you okay?"

"I'm fine. I'm sorry to wake you, but…"

"But, what? Did you remember something?"

"I'd like to get into Caswell's office. Can you do that? Can you get into her office?"

He must really be tired, he thought she'd asked to break into Caswell's office. "*What?*"

"Her office. I want to get in and look around. Can you get in without her knowing?"

"Why d'you want to do that?"

"There's something there, something that relates to what's happening, but I don't know what it might be. That's why I called so late. I figure she won't be there and I could look around. I might find something or remember whatever it is."

Blake rubbed his face. How the hell would he get into Caswell's office? He was sure it was locked because of all the private patient files.

"Christ, I don't know how we'd get in. I can't pick locks."

"Oh, I sort of thought you might know how."

Blake laughed. "I'm a cop, not a criminal."

"My dad always said there was a fine line between…the two. Huh, that was unexpected."

"Looks like things are gradually coming back." He yawned. The sound of her voice made him wish she was lying next to him, that he could just hold her close and…sleep. At last he said, "I'll have to think of a way to get into her office. But in the meantime, would you be willing to go to the site where I found you?"

He heard the hesitation in her voice. "Now?"

"Well, it was dark, not this late, but dark when I nearly hit you. Maybe visiting the site would help you remember something. But only if you're willing to do it."

"Will it help?"

"I don't know, but it's worth a try."

"Are you coming over now?"

"Yeah, I'll snag an unmarked car and text Kaye."

"No. don't wake her up. I can come out of the basement entrance. Text me when you get here."

"Wait until I get to the door of the apartment."

———◆———

ALEX LEFT a note to let Connie and Kaye know she was with Blake. He took her elbow and hustled her out to a maroon sedan, whose interior lights had been disabled. They were silent as he drove off and made his way to Sixth Avenue and headed west.

The sky was beginning to lighten, but it was still somewhat dark when they arrived. Blake retrieved his Maglite.

"Stay in the car until I make sure we're at the site. I'll come get you."

Alex nodded and tried to scan the surrounding area. There was a large rise behind the culvert that looked like a hill made of stacked boulders. It tapered on either end and made her think of a dinosaur's back, which added to her unease. A vague memory of darkness and pain and nausea washed over her. She closed her eyes and waited for it to pass.

Blake approached the back of the car and made his way to the passenger side as Alex opened the door. "We're close—it's a couple hundred feet behind us."

He reached out and took hold of her arm to guide her. She'd worn the tennis shoes he'd bought her and was glad of it when they arrived at the edge of the highway. It had lightened more, and she could vaguely see that the way into the culvert was steep and strewn with rocks.

"I-I don't think I can do this." She pulled back from him.

He grasped her shoulders and said, "Alex, please, unless you just can't manage it, please help me."

She closed her eyes, breathing him in, and after a moment nodded. "Don't let go of me on the way down. I feel a little shaky."

They made their way slowly, slipping and sliding part way until they reached the bottom. Flashes of being carried, feeling the person carrying her slip as she and Blake had done, hit her and made her shudder. By now it was nearly six a.m., and there was enough daylight to see the culvert clearly. Alex stood still and looked around, trying to clear her mind and not let the urgency she'd heard in Blake's voice add to her anxiety.

It was cool, the day's heat hadn't arrived yet. She closed her eyes and listened, breathed in the grassy dirt smell that had been churned up by their descent. Before Blake could prevent it, she dropped to her hands and knees, and moaned.

She was enveloped by cold and dark, pain and nausea washed over her. She was violently ill, losing the dinner Connie had encouraged her to eat.

Blake knelt down next to her, wiping his hand across her mouth and cleaning it on the grass. "Alex, talk to me. What's happening?"

"Hurt—I hurt so bad," she whispered as she swayed on her hands and knees, her head hanging down. "Scared. Have to get out of here. So sick."

He wrapped his arm around her waist and pulled her up to her knees and into him. "I'm here, you're safe. Talk to me."

A face swam into her head, a face that terrified her. She flashed back on him grabbing her around the neck with one large hand that felt like a vise and she clawed at it. She struggled, but her vision was dimming as she saw him pull something from between the seats of the SUV and swing it at her.

Alex threw her hands up to shield her face and head, cried out as if she was anticipating pain, and then collapsed against Blake and fainted. His anxious face hovered over her when she regained consciousness.

"Oh, Jesus! Wake up, Alex," she heard him say. When she opened her eyes he said, "Christ, what happened? Are you okay?"

She blinked and raised her hands, feeling around on her head looking for an injury that was no longer there. She reached up and touched his face reassuring herself that he was real.

"He hit me with something. We…we'd been talking about my sister while he drove. He was heading out of the city, he said she was staying at his house. We were out in the middle of nowhere. I was getting worried. Suddenly he pulled over, said he had to pee, but instead he grabbed my neck. I clawed at his hand, trying to get him to let go, but he didn't. I saw him pull something from between the seats, and he swung it at me. I tried to protect my head, but couldn't."

She held her head with her hands but saw Blake's eyes widen suddenly. "I don't remember much. I remember being carried down, I guess, into this culvert, and dropped onto the ground. I-I don't remember anything after that except a woman's voice in my head urging me to wake up and find help. I think I was conscious for a few moments and then…nothing. I remember coming to in so much pain and being cold and sick."

Blake pulled her gently into a sitting position and held her hands. "His face, do you remember it? At all?"

"Like the woman you talked to said, he was big. With black hair and blue eyes. His hand…it was so large it nearly encircled my neck." Her hand went involuntarily to her neck where the bruises had finally disappeared.

"Would you recognize him?"

She shuddered. "I'll never forget him now. I wish that I could."

"Did he give you a name? Anything?"

"He said his name was Bobby, but I didn't think it was. I don't know why." She paused and closed her eyes for a moment.

"When we talked on the street earlier, he said Suzanne had gone with him a few nights before. He'd taken her to his home and let her stay. He said he felt sorry for her. He said if I was looking for her, if I was her sister, he'd take me there.

"I was an idiot. I went with him. I was so anxious to find her I went with him. The thought crossed my mind that I didn't think Suz would go to a stranger's home, but she'd changed so much, and he seemed like a nice guy. He looked so…normal. I went with him."

"I want you to work with a sketch artist so we can get a picture of him."

She watched him. He seemed fired up about something. "What is it? What do you know?"

"I don't want to say, not until I'm sure. What do you think is in Caswell's office?"

"I don't know. I keep thinking about being there. I dreamt I was searching for something." She shrugged her shoulders. "It's probably some stupid dream metaphor for searching for my memory, but I'd like to look in her office. Can we get in?"

He huffed out a breath. "I don't know. Not during the day for sure. I don't want anyone to know about it and I don't want her surprising us. Maybe tonight. I've got to find someone who can get us in and keep their mouth shut."

CHAPTER FORTY-FOUR

H E FELT AS if he was jonesing for drugs. The adrenaline was coursing through him as he drove her back to Kaye's. They let themselves in through the basement door to face both Connie and Kaye.

"Where the hell have you two been?" Kaye demanded. "You scared the shit out of Connie when she realized you were gone and came and got me."

"I left the note," Alex said, indicating the note lying on the table.

"Which you could have been forced to write. And neither of you answered your phones."

"I took her to the culvert, and I turned both phones to silent to avoid the noise while we were out there. I forgot to turn them back on," Blake said, fishing his phone out of his pocket and turning the sound back on.

"You should have texted me. I was about to send out an APB to find the two of you. Jesus, Halloran, what were you thinking?"

"I'm sorry. I wanted to get her out there while it was still slightly dark."

"Did you set this up yesterday and not tell me?" Kaye was getting increasingly angry.

"No," Alex said. "No, Kaye, he didn't. I called him around four this morning to ask a favor, and he suggested it."

Kaye thrust her index finger at Blake. "Do not pull a stunt like that on me again, you hear me?"

Blake nodded. He took Alex aside and, with his back to Kaye and Connie, said, "I'll leave you to Connie. Thank you…I…" He was at a loss for what to say.

She'd been so brave, he thought. Brave enough to do something that terrified her. He searched her face. She watched him with those trusting green eyes, waiting for him to finish. He reached out to tuck a strand of hair behind her ear and, letting his hand drift, he cupped her cheek and ran his thumb over her lower lip.

Realizing what he'd done, he turned abruptly and said to Kaye, "I need to talk to you upstairs." And he headed for the stairway, followed by Kaye.

———•◆•———

"WHAT THE hell is going on, Halloran? What was that cozy little scene down there?"

"Nothing is going on. She had a hard time out there, a really hard time, but she toughed it out and gave me something that may help me break this case. So, back off."

Kaye watched him with arms crossed over her chest and the frown still in place. "What d'you want to talk to me about?"

"I need you to keep this quiet, but I need to get into Caswell's office tonight when she's gone and things are quiet."

He saw her eyebrows shoot up in surprise. "You want to get in her office without her knowing? What the fuck?"

"Alex thinks there's something in there that would help. I want her to have a chance to look around, without Caswell's interference or knowledge." He squirmed a little, seeing the look on her face.

"I was hoping you'd know how, or you'd know someone who knows how to pick locks. Someone who could teach me. I don't want to involve anyone else. I don't want anyone to get in trouble if this backfires."

"Which it most likely will. Jesus. You don't ask much, do you?" She leaned up against her kitchen counter and thought for a moment.

"I know someone, but you'd have to know what kind of lock she has. He can't teach you all the tricks for all locks in one go around, but he could probably teach you enough to get in, if he knows what kind of lock it is."

"I'll find out. I'll text you. Tell him I'll meet him wherever he wants if he'll help. What'll it cost me?"

"He owes me some favors. I'll call them in and let you know." She eyed him and shook her head. "You're fucking nuts. You know that, don't you?"

He grinned. "Have been for a while, but if this gets me the collar on this creep, I'll risk it."

He headed for the door and heard Kaye ask, "Are you in love with her?"

He didn't turn or answer her. *I guess I am*, he thought as he headed out the door. *Fuck me. I would pick the one woman who doesn't want me.*

———◆———

WITH ALEX occupied talking to the sketch artist, he'd met the guy who called himself Pickman and showed him a photo of Caswell's door lock. He hoped the guy could teach him how to open the lock easily but didn't have high hopes.

"Cool, it's a pin tumbler lock. Those are easy."

Two hours later, he had yet to get a similar lock open. Easy apparently was relative. "Fuck, this is hopeless," he said, sitting back on his heels.

"You keep putting too much pressure on the tension wrench. It's subtle. You haven't got a feel for it yet. Here, insert the wrench again and let me guide your hand."

The guy waited until Blake had inserted one of the small tools he'd shown Blake how to use and placed his hand over Blake's and gently pushed down. It didn't really look or feel like he'd put any tension on it, and Blake finally understood what he needed to do. He wished the guy had done this earlier.

"Now insert the pick rake all the way back and work your way out, using it on each tumbler. I'll show you." With his hand once again over Blake's he demonstrated how to do it, and the lock opened.

"It'd be easier if I had you do it, but I don't want you getting arrested if we're caught."

"Thanks, Halloran," the guy said with a laugh. "I'd rather not have that happen either. Now do it by yourself and let's see if you can open it."

Several more attempts were unsuccessful, but at last Blake managed to unlock the door.

"See, you can do it. Now keep practicing a few more times and I think you'll be set. If you're gonna do this, do it when as few people are around as possible and you won't be in a rush. The first few actual jobs are pretty nerve wracking and it takes longer."

Blake nodded, and did it again several times before deciding he was as ready as he'd ever be and stood up. "I really appreciate this. If you ever need a favor—other than helping you commit a crime—let me know."

"Will do, and good luck."

———————◆———————

BACK AT the precinct he went to the room where the sketch artist and Alex were working and talking. Alex watched over the woman's shoulder, commenting periodically on her sketch. They were so involved in it that they didn't look up until he spoke.

"Can I steal her for a few minutes?"

"Sure, we should take a break anyway. I'll go grab a coffee across the street. You guys want one?"

When she left with their orders, Blake sat down in the chair opposite Alex. He chose not to look at the drawing for a lot of reasons, but mostly to avoid getting his hopes dashed. He was pretty sure who the perp was, but he wanted to wait until he could see the finished drawing.

"I am now minimally skilled in picking the lock that Caswell has on her office door," he said with a grin.

"We're going to have to go to her office after midnight, so there are fewer people here. Fortunately, because of the reasons for cops to visit her, there are no cameras in that hallway, and her office is somewhat isolated. The restrooms are down the hall, though, so there'll be people showing up periodically."

Alex nodded. Pale with dark circles under her eyes, she looked as tired as he felt. Neither had gotten much sleep because of the trip to the culvert. She had been able to sleep for a couple of hours until Kaye brought her into the precinct, but Blake hadn't bothered. He was unshaven and still in the clothes he'd worn yesterday.

"I need to get you up to Caswell's office without anyone recognizing you, so it's good you've got the wig, you'll need it later. I plan to cuff you. I'll take you up the back stairs to avoid as many people as possible. I'll take the cuffs off when we get to Caswell's hallway. If we're seen, people will think you're a suspect."

She bit her lip and her brows drew together, clearly anxious. "Okay. Then what?"

"I'm going to put you by the end of the hall, and I need you to warn me if you see or hear anyone coming. Warn me and then go into the women's restroom and into a stall. If someone sees you, hopefully, won't get a good look at you."

He exhaled tiredly. "I'll work as quickly as I can, but I'm not great at lock picking yet. We may have to abandon it if I can't get it open quickly."

She frowned. "I wish I didn't have to ask you to do this. How much trouble will it cause if we get caught?"

"Let's not go there, let's just get this done." He rubbed his eyes. He felt as if there was sand in them. "I have to get some sleep. I'm going down to the bunk room and try to get a few hours."

He took in her face, lingering on her eyes and then her lips, and sighed. "You look tired. I'll text Kaye when you're done here, and she can take you to the women's bunk room. Get some sleep. I'd save the coffee until it's time to wake up. It'll be cold, but the caffeine will help. I'll text you when it's time."

He was about to say more, when the artist arrived with the coffees, so he left. Arriving at his desk, he told Stevens he was going down to try to sleep.

"Sleep? I thought you did that last night."

"I tried, but Alex called me about four a.m., and we ended up going out to the culvert."

Stevens looked surprised. "She remember anything?"

"Yeah, I about had heart failure when she did. It was pretty traumatic for her, but she's working with the sketch artist now and we'll get an idea what he looks like. So that's something."

"Good job. Go sleep. You earned it. I'll let you know if anything comes up."

CHAPTER FORTY-FIVE

SWEAT COLLECTED ON his forehead and in his armpits. He'd been working on the fucking lock for five minutes now, and it was like he'd forgotten everything Pickman had taught him. He stopped to swipe his forearm across his forehead to keep the sweat from running into his eyes.

You can do this. Take a minute and calm down, then just do it, he told himself as he took a deep breath, wiped his palms on his slacks, and slipped the tension wrench into the lock and began again. Minutes later he felt the last tumbler give and he opened the door.

He motioned for Alex to come and used his shirt tail to wipe the lock, door handle, and the area around it of any prints he'd left. As they entered the office, he closed the door and pulled two pair of gloves out of his pocket, turning back and again wiping the interior door handle.

"Put these on before you touch anything," he said quietly. "I'll close the blinds and then we can turn on the desk lamp."

When she had the gloves on, he handed her a small pocket flashlight. "I don't want to turn the overheads on, so use this to look around."

Alex began going around the room, examining the shelves, glancing at the book titles, and carefully scrutinizing the odds and ends Caswell had on the shelves. Nothing triggered any recognition.

"Maybe there's something in her desk," she whispered to Blake,

Blake moved around to the desk and tried the drawers. All were locked. He sighed. "I'll give it a try and see if I can get them open." He sat down in the desk chair and inserted the first tool into the lock on the pencil drawer.

A few minutes later he crowed, quietly, "Got you, you bastard!" and pulled the drawer open. He turned to Alex. "Here, sit down and go through it. See if anything pops for you."

Alex sat down and her eyes widened when she spotted a face-down photo frame after removing some papers. She pulled it out and turned it over.

"Blake, it's him! I remember now! This photo was sitting on her desk. I only got a quick look at it, but she saw me look. She apologized. She said she never left family photos out for clients to see and she put it in her desk. He's the guy!"

Blake snatched the photo from her and peered at it. Kyle Fucking Jeffries. He'd been right. It explained Caswell's determination to be involved with Alex, and it lent credence to Alex's worries that the suggestions given to her during the hypnosis weren't for her benefit. He pulled his phone out and took a picture of the photo.

"Let's go," he said, slipping the photo into the drawer, face-down as Alex had found it, shuffling papers over it and sliding the drawer shut.

"How're you going to lock it again?"

"I'm not, and it doesn't matter. We'll bring him in under arrest, and we'll bring her in for questioning before she has a chance to come into her office. The outer door will lock automatically. If for some reason she beats us here she may think she forgot to lock the desk drawer. We have the sketch, so neither of us has to admit being in here."

He wracked his brain, then stood up. "We found the photo without a search warrant, so it can't officially be used in evidence. But with the sketch and your memory of her telling you he's family, I can get a warrant to search her office and find it legally."

He stood up and caught her hand, pulled her into a hug, and said, "You're amazing, you broke the case! God, I love you!" That had slipped out without him thinking, so he said brusquely, "Let's go before we get caught."

She stared at him in surprise, her hand rising to cover her mouth for a moment, and then nodded. They left the office quietly, cautiously walking down the hall to the stairwell. When they arrived at Blake's desk in Homicide, he texted Stevens.

<I need you to come in now. I've got an ID on the suspect.>

A few minutes later his phoned pinged.

<Are you kidding me? Never mind, I'm on my way.>

When Stevens arrived, Blake showed him the sketch and then the photo he'd taken with his phone.

"Okay so they look alike. Who is he?"

"Kyle Jeffries."

"Who's Kyle Jeffries?"

"The cop who showed up after I nearly hit Alex. The cop who never showed up at the hospital, probably because he was afraid Alex would recognize him before he could kill her. He's Caswell's family member. She admitted it to Alex. He's gotta be her son."

Stevens' eyebrows shot up then he narrowed his eyes. "Where did you get this photo?"

"I'd rather not say."

Stevens rolled his eyes and moaned. "We can't use it if you got it without a warrant."

"I know, but we've got the sketch and Alex's ID. Let's get an arrest warrant and bring Jeffries in for questioning. She'll get wind of it, and my guess is she'll show up to find out what's going on. We need to ask for a search warrant for her office, then we can get it legally."

"Once she gets wind of him being brought in, she may destroy the photo."

"Doesn't matter. She told Alex he was her family member. My guess is she'll show up and tell us he's her son, want to see him, and we can interrogate her." Blake was pumped. Alex stood nearby and watched him quietly.

"We need search warrants for Jeffries' home, car, and locker at his precinct, and we need one for Caswell's office, car, and home. Who knows whether she knows what he's been doing, but I bet she does."

Blake paced in front of his desk. "My guess is that's why she was so keen on working with Alex. That way she could keep an eye on what Alex was remembering. I think she planted suggestions that Alex wouldn't remember anything and she may have pushed her to try to commit suicide."

"I'll send some uniforms to find him, pick him up, and bring him in. You take care of the arrest warrant and the search warrants."

Stevens sat down at his desk and began making phone calls. "If she doesn't show up after he's brought in, I'll have her picked up as well. I'm going to station a uniform outside her office in case she shows up before we bring her in."

Alex turned to Blake. "I want to listen when they're interrogated."

"I can't let you do that. I don't want to give a defense lawyer any way to throw any of this out. Your testimony as a victim and a witness can't be tainted by listening to the interrogation." He picked his phone up off his desk and texted something.

"I'm going to have Kaye take your official statement and then take you back to her place." He hesitated. "I'll fill you in as much as I can when I'm done."

Alex nodded. "Once he's arrested and in custody, can Connie and I come back to the apartment?"

"Yeah, in fact I'll take both of you back when this is done. You may have to stay at Kaye's another night. These things can take time."

CHAPTER FORTY-SIX

JEFFRIES LAWYERED UP immediately after he was brought in and sat in the interrogation room, waiting for the lawyer to arrive. Before Jeffries had arrived, Stevens had insisted Blake go home, shower, shave, and put on clean clothes. It had been a good idea. He'd caught a whiff of himself as he undressed and realized he desperately needed a shower.

"You smell better," Stevens said with a laugh when Blake got back.

Blake rolled his eyes. "Thanks. Has Caswell shown up yet?"

"Not yet. Jeffries used his one phone call to contact the lawyer, so mom may not know about it yet. I've got a uniform stationed at her office door. He'll escort her down when she shows up."

Stevens flashed some papers in his face. "The search warrants arrived. I've got people waiting near his place to conduct the search. I'm going to wait until the lawyer shows up to serve Jeffries with his. Don't want him saying we violated his rights for some reason."

He yawned. "We can serve Caswell when she gets here. I've asked the crime scene bunch to go with both search teams to help collect and handle any evidence that shows up."

Blake nodded, and watched Jeffries via video in the observation room. The guy didn't move or shift in the chair. He didn't pace or act bored or frustrated. He sat quietly, his face closed off and impossible to read. He wouldn't be an easy nut to crack. But they had witnesses, and they would get DNA and hair samples for analysis to compare against the evidence they currently had. They'd go over his black SUV with a fine-toothed comb and maybe, just maybe, he'd kept trophies.

He might not confess, but they had enough to arrest and convict him. The ADA assigned to the case had reviewed it and agreed it was convincing evidence. With Alex's ID, it would probably make for an easy conviction.

"How long's he been like that?" Blake asked.

"Since he arrived about an hour ago and I escorted him in there. His butt must be numb by now."

"You brought in the women I talked to, right? And got their statements? Did they see the sketch and ID Jeffries?"

"Yep, both of them."

"Good. What's our approach to him? I doubt he'll confess and throw himself on our mercy."

"I'm gonna sit back and let you handle the interrogation. You've got history with him, and neither of you likes the other. I figure you'll be able to piss him off and maybe get him to slip and say something before his lawyer can muzzle him."

Blake nodded, and continued to watch Jeffries. The coldness radiated off him. *Psychopath*, he thought. Almost as if he'd heard the thought or sensed Blake watching him, he looked up at where the camera and sound equipment was installed and smiled, then resumed his stoic position again.

Yep, psychopath, Blake thought. *He's enjoying playing the game. We'll see who wins the game, asshole.*

———— ◆ ————

"MY CLIENT and I want an explanation for why he was brought here for interrogation."

Blake and Stevens had walked in and sat opposite Jeffries and his lawyer. Blake carried the case files with him. Stevens reported who was present and read Jeffries his rights.

"Pretty sure your client knows exactly why he's here. But for your benefit, because I'm sure he hasn't told you, he's here under suspicion of murdering six women and attempting to murder another, twice," Blake said.

"That's outrageous! What proof do you have?"

Blake waved a dismissive hand at the lawyer. "We'll get to that, keep your pants on."

He'd said it intentionally and could see that the lawyer was pissed. Jeffries sat without comment. Blake stared at him until he looked away, smirking as he did so.

"Do you pick up prostitutes, Kyle?"

"To arrest them."

"Not on your off time?"

"No."

"Interesting. I have two women who will testify that you did indeed try to pick them up and offered a fairly large sum of money if they'd come with you."

"Prostitutes lie all the time. Next question."

"Why didn't you follow up with the assault victim, the woman I nearly ran over three weeks ago on Highway 93?"

"I didn't have time to before you jumped in and did my job for me and then had the case sent to you." It was clear that it still rankled him.

"You had plenty of time to go to the hospital that night, get fingerprints, collect evidence, get a statement before I ever showed up. It was your case. Why didn't you do that?"

"I got called to another accident."

Blake shot him a self-satisfied smile. "Mistake number one,

which you should know: Don't lie during a police investigation. There was no other call that pulled you away, we've checked. In fact, your shift was over when the 911 call came in. Kind of above and beyond the call of duty, wouldn't you say?"

Jeffries sat without comment, listening to his lawyer whisper in his ear. He looked at Blake and said nothing.

"At the time, I figured you were a lazy son of a bitch and couldn't be bothered. One of those cops who just puts in the minimum required. Then I thought perhaps you had been called away, but it turns out I was right. You're lazy and careless.

"There's no need for that, Detective."

Blake ignored him and continued. "There was another reason you didn't go, wasn't there?"

"I have no idea what you're talking about. I figured I'd get to it when I had time."

He smirked. "She was a prostitute, probably got worked over by her john, so no point in exerting myself. She wouldn't be able to ID the guy, they never can. It'd keep till I got around to it."

"No, that wasn't the reason. You knew she could identify you as the man who'd tried to kill her, and you didn't want her to see you."

"That's ridiculous, Detective," the lawyer began.

"No, it's not. We have the assault victim's statement that your client, Kyle here, is the man who assaulted her. And we have two other witnesses who back up the fact that Kyle was picking up women on his personal time."

"She didn't tell you shit. She can't remember anything. She probably made it up."

Blake raised his eyebrows. "How'd you hear she was amnesic? From Mommy?"

He could see the anger flare in Jeffries' eyes, but he said nothing. "We have your mother in interrogation, and we're executing a search warrant on her office and home."

Blake reached into his jacket pocket and pulled out the warrant. "Oh, by the way, here's the search warrant for your house, car, and work locker," Blake said, holding out the paper, which the lawyer snatched out of his hand and reviewed with Jeffries.

"Don't answer any further questions. He's fishing, and we're done here." The lawyer began to stand up.

"You might want to sit down. We have a warrant, based on evidence we've accumulated and witness statements, for your client's arrest on six counts of murder in the first degree and two counts of attempted murder of a witness." Blake waited and Jeffries said nothing. His lawyer sat down.

"You may want to rethink some of your answers, Kyle."

"You can call me Jeffries, not Kyle." It was the first glimpse of anger, and Blake intended to get more.

"Nah, I like Kyle. It's friendlier. So, Kyle, back to my question. How'd you hear she was amnesic?"

Jeffries eyed him coldly for several minutes. "It was all over the news. Hard to keep something like that secret, especially since you put her up at a hotel. Did you have fun with her while she was there?"

Blake laughed. "Good try! One point for trying to piss me off." He flipped through several files, and finally pulled the sketch out, leaving it lying on the table for all to see.

"I didn't have fun, as you put it, but you showed up for some when you broke into her hotel room and tried to strangle her again. What's the matter, Kyle? Losing your touch? You fucked up both times and left her alive, and now, she's ID'd you. Guess you need to work on your strangling skills."

Jeffries said nothing, but he was clearly pissed by the look on his face.

"Mommy didn't tell you she had insinuated herself into interviewing and providing therapy for the victim? Or that she talked the victim into undergoing hypnosis so she could plant suggestions that the witness not remember seeing your photo on Mommy's desk?"

"You're fucking nuts. And it's Dr. Caswell to you."

He really didn't like the disrespect. "Mommy didn't keep you apprised of the victim's amnesia status so you'd know if she was remembering things that might incriminate you?"

"Where do you get this shit?"

"From your mommy, Kyle." That was a lie, but Jeffries didn't know it.

"My mother wouldn't say anything like that to you assholes."

"But she has, and we'll be going over her texts and phone calls to you. We have your phone in evidence. When we look through it, I'm sure there'll be corroboration."

Jeffries laughed. "Look away, dickhead. There's nothing on either phone."

"Why? Because neither of you are stupid enough to leave evidence?"

Jeffries smiled at him and said nothing.

"I get why you cut their fingertips off—made IDing them hard. None of them were raped. With them being prostitutes, that didn't make a whole lot of sense, but I wonder why you killed them in the first place." He saw the lawyer blanch.

"I think it's because you can't get it up with a regular woman, and then discovered you couldn't get it up with a prostitute either. That's got to piss a guy off." Blake smiled insultingly at him.

"I mean, it must be maddening when you pay for it, pay someone whose only job is to get you off, and you can't manage it."

Anger flared in his eyes. "I would never have sex with a prostitute. They're filthy and despicable. They're not worthy of anything other than…"

"Than what, Kyle? Killing them?" Jeffries remained quiet. "Who's worthy of your attention? Mommy? Does she take care of that issue for you? Is she the only one you can get it up for?"

Blake was intentionally trying to piss him off. And realized, too late to stop it, that he'd done a great job as Jeffries lunged across the table and grabbed him around the neck.

"You shut your mouth, you piece of shit."

Stevens grabbed him and hollered for the uniform outside the door, and between them they managed to pull Jeffries off Blake.

"You're fucking that piece of trash you're protecting. Don't you dare insult my mother!"

"I guess we'll add assaulting an officer to the charges," Blake croaked as he massaged his neck.

"I think I've heard enough." Stevens said pulling his cuffs off his belt. "Kyle Jeffries, you're under arrest for murder, six counts, attempted murder, two counts, and assaulting a superior officer. Put your hands behind your back."

Stevens cuffed him and walked him to the door, handing him over to the officer who'd come in to help. "Take him and book him. Let me know when it's done. You can go with him if you want," he said to the lawyer, who followed Jeffries out of the room.

He closed the door and turned to Blake. "You okay?"

Blake nodded. "Neck's a little tender, but I'm fine. Let's tackle mommy dearest."

"You want a break? Maybe get some coffee before we question her? The longer she has to wait the more anxious she'll be."

"Only if you want me to do the interrogation."

"Let's get some coffee."

CHAPTER FORTY-SEVEN

THEY'D BARELY GOTTEN down two floors on the back stairs when cops started rushing past them with weapons drawn.

Blake grabbed one by the arm. "What the fuck's going on?"

"There's a problem in booking. A suspect is armed." He pulled away and continued his rapid descent, leaving Blake and Stevens following in his wake. They reached booking a few minutes later, to see Jeffries with a gun held to the head of the cop who'd escorted him to booking.

Blake stepped into the booking area, feeling Stevens grab at his arms and miss.

Jeffries saw him and grinned. "Glad you could make it, asshole. I was hoping you'd show up."

"You know you're not going to get out of here. Put the gun down and let Carson go."

"Nope, that's not how it's going to work. What's going to happen is all of you are going to stand down and let me walk out of here, or Carson gets his brains splattered all over you."

"And you'll be dead the minute you do that."

Jeffries laughed. "Well, I've got nothing to lose at this point. See, I don't give a fuck what happens to him or me at this point.

But I figure you guys do. I figure you don't want ol' Carson here to be splattered all over intake, and the only way that's not going to happen is if you let me go."

"You're going nowhere. You're an idiot if you think you'll walk out of this." Blake heard Stevens suck in a breath.

"Christ's sake, Halloran, don't piss him off," he hissed.

"Idiot, huh? Had you chasing your tail for a good long while, till you got that whore to remember."

"I'm curious, why didn't you kill her the first time?"

Jeffries shook his head. "I thought I had. I strangled her in the truck and hit her with my wrench and she went out. I carried her down the ravine and was getting ready to cut her fingertips off, when a cop car pulled up at the top of the ravine with its lights flashing. Guess the cop saw the SUV at the side of the road and figured it should be checked out."

"All you had to do was stay quiet and he'd have left."

"No, no I couldn't. I could see him sweeping his flashlight over the SUV. He ran his hand over the hood, it was still warm, so he knew the driver couldn't be far. I left her there. I thought she was dead, I didn't have time to make sure. I walked a few hundred feet away from her in case he heard me and shined the light down."

He looked around the room. "Tell them to back off," he said, indicating two cops who had started to move closer. Blake motioned them back.

"I unzipped my jeans and started up the culvert, zipping them up. Told the cop when I got to the top, that I'd had to take a leak." Jeffries looked irritated.

"Moron said next time I should put my hazard lights on, because it was hard to see my black SUV on the side of the road. Then he asked about my hand. The bitch had scratched it pretty badly. I told him I worked at a vet hospital and one of the animals had scratched me while I was holding it for the vet."

"You could have gone back to finish your little ritual with the fingers after he left."

"He wouldn't leave, said he'd wait for me to take off. I didn't like the way it felt, so I left and decided not to return. I thought she was dead, and at that point it wasn't worth coming back to do her fingers. Turns out it didn't matter, you couldn't find her prints in the system."

"Mommy tell you that?"

"Dr. Caswell to you, asshole." He pushed the gun tighter against Carson's temple and Blake saw the man flinch.

"I returned to the station, not sure why really, but I was unsettled and being in uniform makes me feel good. I changed and left in a cruiser. I had been driving around for about an hour when I heard dispatch call for assistance on the 911 call. I responded and said I'd investigate it."

"Must have been a surprise to find she'd made it out of the culvert, and bad luck to you that a cop was the one who found her."

"Yeah, the stupid bitch has been lucky. Got lucky in the hotel as well. She put up quite a fight and that asshole across the hall called the manager, so I took off."

He frowned. "My luck, on the other hand, hasn't been so great. The bugs didn't work like my mother thought they would—never got a lot of information, then they quit working. Even Mom's suggestions to her under hypnosis didn't work like we planned.

"I thought the woman in your car was her. Just no fucking luck once I picked her up. I should have gone back and made sure she was dead. Mom was pissed, said I should never have talked to her in the first place or left her alive at the hotel. She said none of this would have happened if I hadn't decided to tell her about her sister. I was worried she'd connect with the women who'd seen me, or maybe one of them had seen me pick her sister up, so I took her with me."

"Why'd you do it? All the women? Why?"

"I did it for my mother."

"Why?"

"My father used whores all the time, brought STDs home with him and gave them to her. She'd wanted more kids but couldn't have them because of him. I was evening the score, making it so whores couldn't ruin someone else's life like they did hers."

"I'd have gone after my old man, not the whores," Blake said. "He was the one who was to blame."

Jeffries laughed. "He was so proud of me graduating from the academy, you know what he did? He bought a whore for me. I killed him for it and her. They never solved that one, and you wouldn't have solved these cases if it weren't for that bitch."

Blake sighed. "Put the gun down and let Carson go. We can talk to the DA, see if we can work a deal. It's the only way to resolve this."

"Only one way to end this, bro. Only one way."

He raised the gun, put it to his head, and pulled the trigger. Carson dropped to the floor and Jeffries landed on top of him. Blake ran to Carson, rolled Jeffries off him, and pulled him away as cops raced into the area.

"It's okay, man. It's over. Are you hurt?"

Carson shook his head. "It's my fault. I uncuffed him so they could get his fingerprints, and I was talking to the intake cop when he grabbed my gun and took me. Stupid on my part."

Blake shrugged as EMTs arrived and began to check Carson over. "Everybody makes mistakes. I'm just glad you survived. Next time remember what happened and pay attention."

Carson nodded.

"Mommy is still in interrogation. Guess we should let her know," Stevens said as Blake approached.

"I guess so." Blake told one of the cops where they were going and, as they walked out, he said, "I didn't see his lawyer anywhere."

Stevens laughed. "According to Mitchell, he ran out of booking the minute the shit hit the fan. He was yelling loud and clear as he ran out—that's what alerted everyone."

"Let's get this over with."

<hr>

BLAKE ESCORTED Connie and Alex into the apartment building and to Connie's apartment. Connie went in, told Alex to come in when she was finished talking to Blake, and closed the door behind her.

"Tell me what happened," Alex said.

Blake nodded and opened his apartment door, holding it for her and flipping the lights on. He closed it after she took a seat on the couch. He sat down beside her and gave her a brief recounting.

"He wasn't going to shoot me, and he couldn't very well shoot Carson. He would have been dead before he finished pulling the trigger. I think it finally sunk in he wouldn't be walking out a free man. It was either prison or death—he made his choice."

"I'm glad I wasn't there. Are you okay?"

Blake nodded. "Just tired. You were right about his mother. Under hypnosis, she told you that you wouldn't remember the photo you'd seen in her office and that you wouldn't remember anything, ever. Those feelings of hopelessness were all planted by her. She said she began suggesting that suicide was the only solution, and hoped you'd act on it."

Blake lay his head back on the couch and sighed. "At least it's over. She confessed, and says she plans to waive her right to a trial and go to sentencing. I'm not counting on it. She'll probably change her mind after she has a few days to think about it, but we could get lucky."

"Let's hope she doesn't."

"Well," Blake said, sitting up, "you probably should head over to Mrs. H's. You're probably tired, too."

"Did you mean what you said?" she asked.

"About what?"

"In her office, you said you loved me. Did you mean it?"

Blake frowned and stood up, pacing away from the couch. "I meant…I was so fired up about the break in the case…"

"So, you didn't mean it?"

"I—" Christ, he couldn't tell her he loved her and have her tell him to get lost. But he didn't want to deny it either and ended up saying nothing.

Not to prolong the discomfort, she said, "That's okay, I didn't mean to embarrass you." She stood up and walked to the door. "I should get over to Connie's. She'll want to go to bed, and she won't until I return." Alex grasped the doorknob and turned to open it.

"Alex, wait." Blake walked up to her and put a restraining hand on her shoulder. He was clearly uncomfortable, and at a loss for what to say.

"Blake, it's okay. We all say things we don't give much thought to at the time. I just wanted to know."

"What if I did?"

"Did what?"

"Mean it. How would you feel about it?"

"But you didn't, so it doesn't matter."

"It matters to me."

She raised her eyebrows at him. "I have to confess before you'll commit?"

"Alex, I need to know."

"I'd be happy about it."

Blake felt his gut relax. "I'm not good at this Alex, I have a terrible track record, but…I think I do love you. I've never said that before, to anyone."

She smoothed her hand across his cheek and gave him a half smile. "I think I love you too, Blake, but if we're to be together, you have to be sure. We both do. I don't want to keep secrets, and

I don't want to rush into anything. I have things to take care of back in Montana. I think you have some things to come to terms with as well." Her hand stayed on his cheek.

"Connie has loaned me some money. I'm going to take Sharon's and Suzanne's ashes home and try to decide what to do from there."

"I don't know what that means for us, Alex."

"I guess we'll find out. We both need time to think. Based on what I've remembered, I've never done things half-assed. I won't do us half-assed either. When you're ready, if that's what you want, come find me. Tell me about Lindsey, tell me she won't stand between us, and tell me what you want to do." She kissed him softly, dropped her hand from his face, and left, leaving him alone, like he'd always been.

CHAPTER FORTY-EIGHT

BLAKE STOOD IN the kitchen with a forgotten cup of coffee in his hand and stared out the window, his mind drifting. Alex's words came back to him.

"You can talk to me. You don't have to carry all this on your shoulders…"

"I won't do us half-assed either. When you're ready, if that's what you want, come find me."

He shook his head abruptly. "It's what I want, but I'll ruin it. Like I always do."

He thought going back to how things had been before Alex came into his life would be simple. But so far it had been excruciating. He carried an ache in his chest. He wasn't sure it would ever go away.

Clark had finally taken him aside two weeks after Alex left.

"Are you going to let her go?"

"What?"

"You know what I'm talking about."

"She left, I didn't."

He really didn't want to talk about this. Every time he thought about her, he thought about going to Montana. Once he'd made it all the way to Wyoming before he pulled over to the side of the road and sat for an hour before turning around and going home. Fear or uncertainty or his usual reluctance to get close stopped him. Talking about it wouldn't help, it would only pick at the wound.

"So, stop walking around like the living dead and go after her."

Blake grimaced and looked away, clearly miserable. "I don't know if I should. She wanted me to be sure I loved her, that Lindsey wouldn't come between us. I do love her. God, I miss her, but I can't make relationships work. I don't see the point of putting either of us through that."

Clark put a hand on Blake's shoulder. "You can't make relationships work because you never let anyone close enough to try. It's been four years. It's time you let the guilt over Lindsey go. Stop letting her interfere. Lindsey was impulsive, you know that. Her refusal to wait got her killed, not you. Go see Kendall, he's good. He'll help."

Blake didn't look convinced. "Either you love her, or you don't. My wife says that's pretty easy to figure out. I think sometimes it can be complicated," Clark said. "But you're not required to suffer because Lindsey died. You're allowed to have a life. Talk to Kendall."

———— ♦ ————

IT HAD taken Blake another week to make the appointment with Kendall and they'd been meeting weekly since then. Their last session had left him as confused as ever.

"What's your biggest fear?"

"She won't want me 'cause it's taken me so long to decide. She will want me, and we'll be fine for a month or two then she'll leave 'cause I'm not who she thought I was. I won't be able to commit or give her what she wants. How long do you have to listen to all the reasons I should let her go?"

"And letting her go is what you think is the right thing to do?"

Blake nodded. "She deserves better."

"What do you deserve?"

There was a long silence. "I don't know."

"Can you accept that it was Lindsey's impulsiveness that caused her death? That you weren't responsible?"

"You're not the first to point that out to me. I feel like I should have made her wait."

"You tried, she didn't. That's not your fault."

"No, it just feels like it was."

"I know it's hard. You've carried this for a very long time. The only way life will change is if you can accept that you tried to stop her and she ignored you. Let it go and stop isolating yourself."

"If I go to Alex…if I fuck it up…I can't go through losing her again. I don't want to put her through that either. It's easier, for both of us, if I walk away."

"Life's a risk, Blake, relationships are risky, but they're also rich and rewarding with the right person. If you hold yourself aloof from that, refuse to take a chance, you lose more than you gain."

"I'm not sure I can do it. I'll fuck it up, that's what I do."

"This is a tough decision for you, one only you can make, but I would second Stevens' thoughts—if you love her give it a chance. She's a smart woman, giving you time to sort through this was the right thing to do. It's given you a chance to make a decision you can live with, whatever that turns out to be."

Blake wasn't sure he'd ever be able to walk away from the sadness or the regrets he felt for Lindsey. The thought of committing to someone was terrifying. The question was, would he go find Alex or let her go? Did he love her enough to make the effort? Would she want him if he showed up?

He had no idea.

———— ◆ ————

ALEX HAD taken Suzanne's and Sharon's ashes down by the riverbank near Sharon's property where the old tire swing still hung by its now fraying rope, and she'd buried them next to each other. She remembered them, but wished more than anything they were here, that they weren't just memories, that she wasn't completely alone now.

Her memory had returned, gradually, often painfully. Her dreams about Suzanne and Sharon were comforting, but she woke up some nights in a cold terror remembering the assault. Feeling his hands around her neck, remembering the terror of seeing the wrench coming toward her, waking up in the dark, cold and sick. The only comfort was knowing Kyle Jeffries was dead and couldn't hurt her or anyone else again.

Wandering around her father's property, seeing the cellar safe room, and the sad, dilapidated house had brought back unwanted memories of all the unhappiness that had lived there. The smell of the guns as she'd sorted through her father's gun collection triggered memories that left her shaking. Memories of being browbeaten by her father into using guns, being woken up in the middle of the night for paranoid drills of escaping some unknown threat, being ridiculed by the kids in town. Sadly, she was glad he was gone. She'd turned her father's guns over to the sheriff to do as he liked with them, keeping only one that she had often used for target practice.

It had been her father's voice that had haunted her, she realized. His paranoia had shaped her, but hopefully hadn't twisted her as badly as he'd been twisted. She'd put the family property on the market as is. She hadn't had the will to sort through things and be reminded of the misery that had lived there.

Then there were the dreams about Blake. Remembering his scent, his touch, how he'd made love to her, and the yearning she'd seen in his eyes after the blowup and as he'd watched her leave. Once awakened from those dreams, she spent the night in the living room of Sharon's house near the fire, wishing for Blake's arms around her and wondering if she'd ever see him again. It had been nearly two months now, and she'd begun to doubt that he would show up.

"I'm not good at this Alex, I have a terrible track record, but…I think I love you. I've never said that before, to anyone."

"Please come find me," she said as she sat in the dark in front of the fire. "Show me I'm worth it."

Sharon had left her house and property to Alex and named her executor. She'd moved into the house and had sorted through Sharon's possessions, keeping what had special meaning to her and selling or giving away the rest. The memories in this house were happy ones but she wished her sister and Sharon were with her to share them.

If she'd been able to pick the house up and somehow move it away from Freed, she would have. That being impossible, she put it up for sale as well. Sharon's neighbor had taken her horses, and there was no other livestock to sell. She took long walks to exorcise the bad memories and to figure out what she'd do with her life now that it looked like Blake wasn't coming.

Alex waited for the properties to sell and as winter approached, she mourned what she'd had with Blake. She missed him, missed his touch, and missed the feel of him, but refused to contact him. If he wanted her, then he had to be sure and she had to come first. She had no idea who Lindsey was, but Alex wouldn't take a back seat to another woman. He had to decide. If he hadn't shown up by the time the properties sold, then she would leave and let something she wanted badly die.

EPILOGUE

H**E PULLED UP** to the house and parked. It was November. Not a welcoming time of year—trees were barren, it was cold, and the mountains to the west were capped in snow. There didn't seem to be anyone around, and he worried that she'd left, that the trip had been pointless. He'd heard nothing from her and had no idea what her reaction to him showing up would be. He should have called, but he'd been afraid she'd tell him not to come. At last, he forced himself from the car, stepped up onto the porch, and knocked on the door.

His heart was racing, and he was afraid she'd turn him away. It seemed an age before she opened the door. The cold had seeped through his jacket and he was shivering. At least he hoped it was from the cold. She looked surprised and a little flustered, then smiled at him.

"Come in, it's cold out."

She held the door until he entered and closed it behind him. *God, she's beautiful*, he thought. Her hair tumbled in dark red waves around her face, the heavy white sweater she was bundled in looked soft and inviting, her jeans were old and her feet were encased in heavy socks. One hand rested on the door knob and the other lay against her chest, as if she were feeling her heart race or trying to catch a breath.

A weight lifted from him. He wanted to wrap his arms around her and hold her, bury his face in her hair, and he was terrified she'd send him away. He looked around not sure what to do.

"Come into the living room, I have a fire going," she said at last. She showed him into the room and indicated a wing-backed chair opposite an old couch covered in material with faded roses on it. "Would you like something to drink?"

He shook his head no and sat in the chair and watched the fire. *I should say something, anything, and not sit here like an idiot*, he thought, feeling awkward and at a loss. She took a place on the couch and tucked her feet up under her, waiting he guessed for him to say something. Their separation had been torture for him, like some vital part of him had been torn out. But now, he wasn't sure what to say and she sat silently waiting.

The silence stretched for several more moments and then without looking at her he said, "Lindsey was my partner. We'd been partners for three years. We were a great team. She was the best. I loved working with her because we made up for each other's deficiencies. What I didn't know or do well, she did, and vice versa.

"Four years ago, we were responding to a call about an intruder." His voice tightened, his breathing sped up, and he could feel his heart begin to race.

"I wanted to call for backup before we approached the house. She told me we didn't have time, and before I could stop her, she headed for the rear of the house. I was calling for backup as I headed for the front door when I heard a shot. I ran to the back of the house. She'd been shot in the chest, and the shooter was gone.

"She died in my arms." He cleared his throat roughly and sat without speaking for several moments, clearing his throat several more times and blinking rapidly. "I was in love with her, and I never said anything. I didn't want to lose her as a partner, and I didn't know what would happen if I told her. Then she was gone, and there was no way to tell her. Gone in seconds.

"I just shut down after that. I showed up drunk for work one day and was put on a temporary leave of absence. I pretty much stayed drunk the whole time. Then Stevens showed up one night a couple weeks later and found me shit faced in a dark apartment. He sat down and handed me his gun and told me if I was going to kill myself to get it over with. If not, he said he could use a partner, but he didn't want to partner with a drunk.

"He told me to sober up and get my ass into work. So I went back to work. It was what kept me going. He'd pulled me out of a pretty dark place, but I hated him for a while, for making me feel the pain of it all. To avoid that, I decided I was done with any kind of relationship other than my partnership with Stevens."

Blake rubbed a hand over his face. "It worked pretty well—or well enough I guess—until I nearly hit you. On the way home that night I couldn't stop thinking about you. It felt like you were somehow my responsibility. I didn't want you to be, but I kept thinking how not listening to that little voice had turned everything to shit for me. And that little voice right then said I needed to keep you safe. Maybe it was my way of making amends for not forcing Lindsey to wait."

The silence was heavy and at last Alex spoke. "I'm so sorry you had to go through that. Thank you for telling me." It broke her heart. She wanted to take him in her arms and hold him, but she needed to hear him out.

They sat quietly before she said, "It's been a long time. Why are you here, Blake?"

He stood up and walked over to the fire, leaning his arm on the mantle and resting his head on it. "You said when I was ready, to come find you, tell you about Lindsey and whether she'd stand between us."

He turned toward her. "I'm here. I won't pass on the chance to be with you, whatever that turns out to be. I love you. I don't just think I do, I know I do. I won't forget her, but she's gone. I've spent the last four years punishing myself for something I had no control over."

"Do you still love her?"

"Yes, the way you love someone who's passed," he said quietly. "What I loved about Lindsey was more like this deep friendship that could have been more, but never had the chance. We were never lovers. I have no idea how she felt about me other than as a partner. I felt guilty that, somehow, I was responsible for her death. It's been pointed out to me that she was impulsive and that her impulsiveness got her killed, not me."

"Do you believe that?"

He stared at the fire and raised one shoulder and let it drop. "Yeah, most of the time. I think I'll always regret that I couldn't stop what happened."

He ran a hand through his hair, shook his head, and turned to her. "I'm no good at this, I'll probably screw up, but I'm miserable without you, Alex. Something vital has been missing since you left. Please don't send me away. Tell me you haven't changed your mind."

"I didn't think you'd come. It's been such a long time. I figured you'd changed your mind." She unfolded her legs and sat up. "I've spent the last few weeks trying to decide what to do when the properties sold, when I had no reason to hold me here. What I would do if you never came. I've missed you, Blake."

"I'm sorry it took so long. It's taken some work to sort through all the shit I've been carrying around."

He walked over and knelt at her feet. He took her hands in his and kissed her palms, then brought them to his chest and held them over his heart. "I love you, Alex, with all my heart. It doesn't belong to anyone else. Please, give us a chance."

She pulled him in and held him tightly. He felt himself relax into her. "I love you, too, Blake, with all my heart."

"Thank God," he said lifting his head and taking hers in his hands and kissing her as if his life depended on it.

It does, he thought.

ACKNOWLEDGMENTS

FIRST AND FOREMOST, thank you to my fans. Readers are what keep authors going. Many thanks to my beta readers Lois Miller, Laura Cassanova, Lorelei Starbuck, and Mary O'Neale for all their valuable feedback and Laura, thanks for the $50 joke.

Thanks to Cyndy White, LPC, who helped enormously by explaining how PTSD affects police officers and methods of coping with it. Thanks to Catherine Spader, former ER nurse, for explaining the ins and outs of emergency patient care and why slitting your wrists almost never works well. Thanks to Julie Cameron, my editor at Landon Literary Agency who always keeps me on track with insightful and funny comments, especially the one about the sheets and the chopsticks.

Thank you to KB Jensen at My Word Publishing for all the work she puts into getting my books ready for publication and for her proofing skills. And thanks to Gail Cross at Dessert Isle Design for her amazing covers.

This is a work of fiction. The Denver setting is one I know well, however, my apologies for any liberties I may have taken. The characters are fictional as well, although sometimes I wish they weren't. Congratulations to Connie Holtz for winning the 'name a character after you' contest.

Music plays a large part in my writing. The song *Only You* by Yaz seemed to fit this story perfectly.

AUTHOR BIO

HELEN STARBUCK IS a Colorado native, former OR nurse, and author of the National Indie Excellence Award-winning, *The Mad Hatter's Son, An Annie Collins Mystery. No Pity In Death*, the second book in the series, and book three, *The Burden of Hate*, finalist in the National Indie Excellence Awards to which *Kirkus* gave a starred review calling it, "A thriller that offers a master class in suspense." She writes her Denver mystery series from the perspective of Annie Collins an OR nurse. Her standalone romantic suspense novels are set in Colorado.

Visit her at her website https://www.helenstarbuck.com and sign up for her newsletter to be kept abreast of all the news and get subscribers only perks.

Follow her on Facebook https://www.facebook.com/helensstarbuck/ and Instagram https://www.instagram.com/helenstarbuck/

If you like this book, please help other readers find it by recommending it to friends, reader's groups, and discussion boards.

Reviews are enormously helpful to authors as are word of mouth recommendations. Both are greatly appreciated.

Please consider leaving a review on Amazon https://www. amazon.com/Helen-Starbuck/e/B076KPPQ52/ or on Goodreads https://www.goodreads.com/author/show/17197450.